THUNDERCHIEF

TO: John Minshull,

Best Wishes
and good flying

Don Henry

THUNDERCHIEF

Don Henry

PELICAN PUBLISHING COMPANY
Gretna 2004

First edition, 2003
First Pelican edition, 2004

ISBN 1-58980-237-3

The word "Pelican" and the depiction of a pelican are trademarks of Pelican Publishing Company, Inc., and are registered in the U.S. Patent and Trademark Office.

This is a work of fiction. Names, characters, places, and incidents either are the product of the author's imagination or are used fictitiously, and any resemblance to any actual persons, living or dead, events, or locales is entirely coincidental.

Printed in the United States of America

Published by Pelican Publishing Company, Inc.
1000 Burmaster Street, Gretna, Louisiana 70053

THUNDERCHIEF
IS DEDICATED TO THE HONOR AND
MEMORY OF:

My father and uncles who served in World War II but
rarely talked about their experience. After searching
for words to express my own emotions born
out of combat, I now understand.

My mother who was a pillar of strength while
my father served and when I did.

Lieutenant Karl W. Richter, a brave fighter pilot and
friend. He was a man who often talked of duty and honor
at a time when it wasn't popular to serve one's country.
While living his words, his life became
too short...but at the start, had he known
with certainty, Karl would not have walked away.

Author's Note

Thunderchief is a novel in the form of a memoir. It's based on historical events and set in a time and place where my generation of young fighter pilots replaced their innocence with experience. It's as accurate to my emotional memory of the time as I could make it. It contains fictionalized characters and episodes for the sake of narrative, but more importantly to respect the memory of those who died and the privacy of those who did not.

Many of the physical features of Takhli RTAFB (Royal Thai Air Force Base) where I was based in the summer of 1966 and Korat RTAFB where I served in 1967 and 1972/73 have been combined into the base referred to in this work as Korat.

Similarity to any person living or dead is purely coincidental.

Acknowledgments

Many people have contributed to the development of *Thunderchief.*

Lee Bafalon, former Air Force intelligence officer at Korat RTAFB, lawyer, friend and my best critic.

My sisters Sally, Susan and Jeanne who are intelligent, witty, eternally optimistic and always ready to provide encouragement and support.

Those who pointed the way and pushed me along: Lt. General Leroy Manor, *Trends, Indicators and Analysis*, Lt. Colonel Rezk Mohamed, Editor, *USAF Fighter Weapons Review*, and General Bob Russ who, at the Pentagon, put a young pilot on his wing and was infinitely generous on all subjects from national security to the national pastime.

I owe a debt of thanks to Loretta Adams, Pat Hendry, Doug Muir and the many creative writers from Irvine Valley College, Saddleback College, and Santa Monica College who reviewed developing manuscripts and were generous with their comments.

Prologue

The best thing about piloting a single seat aircraft is the quality of the social experience.

—Colonel Moody Suter

For sheer beauty, nothing compares to a single-seat, single-engine fighter aircraft. Especially if it is designed to fly faster than the speed of sound using the wasp-waisted, area rule principle known as the "Coke bottle" effect. And even more so if it is the first fighter aircraft one flew. For me, that was the F-105D Thunderchief, a lumbering giant on the ground but noble and swift in the air—length 64 ft. 5 in., wingspan 34 ft. 11 in., maximum weight 52,838 pounds, powered by a turbojet developing 24,500 pounds of thrust in afterburner and speed over 2.2 Mach or 1400 miles an hour. Nothing in the world could outrun her at low altitude.

It is astonishing how little appreciation existed for what that jet fighter could do, perhaps because of two events which occurred during its acquisition cycle: first, a shift in the Pentagon's central focus on nuclear weapons to include more conventional capability; second, the Secretary of Defense discovered cost effectiveness.

The F-105 was initially designed with one purpose in mind: to be the Air Force's primary nuclear fighter-bomber. However, in early 1961, the Pentagon ordered the F-105 modified to carry conventional ordnance. The new F-105D configuration included an internal 20 mm Vulcan cannon and capability to carry over 12,000 pounds of conventional weapons—a heavier bomb load than the World War II B-17. A cost effectiveness based acquisition approach encourages criticizing the system you have in favor of the new system you want. To save operations and logistics expense, Defense Secretary Robert McNamara wanted the Air Force and Navy to buy the same aircraft. In late 1961, he canceled the Air Force F-105 production after 833 total aircraft and substituted the Navy F-4.

F-105s were used extensively during the Vietnam War, flying 75 percent of the air strikes against North Vietnam during the first four years of Operation Rolling Thunder. In 1966 alone, 126 F-105s were lost for the following reasons: anti-aircraft 79, surface-to-air missiles 5, MiGs 4, unknown 21, and operational 17. The chance of completing a combat tour without getting killed or captured was described by some as "There ain't no way." But fighter pilots refused to believe they could become a statistic and grim fact was confronted with an optimistic retort that became a proverb... "There is a way."

Combat is where the F-105 came into its own. Fighter pilots loved its speed, endurance, weapons capacity, and straightforward handling characteristics. What was obvious to pilots took the Defense Department longer to appreciate. Because of its multi-mission capability, planners thought it would be a challenge to fly and only highly qualified pilots with significant experience in other fighter aircraft were assigned to the initial squadrons. Early combat loss rates revealed the need for a fresh supply of pilots. A great debate ensued in Congress and the Pentagon about whether new lieutenants, fresh out of pilot training, could handle a single seat fighter with the F-105's pedigree. Nevertheless, lieutenants began training at Nellis Air Force Base, Nevada, and a small cadre was sent into combat. Within days two lieutenants were lost to enemy action. Although debate continued, necessity prevailed and the pipeline of young lieutenant replacements resumed after a few weeks.

The result was two very distinct types of pilots flying combat in the F-105D. There were the "older heads" with years, often decades, of experience flying single-seat fighters including many combat veterans of Korea and some of World War II. Then there were the "new kids," young, inexperienced lieutenant replacements, the clueless few like me with six months training in jet fighters and zero combat time. Only these two greatly disparate groups existed; there was no middle ground of experience. Not that the lieutenants weren't talented...they were, but they were thrown into a dangerous environment with much to learn just to stay alive.

A word about technology and the times. The year 1966 was before the digital economy, the cruise missile culture, sensitivity training, and female fighter pilots...before personal computers, the Internet, and e-mail. Aviators in combat had very little contact with loved ones and news from the outside world in general. A telephone call from Thailand to the States was time-consuming to initiate and so expensive it could only be justified for emergencies. A stamped letter was the primary communication tool but most pilot activities were classified and what wasn't often seemed too dull to record. Typically, a box of homemade chocolate chip cookies, lovingly baked and carefully wrapped, arrived crushed so badly we ate them with a spoon. Not much represented home which is probably why pinups were so popular. As Bob Hope reminded us every Christmas, it was nice to see what we were fighting for.

Not only was digital technology lacking in communication it was not yet present in aircraft. The few computers in the F-105 were analog and "smart" weapons were not yet available. All conventional weapon deliveries depended entirely on a pilot's skill. Mission success was solely a product of how well one could fly and think in the cockpit. Fighter pilots succeeded and stayed alive in combat by relying on themselves. Perhaps this explains the jet fighter pilot's self-confident bearing and notorious ego, which, in most cases, was roughly the size of Chicago.

When not flying combat tours out of Thailand, F-105 pilots fulfilled nuclear alert commitments in Europe, Okinawa, and South Korea. "Sitting alert" on Cold War targets, each F-105D was armed with several times the nuclear force expended on Hiroshima and Nagasaki. If launched in anger, no individual warrior in history ever wielded a fraction of the destructive power controlled by one pilot flying a nuclear-armed F-105.

A consequence of this combined nuclear/conventional duty was that many F-105 pilots carried current knowledge of nuclear targets, tactics, and capability with them over enemy territory. Pilots flew their share of combat flights regardless of other responsibilities, which could include duty as a nuclear weapons instructor, nuclear war plans officer, or certifier of nuclear crews and targets. This apparent reproach to security was not lost on the enemy who had a wealth of information parachuting out of damaged aircraft and landing on their hillsides. North Vietnam exploited this opportunity through torture, trade and exchange programs and shared information with the Soviet Union, Communist China, North Korea, Cuba, and other countries.

Wartime is when fighter pilots come into their own, when their actions become meaningful and explicable (though they seldom bother.) Combat brings focus and singularity of purpose that reveals a truckload of unusual traits that seem to go with the territory. In the throes of combat, a fighter pilot seems not to like outsiders very much and is not easy company. One often has no idea what he is thinking and not the slightest notion of what his inner life might be. He appears uncomplicated, unreadable, punctilious, always in control, knowing his own mind, and unusually adept at solving any problem at hand. Then, having succeeded at his task, he smiles that smile, that cavalier, vainglorious, horse's ass smile which seems the worst part about him... as if his vocation were some sort of inviolate priesthood... as if only he knew the right mantra, the right face to show the enemy... as if only he could come to terms with the passion of the moment, the wisdom of the longer view, and the truth that we are more humanly connected with bizarre behavior than we realize.

A fighter pilot is capable of making life or death decisions under the challenge of fear and uncertainty. He wishes he were left to handle any situation on his own, the way it should be handled, and not crippled by an overly-acute sensitivity to the suffering of himself or of others. He uses superior judgment to stay out of situations where he would have to rely on superior skill. He knows that in a time when people are not dying so much he will be more harshly judged because some people who think they understand human nature forget that humans are predators. And he understands that when he tries to explain that concept in peacetime, people will look at him like he is dangerously stupid.

The fighter pilot's I knew considered the enemy an external problem; the internal dilemmas were peer pressure and fear. Zorba was right: "Dying isn't hard. Living is hard." And in the end, I'm happy to be alive to feel the pain and, when things get tough, to keep perspective by remembering—I once had a job where people shot real bullets at me.

THUNDERCHIEF

Chapter 1

East of Groom Lake, Nevada
March 14, 1966

The Russian jet seemed incredibly small as I flew in formation, tucked in so close I could count the rivets on its aluminum skin. The MiG-19 was easy to identify, since I had studied hundreds of intelligence photos. A Plexiglas canopy perched on top of its fuselage like a teardrop and thin wings swept back at a rakish angle. The contour of its vertical fin jutted up like the tail feathers of a bantam rooster, ready for courtship or a cockfight.

The MiG-19 was the first supersonic fighter the Soviets had introduced, but, compared to the hulk of the Mach-2 F-105s Kramer and I flew, it looked like a remote control model. Smiling to myself, I waved to the pilot. He nodded and gave me the finger.

As we turned in formation, sun glint from the MiG's polished aluminum skin flashed in my eyes and caused me to flinch. I reached for my helmet sun visor but didn't pull it down, not wanting to put anything between my eyes and the enemy jet.

This morning I sensed something unusual because Kramer, my instructor pilot, had been smiling too much. In our flight briefing he said I was going to see an "asset", something not part of the curriculum. Since the word asset was a pseudonym for almost anything that didn't exist in the unclassified world, it didn't shed much light on what I would see. Still, Kramer said I wasn't to ask how the asset came to appear at our rendezvous on the Nellis Range or any other questions my inquisitive mind could generate. If I had learned anything in my training as an F-105 fighter pilot, it was that strange and wonderful things flew in the skies over Nevada.

The unclassified part of our mission was to test an airburst bomb. The bomb's fuse contained a miniaturized radar that would cause it to detonate one hundred fifty feet from the target. Kramer carried one test item on the belly of his aircraft, and I flew a second jet as safety chase on his wing. It was a fine way to maintain flying proficiency, since I'd completed F-105 training and was waiting on day-to-day hold for combat orders to Vietnam.

After a while, the MiG driver gave me a hand signal to move away, and I repositioned eight hundred feet to the right of Kramer. The MiG zoomed to a perch five thousand feet above us and set up for a mock gun attack. As he rolled-in, one advantage of the Soviet jet's small size became clear. It would be difficult to maintain visual contact during the knife fight in a phone booth that passes for air-to-air combat.

Kramer flew straight and level so I could observe under controlled conditions. The MiG approached high and from the rear with one hundred knots of overtake. But, instead of breaking off the pursuit, the pilot zoomed under Kramer then abruptly pulled up in front of his nose.

An explosive fireball engulfed Kramer's jet with orange flames and ominous boiling black smoke. In the next millisecond but imprinted on my brain as if in slow motion, a second fireball encased the MiG. Then a concussion shock wave blasted my aircraft sideways followed by a fusillade of metal that perforated my canopy and peppered the skin of my jet. The cone-shaped radome, which formed the entire nose of my plane, sheared off leaving tattered edges resembling high tech composite rags.

I lowered my visor against the terrifying windblast and searched for Kramer and the MiG. They were gone. All that remained were engines falling through the air followed by a trail of debris like the tail of a comet assembled from the blown-apart collage of material that, seconds ago, comprised two airplanes. Falling somewhere amid the rubble, pummeled in ways I couldn't imagine, was all that remained of two fighter pilots.

"Cactus, this is Dreamland Control. We lost radar contact with part of your flight."

Unable to speak, I ignored Control and stared at the pieces until they splashed on the desert floor heaving up sand and smoke. A primal feeling of visceral anguish broke over me leaving me damp and shaken.

"Cactus, Dreamland here. How do you read?"

I punched the microphone button with my thumb. "This is Cactus Two. We got a problem," I said, trying to shout over the wind blasting through my shattered canopy. "Cactus One and the Asset. Both down. No parachutes."

My mind swirled in a numbing trance, not acknowledging the damage to my own plane. There was nothing I could do for the pilots. They had evaporated in front of my eyes and left my emotions grasping for a finger hold in the hollowed out residue of meaningless loss.

Feeling alone and without an alternative, I reluctantly turned south on a course to Nellis Air Force Base. I radioed the Supervisor of Flying, and we assessed the damage. My entire radome was gone and with it my airspeed sensor. Gaping holes ventilated the left side of my canopy. One hydraulic system indicated zero pressure, and the fire warning light had started to flicker.

The SOF diverted an airborne F-105, and, within minutes, he joined up with me to look for damage I couldn't see from my cockpit. The pilot didn't report anything burning so I elected to land. Since my airspeed instruments were unreliable, I flew on the other pilot's wing as he led me back to home base.

Both my plane and my concentration were wounded. My mind kept asking, why? The jets didn't collide with each other. I was certain of that. But how did it happen?

On final approach, I fought with my bucking, rolling jet and tried to stay in formation. Since I didn't know how slowly my damaged plane would fly, I requested the other pilot maintain two hundred thirty knots. My jet zoomed across the approach end of the runway like a rocket. After touchdown, I held my breath and deployed the dragchute thinking it would rip to shreds, but it held together. Still, my jet rolled the length of the two-mile runway before it rumbled to a stop.

In the first quiet moment after shutting down the engine, I patted the instrument panel and thanked the plane for holding together and supporting me like an old friend in a crisis.

Then, behind me, smoke began to percolate out of the engine intakes. I tried to ignore it. Rescue would arrive in seconds, and I didn't want to risk injury jumping out of the cockpit and falling ten feet in my flight gear.

The firemen helped me out and turned me over to the flight surgeon. After a quick check of vital signs in the back of an ambulance, the Doc dropped me off at the squadron. Among the people waiting for me was Grover, one of my classmates. I had hoped he would be there because my hands were shaking. I asked if Grover could attend the debriefing with me, but the asset was close-hold information, and the squadron commander refused.

An hour into the meeting, after comparing telemetry data from the test with my description of events, the test project engineer said he had the answer. The MiG set off the experimental radar fuse when it flew under Kramer. The fuse had armed because a ten-cent clip on a safety wire vibrated loose. Then, when the MiG passed one hundred fifty feet in front of Kramer's jet, the fuse thought the MiG was a target and had functioned perfectly. Those were his exact words. "Functioned perfectly." I felt like jumping out of my chair and grabbing him by the neck.

The bomb had functioned perfectly while still shackled to the plane, seven feet under Kramer. Shrapnel took out the MiG and almost destroyed me.

The last item discussed was the press release. It would report that two F-105s had crashed and both pilots were killed. Of course, there would be no mention of a MiG-19.

Grover had waited for me in the hall. "Ashe, it's your orders. The bad news is you leave immediately on the next available plane. Departs in the morning."

"Impossible," I said. "Jenny's with her mother. Can't leave without..."

"I took the liberty," Grover said, resting his hand on my shoulder, "of calling her as soon as I got your itinerary. I wanted to let her know early in case she could make it back before you leave." He shook his head. "It's not going to happen."

I sighed—for a while not feeling anything and wondering what had happened to my emotions. The timing was awful. I felt uprooted with no chance to be at Jeff Kramer's funeral or to say a proper goodbye to Jenny. Finally, I stared at Grover and asked, "And the good news?"

Grover took a deep breath and held it as he said, "I looked at your jet. You're lucky to be alive."

Chapter 2

I made the seemingly endless journey over the Pacific, sitting sideways, in the web-strap seat of a cargo plane. We were delayed, broken down, and rerouted until my exhausted mind lost track of time. After days at altitude, island hopping over turquoise seas, we descended over the lush verdant Kingdom of Thailand with its checkered rice fields and glittering temples. Korat Royal Thai Air Force Base stood out like a scar of new construction next to a flightline filled with rows of F-105 aircraft. We landed in late afternoon.

A captain in a pickup truck drove up and handed me two 44th Tactical Fighter Squadron patches. "Where the hell you been?" he asked. "You're scheduled to fly in twelve hours."

"Twelve hours?"

"You're Ashe Wilcox, aren't you? We expected you yesterday or the day before. You have to get a few winks, wake up at 0215, and report to the Officer's Club."

"You can't be serious. Takeoff in the dark on my first mission?"

"Not flying. Riding in the back seat of a two-seat trainer. Lieutenant Colonel Erasmus Snow will be up front, but you'll call him Hunter if you know what's good for you."

I shook my head, studying his face for any hint of a smile. "I'm a single-seat fighter pilot. I don't fly in the backseat."

"You do tomorrow," the captain said. "But of course, that's just your new wing commander talking."

"But I'm tired and out of crew rest."

The captain looked at me like I was crazy. "Welcome to the war. Show up at the Officer's Club at 0300 hours in the morning. If you don't want to fly, tell it to Hunter."

As the captain drove, I half-listened as he talked about a mango tree in front of my new quarters and explained how to shake the trunk so ripe fruit would fall. Finally the truck stopped, and I followed him into a building.

He pointed to a rumpled bed. "You sleep there."

After traveling halfway around the world on catnaps, I felt relieved to finally have a bunk I could call my own. Of course, I would have been happier with clean sheets and even more so if the pillow didn't contain a depression of the previous user's head. But then, while trying to think of something sarcastic to say, I noticed a pilot's kit bag on the floor beside my new bunk. An ominous green tag hung from its handle. My gut wrenched while a sickening consequence of combat flying crashed down on me.

As I raised my hand to protest, the captain cut me off. "The pilot's personal effects stay put until a Summary Court Officer takes an inventory. Standard procedure after a shoot down. We're crowded here. No room for his bag anywhere else. Ashe, you're lucky to get his bunk."

My arm quivered as I clutched the handle of my own bag, wanting to set it down yet reluctant. The captain stood rail straight, chest out, and jaw set. He looked stern but there was something more in his features, in his stare—the presence of a hungry predator. A man who would kill because survival required it or, as his eyes betrayed, for revenge.

"He crashed," the captain said. "No one saw a parachute."

"A lot of that going around," I whispered under my breath, thinking it strange he didn't say the pilot's name.

"Our shoot down ratio has dropped below a hundred...statistically," the captain added.

"Statistically?"

"A tour is a hundred missions," he said, turning towards the door. "We're losing a jet every ninety-six. You figure it out."

I pulled off my boots and collapsed on top of the sheets, but

I lay awake, aware of the pilot's bag resting beside me like a discarded tombstone. Throughout the night, I tried to erase it from my thoughts, but the captain's words haunted me. Why didn't he just say it? You're going to get killed here.

His voice had conveyed a tone of wounded resignation—that of an emergency room doctor overwhelmed with more traumas than he could attend. Because the bodies of dead pilots don't return to home base, there's nothing tangible to grieve. I sensed his mourning was a triage of the spirit. Soon, perhaps, it would be my spirit.

Hours later, I lay clutching my head, realizing fear had kept me awake. I had serious doubts about flying my first combat mission with no sleep.

The tin-roofed hooch, one of many buildings arranged in rows separated by community latrines, slept twenty pilots. Sparse lights provided faint illumination for the connecting boardwalks. The most interesting feature of the hooches was that I could see right through them. They had wire-screened walls. I guess the theory was air in—insects out.

In the dim light, my eyes rested on a gecko clinging precariously to the wire mesh. It was stalking a rice bug. The gecko moved with infinite patience, placing one foot, then another, without causing the slightest disturbance in the taut surface of the screen.

I was rooting for the lizard. Bugs, especially large ones, gave me the willies. It surprised me when the insect turned toward its aggressor and sat motionless. Why didn't it sense danger and escape? Instead, it seemed mesmerized, perhaps even compliant with its enemy.

In an instant, the bug disappeared. I thought it had cut and run. Then I spotted the thin outline of wings protruding from the lizard's mouth.

The one-sided skirmish was a tiny release from the tension. It was roughly two minutes past 0200 hours I guessed, not wanting to look at the clock again as I had every five minutes for the past hour. Mission or no mission, my attempt to sleep had ended. I had set the alarm for 0215 hours. No need to let it wake the others, not that the barrack's chorus of snoring, coughing, and farting suggested a sensitivity to alarms.

With my head buried in the pillow, my fingers inched across the footlocker and stretched to find the clock. As I relaxed, my arm brushed the missing pilot's bag and recoiled with a shudder. I leaped out of bed, scooped up a flight suit and shaving kit, and headed to the latrine.

In ten minutes I stood before the mirror, almost ready. I'd been in the Air Force eighteen months and wore the silver bars of a first lieutenant for the first time. Embroidered on my nametag were the silver wings of an Air Force pilot and the name "Ashe."

For as long as I could remember, I'd hated the name Samuel Ashley Wilcox. Perhaps my mother saw *Gone With The Wind* at an influential time during her pregnancy. Out of respect, I never asked. Sam was my preference, but Ashe rhymed with crash, and my pilot peers wouldn't let me forget it. Perhaps they sensed it got to me, and they were right. After winning the Top Gun award in my training class, I put "Ashe" on my nametag, and the rhyming ended.

My removable Velcro-backed nametag and unit patches marked me as a pilot prepared to evade behind enemy lines. A tired and thinner looking fighter pilot, I noted, hunching over to fit my five-foot ten inch frame in a mirror that had been placed on the wall by someone shorter. Months of sun at the Nevada training base had bleached my blond hair to sand and darkened my skin to bronze. The suntan added intensity to my blue eyes but didn't mask the dark circles. Even so, I thought I looked better than I felt. But it didn't matter; I was going to fly anyway. At least I would experience my first Asian sunrise from the cockpit of a jet fighter.

I made a last check in the full-length mirror. Today was the first day to defy flight suit dress regulations in the special ways that would identify me as an F-105 combat pilot. I turned my collar up, pushed my sleeves back on my forearms, and unzipped my flight suit from neck to mid-chest. From the slouching stance of a gunfighter, I did a quick draw on my reflection and said, "So what're they going to do to me, send me to combat?" I shrugged, sensing my own false bravado. I felt exhausted and apprehensive but wasn't in touch with the nature of my fear.

Checking my watch, I left the latrine and made my way back to the hooch. Most of the pilots seemed to be sleeping through the stifling heat and constant background noise as maintenance crews readied aircraft and loaded bombs on the flightline. Twice during the night, I'd heard a scream that would have awakened me had I been able to sleep. In the dim light, I looked through the screened walls into nearby hooches. A few pilots were sitting on the edge of their bunks, having a smoke in silence or staring into the night.

Dew hung like a shroud outside, not moving through the screened walls. Inside, the musty smell of stale cigarettes thickened the air. Two rows of beds and footlockers furnished the sleeping quarters. There were no chairs. A sparse selection of clothing hung from a small bar attached to the end of each bunk.

I'd been given ample advice about what to wear, how much water to drink, and how to avoid social diseases in a foreign country. I felt confident with my training on how to fly, fight, and fornicate, but no one had said a word about handling the fear that gripped me throughout the night and still lingered below the surface of my emotions.

Only two rookie lieutenants had preceded me into combat. Both were shot down and dead within two weeks. Their fate had cancelled my original combat orders. I agonized through weeks of uncertainty at Nellis Air Force Base in Las Vegas waiting for the Pentagon to decide if newly trained lieutenants had what it took to go to war in a single-seat fighter.

When I wasn't flying proficiency sorties, I spent long hours on the Vegas strip. Some routine. Every night, I dined at the Thunderbird Hotel free midnight buffet, watched high rollers place bets I couldn't afford, and played word games with hookers whose unfettered breasts were larger than my means.

Las Vegas had been an interesting diversion at first, then, boring as hell as I waited with no word. When word did come, no one had asked me if I thought I was ready.

Last night I'd set the clock expecting to be asleep as soon as my head hit the pillow. But sleep hadn't come. It was almost time to meet Hunter. Still, I sat on my bunk searching for answers. The odds had taken a terrible turn for the worse. How could anyone make it through a hundred missions? Was I afraid to die? I couldn't admit that—even to myself. But harping in my memory was the image of my bag of personal effects beside the bunk of the next new pilot who couldn't sleep.

Chapter 3

I had heard about Hunter from my first day in fighter training. Because he'd won the Silver Star four times, once for each
MiG fighter he'd shot down, he was a legend and the standard
against which combat aviators were judged. And, if arrogance
and disrespect for authority were any measure of a fighter
pilot, he held the championship on that score, too.

Flying with Hunter would be an adventure. From the back
seat, I could watch a seasoned fighter pilot at work—truly a
rare opportunity since almost all F-105s were single-seat planes.
A few two-seat trainers had been built but rarely used. Most F-
105 pilots had never flown in the same fighter airplane with
another human.

At 0250 hours, I stepped out of the hooch and quietly closed
the screen door. Taking a deep breath, I savored fresh air free
of the pungent blend of stale cigarette smoke and sweat.
Cautiously, I made my way down the dark boardwalk towards
the Officer's Club. The night was hot, and moist air formed
soft rings around distant lights and coated the earth with a thin
mist that glistened like black oil.

A pair of legs illuminated by a small flashlight appeared
from the next hooch and matched my stride.

"Hey, damn dark out," the figure said in a booming voice.

"Yeah," I whispered. Even outside the hooch, I felt I was in a
community bedroom.

"The name's Lucky Slater. Who the hell are you?" he said,
turning the flashlight directly into my eyes.

I pushed the light away. "Ashe Wilcox."

"Don't know you. How long you been on board?"

"Since yesterday afternoon. I've got a full hundred missions to go."

After a few steps, Slater grumbled. "That kind of longevity would be a world record for a lieutenant."

"Thanks a lot, Lucky. I've got a warm feeling now."

"Aren't you the serious one? What you doing out in the middle of the night?"

"I'm on a morning mission. Predawn takeoff."

"You gotta be joshin' me boy. I'm on that mission too. Going to the Red River Valley up near Hanoi."

I stopped in the walkway. "What?"

Lucky shone the light on my face again. "I said that mission's too tough for a new guy."

Half blinded, I resumed walking, "I'm flying in the back seat if you haven't destroyed my night vision."

"You really are confused, boy. The F-105 is a single-seat fighter. There ain't no back seat. You sure you didn't get off at the wrong base? The F-4s are up the road at Udorn. Now, they got back seats."

"No," I replied. "There's a two-seat trainer on the ramp now. It came in from Okinawa to escort a battle-damaged jet back for repair. The wing commander wants me to see a mission from the backseat."

"No way!" Lucky shouted and waved his arms. "That's like practicing bleeding."

Pointing toward the hooches, I whispered, "They're sleeping."

"Who you flying with?" Lucky said with only slightly less volume.

"Lieutenant Colonel Snow."

"Is that a fact? You're flying in a two-holer with Hunter. I'm deputy lead in that flight."

"You know Hunter?" I asked.

"Of course. Everybody knows everybody here except you," Lucky said. "Hunter's notorious. Got shot down and tortured in Korea. Torture is supposed to break people, but I think it just made him spittin' mad. They couldn't keep him out of this war, and we can't keep him on the ground. Volunteers for everything. He's got a set of nuggets the size of watermelons."

"I've heard."

"He's after a fifth MiG, and he'll probably get it too. They sent him to Washington for a big ceremony to get his fourth Silver Star. Got his picture plastered on the cover of Time magazine. If he gets shot down again, the Vietnamese will probably beat him to death with rolled up copies of Time."

"I thought former POWs didn't have to fight again."

"They don't. He volunteered. Guess he's not happy unless he's killing people with an airplane. He's a full-blooded Indian, they say. Makes you wonder how he got a name like Erasmus Snow."

"Heard he never uses it."

"Can't blame him," Lucky said. "Would you want a handle like Erasmus? Calls himself Hunter. Gets real irritated if you call him anything else. Sometimes he talks Indian philosophy for hours at a time. Pretty obscure stuff. I don't understand half of what he says, but he's the king of combat. I'd fly with him any day."

"I've heard some of the stories. I'm supposed to meet him at the club. Want to join us for breakfast?"

"Said I'd fly with him. Didn't say I'd eat with him. You won't have any trouble finding Hunter. Go through that door where it says KABOOM. That stands for Korat Air Base Officers Open Mess. He'll be sitting on the far side of the room at the center table with his back to the wall. I guarantee it. You won't have trouble finding a seat either. He'll be sittin' all by his lonesome."

I nodded. "Thanks, Lucky. I know what he looks like. Saw him back in the States when he picked up that fourth Silver Star. He stopped at the Fighter Weapons School at Nellis and briefed on surface-to-air missiles."

"He's the expert. Should call him magnet ass, the way he attracts hostile fire."

As we stepped onto the lighted porch of the KABOOM, I noticed Lucky's hair was almost white. He looked about thirty-five, tall, and thin as a rail.

Lucky caught me staring and said, "I know what you're thinking, but it was this color before combat."

"Sure you won't join us?"

Lucky shook his head, "Positive. It's gonna be a big day up there. Keep checking your six o'clock. Never know when they'll attack your rear."

Pausing inside the door, I watched four Thai waitresses move between the tables. Their grace and elegant beauty gave sharp contrast to the half-awake pilots in sweat-stained flight suits. The young women looked like royalty gliding gracefully through a herd of unbranded water buffalo. A lone figure sat with his back to the wall, just as Lucky predicted.

Hunter had to be in his late thirties or very early forties, but, as I approached him, he looked older than I remembered. The Lieutenant Colonel's body was trim and wiry with close-cropped salt and pepper hair. A well-worn but crisply pressed flight suit hung loosely on his hard muscular form. His nametag and unit patches were precisely aligned on their Velcro base. Hunter appeared peaceful, but there was something tragic about him as if a wall separated him from the rest of the world. The man evoked a sense of the unexpected. An aura of danger. As I stood in front of his table, he didn't acknowledge my presence. Still, I felt exposed and accessed by some sixth sensor that only he possessed.

Hunter's flight suit, unzipped to mid-chest, revealed gold dogtags on a heavy gold chain. Next to the dogtags hung an odd shaped charm which, according to the lore, was a gilded piece of fanbelt the Korean interrogators had used to beat him like an animal. His sleeves, pushed up on his forearms, revealed deep scars from ropes and irons that had bound him for months at a time.

I broke the silence. "Good morning, Colonel Snow, sir, I'm Lieutenant Wilcox."

Hunter slowly shifted his gaze from the *Stars and Stripes*

newspaper to his coffee cup. Finally his steel gray eyes gave me a brief glance. "Lieutenant, do you come by your military bearing naturally or is it a product of all that college education?"

"I don't understand, sir."

Hunter didn't reply immediately. When he did it was in a growling voice that could easily be overheard. "Why are you standing at attention in the KABOOM dining room?"

"Sorry, sir. I didn't realize I was."

"Great SA, lieutenant."

I had the feeling everyone was looking. "SA, sir?"

"SA, lieutenant. That's what fighter pilots call Situation Awareness. Ever hear of that before?"

"Yes, sir. Of course, sir. But not in the dining room context," my heart sank, sensing how ridiculous I sounded.

"Dining room con...text," Hunter toyed with the word and laughed under his breath as he turned the page of his newspaper. He allowed several seconds to pass then without looking up said, "Well, Lieutenant?"

"Well, what, sir?"

"Well, what do you want?"

I took a deep breath. Why was he giving me the treatment? "Sir, I was told to meet you here for today's mission in your back seat."

"So, you're the guy."

"Yes, sir," I felt annoyed. He had to know.

"It's your first combat mission. You scared, Lieutenant?"

"No, sir. Well, maybe a little, sir. I'm glad this mission is with you. You have experience, and I have a lot to learn. You must take guys like me up in the back seat all the time." I heard myself babbling idiotically. I needed to give him shorter answers.

"You're wrong, Lieutenant. Never done it before. This is something the headquarters staff dreamed up because a two-seat F-105 and a green lieutenant wound up on the same tarmac. I'll tell you right up front, I'm not crazy about the idea. That two-seat model weighs two thousand pounds more than the one-holer. That's two thousand extra, not to mention useless, pounds to carry into combat. How much do you weigh, Shooter?"

"One fifty-seven, sir."

"Well then, two thousand one hundred and fifty-seven to be precise."

"Sir, do you mind if I join you for breakfast?"

"As you can see, Shooter, I'm finished. I'm going down to the squadron and review the mission. See you there, later."

"Wait, sir. I'll walk with you," I said, annoyed he was calling me Shooter.

He raised his eyes just enough to glare at me. "You had breakfast?"

"No, sir. I'll have some coffee at the squadron. I'm not big on breakfast."

"Wrong," Hunter replied in a ringing voice.

For a few seconds, everyone in the room was silent.

Hunter motioned me forward with a crooked finger and in a tone conveying I was peasant and he was king said, "There are two things you should always do before strapping your body into a supersonic jet for a combat mission. Eat a good breakfast and have a good crap. It could turn into a long day." Hunter paused then stiffened. "One more thing, Lieutenant, can you read my name tag?"

"Yes, sir."

"What does it say?"

"Hunter, sir."

"Last time I looked, it said Hunter. Just Hunter. Not Hunter, sir, or Lieutenant Colonel Snow or anything else. Just Hunter. That's what I want you to call me. Hunter."

Chapter 4

After breakfast Lucky and I walked to the Operations Center called "Fort Apache" where he gave me a quick tour of the mission planning area. Somewhere along the way, I swore if I ever again ordered an omelet in the KABOOM dining room, it would be without Thai peppers. After an overview of the day's mission, we took a seat in the main briefing room.

A crusty looking major called Frank Garrett walked to the podium and looked at his watch. "It's 0429, one minute to time hack."

"Anyone seen Roscoe?" Lucky asked as he stood up and headed for the door.

Lucky returned followed by a medium-sized, mixed-breed retriever with a coat that was a blend of gray and tarnished sable. Roscoe jumped up in the chair labeled "Wing Commander" as Lucky fished a napkin from his flightsuit pocket. Lucky held out a strip of bacon then wiped his fingers on Roscoe's paw.

"Thirty seconds to time hack," Garrett said.

I studied the line-up card Lucky had copied for me. Garrett was the mission commander. Much of the data on the card wasn't familiar. Tomorrow I would go to the local aircraft commander's course and everything would make more sense. With my pencil, I tapped the crew box under Hunter's name. Someone had written-in one word: "Passenger."

As I reviewed the weapons settings, an irony of my training

struck me. I was a combat ready pilot but had never dropped a real bomb. In training we used twenty-five pound practice bombs. It had been like practicing basketball without a hoop. I didn't want to say it out loud, but I was relieved Hunter was the real pilot on today's mission.

"Fifteen seconds to hack," barked the mission commander.

"It's time for a nap," Lucky said petting Roscoe as he took a seat behind the mascot. "We want an easy mission, so you sleep now."

From the back row, I noticed sixteen pilots sprawled into theater style seats with no two in adjacent chairs. I wasn't surprised that combat pilots cherished space, perhaps, even when sitting with their closest friends.

"Hack. It's 0430."

The pilots focused on the mission commander as he passed critical information quickly, covering each item once in a rapid-fire process that, for me, was like trying to take a drink from a fire hose. The mission sounded like my entire training program rolled into one flight. I was still writing when the mission commander summarized.

"Our primary goal is to hit the bridge," Garrett said. "So let's do it. Don't get MiG happy and jettison your bombs to engage the enemy. After you drop the bridge, then you can chase down the MiGs." Garret closed with a single Vu-graph that read:

IF YOU ARE PILOTING A FIGHTER IN COMBAT
TODAY...*PREY*

The briefing had raised a million questions, but I knew better than to ask them in this forum. As a new guy, I would ride along keeping my ears open and mouth shut.

Outside the main briefing room, a tall, thin officer with a medical insignia on his flight suit waited for me.

"Lieutenant Ashe Wilcox, I presume," he said as a smile raised the tips of his handlebar mustache until they touched the sides of his glasses. "I'm Doc Morgan, your flight surgeon.

We have a special today on footprints and rectal exams. Which one would you prefer?"

"What?" I replied.

Morgan tapped a large envelope. "Got your records right here. You need my medical sign-off to fly. Relax. Your records are fine except we need to add a footprint to the file."

"I am relaxed," I said, glancing at my watch. "Relaxed but also in a hurry."

"We won't be long. I understand the time crunch. Let's step into the Intelligence shop. They have a fingerprint kit. It's not the perfect solution, but the Doc can make it work. No footprints, no fly, so jettison your boots and socks."

"Why do I need to do this?" I asked while unlacing my boots.

"Lieutenant, there are some questions that are better left unanswered. But if you must know, it's so we can make positive identification in case of terminally acute trauma. Do you get the picture or do you require a more graphic explanation?"

I grimaced. "You mean they are going to identify me by my footprint."

Doc continued. "Most fighter jocks think they have a huge male member, it's going to survive the crash, and everyone will recognize it afterward. If their manhood were half as big as their ego that would probably work. In the real world, we use dental records, fingerprints, and other stuff."

I held up my hand to wave him off, "I think I got the picture."

Doc Morgan inked a flat plate with a roller, positioned two papers on the floor, and began to print my feet.

A hand pressed on my shoulder, and I turned to look behind me. Whoever it was, he was standing in my blind spot.

"Did you eat a good breakfast, my son?" he said in a wavering voice. "Having breakfast is so comforting. Don't you agree?"

"Who's there?" I asked.

Doc Morgan chuckled, "It's Padre Johnson."

"Actually, I'm a chaplain," Johnson said as he walked around and faced me. "Are you right with God?"

I studied his face surprised by the question. The chaplain

was gaunt with the hollow-eyed look I had seen in pictures of holocaust victims. He didn't seem to be present in his own body. I shrugged not knowing how to respond.

"Good," the chaplain said as he turned and ambled towards the door.

Morgan discreetly spun his finger around his temple indicating the chaplain was crazy. When Johnson was out of earshot, Doc said, "I'm afraid our messenger from God is about to crack. He blesses every plane before it takes off and feels personally responsible if it doesn't come back. Don't think he ever sleeps. I may have to send him home. Hate to do that since we're only one deep in chaplains right now."

"So the chaplain's crazy. That explains his behavior. But I met Hunter at the club and he was down right hostile. I'm just a new guy. Why doesn't he give me a chance?"

Doc glance up. "Hunter would probably say you got a chance, you're here, aren't you? You're a lieutenant with no combat experience. This crowd's not going to treat you like the king of fighter aviation on the first day."

"I doubt if Hunter would sugarcoat it that much," I said. "But what do you think? You're the flight surgeon."

Doc Morgan grimaced. "Hostile fire has been tough the last few months. Everyone has lost tons of friends, and I'm afraid it's going to get worse. Still our pilots put themselves at risk everyday. The chaplain handles loss by getting too close. Don't do that. Most pilots handle it by creating emotional distance. Don't do that either."

"But how do I avoid the treatment?"

Doc smiled. "It's simple. Stay alive for a while and folks will like you just fine. Then no one will have to miss a mission to write your parents and send back your personal effects. Most important, at the bar they won't have to take a break in the serious drinking to have a last toast to your fate."

After inspecting each footprint, Morgan taped them to the edge of the counter to dry.

"For this you went to medical school?" I asked wanting to change the subject.

"Actually I have a great job. I get to ride in fast jets and see the world. The only down side is the practice. Pilots don't get sick much, and, if they do, they lie about it to keep flying. If a fighter pilot ever said he was sick, I'd refer him to a mortuary."

"Hurry, Doc, I'm running out of time."

Morgan reached in his medical kit and produced a small bag with a shoulder strap. "Here's a hit-and-run medical pack. It has go pills, stop pills, and some narcotics for emergencies. Sign this receipt for the narcotics and remember the condoms are for carrying water, not chasing the natives."

Doc held up something that looked like a large pill. "This is my own innovation. It's a button compass tied off in a small pouch of condom material."

"Why?"

"So you can conceal it from the enemy, easier to swallow if you're about to be captured. Much easier to retrieve later and more sanitary if you have to recycle it through your system. You can remove it from the pouch and swallow it again. Good as new."

"Yuck," I shook my head. "Please. I got it."

Lucky poked his head in the door, "Hey, Ashe, when you get your boots on, hustle over to the next building. We'll get you checked out on your combat survival equipment."

Morgan nodded to Lucky. "We're done." Then he turned back to me. "You got any snacks?"

"No. Should I?"

"Here's a baggie with a Snickers bar and a package of M&Ms. It's been on a couple of missions and got a little smashed, but it might come in handy."

As I headed for the personal equipment room, I felt caught up in a whirlwind of information with no hope of absorbing it in time. For the moment, my feelings of inadequacy drowned out the fear of a faceless enemy, and I wanted to learn everything as fast as possible.

"Lieutenant Ashe Wilcox," Lucky announced, "meet Sergeant Ricky Smathers. He runs the best personal equipment section this side of Hawaii. Sarge, think you can fix him up?"

"Sure," Ricky grinned. "We checked out the helmet and G-suit you brought from the States and made a few modifications for combat. I'll give you a quick rundown on the survival gear we use here and get you suited up."

I nodded. "Ricky, I'm a new guy. Don't assume I know anything. I'm carrying a Snickers bar that has more combat time than I do."

Lucky patted me on the shoulder. "I'm going to jump into my 'go fast' gear. See you on the aircrew truck."

While Ricky adjusted my survival vest, I looked around. Parachutes hung on racks in the center of the room, and on the walls, camouflage flight helmets appeared like rows of mounted alien heads. The smell of latex oxygen masks swabbed with alcohol permeated the air. The floor sparkled with new polish and every flat surface glistened with fresh white enamel.

"We number everything here," Ricky said. "No names in case of a shoot down. The number twenty-six recently became available, and it's yours now."

I wondered if twenty-six belonged to the pilot whose bunk I'd used last night.

"No lock on our lockers?" I inquired.

"You don't have to worry about losing anything here," Smathers paused for a breath and glanced away. "And it's less trouble if someone doesn't come back."

I sensed Smathers took losses in a very personal way. Not overly so like the chaplain, but it was clear he was moved.

Ricky walked across the room and reached below the counter of the gun cage. "Here's your basic thirty-eight caliber Combat Masterpiece pistol. Here's your basic baggie with six signal flare rounds for the pistol. Here's your basic box of fifty military standard thirty-eight-caliber rounds of ball ammunition. Here's a baggie with your basic blood chit and your basic gold bar. Here's your basic receipt to sign for all this stuff."

"Okay, Ricky, and here's my basic signature," I chided. "This box of bullets weighs a ton. Maybe I shouldn't carry them all. How many does Hunter take?"

"One," Ricky said.

I frowned. "One bullet?"

"Yup," Ricky tapped the box. "We call them rounds here. Some pilots take all they can carry and others think that shooting it out on the ground in North Vietnam is a quick way to get yourself killed. I know one pilot that says he'll throw the gun away while he's coming down in the parachute. Everyone has a different approach."

"I'll take twenty rounds. You keep the rest."

Chapter 5

Drenched with sweat, I stepped off the aircrew truck like a geriatric case under the heavy burden of flight gear and survival equipment. Looking up at my jet, I found the grace of its supersonic airframe interrupted by elements of destruction hanging from her wings and underbelly. Bombs and missiles transformed the restrained elegance of the streamlined fuselage into a haunting specter of annihilation.

Most pilots called the F-105 Thunderchief by her unofficial nickname, the Thud. I used the name but somehow didn't think it fit, especially considering her smooth handling qualities in the air. Thunderchief seemed more appropriate since the plane had the loudest afterburner ever put in an air machine.

A lot of folks referred to Hunter as Thunderchief, too. The name was a convenient combination of his Indian heritage and legendary intensity when driving home a point. When someone used the name Thunderchief around Erasmus "Hunter" Snow, it was hard to know if he meant the man or the machine.

The nose of the Thud was pointing precisely at me. I stared into the 20-millimeter cannon loaded with 2000 rounds of high explosive incendiary ammunition. Olive drab bombs were suspended three-behind-three on the aircraft's belly. On each wing hung a huge fuel tank and a Sidewinder heat-seeking air-to-air missile.

Except for the low whine of generators powering small floodlights on each side of the jet, the flightline was quiet. The light's reflection in the morning mist draped and darkened the brown and green camouflage of the aircraft's skin and turned it into a shiny black cloak. The combat-ready jet commanded a sense of respect that, in my youth, I learned to reserve for a loaded gun.

I wondered if anyone felt prepared as he crawled into a plane for his first combat mission. I suppose some did. Hunter probably did. But my heart pounded with every hesitant step. I felt well trained until now. But nowhere had I learned, or even thought much about, how to cope with the dilemma I faced at this moment. Today's mission was real. What I felt wasn't from a novel or the movies; it was kill or be killed. I had reached an emotional threshold, and there was no turning back.

"Hey, Shooter, get a move on," Hunter yelled. "Put your helmet and parachute by the ladder and follow me on the walk-around inspection. Shortly this tarmac will explode with the sound of screaming jets. I want to be in the cockpit wearing my brain bucket when that happens."

I fumbled and dropped my checklist. Recovering quickly, I straightened up, took a deep breath, and said, "I'm ready."

"Memorize that checklist so you don't have to carry it around," Hunter said, then he hunched down by the nosewheel.

As he stretched, pointing to a hydraulic gauge, Hunter's sleeves pulled up on his forearms. I felt an ominous chill as I saw, at close range, the bracelet of scars on his tortured wrists and his gnarled arthritic hands.

He quickly finished with the plane then turned to the bombs. "If an armed bomb collides with another after release, we're history."

"Roger that," I said, glancing at the small clips holding the arming wires in place and thinking it ironic that life or death in a multimillion dollar warplane hinged on a piece of metal no bigger than a paperclip.

"You got it, Shooter?"

"Checking," I said, bending over the bombs, plucking the arming wires with my finger. I flinched as an explosive noise erupted and dense sulfur smoke belched from the belly of the jet parked next to us.

"Starter cartridge," Hunter shouted in my ear. "Let's move out."

Hunter slapped a handkerchief over his nose and mouth. I didn't have a handkerchief, so I held my breath as I put on my parachute then raced up the rear cockpit ladder. Once in the ejection seat, I pulled on my helmet, snapped on my facemask, and turned the oxygen to one hundred percent. The crew chief stood on the ladder wearing a bandana over his nose and mouth like a bandit.

Acrid sulfur smoke hung in the still morning air until the roaring jet, just a wingspan away, created enough turbulence to clear away its own cloud. My helmet protected my ears, but I could feel the raw noise in my bones. My whole body seemed to reverberate with the screaming jet.

I felt more restricted and cramped than I had ever felt in an airplane. Today, as a passenger, I could eject but had no control over any other part of the flight. Strapped in the ejection seat wearing water wings, a pistol, and a survival vest packed with supplies was like being tied up in a sleeping bag in a sauna. Every movement required extra effort, and I wondered why the training program hadn't included a few missions in full combat gear to prepare for this moment.

Hunter and the crew chief communicated with hand signals. The chief twirled one finger above his head and our aircraft shook as Hunter ignited the starter cartridge. As the jet engine rotated, the aircraft came alive. The cockpit lights came on and a high-pitched hum behind the instrument panel vibrated like a hundred electric motors humming together. As the engine howled at idle power, I heard Hunter's voice on the intercom.

"Ashe, how do you hear in back?"

"Reading you fine," I replied.

"I haven't flown a two-seater for a long time. Forgot to check the bailout light before engine start. I'll test it now so don't eject when it comes on."

"Light checks good," I said as a square red light on the instrument panel illuminated with the words BAIL OUT. I regarded it with curious resignation. It seemed to be an emergency alarm on the aircraft's heart monitor.

As Hunter finished the preflight checks, I gazed into the dark and heard Jenny's voice. At least I thought I heard it.

"I'll miss you," she said through some trick of my mind speaking in a voice clear and soft.

"I love you," I replied. I hate good-byes, never knowing what to say. Especially this time, on the phone, in those pregnant, interminable moments waiting for the plane to board. Jenny probably didn't know what to say either.

We said goodbye three days ago, I thought. After crossing a dateline and a ton of time zones, I wasn't sure how many days it had been. Less than seventy hours, probably. I felt like I had moved to another planet. I was half way around the globe but a world away from Jenny's warmth and compassion. It would be interesting to know what time it was now at her place in Vegas but not interesting enough to actually figure it out.

"You ready to taxi?" Hunter asked over the intercom.

"Roger, could you drive me to the nearest war?"

"You bet, Ashe."

Hunter pushed up the power on our heavily laden jet and called to his wingmen on the radio. "Buick flight, check in."

With crisp radio calls, each acknowledged with his flight position.

"Two."

"Three."

"Four."

Our flight crept in single file for a mile down the taxiway before turning into the arming and inspection area where we joined three other flights of four aircraft each.

We parked in marked angled rows carefully laid out to protect us from each other's exhaust blast. But there was no protection against temperature as the screaming engines created their own brand of tropical heat.

Maintenance and arming crews darted under our jet. They appeared everywhere at once with Mickey Mouse ear headsets and flashlights that drove pencil beams of light through moist air and illuminated safety tape on their clothes in a macabre dance set to the scream of jet engines.

In the midst of hustling arming crews and piercing noise,

Chaplain Johnson stood below the cockpit of the adjacent fighter. He lingered, staring up at a pilot while making the sign of the cross. Heat waves and sickening fumes distorted the air making the unhallowed night mirage appear like the chaplain had been swallowed up and scorched in the heat of hell.

"Put your hands high on the canopy rail so the arming crew can see them," Hunter said on the intercom. "They need to know we aren't going to bump the jettison button and dump bombs on them. It would ruin their whole day."

"They ever going to build a fighter with air conditioning that works on the ground?" I asked. "It's way over a hundred degrees in this cockpit."

Hunter was silent, but I could see his helmet nodding.

I needed another drink of water, but there was no time. The suffocating gear and noxious exhaust from sixteen aircraft were making me ill. If I was going to toss my breakfast, I had to do it before I closed the canopy. Yanking open the seat belt, I pulled myself over the canopy rail as far as I could. Thrusting a finger down my throat, I exploded a stream of eggs and Thai peppers that, for the most part, cleared the canopy rail.

Arching back against the headrest, I wondered if the result was sucked down the engine and hoped any evidence on the side of the aircraft would blow away before sunrise revealed it to our wingmen. Looking down, I saw Chaplain Johnson below wearing Mickey Mouse ear sound suppressors and frantically brushing off his uniform.

"Ford flight is ready," the radio crackled.

In thirty seconds, I would have to lock the canopy closed for almost four hours. Moving quickly I strapped in for takeoff. Sweat soaked my flight suit and the smell of vomit engulfed the cockpit.

"Tower," mission commander Garret radioed. "Olds package is ready for takeoff."

"Olds," the tower controller replied. "Wind calm, temperature eighty-eight degrees. Cleared for takeoff. Cleared to departure frequency."

The control tower reported eighty-eight degrees, but the exhaust-soaked inspection area seemed like an oven. I couldn't breathe.

"Olds package, go departure," Mission Commander Garret radioed. After changing radio channels, Garret said, "Olds" then waited until Nash, Buick, and Ford flights reported in sequence, and all sixteen jets had checked-in.

I listened closely to the quick chain of voices confirming all the radios were working and each pilot was on the correct frequency. But it was more than that. Crisp, controlled radio calls were a measure of a pilot's self-discipline. In the air, radio voice was the only direct contact with another human and much was judged from it.

Among fighter pilots, it was okay to be afraid, as long as you didn't appear afraid: like a duck moves across a lake, smooth and unruffled on the surface but paddling like hell underneath. I smiled at the professionalism of these men. If they felt any anxiety about the mission, it was not written in their voices.

Chapter 6

Mission Commander Garrett led the first four planes onto the runway and stopped in formation with the first two aircraft five hundred feet in front of the second two. His takeoff would begin a daisy chain of sixteen aircraft grouped in four flights that would extend across the night sky for miles. Except in the movies, I had never seen so many airplanes flying together.

Hunter's canopy started down, and I closed mine. I rechecked the canopy latch and gulped deep breaths of 100 percent oxygen while I scanned the instruments. There were dozens of indicators and gauges in the cockpit, but none of them measured my chief concern. Cockpit temperature. There wasn't a dry thread of clothing on my body. Sweat formed a slippery seal against my oxygen mask. If we didn't get airborne soon, I thought I'd drown.

"Garrett's ready to light the afterburner," Hunter said. "It's a real shock especially at night. A genuine wake-up call for war."

Hunter's demeanor had changed. In the KABOOM, he tried to test me to see how I would perform. He didn't seem to give a whit about my level of stress. Of course, the enemy wouldn't care either.

Now, in the airplane, Hunter's spirit appeared to soar, and he provided a steady commentary on events. Most of the information was basic, but I didn't complain. I'd sift through the sentences of the man I thought was the greatest living fighter pilot and find the diamonds.

I watched as the four ships on the runway roared at full power, illuminated with an eerie green and red aura from their navigation lights. As they pushed forward, compressing their nose gear strut, they looked like the offensive line of a football team poised in a three-point stance, snarling and roaring, impatient for the quarterback to hike the ball.

Garrett's afterburner ignited, and his jet thundered down the runway. Every ten seconds, another plane exploded like a giant blowtorch and chased him. As the fourth jet rolled, the second flight of four replaced the first on the runway and repeated the choreographed ballet. An unbroken trail of lights extended across the night sky.

Then it was our turn.

Hunter moved the throttle outboard and the afterburner ignited with explosive force. Our F-105 rolled slowly at first then accelerated surprisingly fast for 24 tons of aluminum and steel. As we rumbled through 130 knots, the jet began to cleave through the air and become stable, feeling more like an airplane than a high-speed tricycle.

"Committed to takeoff," Hunter reported as the airspeed raced through 160 knots.

At 180 knots, he eased back on the control stick and let the wings dig into the moist night air. At 195 knots, we were airborne.

I knew our afterburner's pounding thunder dominated the night. Its roar of fearless self-reliance concealed the vulnerability of a plane that would need another 100 knots of speed before it could make the slightest turn. "Coffin corner," "death valley," and "behind the power curve" were phrases used to describe slow speed flight which, for a loaded F-105, was any airspeed below 300 knots.

As we gained altitude, our three wingmen caught up with us and stabilized in fingertip formation a few feet off our wingtips. As Hunter continued to climb, leading our four-ship formation, the world below became a sparse collection of lights with no visible horizon. I couldn't tell where the lights on earth stopped and the heavens began. Stars seemed grouped in bright clusters. Pinholes in the dark as Jenny was fond of saying.

After two years of star-filled nights, Jenny and I had not come to terms with our love. I had thought about it a lot and knew she had too. But in the end, we used the war as an excuse to delay the ultimate commitment.

Perhaps we would have married if Pete, our friend from F-105 school, hadn't crashed during training. Jenny and I tried to comfort his wife, but the effort put too much stress on our relationship and shattered our plans. Too many unresolved issues happening too fast especially since I was leaving for combat. Our solution was to be engaged-to-be-engaged and resolve our feelings after my tour. I don't know who thought of it first, but we were both drawn toward the idea. Of course, neither of us knew precisely what engaged-to-be-engaged meant.

A lot of things remain unsaid when one goes off to war. On a deep level I felt guilty not making more of a commitment, but I had haunting and unresolved feelings. What would I be asking her to do if I went missing? Perhaps we were both trying to offer an impossible combination of freedom and commitment. Our parting was a clumsy compromise to deal with the unspeakable reality. We were delaying commitment to see if I returned.

The radio jolted me back into the mission.

"Center, this is Olds, request you confirm our tanker," Garrett radioed.

"Roger, Olds. Still checking. Standby," the center air controller replied.

"Standby, standby," Hunter said as he forced an irritated laugh over the intercom. "At a stoplight, I can standby. Pushing these gas hogs through the air at seven miles a minute, I need some action."

Two more minutes went by before center control gave us a flight vector to our tanker.

"Fuel considerations dictate everything," Hunter reminded. "We have to top off and drop off on schedule. Our mission support aircraft will be on station at our target time. If we're late, they won't be able to stick around, and the MiGs will eat us for breakfast."

Hunter made a smooth join-up with our tanker then settled into position 40 feet off the KC-135's right wing. In seconds, the next flight of four jets arrived and assumed their station as a mirror image off the refueling aircraft's opposite wing. I looked side-to-side in wonder as the lumbering tanker and eight bomb-laden fighters flew tight formation at 315 knots in the dark. Also concealed by the night, visible only as a faint cluster of lights five miles ahead, was another tanker refueling the other half of our 16-ship formation.

As Hunter moved in for the first refueling, the expanse of heaven transposed from star-speckled sky to the intensely illuminated aluminum belly of the KC-135. We were so close to the tanker I felt I could touch it.

I heard the roar of the refueling aircraft's engines and saw the expanse of tail framing the face of a sergeant maneuvering the refueling boom. The boom issued a metallic clunk as it locked into the nose receptacle of our jet. Hunter was transferring fuel from the tanker less than twenty feet above us. The two aircraft, locked together, lumbered as love bugs mating in flight.

In three minutes, Hunter disconnected and moved to the right side of the formation. The number two aircraft quickly replaced him on the boom. It would be thirty more minutes before all the planes completed refueling.

The air conditioner finally cooled the cockpit, and my clothes began to dry. I unstrapped one side of my oxygen mask and let it hang from my helmet. Breathing deeply, I felt more relaxed even though the sour scent of vomit lingered. Although Hunter couldn't see into the rear cockpit, he had probably noticed the smell. Fortunately, he didn't comment.

Light from the sun collected below the horizon and resolved into a precisely chiseled line revealing the curvature of the earth. The pre-dawn light grew until a stream of sunlight flooded over the horizon, and it was day. The sun's first ray had revealed itself as a shot of subdued color then instantly resolved into intense hot light. The sun warmed my unmasked face. Towering columns of distant clouds were illuminated and, over the next few minutes, resolved from a shadowy pink to snowy white.

As I witnessed the sunrise, I wished that I could make time stand still long enough to capture the moment. I wanted to take a picture or create a painting that I could savor, hold, refer back to, and crawl into at will.

In dawn's new light, our aircraft pranced in formation, moving and bobbing, maintaining their relative positions like wild horses running easily together. In all of history, only during my short lifetime had anyone witnessed this specter of steel jet steeds galloping through the night sky and into the dawn. I reflected on the unbridled beauty of planes framed by my first Asian sunrise and knew I would remember the moment forever.

Several miles into Laos, at the end of the refueling track, both tankers began a slow, arcing turn back to the south. Our fighters continued north, each four-ship altering course a few degrees to individual headings. Although we would attack the target at the same time, each flight would take a slightly different route.

"Now we need some airspeed," Hunter said, pushing up the throttle and accelerating from the refueling airspeed of 315 knots to 500.

After a few minutes of silence, Hunter said. "Think I'll have a smoke."

Curiously, I peeked around the headrest of Hunter's ejection seat and saw his reflection in the front cockpit rearview mirror. He detached a strap of his oxygen mask and lit a cigarette. I smelled smoke and pondered the effects of a burning cigarette dropped in the cockpit. Deferring to Hunter's experience, I didn't say a word.

Laos unfolded as a carpet of enormous trees. They formed a verdant jungle punctuated with milky-white limestone karst. The karst outcroppings appeared as if huge rough cylinders had poked through the earth's crust and lifted a patch of jungle hundreds of feet into the air. I stared at the dense growth below. As a boy walking in the woods, I found places I thought no one had ever seen before. I suspected the Laotian jungle below had miles of country like that.

"Olds Flight. Let's green'em up," the mission commander radioed, the signal to arm the weapons.

"From now on," Hunter said, "our options for jettisoning include dropping our bombs armed so they'll explode on impact. I like that. Don't want the bad guys digging up my ordnance and using it to shoot back. Shootdown is a risk I can accept, but with my own powder—well, that's a horse of a different color."

"Roger," I said, still staring down at the jungle, seeing no sign of civilization. I couldn't imagine trying to survive in that endless sea of trees. In a way, I felt fortunate to be riding in Hunter's backseat. I would see a much tougher target than if I were in the normal indoctrination program. Mainly I felt safe with Hunter. I still had butterflies and felt ill from the heat, but the odds don't get any better than being with him.

"I can see the Red River ahead," Hunter said. "Keep your eyes peeled. You ever seen anti-aircraft guns or surface-to-air missiles?"

"Never," I said, thinking it a curious question to ask on my first combat mission.

"You will today. Anti-aircraft rounds look like black or white puffs just like the World War Two movies. Since this ain't the movies, you can't hear them. You just see the puffs. I assume at Nellis they taught you what to do if a surface-to-air missile is coming at you.

"Yeah," I said, "And I heard your briefing on SAM's at the Fighter Weapons School."

"Well nothing's changed, Shooter. We've had more experience with SAMs, but it's all been bad. So be on the lookout and try to catch those suckers coming off the ground."

Suddenly I felt thirsty. I pulled the aircraft thermos out of its case. Empty. I had finished the ice water while we were still on the ground, and it went over the side with breakfast. I felt dehydrated, but there was no time to fish around in my G-suit for the emergency water. I glanced at the instrument panel; we had covered the last thirty miles in less than four minutes.

"Time to get your eyeballs out of the cockpit and look for MiGs," Hunter directed. "Check behind us. I'll accelerate to 600 knots and descend right down to the treetops. We'll put this four-ship on the deck and go like a bat out of hell."

"Checking," I grunted, straining to look back over my shoulder while strapped into the ejection seat and encumbered by my vest bulging with survival gear.

"OK, Shooter. Hang on to your socks. We're going to jink. I'll make a hard turn every few seconds so the gunners can't get a tracking solution. The lower we go, the harder we'll jink. It doesn't look like anyone is shooting now, but it's the stuff you don't see that'll kill you. We don't want a hit by the magic golden BB to be our first indication they're shooting."

"Roger," I grunted, trying to reply while being smashed down in the seat by a high G-turn.

"From this point I don't use a map," Hunter said. "Got the last thirty miles memorized so I can keep my head out of the cockpit. And I don't use any of those zippety-doo-dah electronics to navigate either. Keep it simple. Identify checkpoints on the ground and work into the target. Dead-reckoning navigation. The old tried and true way. Now we double check the Master Arm Switch and the weapons pylon select buttons indicating green. That covers it. We're ready."

"Ready," I repeated as Hunter jinked so hard my helmet bounced off the side of the canopy.

Chapter 7

"Buick Flight, Three here. Muzzle flashes at your one o'clock position."

"He's right; they're shooting," Hunter said. "Exploding just above our altitude."

"I hope it's going off above us," I said. "We're only flying at 200 feet."

"Handles great at 600 knots with a load of bombs," Hunter said, to himself or to me; it was hard to tell which.

"I wouldn't know," I said glancing at the blur of treetops. "You haven't let me touch the controls,"

"Standby, Ashe," Hunter said, in a calm, detached voice. "We're five seconds from the pull-up point."

I felt a kick when the afterburner ignited and my body slammed down in the seat, as Hunter pulled 6-G's and sustained the crushing force. My peripheral vision turned gray as my body weight increased to over 1,000 pounds. Then, as fast as he had put on the G-forces, Hunter took them off. We surged upward at near zero-G in a zoom-climb riding on our flaming afterburner. As the periphery of my vision returned, I watched the wingmen reposition until our four jets appeared line abreast and ready to roll-in to dive bomb the bridge.

"OK, Shooter, we're passing through 9,000 feet on our way to 12,000."

The lack of G-forces was a relief as we climbed towards the

top of the pop-up, but, even with full afterburner, we couldn't sustain airspeed with the heavily laden bird.

I looked to the left. At our 10 o'clock position, lay the French built, mile-long Paul Doumer Bridge, named for a Governor General when Vietnam was French Indochina. All supplies moving by rail or truck from China or Haiphong Harbor and over the Red River into Hanoi and thence south to the battlefields funneled through the Doumer Bridge.

A peaceful mud-red river flowed between lush green banks and under the nineteen majestic steel spans. It wouldn't be peaceful long. There were no trucks or cars anywhere. The target appeared deserted except for a handful of people following an ox cart on the southern bridge approach. They were not going to have a good day.

As we climbed through 11,000 feet, Hunter rolled our jet toward the bridge and paused upside down. As I looked down at the target through the top of the canopy, bombs from the first two flights detonated and a span of the bridge was obscured with explosions and plumes of water. Hunter eased back on the stick, pulled our aircraft's nose down through the horizon, and zoomed toward the ground. After a crisp roll upright, he stabilized in a 45-degree dive at the bridge.

My forward view was limited, but I suspected the target was precisely aligned in Hunter's bombsite. The engine wound down as the throttle came back. Even at reduced power the jet raced quickly down hill. We passed through 8,000 feet then accelerated through 6,000. I anticipated bomb release at 4,500 feet, but it didn't happen. A wave of tension engulfed me as Hunter crossed a dangerous line and pressed the attack.

At 3,800 feet and 640 knots, I felt the 750-pound bombs ripple away as explosive ejectors hurled each weapon from our aircraft. An instant later, Hunter's 5-G dive-recovery slammed me down in my seat.

"They're shootin," Hunter said, "shootin' from the right."

Under Gs, I struggled to turn my head but still didn't see a single round explode. Then Hunter made a series of hard turns to evade the gunners. With each jinking turn, my head slammed against one side of the canopy, then the other.

I didn't hear the bombs go off but felt concussion waves hit our aircraft as they seem to lift and thrust it forward. Hunter's low release increased accuracy but also heightened the risk of getting blown up by our own bombs. Why did he press inside the bomb fragmentation envelope? Was he that good or just crazy?

Hunter turned hard to the left so we could assess the bomb damage. Vertical chutes of water and debris hung several hundred feet in the air. Hunter reversed the turn and made a quick check for enemy defenses then rolled back again. Now the bombs from all sixteen planes had impacted. The bridge didn't seem to be down, but it was hard to tell through the debris.

"Damn, those gunners are good," Hunter said, in an excited voice. "We had triple-A going off all around us, Ashe. Did you see it?"

"No, Hunter, sorry to say I didn't." I felt disgusted, having to admit I hadn't seen a single round.

Hunter did a quick aileron roll then after a few seconds said, "This jet feels funny. Look at the left drop tank."

The tank had several holes in it, and, aft of the holes, a ten-inch section of sheet metal stuck out into the wind stream.

"We took some small caliber in the tank," Hunter said. "We'll have to jettison." Hunter pulled the jet into level flight. I felt a bump as the fuel tanks and pylons dropped away from the wings.

When the fuel tank departed, we were traveling 620 knots, far above the safe jettison speed, but I trusted Hunter knew what he was doing. With the damaged tank off of the wing, the plane felt fine to me.

"Let's make sure our flight members are still with us," Hunter said.

I looked to the left then right. Our three wingmen were all in position precisely where they should be. My adrenaline was still flowing fast. I sighed with relief. We had been shot at and hit and were doing fine. I had seen combat and hadn't been frozen with fear as I thought I might be. Suddenly, I felt a strange sense of invincibility. Hunter could get us through anything. I smiled with a child-like feeling that we had gotten away with something as we skimmed along the tops of the trees at over 600 knots.

"Buick Three, this is Lead," Hunter radioed. "Could you slide in here and look at my jet?"

"Roger, Lead."

"Still isn't right," Hunter said on the intercom. "Feels a little goosey. Kind of a low rumble in the airframe."

I tried to feel something but did not.

"Buick Lead, this is Buick Three. You took hits in the belly and you're leaking. Keep an eyeball on your fuel gage."

"Reading 5000 pounds," Hunter said. "That's 2000 less than we should have."

Frantically, I looked for my line-up card to see how much fuel we needed to get home. Another detail I should have committed to memory but did not.

"Buick Lead, this is Three. Pouring out pretty good now. Streaming back along the fuselage."

"Right," Hunter said on the intercom. "I can almost see the gauge going down." Then he said on the radio, "Buick Lead is going burner, the rest of Buick flight stay low and save gas."

Hunter plugged in the afterburner and started to climb. In clean configuration, our bird accelerated quickly and lifted us up and away from the flight.

"Afterburner?" I asked. "Why are we in afterburner?"

Hunter was silent.

"What's happening?"

Still no response from Hunter.

"We're leaking but you're in afterburner using up the fuel we have left. What gives?"

Our jet passed through 5,000 feet climbing at 540 knots. I wondered if the intercom still worked and activated hot mike to override it. "Hunter, can you hear me? What's going on?"

"Roger, I hear you," Hunter said, in a thin voice. "Your intercom works. Now get off hot mike and standby."

Mechanically, I recalled the critical action emergency procedures that I had memorized in training. Then it occurred to me why Hunter was in afterburner. He did it to gain altitude and energy. Better to run the gas through the engine than out a hole in the belly of the jet. I had made a stupid mistake questioning his emergency response before I thought it through. I flipped the 100 percent switch and took deep breaths of cool pure oxygen. But soon my feeling of embarrassment became raw terror. We were deep in enemy territory in a wounded jet with no alternative but to eject.

"Hunter, talk to me," I shouted. "We're going to flameout. If you have a plan, it would be a perfect time to tell me."

Hunter didn't respond, and our jet continued a steady climb. Our fuel gage indicated less than 500 pounds as the rest of Buick flight dropped out of view behind and below. Looking over my shoulder, I could still see the city of Hanoi.

Until now it had seemed unreal: one of the thousands of emergency procedure drills in the simulator where I learned to set aside emotion and concentrate on the next step. But I was not in charge here, and it wasn't a simulation. Nothing had prepared me to function as a second crewmember. We were in serious trouble, and I couldn't understand why Hunter wouldn't talk.

"Buick Lead, this is Buick Three. You have a fire in the aft section. Repeat, aft section fire."

"Roger, Buick Three," Hunter radioed in a carefully modulated voice.

I reviewed the ejection procedures: head back, heels back, elbows in, back straight, pull up arm rests and squeeze the handles. As we descended through 12,000 feet, I thought I smelled smoke. Automatically, I looked around the headrest at Hunter. Again, I felt like a fool. Of course Hunter wasn't smoking, but he wasn't busy either. He sat quite still, helmet visor down, and facing straightforward. Why wouldn't he talk to me?

A muffled explosion buffeted deep within the airframe. Either we took another hit, or the jet was coming apart.

Abruptly the afterburner quit. After a few seconds, the engine began to spool down, and, one by one, aircraft systems dropped offline. An alarming quiet filled the cockpit.

"Zero gas," Hunter said.

"Buick Lead, this is Buick Three. There's a torch, thirty feet long, coming out of the belly of the bird."

"Roger on the fire," Hunter radioed, again in a controlled voice. "And we have a flameout."

Instinctively, I reached for the checklist and opened it to engine failure. I had the critical items memorized but left nothing to chance. My finger traced down the list and paused on the Ram Air Turbine or RAT. Extend for emergency hydraulic power, the checklist said. But the RAT could only be engaged from the front cockpit.

If the RAT didn't extend into the air stream, we would lose power to the flight controls. Without flight controls, the Thud would live up to its name and plummet into the jungle with the aerodynamic characteristics of a boulder. As I reached for the intercom button to remind Hunter, Lucky came on the radio.

"Buick Lead, this is Buick Three. Extend the RAT, hit the restart button, and pick a spot to eject."

I felt a vibration as the RAT moved into the air stream. The hydraulic gauges began to show an increase in pressure but fluctuated wildly with each flight control movement.

"Are we going to punch out of this thing?" I shouted. "Hunter, talk to me. Talk to me!"

"Buick Lead, this is Buick Three. You're burning man. Time to punch out, repeat, eject now."

With airspeed less than 240 knots, we descended toward the trees. Even if an air-start worked, we had only fumes in the tank. Very soon, in seconds, we would have to parachute into the jungle.

I was frantic. "Hunter, you gotta talk to me!"

"Buick Lead, this is Buick Three. You're well below safe altitude, EJECT, EJECT, EJECT IMMEDIATELY. Hunter, EJECT NOW."

"I'll ride this thing to hell before I'll punch out," Hunter radioed.

"That looks like where we're headed," I screamed on the intercom. "Hunter, PUNCH OUT. Talk to me! EJECT NOW."

As airspeed dropped below 200 knots, less than 1,500 feet above the trees, I shook my head not believing. If I'd been flying the jet, I'd have punched out with at least 4,000 feet of altitude. I put my faith in Hunter; now he was going to scrape me off on a tree.

Instinctively, I grabbed the checklist. Then, in frustration, I slammed it to the floor of the cockpit. At 1,000 feet, Hunter eased back on the control stick. The jet slowed then vibrated with the insidious shudder of a terminal stall. Below was a blanket of treetops with one huge limestone karst protruding through it. While I watched, we sunk below the top of the karst.

"Hunter, say something or I'm leaving."

Everything instilled by my training fought against what I knew I had to do. Hunter was about to kill me. I had to leave the apparent security of my cockpit for the unknowns of the jungle below. It would be the most important irreversible decision I had ever made. I took a last breath of pure oxygen as I jerked the armrests into the ejection position and wrapped my trembling fingers around the handles. I yelled, "I'm history," and squeezed.

The canopy from Hunter's cockpit jettisoned upward and flew to the right. Surprised, I turned my head to follow it as the front ejection seat exploded into the air followed closely by my canopy. As soon as I turned my head out of position, I realized I shouldn't have. As my ejection seat detonated, it applied 22 instantaneous Gs propelling me out of the cockpit and 30 feet above the jet. An intense pain shot down my back, as my 157-pound body, for one instant, weighed over 3,400 pounds. My arms and legs flailed at the top of the trajectory...then I began falling...

I was barely conscious when the automatic butt-thruster strap kicked me away from the ejection seat. The next instant my parachute opened. The chute stopped my fall less than a hundred feet above the trees. Before I could look up to check my parachute, pain wrenched through my back.

I penetrated the jungle growth and started falling through the branches, grunting as I absorbed each blow. Tree limbs tore my arms and legs as I ricocheted from branch to branch. Finally, I stopped. I hung with my eyes closed and arms up around my head like a defeated heavyweight expecting the final blow.

It was quiet. Cautiously I opened my eyes. With my helmet visor down everything looked dark. My right arm ached, so I fumbled with my left and pushed my visor up.

I couldn't breath and clawed at my oxygen mask release clip trying to get at the fluid that choked me. Finally, one side of the mask came free. I wiped my face with a gloved hand as I gasped for air. On my glove was sweat and blood from inside my mask. I touched my neck below my right ear. More blood.

I hung far above the jungle floor in a fairly clear area below the major tree canopy. I considered releasing my parachute straps, but the fall would probably kill me. Instead, I decided to drop my brain bucket to judge the distance. Carefully I slid the helmet off trying to favor the pain in my right ear. Holding it straight out, I let it go.

The helmet, still attached by the oxygen hose, arced down and smashed against my knee. A sharp pain shot up my leg and into my back. Unsnapping the oxygen hose, I released the helmet again. By the sound, I thought it fell 60 or 70 feet to the jungle floor. Then I heard a jet engine. It was the rest of Buick flight, I hoped.

The parachute straps dug into my crotch. I wanted to loosen them, but it was more important to establish contact with the rest of my flight. I desperately needed to tell someone I was alive and knew the jets couldn't stay in the area long.

Sharp pains accompanied each movement as I unzipped the radio from my survival vest and turned it on. My finger hovered over the microphone button, but I didn't know what to say. Hunter was Buick Lead, but I didn't have a call sign? Buick

Lead, backseat? No, that wasn't it. Out of desperation, I keyed the mike.

"Buick flight," I radioed. "This is Buick Passenger."

As my radio went into the receive mode, I heard the distinctive YUP, YUP, YUP of an emergency parachute beacon. Someone's down with his beacon on, I thought. Then I realized it was my beacon, and it would block any attempt to contact my flight.

The emergency beacon was on a parachute strap above my shoulder. I tried to reach it but couldn't. As I struggled, I dropped my handheld survival radio. Its retainer cord payed out as it slid towards my feet. I grasped for it, but the radio fell to the jungle floor. The end of the cord hadn't been tied to the survival vest. Fortunately, I had a second handheld unit and could retrieve the dropped radio when I got down.

Next I initiated the seat survival pack that I should have released while descending but didn't. As I pulled the lever, the seat case opened. The life raft dropped below me and started to inflate. It made a loud hissing noise, and I looked around to see if I had been discovered.

Several yards away, I noticed a figure standing by the base of a tree. It looked like Hunter, but I couldn't focus. I strained to see but felt consciousness slipping away. The figure squatted by the tree then rocked back and forth while looking down at something in his hand. It appeared to be a service revolver.

"Hunter, up here," I yelled. "Here, in the tree."

The figure stopped rocking but didn't look up. I yelled again, but he didn't move. Perhaps my eyes were playing tricks. Maybe pain was causing me to see things that weren't real. Surely, Hunter would respond. Except he hadn't in the plane.

I blinked several times, convinced the figure was Hunter. When I yelled again, Hunter stood up, slowly turned away and disappeared into the jungle. I screamed at him, not believing he would leave me hanging in a tree. The throbbing in my back was intense. My pills were in the G-suit but reaching my ankle and unzipping the pocket was going to be excruciating.

I began to pull my leg up, slowly grasping the G-suit material hand-over-hand. Each pull brought my ankle closer and a new threshold of pain. The ankle pocket was almost within reach when a paralyzing lightning bolt shot up my back, and I lost my grip. As my leg dropped, I screamed in agony and passed out.

Chapter 8

A slice of sunshine exploded through the trees onto my face and warmed me to a sleepy consciousness. Raising my head cautiously, I expected pain but there was none. Instead, I felt a calm solitude as I lay cradled in lush, warm vegetation savoring the pungent aroma of flowers and ripe fruit. In the distance, the shrill screech of a bird faded into eerie quiet. I imagined myself lying under palm trees at the Sahara Hotel pool until reality passed through my body like a bolt of lightning.

My eyes shot open as the realization that I was on the ground in a jungle in North Vietnam froze my body with fear. My mind raced as the muscles in the back of my neck burned with tension. Four months ago, I had barely heard of Vietnam. Four weeks ago, I was in Las Vegas embracing Jenny's sun-warmed body. Forty minutes ago, I had never seen Vietnam.

Now I was injured, behind enemy lines, and probably on my own in enemy territory. There was no one to turn to and no one to ask what to do. My heart raced. I could feel it pounding in my chest as my throat began to constrict.

"Breathe," I said, slamming a fist against my chest.

Looking around, I tried to clear my mind and assess my situation. I was out of the tree but had no memory of how it happened. Hunter must have untangled my parachute. My body lay on my folded chute with survival gear neatly stacked within arm's reach. Near my head lay a canteen and two small survival-ration cans I didn't recognize. My G-suit was in a pile by my feet with both survival radios. My emergency locator radio beacon was perched on top of the radios. It had been cut away from the parachute harness where I had strained so painfully to reach it. Hunter must have switched it off.

I scanned the clearing for Hunter but couldn't see him. I didn't want to wait long. Since I couldn't depend on Hunter, I needed to take action and start surviving on my own. Although I wasn't hungry, I recalled from my training that it was important to eat. Obsessively, I ripped two brown camouflage cans open with a key opener and started fishing the contents out with my fingers. As the food entered my parched throat I choked and spat it out on the ground. Opening the canteen, I wolfed down water and tried to control my anxiety. I felt like a crazed fool, like the pilot my survival school instructors laughed about who ejected, was rescued an hour later, and had consumed three days' rations.

As I started to throw the cans into the undergrowth, I held back. Don't eat fast but don't waste it either. I relaxed for a few seconds then stared at the cans. One label read pound cake, and the other, peaches. In smaller letters was printed, K-Rations packed in 1945. Must be contraband Hunter carried since they're too old to be in the survival kit. I began to eat small bites, savoring pound cake canned twenty-one years before and washing it down with juice from the peaches. Finally, I lay back and let the last drops of juice from the upturned can trickle into my mouth. Looking up into the trees, I wondered how Hunter managed to get me down and retrieve all my gear.

Hearing people noises in the distance, I bolted upright and looked around to see what cover my position provided. The last thing I needed was for the Vietnamese to find me before Hunter returned. The noise sounded closer. I rolled up the white and orange parachute and placed it next to the supplies. Then I covered the pile of equipment with an olive drab poncho.

The noise grew louder, and I noticed movement deep within the jungle plants. Hunter wouldn't make noise. This had to be someone else. Drawing my service revolver, I cocked the hammer over a live round and waited. Glancing to the side, I didn't see the rest of my ammunition. The pistol carried only three live and two flare rounds.

As the foliage moved, I raised my weapon and followed with shaky hands. After another crashing sound, the vegetation parted, and I caught a fleeting glance of the intruder. It was a girl carrying what appeared to be a long stick. Every few steps she swung the stick and brought it down to clear her path. She was going to pass dangerously close to my hiding place.

Was she friendly? Impossible, so deep into North Vietnam. What should I do if she saw me? I couldn't kill a kid, and she obviously wasn't a soldier. Was she on a trail or just walking through the jungle brush? She seemed to take forever to go a few feet. Don't move, I thought. Don't assume she saw anything. I waited, praying she would pass quickly.

As the moving undergrowth resolved into the clear form of the young girl, I could finally see that she was alone. I lowered the pistol and rested it on the ground then flattened my body against the mossy jungle floor. She stopped less than twenty feet away and looked around. I didn't think she saw me but couldn't tell for sure. I tried to peer out of the corner of my eye fearing any movement would betray my position. Again I felt my heart pounding, terrified I would choke or cough. Slowly she moved on, giving no indication she had seen me.

I held my breath until she was out of sight then crawled to the area she'd passed through. It was a small path, not beaten down but clearly used. Gathering my gear I looked around. Where was Hunter? If I moved, how would we get back together? I was torn between the need to find a better-concealed position and my desperation to locate Hunter.

I gathered all my equipment in the parachute and hoisted it up waist high. Pain struck again. Moving slowly under the weight of the gear, I crept a few feet up the side of a hill, heard another noise, and stopped. As I hid under a broad leaf plant, I wondered if I'd detected the noise soon enough or had pain distracted me. Squinting with hazy vision, I saw the silhouette of another figure with a stick.

As I reached for my pistol, I found an empty holster. I had put the gun down on the parachute and now it was wrapped in the huge ball of nylon with my gear. The figure walked carefully, making very little sound. It appeared to be searching through the foliage. The figure left the path and crept towards the spot where I had been hiding earlier. I began to see details. It was a man but not in a uniform I recognized. He was wearing pajamas. Black pajamas. And it wasn't a stick he was carrying. It was a rifle.

My eyes frantically searched for an escape route but there was none. I wanted to become invisible. The soldier stood motionless, scanning the bushes methodically, revealing he had not found me. Moisture hung in the jungle air and muffled sounds to an unworldly quiet. Pressing my arms forward, I flattened my body against the ground. The soldier, still scanning, began to walk away from me. I was relieved until he stopped, turned, and again moved in my direction. I pressed my chin into the soft earth until I tasted musty dirt. The soldier approached so close that all I could see were his legs. I closed my eyes and held my breath.

I wrenched with pain as the rifle barrel dug into my back. The soldier shouted in Vietnamese and poked me again. I rolled over on my back in agony. He looked young, no more than a boy, wide-eyed and afraid. He lunged, thrusting the rifle toward my side. I raised my hand to deflect the blow, grabbed the muzzle, and held it away from my body. Surprised, the soldier jerked the rifle back. As I lost my grip on the barrel, he lurched off balance and fell. Recovering, he ran forward again, stopped at my feet, snapped the rifle to shoulder firing position and aimed straight at my head.

The boy-soldier stiffened as his mouth curled into a slight smile or perhaps a grimace. His eyes seemed to lose focus. The muzzle wavered, tracing an unsteady arc as the rifle alternately pointed at my head then my chest. He fired.

Concussion from the blast blew me from a sitting position to flat on my back. Instantly a lighting bolt of pain engulfed me. The soldier took a tentative step forward, his mouth parted as if to speak then his knees buckled and he crashed down on top of me. His body pinned me to the ground as his forehead collided with my nose and smashed into me again and again as he twitched with violent spasms. Finally, he was still.

Too shocked to move, I stared up at the trees unsure of my wounds. Blood gushed out of the soldier's back in spurting torrents, splashed into my mouth and poured off his shoulder onto my chest. A thin hatchet, decorated like a tomahawk with a small posy of bloodstained feathers, was half buried in the base of his neck.

"Hey, Shooter. You alive?" Hunter said.

"I don't know."

"You are. The Gomer missed. It's hard to shoot straight with a tomahawk in your spine, even at close range. Kind of takes you off your aim."

"Hunter, where the have you been? You could've got me killed."

"Looks like you were doing a fine job of that yourself. This is no time for polite conversation. We got to haul ass, find better cover, preferably someplace with a view that doesn't have a dead body in it."

Hunter stood over me and yanked the tomahawk out of the soldier's back, splattering more blood on my face and neck. With his fingers, he scraped off the cutting edge then flipped his hand several times to shake off the blood. After wiping the residue on the leg of his flight suit, he spit on the blade and started to polish it with the heel of his hand.

"Well, Shooter, you going to dance with that guy all day or are we going to make tracks?"

I finally realized Hunter wasn't going to help me, so I rolled the soldier off to the side then stood up. The front of my flight suit was soaked with blood. I could feel it on my face and taste it in my mouth. I spit and gagged trying to get rid of it. Methodically, I patted over my face and chest. As far as I could tell all the blood came from the soldier. I hadn't been wounded, but the piercing pain in my back felt like I'd been run through with a sword.

The dead soldier lay on his back, eyes open and unfocused in a death stare. He looked far too young for war. My eyes lingered on his rifle, his ragged black sandals made from the tread of a tire, and his black pajamas glistening with blood.

His face no longer belonged to a boy. Now he was a man who had experienced all of life that he would live and felt it slip away too early. His tormented expression and all-seeing stare spoke to me in silent eternal phrases. I looked at him wanting to say something in return but not finding words.

"Ashe, snap out of it," Hunter said. "We've got to move. That guy isn't carrying any gear. No water, no bandoleer, no nothing. All I see is a rifle and one clip of ammo. He's not far from his supplies and his people, so they're not far from us." Hunter pointed to the base of a tree. "Dump all your equipment over there and be quick about it. We'll hide your orange and white parachute and we'll use the material from mine; it's the new camouflage type. Hurry! Move faster."

"I can't move faster. My back is hurt."

"How bad?" Hunter snapped.

"Real bad, I can hardly move."

"We don't have time to stick around. Hurt or not you've got to carry your load and haul out of here. Whatever pain you feel now is nothing compared to the alternative. I'm going to give you two pills. They'll make almost anything go away, but we can't sit here until they take effect. You must move now and move fast. And above all, be quiet. Understand?"

"Okay. What do you want me to do?"

"Like I said, Ashe, dump your gear on the ground. The stuff we take we'll carry in sacks I'll make from my parachute. The throw-a-ways, I'll hide with your chute. Take your G-suit with you, either wear it or carry it."

"Why are we taking G-suits?"

"Why! What do you mean, why? You think we're going to vote here? That's the last bleeding 'why' question I want to hear from you. Just do what I tell you, do it fast, and keep your voice down."

Hunter worked quickly, sorting our food, water, medicine and survival gear. He put my survival radios into his vest. Next, he removed one bullet from my pistol and put it into his revolver then tossed my weapon and spare ammo on the throw-away pile. I wanted to protest but decided to keep quiet. Hunter rolled up the discarded gear in my parachute, motioned for me to stay put, and disappeared into the undergrowth.

Hunter returned in a few minutes and cut his camouflage material into two packs that could be slung over our shoulder like bandoleers. Next he fashioned two smaller pieces of material and without speaking directed me to sit with my feet toward him. He packed a thin layer of moss and crumpled leaves against the soles of my boots, covered it with broad leaves, and bound it with parachute cord. Then he wrapped each foot with a piece of cloth and secured it with cord. My feet looked like boxing gloves. Hunter removed his own boots and socks and placed them in his shoulder pack.

"Let's move out," he said. "Follow six feet behind and watch your step. We'll move slowly but you won't have much traction with that cloth on your feet. Don't want to leave a trail, so don't disturb anything."

For the next two hours, Hunter glided barefoot through the undergrowth. I followed limping badly. The wrapping on my feet aggravated my back injury, and pain coursed down my leg with each excruciating step. Soaked with sweat and mouth parched, I moved forward but desperately wanted to stop. As we approached the base of a huge limestone karst with sheer walls that disappeared up through the jungle canopy, Hunter unfolded a map and looked around.

"Stay here. I'll scout the area and be back in a few minutes," Hunter said, then moved toward the dense undergrowth at the base of the karst.

I slumped against the exposed root of a large tree and rummaged through my pack for something to drink. I found one of the plastic baby bottles used to carry emergency water and drank it all. If the pills had eased some of the pain, I wasn't aware of it.

The soldier's blood had congealed into a thick wet mass on my flight suit. Sweat kept it from drying so I pulled the caked material forward to keep it from sticking to my chest. Putting my head back, I tried to rest. After a short while, Hunter emerged from the foliage with a small bunch of bananas.

"We're okay for a now," he said. "Rest until dark and then we'll move out. Take two more pills. They'll cut the pain and help you sleep."

"We're going to walk through this jungle at night?"

"Always at night. Only at night. You're afraid of the dark now, but you'll learn that night is your friend. I'll teach you to live in the dark. You'll be able to see and do much more than you think, once your eyes get used to it."

"Hunter, what's going to happen?" I said in what seemed to me a pitifully weak voice.

"We walk out, get picked up by a chopper, or die. Those are the choices I see so far. Since you got a gimp leg..."

"It's mostly my back."

"Whatever. We may have only two options. We need to make tracks tonight, get far away so they won't find us near the crash site in the morning. They've probably found our plane already, but it will be tomorrow before they can get enough people together for an organized search. By then, we need to be miles from here. They'll expect us to go due south, so we'll head west or southwest and find an area that's remote but open enough for a helicopter. Rescue will have the devil's own time getting a chopper this far north. I don't think it's been done before."

"How long before we get picked up?"

"One thing at a time. We'll worry about staying alive hour by hour. Try to rest. Sleep for a couple of hours, then we'll move out after dark. Now eat your bananas."

"I'm not hungry."

"Eat'em anyway. They're monkey bananas. They have big black seeds that taste bitter so spit them out and eat the rest.

We have four cans of emergency water plus four plastic baby bottles."

"Three, I drank one."

"Good, drink all you want. Just tell me when you do so we can keep track of supplies. Finding more water won't be a problem. I'm going to give you some pemmican. Eat it slowly and wash it down with water. It'll give you a lot of energy but doesn't taste so hot. Eat all the fruit you can, there's plenty in the jungle if you know where to look."

"This pemmican tastes awful," I said.

"Right. I'll call room service and have them send in a steak."

"I'd settle for some more of those peaches and pound cake you set out earlier."

Hunter's brow furrowed. "The what I did earlier?"

"The canned peaches and pound cake you left after you got me down from that tree."

"Well, Shooter, I didn't get you out of a tree, and I don't know anything about any peaches. Now get some rest."

As the pills softened the edge of the distracting pain, I drifted into a half-awake trance. The jungle mist resolved into gentle rain. Hunter covered me with a poncho and set up a second poncho to collect rainwater. He opened a plastic baby bottle for each of us, and while he sipped, he examined the canteen curiously. After a while, he peeled bananas and slowly ate them while he studied a plastic coated survival map of North Vietnam. I watched as water droplets became small rivulets on the poncho and trickled down to fill the plastic bottles. Finally, I slumped against the moss-covered trunk of a tree and passed from pain to sleep.

Chapter 9

My eyes shot open looking for the animal that was in pain. The screaming seemed to come from everywhere at once. As I peered into the dark jungle, a thousand eyes seemed to be staring back at me. "Hunter!" I yelled.

A hand clamped over my nose and mouth. Hunter raised a finger to his lips signaling me to be quiet. I sat motionless until the eerie noise stopped and Hunter whispered, "Welcome to the jungle."

"What going on out there?"

"Birds mainly, but other critters too. Shortly after sundown they screech at the top of their lungs for five or ten minutes. Seems longer, doesn't it?"

"Scared the wits out of me."

"If they don't screech, you should be scared. If a lot of people are around, they wouldn't do it."

"Are those eyes out there?"

"Looks like eyes but it's not. It's a funny kind of moss on the trees that emit a phosphorescent glow for a while after the sun goes down. It won't last long."

"When do we move out?"

"Now," Hunter said. "Everything's packed. How's your back?"

"Don't know," I said as I got up on all fours and tested my ability to stand. Finally I had to admit to myself that I couldn't make it. All my joints were stiff and felt like they had been packed with sand. "Still hurts everywhere when I move."

"Here are two more pills. Take them and we'll leave in about ten minutes."

I rolled onto my back and tentatively began to stretch my stiffened limbs. After several painful minutes of false starts, I made it to my feet and clutched a tree trunk until I recovered my balance. "We might as well do it," I said, trying to sound more confident than I felt.

Hunter strode through the jungle with surprising speed. I followed six feet behind when the foliage was sparse but tracked closer when he held back large branches so both of us could get through. Several times I lagged and was hit in the face with a limb that snapped back into place. As we rested a few minutes each hour, we ate fruit and sipped water spiked with instant coffee. Although limping, I kept the pace—at least for the first three hours. Hunter, wanting to avoid trails, set a course straight across the terrain on a compass heading.

Moving through the jungle was even worse than I supposed it would be, and I supposed it would be awful. Around one o'clock in the morning, rain fell in a downpour. I slipped on wet ground and fell flat on my face.

I tried to lift my head out of the mud, but, as I did, my whole body was seized with pain so sudden and so terrible that I screamed out in agony. I rolled onto my back and lay in a muddy pool trying to move my cramped legs out straight.

Hunter sat beside me for a few minutes then helped me try to stand. Just when I thought I had made it, my legs collapsed, and I fell again.

"It's time for the big guns," Hunter said, as he put a pill in my mouth and held a bottle of water to my lips. I didn't have the energy to ask what I was taking.

The next three hours passed into a macabre memory of trailing Hunter through the jungle. My emotions caromed between drugged detachment and paralyzing anxiety. My life depended on staying with Hunter while he covered ground quickly in the dark. But, it seemed to me, he didn't consider my injuries.

Each time I lost sight of Hunter, even for an instant, I was possessed by terror. My emotions were so rattled with pain and pills, I thought I was going to die. I spoke to God and promised

I would get religion if He let me escape from His jungle.

By 0400 hours, I yearned for dawn's light as pain seared through my body and each step brought an agonizing groan of self-pity. "Hunter, I need another pill."

"Not now. If you make it one more hour, you can have the whole day off. At least the daylight hours."

"I'll try."

"Try is not an option. Shooter, you'll do it."

Hunter showed no hint of fatigue even though he was carrying my shoulder pack. I don't know when he relieved me of the burden, but there he stood, ramrod straight, with both packs across his chest like bandoleers. Hunter attacked the jungle like a hybrid crossbreed of animal and machine. The wetness, mud, steep trails, thick foliage, or dark of night did not bother him. He maintained a cool air of self-sufficiency and never once complained.

At dawn, we stopped while Hunter scouted for a secure hiding place. When safely concealed for the day, he removed the wrapping from my feet, took off my boots and socks, then dried my feet. That's all I remembered before passing out from exhaustion.

Still dazed and bewildered, I emerged from sleep. My first half-awake thought was of Jenny. I felt detached from my own battered body as I imagined her stepping out of the shower and drying with a huge towel. With long strokes, she brushed her hair until it flowed over her shoulder like a waterfall. Then she walked to our bed, pulled back the covers, and snuggled in beside me. Her body was warm and soft against mine as our legs entwined in a lover's knot.

As our bodies melted together, a tearing pain shot through my back and coursed down my leg, causing me to groan with agony.

"Good afternoon," Hunter said.

"What time is it?"

"Almost 1700 hours. You slept all day except for a few times I had to shake you. Snoring you know, enough to wake up the whole jungle.

"What day is it?"

"It's the afternoon of our second day in this God-forsaken place. We've been on the ground about thirty-four hours—of that, we've walked fifteen."

"But who's counting, right?" I said.

"Sleep some more if you want. We won't move out until dark."

Sleep eluded me but while resting in addled quiet, I sipped water and chewed on bite-size morsels of meat Hunter gave me. I thought it might be canned meat until I noticed the carcass of a snake, gutted, cleaned, and sectioned with surgical precision. Hunter sat on his haunches with the serpent's head balanced on his shoulder. The long skin was draped around his neck, flowed down his back, and trailed across the ground. He held a huge section of the reptile with both hands and gnawed on it like an ear of corn.

While revolted at first, I was resigned to follow Hunter's lead. I consumed my portion of raw snake without the slightest complaint or even curiosity about its pedigree. When Hunter offered a second helping, I ate it and reminded myself that raw snake was probably a delicacy. Somewhere.

After the meal of snake sushi, Hunter looked refreshed and unfolded a map, studying it as if memorizing the terrain.

"Hunter, do you know where we are?"

"Possibly."

"That's it? Possibly?"

"Best I can do. I think we're crossing a ridge line north of the Song Ma River," he said, holding up the map and pointing to a river meandering through the terrain. "Right here where it says 'relief data incomplete.'"

"'Data incomplete.' Even the map doesn't know where this place is."

"If we can find the river, we can figure it out."

"And that's all we know?" I asked.

"That's it. Next time you take a hike in North Vietnam, call ahead, reserve a guide."

As dusk fell, I tried to stand but felt weak and stiff. Hunter helped me limber up, working and stretching my limbs like a trainer. Finally, after spending a long time on all fours, I made it to my feet.

After relieving myself behind a tree, I forced down a patty of pemmican and several pieces of fruit. Then I swallowed two pills and chased them with a concoction Hunter asked me to try. It looked like mashed bark and leaves soaked in a bottle of water. As Hunter instructed, I drank the bitter tasting fluid then returned the solid matter to him. Hunter held the mash in cupped hands and made guttural sounds as if singing to the moon. I watched the ceremony with interest but didn't ask.

It was a luxury to have time to wait for the painkillers to take effect. Hunter sat cross-legged in front of a compass and studied the sky as the stars came into view. Except for a few puffy clouds, the night was clear. It hadn't rained all day, and I was dry for the first time.

Finally, after the medicines eased my pain and elevated my mood, I stumbled to my feet and said with some newfound authority, "Let's do it."

The night wore on as another painful drudge of putting one foot in front of the other. I stayed awash in a drugged stupor, alternately lethargic and filled with anxiety. The moon was visible for a few hours, and, later, a passing thunderstorm allowed us to replenish our water supply. At the first hint of light, Hunter found a campsite that was plush compared to the previous night. The moss-covered ground made a fine bed, but I could have slept on nails.

Chapter 10

The sun hung low in the afternoon sky as I awoke from a deep and satisfying sleep. My recovery seemed remarkable until I moved, and every aching muscle recalled the punishing trials of the previous days. The ticking of my body clock forewarned of the closing interval, the next excruciating pain, and I wondered how many pills remained.

The blood on my flight suit had mixed with sweat and cast off the heavy sweet scent of death. My strung-out mind wondered if jungle animals were attracted to the smell like sharks to a bleeding victim.

Hunter wasn't in camp, but I felt relatively secure in the hideout he had chosen. Bananas, mangoes, pemmican and water lay within easy reach. I opened a baggie of pemmican, but, after smelling it, decided to eat a banana instead. I tried to go back to sleep, but a shadowy silhouette walking through the jungle about twenty yards away startled me. The figure walked stealthily, appearing bent over as if carrying something. I thought it might be Hunter, but, through the thick foliage, I couldn't be sure. I looked for our pistol but decided it must be with Hunter. The figure finally disappeared in the undergrowth to my right. Then, in a few minutes, Hunter appeared out of the brush behind me carrying a double armload of fruit.

"Howya doing, Ashe?"

"Did you go by here a while ago?"

"Yeah, I used a circular route. If they track us they'll go in front of our position and have to double back to get to us. We'll have some warning."

"Is that an old Indian trick?"

"It's a trick and I'm an old Indian if that's what you mean. Getting your sense of humor back? Thought it was a permanent loss."

"Me too. You brought more food?"

"Special on bananas and mangoes at the jungle supermarket today. And, as an added treat, we still have that great pemmican paste I mixed up yesterday."

"That stuff really sucks. What's in it?"

"Dried meat and fat but I spruced it up with some chili and onion powder from our survival rations."

"An old Indian dish?"

"No, but it could be. When I was a kid, we ate a lot of dried meat, jackrabbit, and venison. Spiced it up with hot chilies, too. Not my favorite food, but you can't beat it for energy. So eat it. Make believe it's steak."

I sighed, resigned to eat some of the foul-smelling, fat-based meat. It seemed like the better I felt, the less palatable pemmican became. But I would do anything to get out of the jungle alive. I would eat pemmican. I would even ask God for help although I was not practiced at talking to the man upstairs.

Closing my eyes, I searched for a prayer but couldn't think of any. Instead of a prayer, I made a promise. If God allowed me to get back to the States, I would clean up my life and get religion. Maybe become a priest. Oh, I thought. God wouldn't believe that. I didn't believe it myself. I didn't know how to pray or to ask God for anything, but the thought of calling on Him was an undeniable measure of my desperation.

Over the next hour, Hunter occasionally pointed to the food, then to me, as a silent reminder to keep loading calories.

After a while, Hunter picked up the canteen and looked at it with a puzzled expression. "I'm surprised you didn't get hurt worse, landing with all your heavy gear. It's a wonder this canteen didn't beat you to death when you punched out of the jet."

"I didn't have the canteen, Hunter. You left it when you got me out of the tree. You left the peaches and the pound cake too."

"There you go again, talking crazy. Like I said before, I didn't get you down from the tree, and I sure don't know about any peaches."

I took the canteen from Hunter and held it in both hands, trying to piece together the details. Hunter didn't sound like he was joking, but it didn't make sense.

"Hunter, you saw me during preflight and I didn't have this canteen, right? And you say you didn't have it either. How can that be?"

Hunter shrugged. "Beats me."

"There's a lot that doesn't make sense and you need to level with me now, before we go on."

Hunter leaned back against a tree. "I don't have the answer, and we don't have time for a big discussion. We're trying to evade Charlie here. We'll move at twilight and it's going to be a tough night."

Hunter's evasive manner added to my frustration. "I want to know, and I want to know now," I said.

He glanced at me with a semi-tolerant smile, as if humoring a child.

"Hunter, what about it? Talk to me."

"Look," he said. "I already saved your bacon once. That soldier could've killed you, or worse, you could've been captured. I didn't have to save your tail then, and I don't have to keep saving it. If you want to strike out on your own then do it, but if you're going with me, keep your mouth shut so I can get some rest."

"Sorry, Hunter. You may have me on rank and experience, but there's too much that doesn't make sense." I knew I was stepping out of bounds. Maybe it was the drugs. Maybe the anxiety, but I couldn't hold back. "Why didn't you talk to me when we were going down in the jet? Why wouldn't you eject? Your ungrateful ass wouldn't be alive if I hadn't punched us out."

"Keep your voice down," Hunter hushed.

"How did I really get down from that tree?" I yelled, like I was possessed. "And what were you doing with that gun? And where did that canteen come from?"

As my anxiety grew, I continued waving my arms and talking out of control. Finally Hunter lunged forward, clamping his hand over my mouth, and shoving me to the ground. I fought violently until he slammed his knee into my ribs and ended it. I winced with pain, holding my side and gasping for breath.

"One more word out of you and I'll kick your side in and throw your pills in the jungle," Hunter said, still holding his hand over my mouth while he whispered near my ear. "Those pills are probably the reason you're acting crazy. I'll give you the benefit of the doubt but the enemy won't. Be quiet or you'll have every Viet Cong for miles down on us. I don't want to have to shoot you."

"You what?" I mumbled against his hand, not believing what I'd heard. It wasn't enough I was in the enemy jungle; I was with a madman.

"Now be quiet," Hunter directed then turned away.

I lay on my side nursing the pain for several minutes. Finally, I took slow, measured breaths and tried to relax some of the tension that racked the muscles in my side and back.

"I'm sorry," I said, as I fought to catch my breath. "You're right. It must have been the pills. I apologize; I acted crazy. I won't make anymore noise, but I need your help to understand. Will you please talk to me?"

"Depends," Hunter said.

"If they capture us, what happens then?"

"They may take you prisoner, but they'll never get me alive."

"What do you mean?"

"Just what I said, Ashe. Precisely what I said."

"Is that why you carry only one bullet?"

"Could be," Hunter said, then looked off into the jungle.

"I believe you have two bullets now. What's the second one for?"

"It's for you."

"What do you mean it's for me? Don't I get a choice?"

"I told you to keep your voice down," Hunter said in a forceful whisper.

I put my face close to his, "And I'm telling you I don't want you to shoot me even if Charlie walks right into our camp. Do you understand?"

"Calm down. The bullet is for you. I don't care what you do with it. You can put it in your brain or shove it up your butt."

I shook my head in disbelief. "If we're about to be captured, you're going to shoot yourself? Isn't that committing suicide to avoid getting killed? Why not carry a lot of ammo and take a bunch of the enemy with you? Go out in a big firefight. This suicide thing's a chicken-hearted approach. Don't you see that?"

Hunter seemed to grind his teeth, and as his lips parted the muscles in his jaw stood out. "Listen closely, Ashe. I'm only going to say this once. I was shot down and captured in Korea. I spent two and a half years in a cold, rat-infested prison, living among my own feces. We had damn little food, no doctors, no medical supplies, and lived in stinking filth."

Hunter hesitated then continued in a whisper. "Half-alive men sat quietly and watched maggots clean dead flesh from their wounds. It works just like they teach in survival training, but it's a slow ugly process, emotionally degrading, and horrible to witness day after day. For two and a half years, I was tortured, starved, and watched most of the friends I made in prison die a slow painful death."

Listening to Hunter drained away my anger and replaced it with fear and regret. I mouthed off and lit his fuse. Now I would suffer the consequences.

"I had never seen a man die before," Hunter said as he stared into the jungle. "But soon I wanted to die because living was too painful. I did live, but I've died at the thought of that place everyday since. Why did I survive when the lives of my friends ended in unspeakable agony? I'm not going through it again. I won't be captured alive. You think I'm afraid. You're right, I'm afraid, but that's a lot different than being a chicken."

How had I let this happen? I had told the bravest man I had ever known that he was a coward. I wanted to interrupt Hunter and somehow take back my unforgivable words, but I didn't know how.

Hunter continued. "I didn't have to come to this war. If you've been a POW you never have to fight again. I'm here because I volunteered, and because I wanted to fight for my country. But, I know when to fight, and I know when the fight is over."

I shook my head, "Look, I'm..."

"Shut up," Hunter directed. "I'm not finished. I accepted the risk and the consequences of coming back to war, and I don't need any green-ass on his first mission to lecture me on the choices I've made. The only reason you're not scared senseless is that you don't know what's waiting for you. I've earned the right to be afraid, and I know what to fear. You can call it chicken, but until you've been there, don't be too quick to judge. One more thing, I don't shoot it out on the ground because that's not my war. We're alone deep in North Vietnam and have to decide how to stay alive or how we choose to die. That young soldier was the first soul I ever killed when I wasn't flying an airplane. It bothered me to do it, but it was the only way I could save you."

"I'm sorry," I said as I felt my eyes fill with unshed tears. "I made a fool out of myself again. I'm scared and need your help to get out of here. This is my first mission. I didn't get any local classes, no jungle survival, and no escape and evasion training. I don't know how to organize a rescue effort, or who to call on the radio to get it started. Back at Nellis they told us rescue procedures change frequently, and, because of security, we'd get the specifics at our combat base. I didn't get anything at Korat. They put me in the jet with you before any of that happened. Now I'm in the jungle, trying to escape and evade with someone who knows everything I need to know but is going to kill himself before he tells me."

Hunter was quiet for several minutes as he stared into the tree canopy. His silence seem to last forever.

Exhaustion, frustration, and fear washed over me as I put my head in my hands and cried, not wanting Hunter to hear me, but unable to control the sobbing. After a while, Hunter turned toward me but didn't make eye contact. I watched his expression. He didn't look afraid. He looked surprisingly peaceful for a man considering suicide. I studied the wide band of torture scars visible on his wrists. Perhaps I was beginning to see the scars Hunter held inside.

"OK, Ashe. I hear you," Hunter said, in a disconsolate tone. "I can't guarantee we'll get out of here, but we can give it a good shot. I realize this has been confusing, and I can't expect you to understand. Perhaps you're right. We should talk. I'll level with you about anything you want to know. Might as well be straight with each other. We may not be much, but right now we're all we got."

"Tell me, what happened?"

Hunter's voice betrayed his deep resignation. "Starting where?"

"The beginning, when our jet got hit and you wouldn't talk to me?"

As Hunter looked at me, his eyes flared then he looked away. "We were hit hard. I knew it was over when fuel started to leak. I'm a single seat jock, not accustomed to looking out for someone else in my jet, so I clammed up."

"Why didn't you eject?"

Hunter reached in his pocket, fished out a Zippo lighter, and stared at it thoughtfully. "Never occurred to me. Too far north. The risk of capture and all that."

"You were going to ride the jet in and take me with you?"

"I was going to ride it in, but you had a set of handles. You could have used them if you'd wanted."

"I did use them. I mean, I finally ejected when we were so low I thought we would crash. Why did your seat go if you didn't pull your handles?"

"You ejected me, too. The seat system was set up to go in tandem. My mistake, I forgot to preflight it, since I haven't flown a two-seater in years. Besides, no point in setting up a system I didn't intend to use. I was braced for the crash. Next thing I knew, my tired old body was being catapulted out of the jet." Hunter looked up and forced a smile. "You wouldn't let a man die in peace."

"And after you got down, what were you doing sitting a few yards away while I was hanging in a tree?"

Hunter held the Zippo between his thumb and forefingers. With one motion, like snapping his fingers, the top popped open and the flame lit. "Unlike your experience, I had a good landing. My chute didn't snag and branches slowed me up without tearing me to pieces. I touched down a lot easier than I did in Korea. I gathered up my equipment and turned off my locator beacon, but when I tried to radio the rest of Buick flight, your beacon blocked out the emergency frequency."

"I know. The way I was hanging, I couldn't reach it."

Hunter closed the lighter with a slight flip of his wrist. "You were a few hundred yards away and easy to find, making all that noise like you were. Since you were up high and didn't have your tree rope deployed, I didn't see any way to get you down before someone found us. So I sat under a tree, because... I don't know. I guess I just froze up. I didn't see any way out so I unholstered my pistol. I almost ended it right there, but I decided to gather up my equipment, withdraw a half a mile, and hide for a while."

"So you had a change of heart?"

"Not exactly. It occurred to me, the bad guys would expect to find one pilot from an F-105 crash. After they found you they'd go away, and I'd have some time. In the end, I couldn't bring myself to let them get you. Only the Great Spirit knows why. When I returned, you were out of the tree, lying on the ground unconscious. I started to wake you but heard someone coming, so I hid. Then the parade started, first the little girl, then the soldier. The soldier found you, and you know the rest."

"Are you on the level?" I said. "You really didn't get me out of the tree?"

"Honest Indian, if you'll excuse the pun. When I came back, I found you on the ground. Maybe you got yourself down and can't remember. Perhaps you got a bump on the head."

"I did get a bump on the head. I got bumps all over, but I couldn't have done it myself."

"Sometimes people do superhuman things in desperate situations."

"You don't believe me, do you?" I said.

Hunter forced a smile. "If I thought about it for a while, I probably wouldn't."

"Hunter, I didn't do it. I couldn't have."

"Okay. You didn't do it, and I didn't do it, and you can bet Charlie didn't do it. So, we can't explain how you got down. Maybe you'll remember later."

"How do you explain the canteen, Hunter?"

"I can't explain that either. I'd tell you if I could."

We rested in silence until the sunlight began to fade. Then Hunter talked through a plan of the night's activities. We would walk until we found a river then cross over and look for a clearing both remote and open enough for a helicopter pick-up. Hunter had made radio contact while the morning bombing flights were airborne and had initiated a listening schedule. Friendly forces would monitor the emergency frequency every four hours at fifteen past the hour. They would contact us only when necessary to pass on important information.

As night fell, we prepared to move out. The day's rest helped, but I realized something was wrong in my right ear. It felt full of fluid, and my sense of balance was off. It seemed as if I was walking sideways. The sky cleared and the moon cast pale light in the jungle. It was enough to see several feet. More importantly, the luminous crescent provided a navigation aid, and Hunter seldom had to look at his compass. In the middle of the night, we broke through the jungle and found a riverbank.

Hunter thought the sky was too bright for us to cross, so we hid until moonset. Then we inflated our G-suits, tied them together with a length of cord, and used them for flotation as we paddled toward the other side. As the current carried us downstream, Hunter frequently stopped paddling to study the riverbank.

"Trying to pinpoint our position on the river?"

"Not exactly," Hunter said, as he rested his chin on the inflated G-suit and bobbed in the water. "I'm trying to figure out what river this is."

"You don't know?"

"I think it's the Song Ma, but I'm not positive. I never planned to walk out of here."

We drifted downstream for about a mile before touching the silt-strewn bottom on the far side where we waited silently in shallow water. We listened for bone-chilling minutes before crawling onto the bank to find a hiding place in the undergrowth. I remained undercover while Hunter scouted the surrounding area. He returned within an hour.

"I think I know where we are," Hunter reported. "I'll show you on the map after daybreak. But we have to move further inland. We're too close to a village. Probably two more hours, before we can hide out for the day."

Hunched over, we moved quickly in the dark. Hunter didn't feel comfortable crossing open rice fields and set a pace around the edge that exhausted me in the first hour. Pain returned, and I stopped for pills. Another hour went by and still we hadn't found adequate cover. In predawn light, a large limestone karst loomed out of the jungle beyond the rice fields. We headed for it.

By dawn we had entered the dense jungle again, and Hunter maintained a compass heading toward the karst. Finally, after another hour, we found cover, and I dropped into a heap on the ground.

Hunter took off his gear and said, "Sit tight. I'll have a look around."

Exhausted, I fell asleep and awoke with a hand clamped over my mouth.

"Stop that noise," Hunter whispered. "You're snoring again."

"How long you been gone?"

"About two hours. It's mid-morning. We'll be okay here. I looked for a path to the top of the karst, but it's too steep. I'll make contact on the radio today and see if we're in chopper range. If we're lucky, pickup will be at dawn tomorrow."

"And if we aren't lucky?"

"Well, I don't know. If they can't, they can't, and we'll walk some more. You act like you're not having a good time in North Vietnam."

"I want to go home in the worst way."

"Well, Shooter, if we get out of this jungle, you can go do just that. You can go back to the States and get a nice cushy job flying for the airlines. Probably make a pile of money."

"Whatdaya mean?" I said.

"You were shot down and spent overnight on the ground in North Vietnam behind enemy lines, so to speak. For that, they're going to award you a Purple Heart, pat you on the butt, and you never have to fly combat again. It's a free ticket home. Then you can go back to the States and join the airlines. But first you have to get out of this jungle."

I recalled hearing something about that in training, but I hadn't given a single thought to the future. "Sounds like you hate the airlines."

"Nope, what I hate is any hotdog who signs up to fly jet fighters, accepts millions of dollars worth of training, then tries to avoid combat. There aren't many, but I know of one jock that ran for cover when the shooting started. But that has nothing to do with the airlines. The Air Force could learn a lot from the airlines. They hire people who like to fly and keep them in the cockpit for their whole career. The Air Force plucks exceptional fliers out of the cockpit and tries to turn them into staff officers and managers as if being a combat leader wasn't a big enough job. I don't think the Air Force understands its real mission and that goes double in peacetime."

Hunter had climbed on his soapbox. I couldn't imagine where he got the energy and decided to change the subject.

"You mean I can go back to the States after this?"

"You can choose to go home. It's your decision. That's when we find out if you're a real fighter pilot or just a lily-livered lightweight."

"No guilt trip here," I said.

"You can go home with a medal on your chest and tell your grandkids how you flew half a combat mission in Vietnam. That's probably worth a war story or two. Or, you can stay for the rest of your tour and risk not living to have kids or grandkids. No sense fretting about it now, Ashe. The enemy will probably kill you before you have to make a decision."

Chapter 11

Hunter stashed two emergency radios and a map in his survival vest and left camp. Since he took no food or water, I expected him back in a few minutes, but he didn't return until late afternoon.

I shook my head as he offered me a thin strip of half-dried meat that was rapidly becoming snake jerky. He ripped off a chunk with his teeth, leaned back on his elbows, and grinned like a mischievous kid who had just gotten away with something.

"The rescue is on for tomorrow morning," he said.

"Great news."

"I gave the rescue folks the coordinates of a point on the river. Don't know what the force will look like, probably four A-1E Skyraiders with guns and bombs to suppress enemy fire and one or two Jolly Green helicopters to pick us up."

I looked around taking in the dense foliage. "How will they find us?"

"As soon as we hear their engines, I'll establish contact on the radio and vector them to our position. There's a clearing about a mile to the east. The pick-up will happen there. We'll stash our extra gear so we can travel light."

"To make a clean getaway if the rescue goes sour?"

"Exactly. If we don't get picked up, we'll come back and recover our supplies."

"I'm surprised we haven't seen any soldiers or many locals for that matter."

Hunter shrugged. "Fortunately, we came down in a dense patch of jungle then hit the ground running. The first twenty-four hours were the most critical. We're well past that point and haven't been discovered. If Charlie had a clue about our position, the place would be crawling with soldiers. I think we put enough distance between the crash site and us, and we did it fast enough to throw off the search. Speed equals life on the ground just like in the air." Hunter sat quietly for a minute. "Of course, luck plays an important part. We've been very lucky that we haven't stumbled into a village or an enemy camp."

"But if the pickup does go sour, it may give away our position. Right?"

Hunter nodded, "We moved like a bullet before, and, if we have to, we can do it again. Speed is life."

"Perhaps we can do it again. I don't know how much I have left. I'm worried. Can rescue really get us out?"

Hunter stared into the trees. "Hope so. Don't believe they've pulled off a success this far north. I've got to level with you, Ashe, our chances aren't good."

A few encouraging words might have soothed the ache inside me, but Hunter wasn't about to sugarcoat anything. I don't know whom I feared most: Hunter or the Vietnamese. I began to accept as fact that Hunter would kill me rather than allow me to be captured.

"What if it doesn't happen tomorrow?"

"Our only option is to keep moving south. But the more we move, the more likely we'll be discovered. We don't exactly look like locals. That's why we travel at night."

"What about all that scouting you do in daylight?"

"I'm an Indian, remember, but I can be a tree if the situation calls for it. It's too risky for both of us in daylight."

"Hunter, what happens if they capture us?" immediately I regretted asking the question.

Hunter was silent for a long time then moaned like he had picked up a heavy burden. "Like I told you, they ain't going to capture us. Not me at least. If they capture you, you'll be starved and tortured until you wish you were dead. Your pain will be so intense it can't be described. Eventually you'll say or do anything they want.

"You'll try to give only your name, rank, and serial number. But, they'll eventually win and you'll feel guilty because you gave them more than you thought you should. If the Vietnamese think you know enough, they may trade you to the Soviets. No one survives that experience."

"Russians. No one briefed me on that."

"And they won't, but it makes perfect sense. A lot of Russians are in North Vietnam training the Vietnamese to fight with MiGs, SAMs, and the other arms they provide. We know Soviet pilots fly some of North Vietnam's combat missions because our spooky guys get their radio transmissions."

"I didn't know. They should've told me."

"Should, indeed, but it's above your clearance level. We should be destroying the Doumer Bridge. We should be bombing their air bases and the Port of Haiphong. We're not doing a lot of things we should be doing."

I wondered if there was any clearance level high enough to understand it all, or was everyone in the dark about something. At least Hunter knew about Soviet pilots. "I guess it doesn't matter who's flying the MiGs, Russians or Vietnamese, our tactics would be the same."

Hunter nodded, "Last month a Soviet MiG pilot bailed out near a target our F-105's had bombed. He spoke only Russian, and the locals didn't recognize the language. They thought he was American and killed him. How's that for motivation to learn a second language? Anyway, you can bet American flyboys have tons of information the Russians would give their eye teeth to know."

"Would they send me to Russia?"

"I think they'd want someone who's been around the flagpole a little longer, like old heads who have committed nuclear targets to memory and know the number of bombs on alert and other information that doesn't change frequently."

"You know that stuff?"

"Of course, all of us that were in operational squadrons are certified on nuclear targets. Some crewmembers, like weapons officers who know a pile of targets and all the bomb settings would be even more valuable. Also, electronic warfare officers trained in Strategic Air Command. They know details of the whole electronic warfare pie."

"Who else would be a candidate?"

"Test pilots or aircrews who were project officers on advanced programs in the Pentagon...well, you get the picture. At the rate we're losing pilots, the Russians have a real menu of talent to choose from."

"Hunter, if we get out of this jungle, what'll you do?"

Hunter reflected for a while then smiled. "The first thing I'd like to do is saddle up the nearest fighter plane and bomb the Doumer Bridge into the river." Then he laughed and his eyes sparkled, "We could order another two-seater from the States and do it together."

"No thanks," I said. "I thought you might want to go back and get the gunner that shot us down."

"Nah, not him. He just did his job. You have to give him credit. He got us, didn't he?"

"I suppose you'd respect him more if he'd killed us?"

Hunter nodded. "Actually, I would. He did leave that bit of unfinished business."

"So what's with the bridge?"

"The Doumer Bridge, we should have targeted it first thing. Instead, our own government placed restrictions on it until a few weeks ago. It's a tough target to hit."

"It's a mile long. How tough can it be?"

"But only 38 feet wide, that's the problem. It's easy to find but hard to bring down. You have to place a bomb on that narrow ribbon of cement and steel. If you miss, the bombs explode in the water, and all you do is get the bridge wet. We're sending sixteen-ship formations into the world's heaviest defenses to do what one dedicated pilot could do."

Without knowing it, I had hit a nerve. Hunter talked about

the bridge for hours. I tried to change the subject, but he wouldn't take the hint. He covered everything from boring engineering details to the aesthetic beauty of its French design. He had invented a tactic to slip through the defenses and bomb it with a single jet. Of course, he would fly the jet. I had to admit the idea had more than a modicum of merit. Out of five sixteen-ship raids, Korat had lost six pilots and barely scratched the bridge.

For a while, I thought Hunter talked about the bridge, apparently, to pass the time. Perhaps a technique he picked up while a prisoner of war. I had heard they told movies from memory because there was no other entertainment. But as the afternoon wore on, I came to believe the bridge obsessed him.

When he walked into the jungle to relieve himself, I feigned sleep. I pretended so well that I didn't wake up until sundown. Facing the night with nothing to do, I stayed active to divert my mind from the fears gathering in the subterranean pit of my emotions. I inventoried supplies and planned a ridiculously detailed breakfast for morning. The menu included fruit, pemmican, and four individual packets of coffee to be mixed with jungle temperature water. Next on the planning menu came several sticks of gum and my smashed Snickers Bar. For drinks, I topped off four water bottles from the condoms, now extended like water balloons, that Hunter had set up to trap rainwater.

In the last light of evening, I held up a small signaling mirror and studied my face. At first, I didn't recognize my own reflection. I looked like something from a horror movie. Three days of whiskers couldn't hide the cuts and bruises that seemed to cover every inch of my skin. I didn't look like myself, or anyone I wanted to know.

As darkness fell, insects came out in droves, crawled into my flight suit and attacked my legs and body. I thought it strange; I hadn't noticed bugs until tonight. As I applied repellent, I found old welts and bites all over my body.

Hunter seemed immune to the creatures as he sat in a meditative-like trance. He appeared peaceful, seeming to gain focus on our trek rather than lose strength. I closed my eyes and passed the time eating M&Ms one by one, savoring the flavor, making the sensation of each last as long as possible.

Tonight would be the first night I could sleep through since I had left the States. It was a luxury I cherished even though my bed was the damp jungle floor.

Hunter woke me at 0430 Hours. We had breakfast in the dark and once again reviewed the planned rescue with the same structure and formality as a flight briefing. Hunter provided an overview of the day then focused on the role of rescue crewmen called PJs, because of their Parachute Jumper qualification. He explained what to do if the PJs came out of the chopper to help us and what to expect if they did not. Most of his overview repeated his briefing last night, and I had committed it to memory. I approved of it all except my mind balked at the idea of leaving Hunter behind if he became injured or wounded. It made sense, and I wasn't going to make an issue out of it, but I didn't know whether I could do it. Hunter left me with the strange suspicion there was something he wasn't telling me.

At 0510, we hid our stash of provisions and moved out at precisely 0520. Walking stealthily, we made the rescue pickup point by 0620. The dawn light revealed no hint of morning fog as we hid in tall grass at the edge of a clearing. Hunter put on his socks and boots for the first time since we started our trek, and I removed the tattered cloth covering the cleated soles of my jungle boots. We each took out a survival radio, checked the battery, and placed them together on the ground. At 0715, we mixed our last brew of jungle temperature coffee and stuffed ourselves with mangoes and monkey bananas. I was too excited to be hungry or thirsty, but Hunter had scheduled everything.

Again, there was nothing to do but wait. I pulled the center out of a stalk of grass and held it in my teeth while leaning back on my elbows. The sky was peaceful with a smattering of white, fluffy cumulus clouds in the distance. I stared at the expanse of sky above the clearing. It was 0820 hours.

I saw the F-105 an instant before the jet's screaming noise reached me. The low flying fighter thundered across the south edge of the clearing as another appeared to the north. My heart raced, and Hunter lunged for a radio.

"Thud flight, this is Buick. How do you read?" Hunter transmitted.

A reply came immediately. "Buick, this is Sandy, I'll be talking at you, copy?"

"Roger, Sandy, Buick copy loud and clear. Go ahead."

"Those Thuds were your wake-up call. Sandy is a flight of A-1Es approaching from the south. Did you transmit as soon as you heard the jets?"

"Roger, Sandy. When the first bird passed over us."

"Roger that. We'll fly down the same track. When you see or hear Sandy, give us a shout, understand?"

"Roger that, Sandy."

"Buick, Sandy here. Request you authenticate for positive identification before we bring you in. Buick, authenticate Whisky, Papa, Alpha, November."

Hunter held a small crumpled paper by the radio and appeared to curse under his breath, "Sandy, we spent some time in the water. Our authentication sheet is unreadable. Just come in and get us out of here."

"Not so fast, Buick, who is your favorite dog?" Sandy radioed.

"Sandy, I don't know," Hunter shot back. "We don't have time for this. Get in here. Get us out."

"What's the name of the dog at your home base?"

Hunter nodded and smiled, "Roscoe. Sandy, it's Roscoe."

"Close enough, Buick. We're coming in," Sandy said.

In the sky over the clearing, two A-1Es appeared at 1500 feet with two more trailing high in loose formation.

"Sandy, we're at your twelve o'clock now," Hunter radioed.

"On the east edge of the clearing just below your nose."

"Roger, Buick, got your approximate location. The Jolly Greens will be here shortly. Stay under cover. We'll fly past you and not compromise your location until the choppers are ready. Understand you got two souls for pickup, both mobile."

"That's affirmative, Sandy."

"Roger, Buick, you have smoke?"

"Roger on the smoke, Sandy."

To the east, I heard exploding bombs. Then the unmistakable sound of several F-105s firing their 20-millimeter cannons.

"Probably creating a diversion," Hunter said.

"Buick, this is Sandy. Choppers are ready. Request you pop a can of smoke."

Hunter pulled the ring and shook the can until smoke billowed into a bright orange cloud. Then he flung the can into the clearing.

"Roger, Buick, I see your smoke loud and clear. You'll be talking to the Jolly Green now. Jolly Zero One, you got it."

"Buick this is Jolly Zero One, we're coming in. Move into the clearing on the double. When Jolly gets over you, it's going to be loud. You won't be able to hear our radio transmissions."

We moved into the clearing, and immediately gunfire flashed from the jungle on the far side. Hunter yelled and shoved me to the ground. As the Jolly Green parked in a hover, thirty feet overhead, the wind and noise became intense.

Hunter was prone on the ground shouting into the radio. "We're taking ground fire, Jolly, ground fire."

The helicopter's rotor wash blew up a blinding combination of grass and dirt. Hunter looked up at the chopper and pointed toward me. A rescue crewmember descended on a cable and with a quick motion slid his horse-collar harness off and placed it over my head and arms. Next he pulled my hands together and mouthed the words, "Hang on."

As he gave a thumb up, the chopper jerked me up and turned away from the clearing. I swung wildly and hung on with all my strength. At six hundred feet moving quickly across the ground, a strong arm grabbed the material of my flight suit and swept me into the chopper.

A crewman slipped an intercom headset on me. Then he said, "I'm a medic. You injured?"

"Nothing new," I shouted. "Where we going? You got to get Hunter!"

"We're taking hits. Have to leave the scene. Left your buddy and our PJ on the ground but don't sweat it. We'll suppress the shooters and go back in."

The Jolly Green withdrew to a position over the top of a karst monolith that offered protection and a panoramic view of the battle below.

The medic pointed east, "We got a lot of air support. You can see a flight of F-105s bombing the stuffings out of something. We've got more Thud flights and F-4s waiting in the wings. Also, more Sandys and another Jolly Green that's armed to the teeth. MiG cover too. It's our own private war. I love the smell of gunpowder."

The A1Es began to strafe gun positions across the clearing. From the karst looking east, eight aircraft were making bombing and strafing passes while explosions expelled large clouds of dirt and debris into the air. The second Jolly Green pumped automatic weapons fire into the edge of the clearing where the enemy had launched their first volley.

"OK, crew, we're going back in," I heard on the radio.

The huge chopper flew an arcing path back to the pickup point and hovered over the clearing. The Sandys continued relentless strafing passes even though the enemy had stopped firing and the edge of the clearing was burning.

The PJ leaned out of the chopper door. "Stabilize now," he said. "They're running for the cable."

Suddenly the Jolly Green lurched, and the PJ fell out of the door and dangled in the air by a cable connected to his safety harness. As the chopper rolled back to the right, the PJ slammed into the fuselage of the chopper and fought frantically to pull himself back inside. The engines roared to full power and the Jolly Green gained altitude quickly.

"Medic," the copilot screamed on the intercom. "Medic, get up here. The pilot's hit."

I could hear the intercom conversation between the pilot and the medic as well as the lead Sandy directing the action on the radio. The pilot, although wounded in the left arm, insisted on staying in command of the rescue while the copilot flew. There was a short, terse radio exchange about the second Jolly Green making the pickup, but the Jolly Green 01 command pilot wouldn't hear of it.

Sandy 01 instructed a flight of fighters to attack the far side of the clearing. Then Sandy 01 directed Hunter to pop another smoke can so the friendly forces could locate them. A flight of four F-4s peppered the far edge of the clearing with cluster bombs until it seemed like thousands of hand grenades had blanketed the area, tearing down vegetation and medium-sized trees.

Next, Sandy 01 called in a flight of four F-105s. Each jet carried two 3000-pound bombs with fuses on three-foot tubes extending forward. The bombs, called daisy cutters, detonate before penetrating the ground and emit enormous shock waves that stun into inaction what they don't kill. Sandy 01 instructed the PJ and Hunter to cover their ears and keep their mouths open against the shock. When Sandy 01 unleashed the Thuds, the exploding daisy cutters looked like nuclear blasts, creating enormous shock waves visible in the moist jungle air. The bombs dug craters in the earth and flatted the jungle into pockmarked rubble. The target area looked like the surface of the moon.

Next Sandy 01 called in a napalm attack to the center of the clearing. Our Jolly Green landed behind a dense cover of napalm smoke. A crewmember jumped out and helped the stunned PJ and Hunter into the chopper, then he threw them on the floor, falling on top of them to brace against the powerful takeoff. Protected by deadly covering fire laid down by friendly forces, the Jolly Green withdrew toward Laos.

Hunter and I sat looking at each other as the chopper crossed the border from North Vietnam into Laos. Alternately through tears and laughter, we exchanged the thumbs up sign.

Somewhere over Laos, Hunter scratched out a note then handed me a small ball of crumpled paper. It was a bullet wrapped in our washed-out authentication paper. The note read, *Here's your bullet back, Shooter.*

Chapter 12

As we traversed the relatively safe airspace of Laos, I began to feel dizzy and nauseated from the smell of decaying blood on my flight suit. I'd washed off the worst of it in the river, but the sickening-sweet aroma of death lingered. It hadn't distracted me while we were trying to evade; there had been more important things to worry about. But now, out of immediate danger, I became obsessed with the ominous dark stain.

Leaning forward, I thrust my face into the windblast that roared through the helicopter's bullet-shattered windscreen then whipped into the passenger compartment. My heart raced as I began to accept the reality of our rescue and, with each fresh breath, gained confidence the damaged chopper would make it across Laos to land safely in Thailand.

My memory of evading the enemy seemed strangely vague as if it had happened to someone else. Only the grotesque aroma of death tugged me back towards the reality of the event.

The medic laughed and pointed out the door, "That's the Mekong River. You can see Naked Fanny on the other side."

I had heard about the highly classified Nakhon Phanom Air Base nicknamed Naked Fanny. Its location, a stone's throw on the Thai side of the Mekong River, provided the nearest sanctuary for wounded crews and damaged aircraft limping out of the combat zone.

The Jolly Green crew ignored the normal air traffic pattern and flew straight over the base at low altitude toward a covey of emergency vehicles parked on the ramp. As the aging buildings of the small base passed beneath my feet, I searched for evidence of highly classified operations, not knowing what to look for.

The aircraft parked on the tarmac below seemed old. The only jet was an F-105 sitting on its belly in the dirt between the runway and the taxiway. It saddened me to see the discarded hulk of a great airplane, covered with mud and waiting to be cannibalized for parts.

The medic nudged me, "Check that furrow in the dirt off the end of the runway? The F-105's drag chute failed. It needed 8,400 feet to stop. Trouble is, we've only got 8,000 feet of runway here."

What do they do with these old propeller-driven airplanes, I wondered but didn't ask. I sensed it was another piece of information too highly classified for general conversation especially with a pilot who might get captured. However, secret operations were not complete secrets, and I had heard rumors about CIA operations.

Parked at the far end of the ramp were B-26s, A-1Es, C-54s, and Caribou transports as well as Cessna and Beechcraft aircraft with no identifying markings. I had heard the pilots flew for front companies called Air America, Civil Air Transport, and Byrd and Son. They airdropped supplies to friendly forces and inserted long-range patrol teams deep into enemy territory. I had been told the CIA employed Air America pilots to fly clandestine combat missions for Laos and, as whispered rumors had it, to smuggle drugs.

Our Jolly Green made an abrupt touchdown in front of three ambulances, two blue staff cars, and several small pickup trucks.

"Friendly turf," I shouted as I slid out of the chopper, relieved to be on an American controlled base and out of immediate danger. I staggered on unsure legs, and Hunter put out his hand to steady me. "Thanks," I said. "Feels like I'm about to spin out."

I leaned on Hunter while a medical team swarmed around the wounded chopper pilot. Blood, debris, and shattered canopy Plexiglas littered the cockpit. The pilot, one arm limp and covered with blood, fought efforts to put him on a stretcher. Finally, supported by a nurse and a flight surgeon, he walked with a halting gait toward a waiting ambulance. A colonel, the wing commander, I guessed, talked to the copilot who didn't appear to be wounded and gave him a thumbs-up as he climbed into one of the waiting staff cars.

A one star general, two nurses, and two men in civilian clothes approached. I started to raise my right arm to salute but winced with pain. With a slow tortured motion, I instinctively raised my other arm.

"Sorry, general, my saluting arm's hurt." I paused, noticing no one else had made the gesture.

"Son, that's not necessary on the flightline," the general placed his hand on my shoulder. "You hurt bad?"

"No, sir. I'll be okay," I said, realizing my words weren't convincing.

The general pointed to my chest. "You gotta hell-of-a-lotta blood on you for okay."

I forced a smile, "Really, sir. I'll be fine."

The general spoke in a low and gentle voice. "We're going to take you both to the hospital. I just want to welcome you back to safe territory. I'll call your wing commander and tell him I talked to you."

The general shook Hunter's hand, cupping it warmly in both of his. "It's been a long time, Hunter. Good to see you in one piece. If you need anything, call the command post. They'll find me."

The general patted Hunter on the back then walked towards a staff car bristling with antennae.

I nudged Hunter. "Wish generals wore nametags. Don't know who the hell I just talked to."

"General Thompson," Hunter said. "Runs the whole Naked Fanny operation. We flew F-86s together in Korea."

A man dressed in fatigues with a stethoscope dangling from his neck stepped in front of me and said, "You're next." He pulled my eyelids apart and peered into one of my eyes and then the other. "I'm Doc Cross, your attending flight surgeon."

The Doc helped me into an ambulance, asked me to lie down and began an examination. Also hovering in the cramped quarters were a nurse and one of the men from the ramp dressed in civvies.

Doc Cross unzipped my flight suit and peeled the stiffened blood stained fabric away. "Where were you bleeding?"

"From my right ear, but it stopped. Still can't hear much on that side. And I have some vertigo."

Doc Cross checked my ears and mouth. "Yeah, I see a problem with your ear, and there's a good sized cut on your jaw. You have a wide assortment of cuts and bruises pretty much all over, but the blood on your flight suit, where'd that come from?"

I looked down at my chest and grimaced at the macabre reddish brown stain. "That's not my blood."

Doc seemed impatient, "What do you mean?"

The civilian moved his face close to the flight surgeon's ear. "Hey, Doc, he said it wasn't his."

"Where'd the blood come from?" Doc Cross persisted.

"Doc, stick with the medical stuff," the civilian interrupted. "I'll cover that in debriefing. Remember our discussion."

"Back off," Doc said. "This is a medical examination. I'll thank you to be quiet while I do my job. Then, I'll be quiet while you do yours. Whatever that is." Doc turned back to me. "Now, lieutenant, let me rephrase the question. Are you sure the blood on the front of your flight suit is not yours?"

I nodded. "Positive, Doc."

When we arrived at the dispensary, Doc Cross continued with almost an hour of tests and x-rays. The civilian stood in the room, watching the exam in silence.

"You have a perforated tympanic membrane," Doc reported. "In plain language, your right ear drum's broken. It's a small rupture, probably caused by a change in pressure. Could be overpressure, like an explosion, or result from negative pressure like a smacking kiss. Hunter didn't kiss you on the ear while you were in the jungle, did he?"

I rolled my eyes. "No way."

"Good. That'll save a lot of paperwork."

"Doc, how do you know Hunter?"

"Everyone knows Hunter, lieutenant."

"I mean how did you recognize him. Our uniforms are sanitized. All our identification and nametags are back in a locker at Korat."

"How many combat pilots get their mug on the cover of Time magazine?"

"Popular guy." I said.

"Notorious is a better word. Did you have a sudden severe pain in your ear followed by bleeding?"

"Yeah."

"You may still have some symptoms, nausea, blurred vision, and vertigo. I relieved the pressure, but it's still swollen. The symptoms should ease up soon."

"How serious is it?" I said, leaning forward, eager for an answer. "Will I be able to fly again?"

"If it heals with no complications, and your hearing comes back within range, it'll be OK. Probably take three weeks, give or take a few days. It's not as serious as you might think. Before aircraft were pressurized, some German fighter pilots had their eardrums punctured on purpose so they wouldn't have to deal with pressure changes. Sounds like a terrible procedure but, if done correctly, leaves only a small scar on the ear drum and surprisingly little loss of hearing."

"So why can't I get back on status right away?" I interrupted.

"Not so fast. In our Air Force, you must heal before you fly. I'm going to put you on DNIF. As you know, that's Duty Not Involving Flying, but in your case it's more than duty. You can't even fly as a passenger on anything, including a civil airliner. The ear is the worst of your problems. The muscles in your back and shoulder will be painful for a while, but no bones are broken. Your muscles will heal long before your ear."

"So, I'll fly again?" I said, sitting motionless, waiting for reassurance.

"Chances are excellent," Doc said. "We're talking a few weeks, not months."

Doc Cross and the nurse left the room. I got up slowly and walked unsteadily towards the door.

"Sorry, Lieutenant," the civilian ordered. "We need to talk before you can leave the room."

I felt an instant flush of anger. "I'm going down the hall and find Hunter."

"No, Lieutenant, we need to talk before you contact anyone else."

The civilian stood blocking the door. I was angered with the abrupt treatment by someone I didn't know. As I stood glaring at the civilian, contemplating my next move, the door burst open, smashing him in the back and knocking him off balance. Hunter bolted into the room followed closely by the other civilian.

"Ashe, don't answer any questions," Hunter directed as he positioned himself toe-to-toe with the startled man, shouting in his face, spewing anger with every word. "The goon with me says you're in charge. If so, you better whip out some identification and do some powerful explaining, or we'll call the Office of Special Investigations. You want to talk to the OSI?"

"I'm agent Dan Webster and this is Bob Andrews. Didn't agent Andrews show you one of these?" Webster inquired, thrusting his ID towards Hunter.

Hunter nodded. "Yeah, he flashed some ID I've never seen before and asked about our mission. Everything about our mission is classified. We're not talking unless we're sure you have a need to know. It's your nickel. Convince us," Hunter said, looking at Webster's ID. "This says you're Daniel Webster, CIA. Is this a joke?"

"It's no joke, Colonel Snow, I'm Daniel Webster with the CIA and Mr. Andrews is a colonel in the Special Forces."

"Don't call me Colonel Snow, it's Hunter, just Hunter."

"Your name is Colonel Erasmus Snow unless I'm mistaken," Webster said as he traded icy stares with Hunter.

I broke the silence. "It would be a lot simpler if you would just call him Hunter."

Webster continued, "Okay. Colonel Hunter..."

"Not colonel," I interrupted. "Just Hunter."

"Okay, boys. Let's try this again from the start. Hunter, I'm Daniel Webster with the CIA."

Hunter continued to glare at Webster. "Even if your ID is valid, we still have to verify your clearance level and need to know."

"If you want to verify it through the wing commander we can call him," Webster countered.

"Good idea," Hunter said as he bolted out of the room with Webster in close pursuit. I fell in after them with Andrews following in last place. The party moved like a flight of aircraft, rat racing through the hospital halls in trail formation. We followed Hunter to the hospital commander's office where he picked up the hot line to the Command Post then directed the duty officer to connect him with the wing commander at Korat Air Base.

"You don't have to call Korat," Webster protested. "I've got the local wing commander's number right here."

Hunter looked out the window and ignored Webster as he waited. The conversation was short and congenial. Hunter put the phone down and nodded, "Seems like you're OK. Let's get this over so we can get back to home base."

Webster pulled a small tape recorder out of his pocket and placed it on the desk, "I would like to talk to you first, Colonel, and then to the Lieutenant."

"No way," Hunter shot back. "And don't call me Colonel again. You can debrief both of us at the same time and do it right here in this office. And you can forget the recorder."

Webster glared daggers at Hunter then sat on the edge of the desk. "Now, Hunter, I assume your wing commander said to cooperate with us. We do have procedures."

I looked at Hunter, wondering what his next salvo would be.

"The wing commander said debriefing," Hunter snapped. "He didn't say interrogation. We're a crew of two. You can debrief us together or not at all."

"You seem overly sensitive to the term interrogation, Colonel."

Hunter shot back. "If you knew anything about me at all, which you apparently do not, you could answer your own question. If you think I'm impressed by a CIA badge and feel the need to cooperate, you're wrong. There's nothing you can do to me. If you want anything to move forward, it's going to happen in the cold light of day. That means sitting down together and being open with each other. You're not going to talk to us separately and you'll answer our questions if you expect us to answer yours."

"OK, Hunter," Webster relented. "I won't call you colonel and we'll do it your way. Now would you like to sit down with us and get started?"

"My pleasure," Hunter grinned through clenched teeth. "Tell us why you're here?"

"To find out what happened while you were on the ground up north," Webster explained. "Who you came in contact with. If you saw anything out of the ordinary."

Hunter sat down at the hospital commander's desk, "What's that got to do with the CIA and Special Forces?"

"You might say raw data," Webster replied. "We need it for intelligence purposes."

Hunter stood up. "That's bull. You can read our intelligence debrief for that. Are you going to level with us or do we walk?"

Webster sighed. "You give us no choice but to read you into a very sensitive program. For your own safety, I'd rather not."

Hunter plucked a pack of cigarettes from the commander's desk, made a perfunctory gesture of offering it to others, then pulled one out for himself. "I'm not talking until I hear the details. Ashe, you have a choice in this, too. What do you want to do?"

I looked at Webster then to Hunter. "What does he mean for our safety?"

Hunter took a long drag and watched the smoke rise, "If you're captured and tortured, you'll know more than you need to know. The enemy could become aware that you have a special kind of knowledge."

"How could the enemy become aware?" I said, suspecting I knew the answer. "The CIA wouldn't tell them. Would they?" It seemed as if I had read his mind.

"Probably not as a matter of policy," Hunter said. "But the CIA is a bureaucracy. All bureaucracies are more like a sieve than a safe."

"Could this lead to one of those all expense paid trips to Russia we talked about?"

Hunter forced a thin smile. "It's possible. If the program is important enough. But you don't need to be briefed-in. I'd recommend you don't do it."

"But you're going to do it, right?"

"Right," Hunter replied.

I drew air through my teeth with a sucking sound. When in doubt, I thought, do what the big guy does. "Then count me in."

Webster opened a slim briefcase. "Each of you will have to sign a paper saying you will never reveal what we discuss here. Not to your Air Force Intelligence debriefers, your commander, your families, or anyone else. Ever."

Unless someone tortures the answers out of me, I reflected.

Hunter sat down again and leaned forward. "Where do I sign?"

Webster placed two in-brief forms in front of Hunter and another two in front of me. At the top of each was stamped "CLASSIFIED CODEWORD PROGRAM". The papers didn't explain what the code names "ZEPHYR" and "SPARROW" meant, but they did have a lengthy paragraph explaining penalties under the Federal Espionage Act for revealing codeword classified programs. Hunter signed the forms without reading them then shrugged and gestured for me to sign.

"Aren't you going to read it?" I asked.

"Nope," Hunter sighed. "You can if you want. I've signed a ton of these. They all say the same thing."

"Let me put this in a nutshell," Webster said as he placed his hand to his forehead, appearing to go over a list of mental notes. "We have some people on the ground up north. They're on a highly classified and very risky covert mission. Our government has complete deniability. If they're captured, they don't exist. The team gathers intelligence about activity in North Vietnam. First-hand information on airfields, power-plants, facilities, troop movements, storage areas and truck parks. In short, any vital intelligence. They also disrupt activities through direct but very quiet attacks on facilities and operations."

"How do you keep an attack quiet?" I inquired.

"Make it look like an accident or coordinate the explosion with a night flyover to make it seem like a bomb was dropped from a jet. Those are just two examples from a very large bag of tricks."

I leaned back in my chair, "Clever, we get credit for bombs we don't even drop."

"Our team was in the middle of an important operation when you practically landed in their camp. Needless to say, your ejection and the plane crash brought a great deal of unwanted attention into a normally quiet clandestine operation. Our operatives had no choice but to shut down and go undercover. As luck would have it, they needed to use the radio frequency that was blocked out by the lieutenant's parachute beacon. Normally a beacon wouldn't be a problem, but this one was too damned close."

"Oh no," I groaned. "You mean I closed down the whole show? How many on the team?"

"Twelve," Webster reflected. "They're still up there. When it became apparent you weren't going to turn off your beacon, our guys did it for you. They could have turned it off and left you hanging in the tree. That kind of cautious approach would have been best to keep their operation secure. Instead, they played hero and cut you down. They would have helped you more, but there wasn't time to do so without compromising their position. So, they left you and moved their operation."

I shook my head and stared at Webster. "I don't want to seem ungrateful, but they left us to be captured."

"I'm sorry they had to leave you, lieutenant. As for Hunter, they didn't know he was there. They didn't see him and weren't looking for two pilots since the F-105 is usually a single-seat jet. It was strictly a matter of mission priorities, nothing personal. The lives of twelve team members were at stake."

Hunter was using the commander's pen to pick mud out of the cleats of his boots. "So why are you talking to us now?"

"Because we don't know how much you saw. We don't want you to tell the Air Force Intelligence debriefers about our agents up north. We want you to leave that out completely."

"You needn't have worried," I suggested. "I don't remember seeing them at all. I didn't know how I got down from the tree, but I never dreamed of anything like this. I realize now, they left the canteen, the cans of peaches and the pound cake. Hunter and I couldn't figure out where they came from. We each thought the other was crazy."

Hunter looked up. "How come they had field rations from 1945?"

"The teams use surplus rations from World War Two," Webster laughed. "The meals are still good, but here's the best part. You can still buy them on the black market in North Vietnam. Our boys are carrying US rations that can't be traced to US forces. It allows perfect deniability. Like the team never existed."

"The team must be overjoyed," I said. "Suppose you could get us a case of peaches and pound cake for the road?"

"Not likely," Webster said. "I'm about finished. Since you can't remember seeing our team, there's no need to brief any more details. You have any other questions?"

"Don't think so," I said, struggling with my feelings. I wanted to know more but didn't want the consequences that might come with the knowledge.

Webster folded his hands. "Good. Then you won't have any trouble reporting that you were unconscious and didn't see a thing."

"Yeah, I guess so," I agreed.

"Wrong," Hunter objected. "If he admits he was unconscious, the flight surgeon has no choice but to zap him off flight status permanently. You said they gave him first aid. Did they give him a shot of something that knocked him out?"

Webster turned and looked at Andrews.

"It's possible," Andrews said. "They have a full medical kit. But I don't know if they did. That level of detail wasn't passed on. You have to understand, we have very limited communication with these teams. It's risky."

With raised eyebrows I looked at Webster. "These teams? As in more than one?"

"No comment," Webster said then pointed to my chest. "What about that bloodstain on your flight suit? I think I know the answer, but I'd like to hear it from you."

"A soldier found me and was going to shoot..." I glanced at Hunter and felt uneasy. "Would you like to field this question?"

Hunter pulled the small tomahawk from the ankle pocket of his flightsuit and tossed it onto the commander's desk. "I killed him with this and he bled on Ashe's flight suit. In bad taste, don't you agree, to bleed on your adversary's flightsuit?"

Webster bent down to get a closer look at the tomahawk with its crumpled bloodstained feathers. He moved his hand to touch it but withdrew before he made contact. "And no one else saw you? No one that lived?"

Hunter shrugged. "Not as far as we know. A young girl went by, but I don't think she saw anything. That's it until the rescue choppers arrived, and we were attacked."

"Yeah," Webster hesitated. "I think we've covered everything."

I sighed and said, "So that's it?"

"Yeah, that's it," Webster said as he picked up the signed forms. "Providing you agree to cooperate and never breathe a word of this to anyone. That's essentially what these debrief forms say except for the added part about putting you in jail and throwing away the key."

Hunter picked up the tomahawk and pointed it at Webster, "And you never say a word about the lieutenant being unconscious."

Webster raised his hand in resignation. "Agreed."

Chapter 13

Feeling exhausted and fed up with answering questions, I slumped onto the hospital commander's sofa and watched Webster and Andrews disappear down the corridor. "Did you hear those CIA flatfoots talk about sending us to jail?"

Hunter yawned and rubbed his temples. "Scare tactics. What can they do? Send us to combat? I'm surprised they told us as much as they did."

A laugh started deep in my gut. "You didn't give 'em much choice. What's next on the agenda?"

Hunter stretched back in the commander's chair and opened a small refrigerator behind the desk. "Beer. We scored a bullseye on the CO's supply."

I leaned over the commander's desk and selected the Command Post hotline from a bank of switches on the speakerphone.

"Roger, sir," a voice immediately responded. "Captain Anderson here. What's your pleasure?"

I smiled and assumed an official sounding voice. "What's the status on transport to Korat for our two rescued pilots?"

"Sir, we've got a chopper standing by but no departure time from your medical folks. I was about to check with your people at the hospital."

"I'm checking now." I motioned with a thumb up to Hunter. "Departure time is ASAP. If anyone needs a confirmation on that, tell them to call the hospital commander's office."

"Will do, sir."

"The crew is unwinding over a couple of post rescue beers. They'll be released and on the ramp as soon as they finish."

The duty officer paused. "Post rescue beers, sir?"

I looked at Hunter with a sly smile. "Yeah, it's like mission whisky, only it's beer. Strictly medicinal of course. Any more questions?"

A sigh came over the hotline, "Tell them to have one for me, sir. I'll pass your order to operations right away."

"I thought you handled that well," Hunter said, tossing a can to me.

Making a one-handed catch, I popped the top, and a stream of foam sprayed on the couch. "Think we can finish all of the commander's beer before we get to the chopper?"

Hunter raised his drink to me. "Son, we may make a fighter pilot out of you yet."

Doc Cross stopped in the doorway. "Into the CO's private supply, I see. Didn't mean to leave you on your own so long, but the helicopter pilot's arm is in bad shape. A bullet shattered a bone. I'm going to finish your medivac paperwork, and, as soon as we can get transport, you'll be on your way. Because of your ear, Lieutenant, remind the chopper pilot to fly no higher than 500 feet."

I nodded and pointed my beer at the Doc. "When can I fly fighters?"

Doc Cross raised his eyebrows. "Didn't we discuss that?"

I shrugged. "Grounded for two or three weeks?"

"Closer to three, Lieutenant. The final call belongs to your local flight surgeon. Colonel Hunter, you'll be grounded for twenty-four hours then probably be right back in the air. Any questions?"

Hunter threw an empty can in the trash. "Yeah, Doc. Want a beer?"

Doc waved his hand. "Thanks. But I can't right now."

I felt the beginning of a warm glow. "Don't mind if I do."

Hunter tossed another can to me then turned to the Doc.

"Can we talk to the Jolly Green pilot? He saved our ass."

Doc shook his head. "Still in the operating room. He won't be in any shape to talk before you leave."

As the ambulance drove toward the helicopter, I saw the blue staff cars of the wing and hospital commanders. Both colonels were standing on the ramp with Doc Cross. I motioned to the ankle pockets of my flight suit, bulging with beer cans. Hunter, also bulging at the ankles, waved me off and gave a thumb up. We got out of the ambulance and walked slowly so the weight, low on our legs, wouldn't flop around.

The hospital commander stroked his chin thoughtfully. "Doctor Cross forgot to tell me you hurt your ankles. It's wise to put cold cans on them to keep the swelling down. Consider them a prescription."

I carefully weighed the sarcasm and looked at the hospital commander. "If you ever get to Korat, we'll buy you a beer. I think we owe you a case."

I had mixed emotions as the chopper approached Korat. Four days ago I arrived to fly combat. I flew only half a mission and had spent more time on the ground behind enemy lines than in friendly territory. Although Hunter was flying the plane, I felt guilty because I had been on a crew that lost a multi-million-dollar fighter jet. But it wasn't just the money. Pilots have a deep love for a fine airplane, and I was having trouble resolving my feelings about the loss.

I remembered a horse named Beauty on my grandfather's farm. As a child, I had cried while the magnificent animal struggled, its lathered palomino hide caked with dirt as it rolled on the ground and thrust its head in vain attempts to stand on old crippled legs.

As my grandfather loaded a rifle, I pleaded with him to stop and finally lay beside the animal with my arms clinging around its neck. As soon as I touched Beauty, she became quiet and stared at me with wide fearful eyes. I sensed she thought I could save her, and I clung to her with the blind hope of youth.

Grandpa was gentle at first but, as time wore on, his patience ran out. "Git the hell away," he yelled. "Go back to the house, you little sucky teat."

Still I didn't let go. I hung on to Beauty with all my strength until Grandpa grabbed my feet and yanked hard enough to break my grip. Years later, after I had grown and Grandfather was gone, I realized there was nothing I could have or should have done to save Beauty. But only my head acknowledged the mercy of her killing and acquitted me. In my heart, I still felt responsible for the summary execution of a great and wonderful horse. Beauty and my plane both seemed to be vibrant spirited animals. In my head I knew a jet fighter didn't have flesh, blood, and a soul, but in my heart, I was less sure.

In addition to losing the airplane, I had made dumb mistakes while evading the enemy and during the rescue. Now I felt the other pilots would hold me accountable. I would rather confront another Vietnamese with a gun than face a review by my peers. As the airbase came into view, I crumpled my beer can and hoped the criticism wouldn't be too brutal.

As the chopper approached the ramp, I was surprised to see a crowd of combat crews on the tarmac with small American flags in one hand and drinks in the other. After landing, a medical corpsman attempted to steer me to a waiting ambulance, but the crowd lifted Hunter and then me into the bed of a small pickup truck. With our truck in the lead, a parade of horn-honking vehicles snaked through the enlisted barracks area, the officer's hootches, and then to the KABOOM bar.

As the mass of beer-drinking pilots roared, I felt proud to be in the welcome home celebration with Hunter and to hear the deafening cheers of the operations and maintenance personnel. Clearly the party had started well before we arrived. The crews were most likely drunk and would applaud anyone for any reason, but it didn't matter. I felt a chill of relief and pride.

At the KABOOM bar, toasts were offered to both Hunter and me. Also, the crowd raised their glasses to the F-105 pilots who had flown on the rescue mission. Lieutenant Colonel Mike Parker, our squadron commander, congratulated me and told me to party tonight but, in the morning, report to the flight surgeon for another checkup and to Intelligence for a complete debriefing.

I woke up at ten o'clock in the morning with a serious hangover. I wasn't sure how I navigated from the Officers' Club to the hootch last night. I suspected I had help. My shoulder hurt like hell, my body ached, and the bug bites itched and hurt. I soaked under a hot shower until I felt awake and limber enough to walk to the medical clinic.

A wide smile raised the tips of Doc Morgan's handlebar moustache to the rims of his glasses. "Congratulations, you're alive."

"Yeah, I survived North Vietnam."

"I'm talking about the bar last night. How do you feel?"

"Like my head's going to explode."

Morgan handed me a plastic bag of pills. "Knee-walkin' drunk would be my medical diagnosis."

"What's this?"

"Hangover kit. Vitamins, Tylenol, and aspirin. Take them with lots of water. The paper cups are by the sink."

The medical evaluation included a long phone call with Doc Cross to discuss results of the tests at Naked Fanny. Morgan's summary was short with no surprises. "Your shoulder and arm problems are muscular and will heal in a few days. Your eardrum should heal in about three weeks. After that your future flying status will be evaluated."

Morgan filled out an Air Force form and placed it in front of me to sign. In the remarks it said, "Status is Duty Not Involving Flying. DNIF to include no flying as a passenger on any aircraft. Other duty not restricted."

I had a sinking feeling in my gut. I had to sign a paper that removed me from flying status. I didn't want Morgan to see my hand shake as I picked up the pen. "How's Hunter?" I asked.

Doc Morgan twisted one side of his moustache, looking over to watch it snap back in place. "He's fine. Cleared to fly."

I shook my head. "How can that be? He went through the

same damned experience I did. He even walked barefoot through the jungle."

Morgan nodded. "And hardly a scratch. Last night, a pilot in the bar was hurt worse than Hunter was injured during your whole affair. That Indian guy's a survivor. He smokes and drinks a lot but, if good behavior was a criterion, who'd fly combat?"

I walked to Fort Apache and found Hunter waiting on the steps of the Intelligence debriefing shack smoking a Camel. I wondered if Hunter had an additional gene in his system that allowed him to drink most of the night and still look clear-eyed.

A major and a lieutenant wrote up our Intelligence debriefing. Hunter did most of the talking but turned to me to explain my parachute landing and descent from the tree. At first I was at a loss for words. I had signed the CIA paper, and now I couldn't tell the truth.

After an embarrassing pause, I said, "I followed normal procedures, and it worked just like advertised."

When the debriefing was finished, I was tired and wanted a nap. I returned to the screen-walled hootch, but the heat was stifling. The one-speed ceiling fans were too sluggish to move much air. It had been cooler in the jungle.

The duty officer awakened me about sunset to tell me that Colonel Parker wanted to see me in his quarters. With sketchy directions, I set out for trailer number eight. The flimsy structure looked like a small mobile home with two windows—an air conditioner in one and frosted glass in the other. The air conditioner ran full blast against the hot, humid air. As I approached, the door reminded me of the entrance to a meat cooler.

Mike Parker was well tanned, slim, and spoke with a slight Southern drawl. He was a man that looked you square in the eye when he talked and listened with his whole being when you did. Inside the trailer was one main room plus a bedroom and small bath. It was Spartan and cramped, but the air conditioning was a Godsend. A card table served as both a desk and dining table. We sat on Government Issue metal chairs. There was a sink and a hot plate, but the only visible food was a package of unpopped popcorn.

Parker opened a small refrigerator. "How about a drink?" Without waiting for a reply, he plucked two glasses and a bottle of Tanqueray out of the freezer. The icy gin poured thick over a plug of ice that had been frozen into the bottom of each frosty glass. We toasted to my successful rescue.

The cold gin went down my throat like velvet. "Sir, that's soft as a baby's bottom."

Parker balanced his glass on the heel of his hand and stared into it like it was a crystal ball. "Tanqueray, the colder the better. It's one of my few joys in life here. Gin's up to a dollar-ten a quart at the Base Exchange. Used to be ninety cents. What's the world coming to?"

I took another sip, and my drink was gone.

Parker opened the refrigerator. "Don't be bashful. I'll pour you another, then you're on your own. Pour 'em small and change 'em often. I have a whole freezer full of iced glasses, so help yourself."

"Sir, I'm sorry I didn't get to talk to you before I flew a mission and got shot down."

Parker looked at me with a pained expression. "That whole mess was screwed up. It wasn't your fault, Ashe. We almost got you killed. I didn't like the idea, but I didn't get to vote. This thing about new lieutenants flying combat in single-seat jets is political dynamite back home. You should've seen our hotlines light up when Washington found out another lieutenant was on the ground. It's tough to explain how a new lieutenant arrives on station and the next day is walking around in North Vietnam. Especially since you didn't have the local training that is supposed to be mandatory before you fly. I heard no one told you how to initiate a rescue or even how to authenticate, to tell the good guys you were friendly."

"Unfortunately, that's true, sir."

"We almost got you killed, Ashe, and for that I am truly sorry. I have a young son, much younger than you, but I thought of him many times while we were trying to get you out. Especially early in the game when you and Hunter were evading and we had no contact."

Parker's eyes welled up with unshed tears, but I sensed he didn't want to embarrass either of us.

"Ashe, for a long while we didn't know if you were dead or alive. I apologize for the stupid system that let this happen to you, and I'm sorry you had to go through it."

"Colonel Hunter took care of me, sir. I came through just fine."

Parker chuckled. "Colonel Hunter, huh. I appreciate the protocol, but you can call him Hunter in front of me. I guess you know better than to call him colonel to his face?"

"I guess I do. We learned a lot about each other in a short time."

"Really, Ashe? Then why is it he hates to be called by his rank?

"I don't know why. I just know he does."

Parker shrugged. "Damned if I know either, and I've known him for over twenty years. He's probably the best fighter pilot that ever flew, but since he got out of the slammer in Korea, he's been one of the most mysterious. It's hard to figure what motivates him. I guess he was different before he was captured, but now he's changed even more."

"How do you mean?"

"He's driven. He hates anything not directly connected with combat flying, like staff work, bureaucracy, and especially any request, regardless how small, from headquarters. I can't tell you how many times we've had to save him from himself."

"But he's one of our most highly decorated pilots."

"Right. However, I thought his last trip to the States, to receive his fourth Silver Star, was going to do him in for sure."

"You mean his picture on cover of *Time?*"

"No. I'm sure he didn't know about that in advance. There's

not a political bone in his body. But when he stepped off the plane in Washington, he told reporters that he could really kick ass and take names if the stupid elected officials wouldn't hold him back. You probably saw him mouth off on television."

I groaned. "Yeah. At the time I thought it was funny."

"After that speech, he couldn't go to the crapper without a public relations team. Then they arranged for his wife to accompany him and that was a key move. She's the only person he listens to. She's English and must be a saint of a woman. I don't know how she's put up with him all of these years."

I began to feel mellow from the cold gin as the pain of my hangover finally melted away. "He's a great pilot. It was a pleasure to fly with him. Even if it was only half a mission."

Parker leaned forward. "I read your Intelligence debrief. Why did you guys eject so low?"

"I don't know. We just did. It all happened so fast."

"Didn't you talk to each other? Didn't you tell each other it was time to go?"

It seemed like Parker had an agenda, and I felt uncomfortable trying to explain Hunter's behavior. "We couldn't communicate very well. I guess it was an intercom problem. Anyway, we did punch out a lot lower than I thought was comfortable."

"There was a transmission before you ejected. Something like, I'll ride this thing to hell before I'll bail out. Did you say that on the radio?"

"I don't remember that in our debriefing report." I said. As Parker shifted in his chair, I could tell he sensed I was evasive.

"It wasn't in your report, Ashe. It's not in anyone's report. But, the rest of Buick flight thought they heard it. One of the pilots had a tape recorder patched into his microphone cord. He played it back for me."

My heart sank. "He did?"

"It's on tape. I heard it." Parker paused taking another sip. "I'm your squadron commander. I know you haven't been here long, and you don't know me. But, you can trust me. I'm on your side. Now, did you say it on the air?"

"No, sir. I didn't say it."

Parker sighed. "Did Hunter say it?"

"Sir, I don't know for sure. Like I said, we had some sort of communications problem. I think I heard it too, but I can't be positive who said it. Why don't you ask Hunter?"

Parker nodded. "I will. Doc Morgan says you're out of the cockpit for a while. You'll probably get back on flying status, but you need to be prepared if you don't. We're going to put you on the Rest and Relaxation schedule until you're cleared to fly. That is, of course, if you want to fly combat again."

"How's that?" I said, thinking I knew where this was leading.

"Since you were shot down and remained in enemy controlled territory for an extended period, I'm required to advise you that you can go home and never have to fly combat again. I don't need your answer tonight. Go on R&R. Let the ear heal and you can tell me your decision later."

"What happens if I get back on flying status and choose not to fly combat? What kind of flying assignment could I expect?"

"Hard to say, but it wouldn't be fighter jets. This is not a flying club. Flying fighters is a privilege, and we're all volunteers. If you remove yourself from the combat eligible list, you're out. To stay in fighter jets, you have to want to fight."

I stared into my glass of gin as the chilling reality soaked in. "Doesn't leave me much choice if I want to fly fast jets."

"You got it, and it won't be a picnic either. Soon the weather up north will improve and we'll go there more often. Unless a miracle happens, our loss rate will only get worse.

"I appreciate your honesty," I said, trying to appear more relaxed than I felt.

Parker continued, "You don't have to answer now. Tell me after R&R. Its not often that someone gets the opportunity to make this kind of decision. Of course, everyone so far has made the right choice."

My eyes shot to Parker's face. With a Southerner's economy of language, he had revealed a fundamental precept of combat leadership: a clear division between right and wrong, respect

and contempt, combatants and cowards. He was not the old
style I-won't-listen-to-any-excuses type of leader. Parker's skills,
honed in the space age Air Force schools of leadership, placed
value on empathy, understanding, and patience. As a result, he
would listen to excuses until the cows came home, but he still
wouldn't accept any.

"I'll be surprised if you don't stay," Parker said. "You have
valuable experiences to teach already, and I'd like you to talk
about them at the next squadron meeting. We don't have
many pilots who live through a low altitude ejection, land in a
tree, use the tree rope to get down, are held at gun point by
the enemy, escape and evade for three days and get picked up
by Jolly Greens in a hail of gunfire. The odds are the rest of
your tour will be a piece of cake."

"What about Hunter? Does he have a choice?"

"Sure he does, but you know what he'll do. Last month he
submitted paperwork for another tour even though he's facing
a pile of resistance from the Pentagon. It would be his third tour,
back to back, and would guarantee his future: war college,
squadron commander, and promotion to full colonel. Three
tours are probably too much for anyone, even Hunter. And if
three becomes a standard for success, how could they refuse
anyone else?"

I had sipped a lot of gin and was feeling unsteady as I left the
CO's trailer. For the first time in days, I wasn't feeling pain anywhere in my body. I liked Parker and was surprised how open
and easily he talked for a fighter pilot. It seemed like, to him,
everything was so clear. I felt none of the sense of competition
in him as I did in most other pilots. I had seen real tears in
Parker's eyes, and I trusted him.

I wandered into the KABOOM dining room looking for
Hunter. He wasn't there so I went in the bar. It was early, and
only a handful of pilots were in the room. In the crowd last
night, I had failed to notice the rich teak and mahogany wood
that gave the room a regal quality. The bar was the longest piece
of solid mahogany I had ever seen, and its oiled wood glistened

under the overhead lights. On the wall was a large plaque with
the fighter wing patch in the center and the words:

"YOUR MISSION IS TO FLY AND FIGHT AND DON'T YOU EVER FORGET IT."

I found Hunter sitting on the front steps of the hootch reading a letter. He motioned for me to sit down.

"Got any plans for the next few days?" he said.

"I'm grounded until my ear heals."

Hunter's cigarette dangled from his lips. "Hell, you could go
to Bangkok and get laid. It would take your mind off your ear.
Might take your mind off the war."

I hesitated. "Think I'll just rest for a while. I talked to our
squadron commander. I've got to do some thinking."

"What'd he say?"

"He wants to know if I'm going to stay and fly combat or go
home."

Hunter's head snapped toward me throwing the grayish-
white residue of his cigarette on my leg. "I don't know why
Parker bothered to ask. What kind of pussy does he think you
are?"

I brushed away the ashes and tried to change the subject. "He
wants me to brief my survival experience at the next squadron
meeting. What do I say if they ask me how I got down from the
tree?"

"It's simple. Tell them how to get down from a tree. You
were up in a tree and now you're down, so you're the expert.
Don't sweat the details. It's not like a bunch of fighter pilots
will hang on every word."

"The CO said you are signing up for a third consecutive
combat tour. There anything to that?"

"Yup. Getting a lot of heat about it too. Heat from the
Pentagon, not to mention heat from my wife. I did some poli-
ticking in Washington when I went back there. Just have to wait
and see how it goes."

"And your wife?'

"Unfortunately, she won't wait. She's flying in to see me. That's what this letter is about. She's coming and I expect she's not bringing good news."

"Trying to convince you to go home?"

Hunter grimaced. "We'll see. I need a favor. Since you have some time, how about meeting her at the Bangkok airport? There's a driver we use for R&R, I'll hire him to take you there. You can go early, see the sights, and ride back to Korat with her. I'd go myself but there's a big push going to Hanoi as soon as the weather breaks. I don't want to miss it."

"You don't want to miss a chance to shoot down your fifth MiG, right?"

Hunter paused and studied four jets as they flew over the base in close formation and pitched out into the landing pattern. "Yeah, something like that."

Chapter 14

Hunter steered the Toyota pick-up truck with one hand as he yanked an oversized envelope from the ankle pocket of his flight suit. He tossed the torn, crumpled package on the seat beside me.

I didn't pick it up. Instead, I studied Hunter's hard-cut face, thinking how to phrase my question so it wouldn't offend. "What's she going to say when I show up instead of you?"

Hunter patted the envelope. "Don't forget this. You'll need it."

Frustrated, I looked out the passenger window. If Hunter's wife was flying all the way across the Pacific, the least he could do was meet her at the airport. I understood that Hunter needed only one more kill to become an Ace, but couldn't he take one day off?

"I know it's none of my business," I said. "But what should I say to your wife when I show up and you don't?"

"She'll understand. She wants me to be the first Ace in this war. No explanation required."

"No woman I've ever met would understand."

Hunter shook his head. "You haven't met this woman, and you haven't been keeping score."

"Score? Of what?"

"An F-4 Weapons Systems Operator is in the race for Ace, but we can't let that happen. A single-seat fighter pilot has to be the first Ace, not a WSO operating a radar from the back seat of an F-4."

I knew Hunter resented the F-4 and any other fighter jet with two crewmembers. Many of the old heads had been vocal against the recent decision to award WSOs equal credit for MiG kills. Since WSOs didn't always fly with their assigned pilot, the practice had allowed a WSO to accumulate four kills while, ironically, no pilot other than Hunter, had scored more than two.

"It's come to this," Hunter said, not hiding his disgust. "A WSO, who doesn't know beans about piloting an airplane, could become the first Ace of the war."

"Really," I said, trying not to show my sarcastic smile. "Can't let that happen."

Hunter nodded, staying focused on what he must have thought was a travesty. "That's why I'm staying."

I knew I was stepping over the line but couldn't hold back. "And, you're going to save the day for fighter pilots?"

Hunter flashed an irritated look. "Are you joshing me, boy?"

"Not exactly," I said in a voice that betrayed my agitation.

Hunter ignored my comment and continued. "If we allow this to happen, the next step will be pilotless planes with WSOs directing attacks remotely from the ground. The research eggheads already have money to study it."

"Get off it, Hunter. What kind of Buck Rogers talk is that?"

Hunter laughed. "Mark my words. It'll happen. Then politicians wouldn't have to send American boys into combat. They could wage bloodless wars, at least bloodless on our side."

I shook my head. "And your wife understands and supports all that?"

"Sure."

Fat chance, I thought.

Hunter stopped the squadron truck short of the base gate. An old, beige Mercedes waited on the other side.

"No squadron vehicles allowed off base and no taxis on," Hunter explained then motioned the Mercedes driver to walk over.

Caupouy spoke passable English as he spelled out his Thai given name then politely asked me to call him by his nickname,

Cowboy. A thin man with intense, hollow eyes, he seemed to be late middle age. A western hat, a size or so too small, perched on his head at a rakish angle.

Hunter handed Cowboy a paper bag, tipping it so I could see two bottles of Black Label and two cartons of Camels. I assumed that Cowboy would sell the scotch and smokes on the black market. Hunter had explained the trip and the fare but not the mechanics of the transaction.

Cowboy would drive me to the Princess Hotel in Bangkok, sleep in his Mercedes, and be available night and day to take me anywhere. Hunter stressed that Cowboy was a number one driver, knew Bangkok, could recommend restaurants and bars, and arrange anything a man could want.

"If you want a woman, he'll get one. If you want a car full of Thai girls, he can get that too."

I paused for a few seconds, bothered that I couldn't account for my feeling of unease. Although I had fantasized about sex on demand, Hunter's reference to it seemed crude and out of place. Particularly since I was going to Bangkok to escort his wife. I decided to change the subject. "How will I know who to meet at the airport?"

Hunter slapped me on the back and pointed to the battered envelope. "Julia's her name. The rest is in there with some stuff that may come in handy."

Cowboy placed my bag in the trunk then held the door while I got into the back seat. The car had comfortable leather upholstery, a small fan that foreshadowed the lack of air-conditioning, and a reading light mounted on flexible stem attached to each of the rear seat headrests. I had always felt uncomfortable with personal service and remained silent as Cowboy drove slowly down the narrow bumpy road away from the gate.

We passed by a line of roadside houses—small, wooden hovels, elevated on stilts with open spaces for windows and trash strewn around the yards. A mongrel dog, head hung low and ribs visible through his hide, wandered about looking malnourished and dazed. From the stifling smell, I guessed the open trench at the side of the road served as a sewer.

The car, clean and polished to a high sheen, ran well and looked younger than its years. Several strings of fringed cloth with beads dangled from the rear-view mirror like religious symbols. I had hoped for air conditioning and even more so as wind boiled through the windows dripping with humidity. The air seemed thick and hard to breathe, as the sweet-sickening sewer smell became overpowering. Since heat was the more immediate problem, I reluctantly put my arm out the window to direct more of the offensive air inside.

Five minutes later Cowboy turned onto a highway and accelerated to road speed. The stench lessened then melted into the ripe aroma of pastures dotted with water buffalo. The heat seemed less oppressive as wind whipped through the Mercedes and began to dry my sweat-soaked shirt. I wanted to ask Cowboy why he didn't seem to sweat but decided to start with simpler questions.

Cowboy was married, had three children, and lived in Korat City. He owned the taxi with some relatives but was vague on details. I didn't press for information although I was curious how scotch and cigarettes could pay for a Mercedes Benz as well as support a family and investing partners.

After Cowboy lit a cigarette, the smoke blended with exhaust fumes from a diesel truck and added another dimension to the toxic tapestry that passed for country air. I tried to settle back for the ride but felt uneasy driving on the left side of the road. Trucks and cars seemed to zoom along the highway with reckless speed and apparent disregard for safety. I felt even less in control in Cowboy's car than I had in Hunter's fighter jet.

I opened Hunter's brown envelope and dumped the contents into my lap. There was a map with Thailand on one side and Bangkok on the other, a picture with the name "Julia Snow 1964" on the back, and a pamphlet titled *Customs and Courtesies for U.S. Military Personnel in Thailand.* Also enclosed was a card listing the addresses of hotels and restaurants and six condoms in individual foil packets. I wondered if Hunter assembled the package especially for me or was it his own survival kit for R&R in Bangkok.

I regarded the picture of Julia. She had strawberry blonde hair, haunting blue eyes, and an air of peaceful confidence. She looked as if she had seen much in life and understood it all. Perhaps conversation on the trip back wouldn't be too boring.

Someone had annotated the map from Korat to Bangkok as if he was flying. Tick marks defined ten-mile increments on a route that ended with a triangle target symbol over a hotel near the Chao Phraya River. I smiled to myself as I saw a scribbled-in data box listing the heading, time, and distance to travel beside each leg of the route.

The map contained hieroglyphic evidence of an aviator's need for situation awareness. Pilots always want to know their exact position whether in a car, bus, or plane. It's a built-in need to navigate and time progress across the ground. My finger traced the initial navigation leg down Thai Highway Two, heading southwest at 240 degrees toward Saraburi, then south on Highway One, the "Friendship Highway," to Bangkok. Total distance, 139 miles. At 480 knots, a jet could travel 8 miles a minute and cover the distance in less than 18 minutes.

As we approached Bangkok, traffic slowed, and the acrid smell of open sewers returned. Cowboy patiently worked his way through lines of cars, bicycles, and three-wheeled bike taxis called tuk-tuks that blocked every intersection. Stifling smog hung in the air, and the heat seemed even more intense than before. Cowboy said the hotel would be cooler. Air conditioned, I hoped.

Cowboy parked the car half on the sidewalk in front of an old flat-faced masonry building, which stood in a row of storefront businesses. He pointed to a faded blue sign with chipped white lettering. "Princess Hotel," he said. "Number one hotel for you."

I walked through an arched entrance into a small lobby lined with potted plants and palms. Rooms were stacked on four-story decks encircling a center courtyard with a pool partially shaded by graceful palms. The lobby was open to the street and not air-conditioned. I was assured at the desk that my room would be.

The path to the staircase wound past the pool where three women were sunbathing. I tried to act nonchalant, but couldn't help staring at one of the women, a stunning blonde, wearing a wisp of a bikini top that barely covered her full, firm breasts.

"Guten tag," she said.

Caught in mid-gaze, I nodded and moved on, thinking her next words might be "quit ogling my knockers."

My small room on the second tier had two single beds and a bath. Because the closed-up room felt like a pressure cooker, I walked straight to the window air conditioning unit, turned it on high, and retreated to the balcony overlooking the courtyard.

Looking down at the fraulein, I became entranced. The woman had a blend of beauty and vulnerability that radiated sensuality. Although our eyes met, I didn't want to meet her and reflected on the irony. The last time I talked to a stunningly beautiful woman it was a sad disappointment: a child residing in a woman's body. She had become a victim of her own beauty. Now I can't even recall her name. The experience left me feeling that sometimes it was better to keep the dream than live with the meeting. Gazing upon Ms. Guten tag in the courtyard, I photographed her with my eyes in a sensuous appreciation of form.

Reconnaissance taken to a new level, I thought. But then I felt exhausted, far from home, and a little sad. I would have to dream later. I wondered if she had dreams too.

"Hey you," a voice yelled. "The Yankee air pirate. Want a beer?"

I glanced left on the balcony. Two men, obviously American military, sporting mustaches, and wearing baseball caps that said UDORN, walked toward me. "I'm a Thud pilot out of Korat. How did you know?"

"Must have been the haircut, but positive ID was tough without a brew in your hand. How about a cold one? Here, catch."

Out of the corner of my eye, I saw a bottle of Singha in mid-air. Instinctively, my hand flashed over the balcony rail and grasped the beer before it fell to the pool deck below. "Hey, watch it. You could hurt somebody."

The stranger staggered close and whispered with stale breath. "Just checking to see if you got reflexes like a real Thud pilot. I'm Mike. This here's my WSO Dave, and down there's the best set of knockers on this side of the Pacific."

"Mike," I said. "They could use your breath as a chemical weapon. You guys on R&R?"

Mike spit over the balcony rail. "Yeah. We're going to Patpong to get laid. Want to go?"

I watched Dave adjust his posture in a drunken attempt to hide his condition. "I don't think so," I said. "I'll just stay here and rest."

Mike made a jerky motion towards the pool. "Bet you'll try to nail one of those stewardesses, right?"

"Nope, I'm the sentimental type with a girl back home," I immediately wished I hadn't mentioned it.

"Girl back home," Mike shouted. "You're in the middle of the world's biggest sex smorgasbord, and you got a girl back home. Hell's bells. You're half way around the world from your poontang at home. You can buy a woman here for less than a carton of smokes."

I held up my hand. "Save it. I'm going to stay here."

Mike didn't get the hint. "Forget that stewardess, too, unless she'll go straight to your room. For the price of taking her out to dinner, you can buy a couple of women who will do anything you want. What a great place to fight a war."

"Thanks for the economics lesson, but I'll pass."

Mike shrugged then stumbled down the steps and headed for the sunbathers. The women seemed friendly at first but noticeably cooled when he yelled, "Show us your tits!"

Dave followed, still grinning and clutching a beer bottle tightly to his chest. He had not uttered one intelligible word.

I shook my head as I went back into my room. The air conditioner had begun to cut the heat. I turned on the shower and stood under the water, sipping the cool Singha. I soaped up and washed off several times then stood motionless letting water wash over me. After a long while, the label soaked off the beer bottle and dropped to the floor of the shower. Still, I didn't feel clean.

I put on a fresh shirt and slacks and set out for a walk. I nodded a greeting as I approached the women by the pool.

"Are you a fighter pilot?" the stunning blonde asked in English with a German accent.

"Yes, F-105s from Korat."

She smiled. "The F-105 is called the Thud. Right?"

"Right. The Thud, or Thunderchief."

"Are you here with your flight?" The dark haired one asked, sounding distinctly American.

"No, I'm alone."

The American pulled down her sunglasses. "Then those guys from Udorn aren't friends of yours?"

I grimaced. "Thought they were with you."

"No way," she smiled. "I'm Tibby and this is Utta and Marlene. They're stewardesses with Lufthansa. They live in Frankfort."

"And you?" I strained to keep eye contact with Tibby as Utta rubbed lotion on her shoulders, often slipping her hand under her bikini top. "Are you with Lufthansa?"

Tibby pulled the back of her chaise lounge up a notch. "I wish I were. These are my new friends. They've been helping me with my German."

"She is too modest," Utta said with her hand still inside her top. "Tibby speaks excellent German. Did she tell you she once lived in Landstuhl near the American Air Base?"

Utta was making me nervous, and I suspected she knew it. "Really," I said. "She didn't say anything about herself, so I thought she was with the CIA."

Tibby faked a pout. "Well, you don't have to tell everybody."

"Tell everybody what?" I asked, sure that she knew I was joking.

"That I'm with the CIA."

"So what do you do, really?" I asked.

Utta interrupted. "She is with the CIA. At least her husband is. He works for Air America, and they live in Vientiane, Laos."

"My husband does work for Air America and we do live in Vientiane, but I never said he was CIA."

Utta frowned. "But everybody knows who owns Air America. Everybody knows."

Tibby seemed to want to change the subject. "So why are you in Bangkok without your flight buddies? I heard fighter pilots do everything in formation."

"A double-entendre?" I said, watching Tibby's face for a reaction. Seeing none, I regretted that I said it. "I was shot down. I'm here recuperating."

Utta's eyes widened. "Is that how you got all those cuts and bruises on your face? You must tell us all about it."

They listened through several rounds of drinks and probed with questions when I showed signs of slowing down. They expressed shock that I had been in Asia six days and, so far, had spent half of my time on the ground in North Vietnam. As the tiers of rooms began to cast a long shadow over the courtyard, I felt tired and rubbed my eyes.

Tibby, perky and full of life, said, "Let's all go to dinner. We'll treat you. You can be our hero tonight."

"I'm not a hero."

"You are to me," Tibby said. "I had an uncle that was a fighter pilot in the Second World War. I never got to meet him. He's buried in the American Cemetery near Cambridge, England. I visited the gravesite several times."

"I'm sorry for your loss," I said as we all looked at Tibby for a few seconds. "I'm also sorry that I'm exhausted. Could I take a rain check?"

Tibby nodded with a sly smile. "Anytime, flyboy."

I turned to walk away then stopped. "Do you have a car?"

Utta looked surprised, "No, it's not good to drive in Bangkok. We'll hire a taxi."

"That's not what I mean. I have a car and driver I'm not going to use tonight. You're welcome to have it. And my driver will take good care of you."

I located Cowboy and introduced him to the women. Then asked him to get some beer and food and bring it to my room while they got ready. The women thanked me for the car and each gave me a big hug and apologized for my unfortunate first few days in Asia as if they had something to do with it.

Cowboy delivered Singha beer, fried rice and another dish I thought might be chicken. I placed the food on the small dresser and opened a bottle. I stripped down, took another cool shower and was asleep as soon as my head hit the pillow.

Chapter 15

Startled out of a panic-stricken dream with the macabre death-face of the young soldier fresh in my mind, I shot up on one elbow, trembling, soaked with sweat, and trying to make sense of my surroundings. I recalled the frightening look on the young soldier's face the moment life left him. He was dead. I hadn't dreamed it although now it seemed like a distant dream. My brain had ways of suppressing horrible events, but sometimes they came back and confronted me with undeniable truth; I could have been dead in his place.

The door opened slowly. Tibby peeked inside wide-eyed and smiling. "Hello. It's me," she sang out.

I shook my head trying to clear my eyes. "Is it morning?"

"No, just a little past midnight. Your light was on. Thought you were awake. Should I leave so you can sleep?"

I squirmed at the thought of being alone. "No, don't go. Did I leave the door open?"

"It swung open when I knocked. You shouldn't do that here in the big city."

Realizing I was uncovered, I pulled the sheet up half way. "I must have been really wasted."

Tibby held a glass in each hand. "I brought Bloody Marys. We're having a nightcap at the bar. I'm here to thank you for the car and invite you to join us."

She looked elegant in a simple black dress, pearl choker, and oversized gold bracelet. Her eyes locked onto mine as she strolled towards me, coy, confident, playing the coquette. She placed both glasses on the small bedside table.

"There," she said, straightening up to full height and turning toward me. As she threw her shoulders back, the basic black dress drew taut against her breasts.

I started to reach for the drink but grabbed my shoulder as pain shot through it. "Muscle clanked up again. I have to get some pills from my shaving kit."

"Lie still, I'll get them," Tibby said, as she retrieved the bag from the second bed. "Is this it?"

I nodded. "I don't have a robe. Could you hand me a towel?"

Tibby glanced at me with a mischievous smile and ignored my request. "You think I've never seen a naked man?"

"You've never seen me."

"Did when I came in. You look fine except for the cuts and bruises all over. Did the ejection do all that?"

"Ejection was okay, but I landed in a tree."

She opened the pill bottle and handed me a tall glass with a posy of celery perched on top. "You need some tender love and care."

I sipped some of the Tabasco flavored juice. Then, ignoring the burning sensation, I took a gulp. The bouquet of celery was a welcome change from the lingering scent of soy sauce and untouched food on the dresser.

"Poor baby, take your pills, and I'll give you a rub. We'll see if I can make it better." Tibby sat beside me and stroked my shoulder. "Tomorrow we'll take you out for a steam bath and massage. It's an Asian specialty. Have you had one?"

"No. Just a little physical therapy at the clinic," I said as I closed my eyes and stretched against the pressure of her hands. Several minutes passed in silence before she tugged at my shoulder.

"On your stomach," she directed then pushed me face down on the bed. "I need a better position."

Turning my face to the side, I watched her in the mirror. With a single motion, Tibby hiked her dress up to her waist and straddled my hips. Her bare legs tightened against my thighs, riding and pushing against the tension. I felt an involuntary spasm as her fingers dug into my back.

She paused. "Did I hurt you?"

I fought off a second shiver and recognized a warm surge of emotion vying with the pain. "No. You're doing great."

Closing my eyes with a grimace, I arched cat-like against her hands. A dizzying sensation of pleasure held me very near the sharp edge of pain. Letting her take control, I felt safe in her hands and began to relax for the first time since I'd been in Southeast Asia.

As her expert fingers massaged, I reflected on my brief combat experience and the weeks of waiting while politicians decided if new lieutenants could fly combat in single-seat fighters. I had been the third lieutenant to get shot down very early on his tour. I wasn't dead, like the others, but Hunter had saved me when I couldn't save myself. Although technically it wasn't my fault, I worried that I had disgraced my peers by adding fuel to the political fires in the Pentagon.

The unknowns and anticipation facing me before I left the States were all history. The terrifying experience of the shootdown was behind me. A scary but exhilarating feeling lingered now that it was over.

At the pool, I had enjoyed the look on Tibby's face as I told her the story. The other women were attentive, but it was Tibby that hung on every word. She'd made me feel like the most important person in the world. I didn't have to explain things to her. She understood flying and the war. She made me feel I could talk to her about anything. It seemed as if she had asked a thousand interesting questions.

I had told her about my fear. It just came out. I hadn't considered the two Germans were also listening. I had felt as if only Tibby could hear. I had been afraid. I actually said it out loud and remembered being surprised by my own words. In my lifetime, I never expressed that thought to anyone. Not even to myself.

Hunter's words raced through my head, "Death or something worse than death." But I didn't die and I hadn't been captured. For the moment, I was alive in a Bangkok hotel room and being brought more alive by Tibby.

Could I go back into harm's way? Could I finish ninety-nine more missions being shot at and knowing what waited in the jungle? If events had been slightly different, instead of a massage in a Bangkok hotel, I would be fighting for my life in a North Vietnamese prison. Interrogators would be using ropes to break my limbs and pull my arms out of their sockets. The mental image of torture caused my body to tremble.

Tibby stopped. "What's wrong, did I hurt you?"

"Just thinking how lucky I am to be here with you instead of in prison up North."

"Bad dream, right?"

"Could have been a long term nightmare."

"You're safe with me. You need someone to be good to you," Tibby said as she bent low over my back and placed kisses on my neck.

I savored the subtle aroma of her perfume as her silky hair lightly brushed against my shoulders like the breath of an ardent angel. Her fingertips stroked my skin in tiny circles, ever so lightly. "How do you know what I need?"

"Don't worry. I just do," Tibby whispered. "You need someone to lose yourself in for a while. Someone with no conditions. Someone you can trust."

My eye lingered on her reflection in the mirror. Gently she moved my arms above my head. Beginning in the small of my back, with long, slow strokes of the heels of her hands, she traveled up my spine, over my shoulders and the full length of my arms. As her hands stretched toward mine, I savored her balmy skin and delicate fragrance. I felt the fullness of her as she moved, side to side, slowly, sensually teasing my back. Her moist lips gently touched my ear.

"You're tense," she whispered.

"Who wouldn't be?"

"Relax. I'm here for you," she breathed, playfully biting my ear. "You can have anything you want."

I thought I was dreaming. How many times had I fantasized about a moment like this? A voluptuous woman waltzes into my life and offers to fulfill any lascivious desire. Who was this woman I could talk to so easily, who swirled my shallow thoughts into deep eddies? We met only a few hours before, yet she was the only human on the planet with whom I had shared my fears.

I couldn't shut out the softness of Tibby's caresses, the low moaning sound of her whispers or the amatory aroma of her skin. Again she traveled the distance of my back until stretched out full and flat against my body. Her face pressed next to mine. Her mouth parted, gently biting my lower lip then holding it captive as her tongue explored. My desire became urgent and undeniable, but a word echoed in the back of my mind and intruded on my thoughts. Married.

"Relax, Ashe. It's okay," Tibby said, seeming to sense what I was thinking. I want to help you forget your bad experiences. It's not the rest of your life or mine. It's just an R&R in Bangkok. Oh, I'm not saying this right. Ashe, I want you. I need to help you tonight. I've had a few drinks, but I know what I'm doing. I want us to get lost in each other."

"I think my emotions are numb," I said. "Afraid to feel. Afraid to let myself go."

"Ashe, all that matters is our time together here and now. There's a war on, and we could all die tomorrow."

I propped myself up on one elbow. "Isn't that supposed to be the guy's line?"

Tibby laughed. "I know, Ashe, but it's true. You're going back into combat. You had a narrow escape on your first mission and you have ninety-nine to go. Let's make every minute of our time count."

"But what about you. Aren't you..."

"Married," Tibby interrupted. "Is that what you mean? That's for me to keep straight in my head. Tonight I'm here for you. There must be thousands of guys who fantasize about a night like this on R&R in a war zone. Guess those gunners didn't scare you enough."

"They scared me plenty."

Tibby kissed my cheek. "I think I scare you, too, fighter pilot."

I sighed then sipped on a Bloody Mary until the glass was empty. Tibby opened a beer and poured it into the Bloody Mary glass. Singha, over ice, flavored with a hint of tomato juice. It tasted better than I expected. A lot better. After a while, she nudged me onto my back and planted soft whispers of butterfly kisses on my chest.

Her breathing deepened as she moved easily and softly over me, kissing, touching with her tongue, softly biting, and caressing my skin. She straddled me again, her body bending over mine, lightly brushing against but holding back. Then her lips half-parted over mine, hovering, not touching.

We moved together then, pulled back slightly, teasing, and pretending to resist. Suddenly, I closed my arms around her, drawing her near, locked in a deep kiss. I was caught in an unexpected storm of emotion that engulfed me in a great wave.

A flood of anxiety and fear poured out of me as unintelligible sounds resonated deep in my throat. She pulled back, then clutched me tighter. We clung together, absorbing each other's pain, fulfilling each other's longing, and collapsing into the safety of each others arms.

We kissed again and again in timeless attempts to hold on to the feelings of warmth and security. A consummate lover, she offered herself as a gift. I wished I had more experience, wanting assurance I had satisfied her. I lost myself while cuddled up beside her. I cried, and laughed, and wanted it to go on forever.

Towards morning, Tibby nestled close, crying softly on my shoulder. I tried to comfort her. After a while she slept in my arms. Overcome by her presence, I lay awake and held her until full morning light.

I felt at once both secure and confused by our relationship. I sensed that I could talk to Tibby. Words in half-formed thoughts poured out of me and began to coalesce as she listened. I tried to sort things out in my mind but probably wasn't making any sense to her. Only one thing was clear. It was not the past that troubled me. It was the future. Finally, I talked myself out and stared at the ceiling in silence.

Tibby held me tight and nuzzled my shoulder. "I want you to feel safe in my arms."

"I do," I whispered and drew her closer. My fingers traced up the lacunae of her lower back, traversed the hollow of her shoulders, lingered lightly at the nape of her neck, and finally settled into her hair. "Did you sleep well?"

"Yes, but we didn't sleep much," she said. "I want to spend the morning in bed with you, playing, and sleeping, and playing."

"You're repeating yourself."

Tibby snuggled against my chest. "I would love to repeat myself."

"Fortunately, I have some time before I meet Hunter's wife."

"Sounds delicious," Tibby said. "Then what'll you do?

"Take her to see Hunter. We'll head for Korat from the airport."

"Oh, Ashe, when will I see you again? When is your next R&R?"

"I won't be coming back," I said, bending my head forward. Suddenly I drew a breath, realizing the full impact of my thoughts by hearing them for the first time.

Tibby pulled back and looked into my eyes. "What do you mean?"

"I mean, I probably won't be flying combat again. So, I won't be returning to Bangkok on R&R." I said, searching but not finding a way to make my earlier statement sound softer and less precise.

Tibby pulled me close. "Oh, honey, I didn't realize you wouldn't be able to fly again. I am so sorry. I didn't know you're permanently grounded."

"I'm not permanently grounded."

"Ashe, I don't understand."

"I was shot down and evaded in enemy territory. That's a free ticket home if I want to go."

Tibby's brow furrowed. "I see."

"I've been thinking about it a lot. Being with you has helped me understand it's okay to be afraid. It's normal and natural. I'm sure there'll be pressure to stay, but the regulation is clear. I don't have to risk facing those enemy gunners again."

Tibby pursed her lips. "When could you fly again?"

"Probably three weeks. When my ear heals."

"So you'll be able to fly combat, but you're not going to because the Air Force won't force you to do it? Is that what I hear you saying?"

"I don't have to decide for another two weeks or so. This has bothered me a lot, knowing I have to make a decision. I've been cooped up with other pilots and fighter guys aren't easy to talk to. Tibby, you brought me out of that narrow world and back to a place where there's warmth, beauty, and love. Knowing you has allowed me to find my own feelings and get in touch with them."

"And what will your decision be? Tell me again."

"Before, I believed there was no alternative. Now, after being with you, I think the only reasonable thing to do is to hold on to life and go back to the States. After all, my luck may be running out. Thanks to you, Tibby, I'll go back home and live a long happy life."

Tibby smiled and moved slowly as she got out of bed and stood in front of me. She swayed slowly and made low moaning sounds as if to some inner music. She stood full in front of me, outlined by dim light from the shuttered window. I pulled myself up to a sitting position on the edge of the bed, despite the ache in my shoulder she had tried to massage away. Cradling my head in her hands, she nuzzled my face against the soft skin of her stomach.

With almost imperceptible movement, she began to turn sideways at the hips. I raised my eyes to better see her as I placed light kisses on her taut skin. She continued to turn as far as she could with her feet squarely facing me. Her delicate skin stretched tighter as, with slow, steady motion, she lifted her arm to eye level. She paused, motionless, as I drank in her fragrance and revered the outline of her body against the soft light.

In the next instant, her beautiful form became a blur as I saw what was happening too late to believe it. Her clenched fist hit my cheek like a cannonball and drove my head against the cinder block wall behind the bed.

"You wimp," Tibby screamed. "You lily-livered pansy. How could you think of going home after one mission? I offered myself to you, thinking you had balls like a real fighter pilot. I thought you would die for your country, die for your buddies, or whatever you fighter pilots are supposed to die for. You have ninety-nine missions left and you're going home and leave your buddies here to fly them for you. You're not my hero. You're just a coward. A revolting coward."

With blurred vision, I watched Tibby move toward the door while straightening her dress. Then, as she ran down the stairs, she shouted again. "You coward. You miserable, dirty, rotten coward."

Chapter 16

A thin stream of passengers began to trickle through the customs gate at Bangkok's Don Muang Airport. The plane had been on the ground over an hour. I had watched it sitting on the ramp, but the processing of travelers had been painfully slow. Weary of waiting, I pulled Julia's picture from my shirt pocket then finally put it back without looking at it. Cowboy stood beside me, hat tipped back on his head, holding a hand-printed sign labeled, "JULIA SNOW."

My reflection in the window displayed an impatient scowl, and my jaw hurt like hell. Tibby had made her desires known and left a painful reminder of her position. She wanted me to finish and didn't distinguish whether the end meant my tour or my life.

Fortunately, her unexpected blow landed on the left side of my face instead of my damaged ear. A darkened knot had appeared between my eye and swollen jaw. I tried to make the new bruise blend with the old by covering it with Clearasil. Cowboy had been discreet and not mentioned the fresh wound although I caught him glancing at it.

I retrieved the picture from my shirt pocket once again and stared at it. Julia wore a loose casual blouse, very little makeup, and hair pulled back tight. She had a knowing smile and none of the rough edges that were apparent in Hunter. Mostly, I liked her sparkling, mischievous eyes, the way they revealed both vulnerability and strength.

Cowboy pointed towards the customs exit. "Lieutenant Ashe, that be her."

At first, I was unsure. She approached down the corridor pushing a luggage cart. How had Cowboy known? Her hair wasn't pulled back like in the photo. It was loose, full, and blonde, with a slight red tinge, strawberry blonde, perhaps. Her complexion looked darker in the distance, but, as she approached, resolved to be fair and punctuated with a soft hint of rose freckles. She wore a light, flowered, spring dress and walked with easy confidence and uncommon determination.

Stopping directly in front of me, she hesitated, lifting her head until her penetrating eyes met mine. "I'm Julia Snow and you're an American, here to give me a lift to Korat, I presume."

I tried to mimic her correct British pronunciation. "I am Lieutenant Ashe Wilcox and your presumption is correct. How did you pick me out of the crowd?"

She tossed her head back and laughed. "Surely you jest, American shoes, polyester pants and the haircut. Who else could it be? There's another clue, as well," she whispered. "Your manservant is holding a sign bearing my name."

I turned, "Oh, of course. Let me introduce Cowboy. He'll take your bags and meet us with the car."

After the long wait, I sighed with relief as we began to walk out of the terminal. I had expected Julia to look older, like my vision of Hunter's wife, not this stunning, vibrant woman. Her piercing eyes seemed to look into me rather than at me. She had an easy smile and intriguing British accent. After a few minutes with her, I felt a strange connection that I couldn't identify and didn't want to reveal. Taking care not to let my eyes linger too long, I realized she was a woman who would show up in my dreams. I shook my head, not believing I had those kind of thoughts about Hunter's wife.

I don't know why, but I felt I needed to apologize for Hunter. "Lieutenant Colonel Snow would like to have been here to meet you, but he had to stay at Korat."

Julia's eyes narrowed. "You mean Hunter, don't you? You

need not make excuses for him. It is you who has been put to the inconvenience, not I."

"We have a good driver and should arrive at Korat by midafternoon."

"Oh, I'm so sorry. We weren't able to discuss an agenda beforehand. I have a booking at the Oriental Hotel. But, there's no need to look after me. If you must return to Korat, please feel free to take the driver and do so. I'm perfectly capable of arranging my own transportation and looking after myself."

"But I'm here to escort you to Korat," I said, trying to act nonchalant but being surprised she was in no hurry to see Hunter.

"I don't require an escort. However, if you do stay over, I invite you to dine with me tonight at the hotel. I'm told they have a superb restaurant."

"Actually, I have no time constraints. I'm temporarily grounded."

Julia looked at me in wonder. "I understand now. You're not a lieutenant. You're the lieutenant; the one flying with my husband when he was shot down. My poor dear, I wondered about your face. Hunter said you were hurt far worse than he."

I turned slightly to make the new bruise less visible. "I'll be fine in a few days."

She cocked her head to one side. "I sense you had two calamities, one in an aircraft and one with a woman."

"I can't believe this. How did you know?"

"Simple, my dear. You have been struck recently by a woman."

"But how could you possibly know that?"

Julia's voice softened. "In all my years around fighter pilots, I have never seen one marked by another man. Pilots avoid fisticuffs at all cost, not wanting to risk their flying careers to senseless injury. Only a woman can get close enough, in an unguarded moment, to inflict damage such as the fresh bruise you're sporting."

Fortunately Cowboy pulled up with the car before I felt the need to explain. I hurried to the driver's side to discuss the change in plans. Cowboy drew air through his teeth, making a hissing sound, and said the Oriental Hotel was "mach mach baht" meaning very expensive. He suggested I return to the Princess, pointing out that it was only two city blocks from the Oriental.

The morning haze was burning off as Cowboy chauffeured the Mercedes on a halting journey through heavy traffic. I realized it would be painfully slow going as the sun's heat broiled us in a toxic mélange of humidity and exhaust fumes.

Julia appeared cool, relaxed, and refreshed, especially considering her long flight from the States. She had a regal presence, perfectly blended with an earthy English humor. She gave conversation an edge by combining a proper English accent with a smattering of American slang.

I had little confidence in my own conversational abilities, not for lack of intelligence but experience. Julia appeared worldly, and if she wasn't, she made up for it with confidence and enthusiasm. She talked easily, and I enjoyed her company.

Julia seemed to be captivated by the streets and storefronts as they passed. "What do you think of Bangkok?" she said.

I thought of Tibby and how my impression of a place often hinged on a woman met there. "Hot and sweaty. I like it a lot, but I've spent most of my time in my room. Sleeping."

Julia nudged my arm. "You'll ruin your fighter pilot image, admitting you slept away your R&R. Bet that's not what you'll tell the boys at the bar. I won't presume to ask if you were sleeping alone."

Julia was direct in a way I hadn't experienced in a woman who commanded my respect. My face felt flushed. "Fine," I nodded. "There's probably no right answer to that question."

"Perhaps not." Julia said, with a sly smile. "Fighter pilots have enormous egos. They lie a lot, but most women are smart enough to see through it."

I studied her face, realizing I was not in control of the

conversation. "But you married a fighter pilot. There must be some attraction?"

"Of course there is. They have wonderful qualities: intelligence, humor, coordination, enthusiasm, and so forth. They also share many of the playful qualities that make little boys lovable, don't you agree?"

"Not particularly."

"I like the whole fighter community, and Hunter is really very special, as you perhaps know."

"He's a legend."

"As we English say, he's a one off. I have never met anyone like him and, perhaps, never will again. It's odd. What draws you to a person and what keeps you happy together are often very different things. Don't you agree?"

I paused feeling uncomfortable. "I wouldn't know, really, I wouldn't. How did you two meet?"

"We met in England shortly after the Korean War. He was a prisoner in Korea, as you may know. He had been tortured severely, starved, and had developed Korean hemorrhagic fever. He suffered great pain as a prisoner and the fever nearly killed him after he was repatriated."

I grimaced. For the first time I began to think of our shootdown through Hunter's eyes. Perhaps I could understand why he considered killing himself rather than be captured and tortured a second time. "How did he come to be in England?"

"After he recovered physically, the Air Force reinstated his flying status. They posted him to the American Base at Woodbridge, England. I lived in Tuddenham, a village near by. American pilots represented their base at local events, and we met at a Tuddenham fete. I remember the first time I laid eyes on him. He looked uncomfortable in the crowd of strangers so I came to the rescue. We had a jolly time. Perhaps we hit it off because I had been interned myself. I understood what he had been through."

I stiffened. "Wait. You were a prisoner too?"

"Yes. My whole family was interned."

"Please, tell me about it. If I'm not intruding too much."

Julia sighed, "My father worked as a civil engineer in China before the Japanese occupied the country during the Second World War. The British had many engineers in China, and we lived in Shanghai. One day, the Japanese came to our house and arrested our whole family."

I didn't reply at first, trying to imagine what it would be like to have the enemy show up at your doorstep. Then she stopped and looked at me, apparently waiting for me to understand.

"How did you feel about that?" I asked.

"Scared out of my wits at first, but then all my childhood mates and their families were taken prisoner as well. The adults tried to comfort us and told us we would go home soon. We were held under guard in an old gymnasium with a huge curtain drawn across the center. Men and boys lived on one side and women, girls, and young children on the other.

"I didn't completely understand what was happening at first. I was just a child, and all my friends were around me. But as time passed with no hope of release, I could see the adults were afraid. Soon I felt the terror. We had barely enough food and few medical supplies. Water was plentiful, but contaminated from time to time. There was much illness."

"Were you sick?"

"Sometimes. But not as bad as others." She took a deep, seemingly painful breath. "My older sister died in the first few months. My father gracefully endured the agony of a long illness. Although he lived to be repatriated to England, he was forever physically and spiritually weakened. He died two years later. Only thirty-six."

I shook my head. "I'm sorry. What a tragic loss."

Julia's face turned toward the window. "When my mother grew old, she told me stories about the prison. There wasn't much physical torture in the classic sense, but there was torture of a different sort. The guards controlled all of the food and medicine. My beautiful mother had to exchange sexual favors for necessities to keep my father alive. That is how they say it, isn't it, to put it in the best light, exchange sexual favors?"

I was stunned and couldn't respond. I felt uncomfortable like an intruder into the intimacy of her past.

"Mother did it to keep the man she loved alive. God, she loved him. She never told him. She never told anyone, not even British Intelligence during her repatriation debriefing. She never wanted him to know and carried that burden silently and alone until after he died and I was grown. I'm the only person in the world with whom she shared her secret."

"I don't know what to say. By comparison, my life's been very sheltered."

Julia looked at me with sad eyes masked by a hint of a smile. "I would have traded anything for a sheltered childhood. However, on a positive note, it may have been the reason Hunter and I came together. We each carried quite a bit of pain, and our common experience helped us to understand each other in ways that few people can. He has been through far more than anyone I know. He has suffered many losses and with each has become more focused.

Julia looked ahead and smiled. "I believe we're approaching my hotel." Then her voice turned bright and cheerful, completely changing the mood. "Dine with me tonight," she said. "I promise not to bore you with any more heavy conversation."

The idea excited me, but, wanting to appear worldlier than I felt, I tried not to show it. "It would be my pleasure."

"Smashing. We shall meet in the Author's Lounge a tad before eight then repair to the dining room? Well then, it's settled. You need not see me to the lobby. The bell captain will care for my grip, and I'll meet you this evening."

I stood with Cowboy and watched Julia disappear into the hotel. Cowboy was right. It looked very expensive. I beckoned to a bell captain dressed in a white uniform with matching bobby cap and inquired about a dress code. He said a tie and a jacket were desirable. I had neither. Cowboy volunteered to round up a tie while I checked in.

I sent the Mercedes ahead while I stretched my legs on the brief few blocks between the Princess and the Oriental hotels. My thoughts turned to Tibby as I made my way through the mass of humanity on the sidewalk. At the Princess Hotel desk, I discovered I was too late. Mrs. Tibby Barnes of Vientiane, Laos, had checked out.

By six-thirty I had napped and dressed. Regarding myself in the mirror, I thought I looked like a clown. I wore a short sleeve shirt, brown pants, and the tie Cowboy had selected. How long would it be, I wondered, before oversized blue and yellow polka dots would be back in style. I pulled the tie knot loose, hoping to find a more suitable one before dinner.

With some time to kill, I unfolded the map of Bangkok and walked the short distance to the Sathorn Bridge on the Chao Phraya River. I passed several mobile carts where merchants sold skewers of meat cooked over charcoal fires and offered bamboo trays of flat pastry, dried fruit, and nuts. The aroma of barbecued meat, peanuts, and soy filled my senses and piqued my hunger. Not knowing what was safe for me to eat, I passed the stands and waved off the sellers.

The Chao Phraya didn't flow quietly and peacefully as I remembered the rivers of my youth. The water supported a teeming marketplace of constantly rocking crafts of commerce. Strangely, the occupants seemed peacefully detached from the rolling action of the waves.

From the bridge I watched hundreds of colorfully decorated boats that partially obscured the murky brown river. Many appeared to be water taxis, racing back and forth to landing piers on each bank. Others had a large motor on a long pole, controlled by a nautical acrobat balancing precariously on the stern.

A group of boat women, each shaded by an up-turned basket hat, hawked wares and tended flat skiffs filled with fruit, grain, greens, fish and live eels. The women sellers kept twenty or so boats grouped together with no sign of line or anchor. I watched the occasional hand dart out to correct the position of their craft.

I smiled at the automatic station keeping the women accomplished, seemingly without looking.

At water's edge, a few feet from the boats, a woman brushed her teeth as a group of people in loose-fitting sarongs soaped themselves nearby. I felt like an intruder in a community bathroom. The sun hung low in the sky as I walked back down a short stretch of street past the Princess Hotel and headed toward the Oriental. A breeze, blowing in from over the Chao Phraya River, felt refreshing as long as I didn't breathe too deeply. White egrets sat on pier posts and other solitary birds flew elegant approaches out of city noise into the relative safety of the river.

My thoughts turned to Julia as I approached the hotel. Unlike anyone I'd ever experienced, she seemed completely open and candid about intimate details of her life. Her kind of sharing drew a dramatic contrast to my experience growing up in the stoic Midwest where personal trials remained deep family secrets. She seemed so much more of a complete woman than Tibby. And—dare I think it—than Jenny.

Perhaps because Julia was older and more experienced, I felt like she understood everything that I said or even thought. She conveyed her feelings in subtle ways with a touch of her hand or a glance. I couldn't begin to figure her out even though she seemed to share all available evidence about herself. Clearly she radiated immense quality and depth. I thought her a strange match for Hunter.

The Oriental Hotel doorman opened the huge glass entrance, and I strolled into the air-conditioned lobby towards a Thai man in a white uniform topped by a feather-plumed hat.

"Could you direct me to Art's bar?" I asked.

"Perhaps you are looking for the Author's Lounge, sir," the white cap said, setting forth each syllable slowly and precisely. "Are you staying with us or meeting one of our guests?"

"Yes, of course, the lounge. I'm meeting Julia Snow."

Chapter 17

Julia entered the Author's Lounge as if she owned the hotel, breezing through the door, heading straight for my table. I laughed as a headwaiter rushed to attend her. To me, he had been condescending, letting his judgmental eyes linger too long on my bruised face and the tie Cowboy selected. He made no similar mistake with Julia, directing his staff to her as the woman of quality her appearance suggested. By the time she arrived at my table, an entourage of three followed. I stood to receive her. The headwaiter looked disappointed as Julia warmly embraced me.

As she turned to be seated, I leaned toward him, forced an exaggerated grin, and said. "It's the tie."

As the staff dwindled to one waiter, Julia looked straight into my eyes. She had a way of defining a moment with a smile. "Please accept my apologies for being late."

Suddenly I felt nervous. "You look very nice," I said, thinking she had a wonderful sensual beauty but "very nice" was all that came out. I made a self-conscious effort not to stare at her, but she completely captured my attention. She had a stunning aura of confidence. She was the kind of woman that could surface insecurities in almost anyone.

"A refreshing drink, Madame?" the waiter asked.

"Perhaps soda with a touch of bitters," she said without letting her eyes waver in the slightest from mine.

While we made small talk, I searched for an opportunity,

wanting to know more about Hunter without appearing too obvious. She seemed practiced in the art of polite conversation, but I had an agenda.

"What about Hunter?" I finally blurted out, then punched myself on the leg for my lack of verbal foreplay.

Julia diverted her eyes to the window. "How so?"

"I mean," I hesitated. "What can you tell me about him?"

It seemed like minutes before she looked back at me. "Strange. I was about to ask you how he is since you saw him yesterday, and I haven't seen him for several months."

"He's fine," I said. "For a man who was shot down and evaded the enemy for three days. He survived the trek far better than I did. Of course, he'd had the experience before."

"Unfortunately, he was not rescued in Korea."

"I know and he saved me from being captured this time. He knew exactly what to do to get us out. I owe my life to him but feel like I don't know him. I'm not trying to pry into your life. I just want to know more about the guy who saved mine."

"As you are perhaps aware, Hunter doesn't talk easily. Never has. Not even to me," Julia said in a tone suggesting she was hurt. "On the other hand, I have known him longer and better than anyone. Considering the circumstances, your question seems fair. What do you want to know?"

"I'll leave that to you. As much as you feel comfortable telling me."

"Sorry, it won't work that way. I'm too close to him. It is best if you ask questions."

"I apologize. I'm prying. I have no right to ask you to do this."

Julia smiled, apparently trying to put me at ease. "Your request is not unexpected. Many have been curious before you. I feel I have become the great explainer of Hunter since he doesn't speak for himself."

Julia smiled in silence while the waiter placed her soda and bitters then refilled my glass with Singha beer. She looked out the window then drew me into conversation by asking me questions about myself. I became impatient waiting for her to take my invitation to talk.

Finally she said, "So, my dear. What can I tell you about Hunter?"

"I hear he's a full-blooded Indian."

"Yes, both his mother and father lived on the Shivwits Indian Reservation near Snow Canyon."

"Snow Canyon?"

"Near Saint George, Utah. I traveled there several times with Hunter. He's very attached to the Canyon and the woods in Pine Valley close by. Perhaps you have flown over the reservation? There's a radar target in the town nearby. Saint George Radar Bomb Scoring Site, I believe it's called."

"I've flown on that site several times, but I don't recall a reservation."

"Not much to notice," she said. "It's small and probably doesn't look like much from the air, a few huts and little boxes for houses. I saw it after the Indians had moved into a government housing project nearby. Hunter explained what it was like living there as a child. Very depressing."

"What about family?"

"His father's ancestry remains a mystery. Indian, but not of the Shivwits tribe. Hunter doesn't look like the Shivwits. He has physical traits of tribes further east, perhaps Navaho or Ute around the Grand Canyon. His father died of alcoholism, we believe, when Hunter was an infant. What happened to his mother is less clear. By the time he was five, both parents were gone. Then he was boarded with a Mormon family on a farm a few miles from the reservation. He never knew why. They raised him and provided the necessities, that is, if you don't consider love and affection necessary for a child.

"They changed his name to Erasmus Snow and wouldn't allow him to use his Indian name. Now, he detests his Mormon name and won't answer to it because he felt like an outsider and never part of the family. Everyone worked hard on the farm, but, for

Hunter's efforts, the father beat him and humiliated him for being an Indian."

"It's hard to take it all in," I said, feeling my face flush with anger. "He's had his share of life's trauma." Emotional wounds I would never understand had shaped Hunter. I recalled the withdrawn, detached look I had often seen on his face? What were his memories? He would have been about my age now, twenty-four, when the Koreans tortured him for two and a half years. I felt sick to my stomach.

"Shall we repair to the dining room?"

I was jolted back into the moment, "Sorry?"

Julia frowned. "Oh dear. I've made you uncomfortable again. Or worse, I've been a bore."

I sighed. "I sense you are many things but boring isn't one of them. Please don't stop. I want to know more, unless of course, talking about Hunter is uncomfortable for you."

Julia shook her head looking relaxed and peaceful. "I understand your desire to know him. I also sense you have experienced a great deal of emotional pain recently."

I looked at her wondering how she knew things about me that I hadn't completely admitted to myself. "You must be a mind reader."

"One doesn't have to be psychic to know your last few days and perhaps weeks have been a trial." Julia nodded toward the door. "I'm anticipating a wonderful repast. Shall we dine?"

I enjoyed the proper and playful way she talked. Julia put her arm in mine as we left the lounge and made our way to the Normandy Grill. Once again, close to her, I became aware of her subtle but intensely sensuous perfume. I started to comment on it but didn't until we reached the top floor. "What are you wearing?"

"The perfume? Quadrille. Do you like it?"

"Very much." I said, understating my true feelings, which involved licking it off of her neck.

The restaurant appeared to float high above the city as an elegant island of mahogany, glass, gold, and brocade. Julia paused for a minute to absorb the panoramic view of the Chao Phraya River unwinding through the markets and temples of Bangkok below.

"Monet," she said, blowing a kiss to the city. "The haze looks like the soft pastels in his paintings."

"Looks like smog to me." I said, relying on cynicism instead of sharing the emotion of the moment.

"How unromantic," Julia said as she tossed her head back and laughed.

An impeccably dressed gentleman, probably European, approached. "Sir," he said. "I'm so sorry, but a jacket is required for dining."

"Ashe, would you excuse us for a moment?" Julia asked, as she stepped in front of him, took his arm and guided him a few steps away.

When they returned the gentleman smiled and said, "I'm so pleased you decided to dine with us this evening. Our maitre d' will be with you in a moment.

"What did you say to him?"

Julia smiled and put her arm in mine. "Just enough to guarantee an excellent table."

"Wow," I said. "You sure handled that guy."

"Wow, indeed," Julia replied, as she surveyed the room then directed the maitre d' toward a table near the window.

The city lights unfolded into the distance creating the illusion of looking down from heaven.

A waiter approached immediately, "Something from the bar?"

"Kir Royale please, preferably with Louis Roederer Cristal," Julia touched my hand. "Care to join me?"

I leaned forward. "I don't know what that is."

"It's a fine champagne with crème de cassis, a liquor made from European black currants."

"I'll just have a Singha beer."

As we studied the menu, I was conscious of our position high above the sea of millions of people who lived in Bangkok. I was in a magnificent restaurant with an elegant woman, isolated and immune above the pungent pollution and poverty I had witnessed on the streets and river below.

"I have decided," Julia announced with zest as she closed her menu and patted it lightly with her hand. "This is wonderful."

"Do you have a recommendation?"

"A starter of mussels bisque, an entrée of curried lobster béchamel, then a small green salad. Perhaps after, oh yes, we must do this, mango pie with slices of fresh mango on the side."

I glanced up with a look that must have appeared less than enthusiastic. "Mango pie?"

She laughed. "It's wonderful. It has a crumbly, buttery crust. Mango is slightly acidic, but the custard mellows it out. The fresh mango is to sharpen the taste, as we like. You must have it."

"I don't think so. I just heard mango and acid in the same sentence. Maybe I'll have a steak."

"Perhaps you would like to try something more interesting. Something you can't have at home."

"Appreciate your concern, but I've had enough of new and exciting in my short stay in Asia. Your husband served an especially tasty snake supper while we were in the jungle."

"Did you find Hunter an adequate cook?"

"He served it raw. A fire would have revealed our position."

"How disgusting."

"My thoughts exactly. I'll stick with steak and beer. No offense to your tastes or Hunter's talent as a chef."

"None taken."

"It's a long road from an Indian reservation to fighter pilot," I said.

"Yes, and it's interesting how he did that. When he was twelve, he lived with a second Mormon family and things were different. The father took an interest in him and reintroduced him to his Indian heritage. They visited the reservation often, and he was able to learn from the few remaining elders of his tribe and study their ways. It made a deep impression, and he developed a sense of identity for the first time."

"I hoped there'd be a positive chapter in his story."

"His life hasn't been a fairy tale," Julia conceded. "More like a Greek tragedy where the hero is blind to the fatal flaw that ultimately undoes him."

"What's the fatal flaw?"

Julia laughed. "You're too anxious. Do you peek at the end of novels?"

"Do I have to confess everything?"

"Hunter learned about the Indian code readers in World War Two. They conducted radio communications in their native language, which was impossible for the enemy to decode. Learning about their success led to two things. It rekindled curiosity about his native language and sparked his interest in the military. He joined the Air Force as soon as he was old enough. After a while, they sent him to a program called Aviation Cadets. After several months, he qualified as a pilot. Flying became the first thing in life that was truly his own and allowed him to compete equally, or as they say, on a level playing field."

I could relate to her comment. As a child, I was often the smallest member of the team and got battered and bruised for my efforts. But later in life when strapping into a jet fighter, I felt equal to anyone.

As though reading my mind, Julia said, "The machine becomes the great equalizer. It was the first time Hunter could compete as an equal in society. Lord knows, he relished the competition. He became the Top Gun in his fighter training class and never looked back. After that, he won everything. He won the respect of his peers. Most importantly, he won respect for himself, at least for his abilities as a pilot. He was good at flying. God, was he good at it."

"And still is."

"He was assigned to Nellis Air Base for several years. Las Vegas is a few hours from the reservation and we frequently went there. I'll always remember seeing him stand silently staring at a mountain and saying, "Listen, you can hear the mountain breathe.""

"Did you hear the mountain breathe?"

"No, but I never doubted for a minute that he did."

I took a long sip of Singha. "He's been so successful in combat, I think they'll put him on track to become a general."

"His worst fear is precisely that scenario. His desire is to remain in the cockpit and fly combat, or, if there is no war, to instruct others. He's fond of saying he's a warrior, not a manager. Lord knows he is not political or seeking advancement. Yet, with his combat record, he'll certainly be promoted to full colonel, be selected for War College, and be granted command of a flying unit. He fears that will be the end of him. I'll deny ever saying this, but he doesn't feel capable of leading others except from the cockpit of a jet fighter."

"What do you fear?"

Julia's eyes glowed with the mist of unshed tears. "I fear I've lost him either way. If he stays in combat, I can't be with him. If he comes home, his career will change, and he'll be a different person. The only thing I know for certain is that he'll fly combat as long as there's a war."

"Isn't there a limit as to how many tours someone can fly?"

"My dear, you should know better than I, but I think not. At least no hard and fast rule that's been put to the test."

I spoke softly, knowing I was on tenuous ground. "And you're here to convince him to return home?"

"I should think not. I believe he made that choice some time ago. He'll fly combat as long as they allow him, and that could be years. He has a lot of general officer friends behind him. They'll help him stay because they like him and need him in combat. I can't ask him to choose. I merely need to tell him that I must choose."

"Are you going to stay at Korat for long?"

Julia lowered her voice to a whisper. "No. I'm aware of the attitudes toward wives visiting combat bases. I'll respect that, but I must talk to Hunter for a few minutes."

I was startled. "A few minutes? Excuse me, but I thought I heard you say you came all this way to see Hunter for a few minutes."

"You heard correctly. Recently he applied to fly another tour. I love him dearly, but I need to get on with my life. I suppose I always knew what he would do if another war started, but I didn't count on one occurring before he retired."

Chapter 18

Gusty winds from a rapidly building thunderstorm buffeted the Mercedes as Cowboy sped down the rain-soaked highway towards Korat. Clouds darkened the sky ahead and I felt adrift on the lush, green landscape of Thailand. Cowboy was working in his vocation, and Julia was traveling to meet her husband. I felt like a homeless wanderer, not belonging, no longer in training, not yet accepted as a fighter pilot, and uncertain about my pending decision. Most of all I felt a deep longing to go home, not knowing if home was back in the States with Jenny or here in this strange land, flying combat.

Julia and I were sitting in the back seat with no air conditioning and windows rolled up against the rain. Cowboy, perhaps with respect for Julia, had not been chain smoking but finally lit a cigarette. I faked a cough hoping he would catch the hint. He didn't. Finally, I tapped him on the shoulder, and he put it out.

Julia dug a novel out of her shoulder bag and with a wry smile said, "Escape literature. Do you mind?"

I shook my head, settled back, and closed my eyes. I welcomed the chance to think about yesterday's conversation. Julia's openness had tempered my feelings about Hunter. I'd been angry. After all, Hunter had abandoned me in the jungle. Even though he finally returned and directed our rescue, I had been filled with unresolved rage. Even now, in the back of my mind, I wondered how Hunter could have left me alone, vulnerable to the enemy, hanging in a tree.

Hunter's strong silent personality was like the characters in western movies, and like men I knew when I was growing up—always displaying a cool demeanor, appearing to be on an even keel, hiding pain and burying sadness with silence or ironic humor. I imagined Hunter could laugh in the face of any anger, shake his head and walk away in the stoic manner I had come to understand. But Julia was right. Hunter had his own set of fears. Hunter's demons were very different than other people's. They were more intense and hidden beneath more elaborate facades.

Julia had a gift for condensing life into short sentences. "Hunter is on friendly terms with death, being in and out of its clutches so many times," she had said.

But not on such friendly terms with torture, I had wanted to say, but thought it an unnecessary burden for her. I had come to realize death was not a prime motivating fear for Hunter. He feared capture much more and would give up his life to avoid torture and prison. I wondered if other pilots, those who had not been prisoners, felt the same way.

Another one of Julia's gems spilled-out when she talked about their marriage, "Hunter doesn't think he is lovable, so he never forgave me for loving him."

Before Julia's comment it had never occurred to me that Hunter's self-image wasn't strong. Julia certainly had no lack of self-respect. I thought her capable of surfacing feelings of inadequacy in any man, not vindictively, but she was intelligent, sure of herself, and revealing of her own life in an intimate and personal way. I couldn't begin to be as open with her as she was with me. She was skilled in ways I was not—not in the giving and not in the receiving.

Obsessed with my pending decision, I wanted her opinion but was wary of her response. Tibby's violent reaction lingered and haunted my memory. But perhaps, just perhaps, Julia would understand.

"I have a choice to make," I finally said, glancing toward her and taking an enormous leap of faith. "About returning to combat."

"I know," she said, as she put down her book and turned toward me. "Would you like to talk about it?"

"I don't know if I can. I feel so much pressure."

"You're aware Hunter had the same choice?" she smiled.

"But he didn't consult me."

I took a deep breath. "I'm afraid, but I'm not a coward or anything like that."

Julia touched my hand. "Of course not."

"They tell me I have a choice, but I feel stuck with no alternative but to stay and fly."

"I know it must feel that way," she said. "Have you made a decision?"

"Not yet. When I left Korat to meet you in Bangkok, I thought I would stay and finish my tour. Then, I spent the night with an American woman I met at the Princess Hotel. Being with her, the warmth of it all, made me think about life and what I would be missing."

Julia looked at me and shook her head. "My, but you're a fast operator. Bedding this woman at first meeting."

"No, it wasn't like that. I didn't try to hustle her. She just came up to my room to talk."

"Sorry, I thought you implied you slept with her."

I flinched. "Well, I guess I did."

Julia looked at me with a coy smile. "You did imply or you did sleep with her?"

"Oh, you know," I said in frustration.

Julia put her hand to her mouth and laughed. "I see. Perhaps we should return to your decision."

I looked out the window, annoyed at Julia or myself. I didn't know which.

"Were you able to talk to her about it?" Julia asked in a more serious tone.

"Yes, I told her I was leaning towards going home."

"And her reaction?"

"This," I said, pointing to the bruise by my eye. "And she called me revolting. A revolting coward. Isn't that redundant?"

Julia laughed again. "My poor dear." Reaching with both hands she turned my scowling face towards hers. After a while she placed a light kiss near the bruise.

My anger turned to embarrassment. The car was hot. My face was sweat-soaked and probably repulsive. She didn't appear to be put off as she held my face in her hands and stared deep into my eyes for, what seemed to me, an endless moment. My body was unhinged as my mind swirled through a torrent of emotion. After all, she was Hunter's wife.

"Now, love," she said, softly. "We've had our fun, mostly at your expense I might add. It's time we talked seriously." Julia picked up her book, placed a marker in it, and folded her reading glasses.

We sat in silence until I couldn't stand it any longer. "I don't know where to begin. What do you think I should do?"

"As you know, I've never flown combat, but I've known whole squadrons of fighter pilots for many years. You said you were afraid, didn't you?"

"Yes," I said averting my eyes.

"Good. That makes you normal."

I exhaled and forced a smile.

"Every single-engine fighter pilot is a little scared on every flight, if not by the enemy, then from concern his engine will quit at the worst possible time."

"I can relate to that," I said. "Although I don't think about it much anymore."

Julia patted my hand. "I'm guessing you're about twenty-four."

"Exactly," I nodded. It sounded so young when she said it. I pulled back slightly, wondering if her affection was just a mothering instinct. I was unsure what I wanted from her but knew what I did not.

"You've traveled a long distance to get to this crossroad. If you refuse to fly combat you'll give it all up—flying, friends, career. You've been through college, flight training, advanced training in the F-105 and flown your first combat mission. The dress rehearsal is over. It's time to use the tools you've acquired and invent yourself. You can't start that process by running away."

"So, you think I'd be running away?"

"Yes. Not that anyone would blame you. Your introduction to combat has been more severe than most, being shot down, almost killed or captured on your first mission."

"Korat Base ahead," Cowboy said, pointing up the steaming highway.

"Perhaps we can finish our talk later," Julia said.

"Yes, I'd like that. I can escort you back to Bangkok, if you'd like." I said, anticipating her response. "Of course, I'm aware you're perfectly capable on your own and you don't require an escort."

Julia patted my hand. "I would love your company."

"Good, when are you leaving?"

"Late this afternoon, my dear. I didn't check out of the Oriental."

"This afternoon? I know you told me you weren't staying long, I guess I didn't believe it. Why only a few hours? If that's not too personal a question."

"We can talk about that later if you choose to accompany me back to Bangkok."

At two o'clock in the afternoon, I sat alone in the KABOOM Bar, nursing a beer, staring out the window at the steady drizzling rain. The wet mango trees and habu grass hung drenched and lonely. Distant rumbles from an approaching storm blended with the rolling thunder of afterburners as a flight of four F-105s departed on an afternoon mission. I studied the second hand of my watch and reflected on the actions that I knew each pilot was making in the cockpit. At one hundred sixty knots, ease back on the control stick. Airborne by two hundred, landing gear then flaps up. Climb out following the lead aircraft on radar until above the clouds. Then, join up in close formation. I closed my eyes, mentally flying in the formation of jets, streaking side by side, above the clouds, traveling four hundred twenty knots through crystal clear air flooded with sunshine. Wake up, Ashe," a startling voice shouted in my ear.

"Grover," my eyes shot open, recognizing the Southern drawl as the command voice Grover insisted he had honed by yelling at coon dogs. I was so pleased to see a classmate from F-105 training that I jumped up, shook his hand, and hugged him.

Grover, a thin, lanky, slow-talking pilot from a small town in east Tennessee, wore his hair short, almost shaved, and told tall stories about growing up in the hills. I had heard many of his down-home stories and suspected the reason I couldn't remember the name of his hometown was that Grover kept changing it. He never let facts get in the way of a good story. "What the hell you doing here?"

"Heard there's a war on," Grover said. "Got here the day you left for Bangkok they tell me. Whatcha doin' back so soon?"

"Long story," I said. "Tell me about you."

"Forget me. You're the one who's been shot down in North Vietnam. You're Mister Excitement, go to Hanoi on your first mission." Grover paused, squinted at me and then lowered his voice to a whisper. "You okay?"

"I'm fine."

"Looks like you fell head first into a bucket of ugly," Grover said. "Your face ever going to heal?"

"Probably," I shrugged. "You flown yet?"

"Yeah, this morning, no thanks to you. The new guy checkout program has changed forever."

"But you flew pretty quick?" I said, wondering what the scuttlebutt was on my shootdown. Were there stories about my screw-ups during evasion in the jungle? Had Hunter said anything? Maybe I would ask Grover later.

Grover held up my beer and studied it like a urine sample. Taking a sip he grimaced and pointed to the glass. "Don't bet on this horse," he said then sat back in his chair. "My mission was an indoctrination in a low threat area. Closely supervised by a flight leader, mind you."

"Sounds like a reasonable first mission to me."

Grover shook his head. "Jungle, all I saw was trees. No roads.

No buildings. Especially no target. We bombed those suspected Communist trees."

"What was the intended target?"

"Suspected truck park. The parrots and monkeys down there'll be picking shrapnel out of their butts until Christmas."

I looked up at the ceiling and sighed. "But you were flying your own jet. That's worth something. At least you showed them a lieutenant can fly without getting shot down."

"Yeah, I guess. We did lose one while you were away. Dave Hastings. They tried the Doumer Bridge again. Sixteen flew away, and Dave didn't come back."

"He get rescued?"

"He's gone, Ashe."

"They get the bridge?"

"They got it wet but that's about all. Blew away a little superstructure. Nothing important. Charlie had it back in operation by the next morning."

"Dave Hastings," I said, the name seemed to hang in the air.

"A major. I didn't know him either. Had a wife and three kids, probably a dog and a mortgage. You know, the full catastrophe."

My emotions were out of focus, somehow detached. I should feel sad but instead felt only confusion. "You know, Grover, I never thought to ask what happens when a pilot is lost. What about a service? Did they do anything?"

"It's weird. There's no chapel here. They gathered at the KABOOM Bar. Vespers they called it. Someone said a few words then added, 'Let's drink to Dave.' The crowd raised their glasses, answered 'Here! Here!' then got on with the business at hand which was more drinking."

"I've heard about that one drink at the bar ceremony." I stared off, stunned by thoughts of where Dave Hastings' body might be at that moment.

"I gotta have some suds," Grover said then walked to the bar and returned with two draft beers.

We sat in silence watching the rain. Two weeks ago we were

both in Las Vegas. A lot had happened since. I thought Grover looked older already and slim in the manner of a Southern gentleman which he could be but usually wasn't unless in the presence of a woman. His flight suit hung on his body like it was draped on a fence. His dark eyes sparkled as if he were a little boy and highlighted his infectious smile.

"Anyone else from our class here?" I asked.

"Nope, the other three will be here sometime next month."

I wondered if the squadron commander called Grover in as my replacement since I didn't volunteer, on the spot, to continue flying combat.

"We're both assigned to Hunter's flight," Grover said. "They formed it for us new kids. They're talking about checking us out together. That means delaying my checkout until you can fly again. So hurry up and get well!"

"Delay your checkout? You mean not fly until I do?"

"I'll be flying plenty but not combat. They want me to ferry some battle-damaged planes to the Taiwan repair facility. Someone has to do it, and I'm the new guy." Grover finished his beer in several large gulps and slammed his glass to the table like he was in a contest. "When can you fly?" he asked.

I looked at his beaming smile. "I've been thinking," I began, feeling at a loss, clearing my throat, wanting to talk with my friend about returning to the States but fearing disapproval.

"About what?" Grover asked.

Chapter 19

I sat staring out the window, not talking to Grover. How could I tell my friend I was thinking about going home after one mission and leave him to fly combat for a hundred? Searching for words, I gripped the mug of beer so tightly my hand shook.

"Hey," Grover said, appearing uncomfortable with the break in conversation. "Sorry I hacked you off. It's not your fault you were shot down. Not that it was Hunter's fault, or anyone's fault. Hell, you know what I mean."

"That's not it," I said, trying to ease his frustration without revealing too much of my own. "It's something else."

"What else?" Grover persisted.

"I don't want to talk about it," I fired back.

"Grumpy," Grover replied with a knowing smile. "Bet it drives you nuts, not being on the combat schedule. One mission and boom, you're grounded. I'd be cranky too."

I was sorry I tried to raise the issue with Grover. My medical grounding gave me too much time to think. My idle mind was playing tricks, dwelling on fear, and treating every possibility as a probability.

At this point, I didn't want a choice. I wanted a clear-cut rule. The shootdown provided license, but I needed absolution. I had lingering doubts that I could make it through a combat tour alive. If only I had permission to go home. A permanent medical grounding would do it, or a visible injury, not serious, but just bad enough. I felt my face blush. Tibby was right. I was thinking like a coward. No wonder I had trouble sharing my thoughts. I couldn't stand them myself.

Perhaps I would always have self-doubts, feeling I was running out on my buddies. I had no one to trust with my feelings. Hunter was faced with the same choice, and he had made it instantly. I knew I couldn't talk about my decision to Hunter or anyone else on the airbase. Surrounded by military people, I felt we were one big indoctrinated family—a family that I knew would oppose, on principle, what I was feeling in my heart. Looking toward Grover, I felt lost in self-doubt and indecision.

Grover raised his head sharply. His eyes moved up and beyond me. "It's Hunter," he whispered.

Hunter looked grim and approached slowly. As he stood over us, he focused his gaze out the window. "Grover, mind if I have a word with Ashe?"

"Sure, Hunter," Grover replied, promptly moving to the bar, then leaving almost immediately by the side door.

Hunter slumped down in Grover's chair, still avoiding eye contact. "Julia's going back to Bangkok this afternoon," he said, in a halting, almost fragile, voice.

"So soon," I feigned surprise. "I'll escort her back if you like."

I felt a chill down my spine as Hunter looked straight at me, revealing eyes filled with unshed tears. "Thanks. I would appreciate that," his voice choked. "I can't bear to go with her, but I can't let her go alone."

I blinked, risked a second look, then nervously turned away out of respect for the pain written on his face.

"Julia has a lot of honor," he reflected. "She flew all this way to tell me rather than send a letter."

Tell you what? I wanted to ask but searched for something else to say. I was looking for, but not finding, a graceful way to leave. Hunter appeared defeated. My concept of a warrior didn't mesh with the tormented pilot I saw before me. I sensed raw emotion from a complex man who, in his pain, didn't seem to care about my expectations.

A man's decisions aren't isolated, I thought. They leave a legacy that spreads like the wake of a ship, washing over loved ones. Hunter had made choices: stoic, manly decisions and remained revered by combat pilots. With the same breath, he had eclipsed the life of the woman he loved and who loved him enough to bring him face-to-face with the consequences.

In muted light, tempered by the passing storm, we watched droplets of rain gather into rivulets and stream from the broad leaves of lush green plants. We sat in silence, as stoic men do, leaving our feelings unsaid, relying on each other's respect for silence. Each of us held the burden of his own emotions. Combat pilots who value companionship but treasure psychological isolation.

After a while, Hunter stirred in his chair. "Thanks, it helped to talk."

I smiled to myself.

Hunter continued. "As soon as the flight surgeon gives the okay, we'll put you back on the schedule. I know it's tough, being here and not flying."

"Right," I said, thinking how much more complicated my decision would be if I had married Jenny. I wondered what motivated men with wives and families to put everything at risk flying combat. How did others overcome fear? How did their families?

"Cowboy will be here in an hour," Hunter said. "Is that too soon?"

"That's fine," I replied. "I haven't unpacked. I'll just throw in some clean shorts."

In an hour, the storm had passed, I had showered, changed and was waiting. Hunter drove up in the squadron pickup truck with Julia. I climbed in the back with my bag. At the base gate, Hunter and Julia embraced and said their good-byes while Cowboy and I waited a respectable distance away. Then, we were off to Bangkok.

Julia was silent as she looked out the window, occasionally lifting a handkerchief to her eyes. It was almost an hour before she said, "Thank you for being here. It's a comfort not to be alone."

I chose my words carefully. "I know this is none of my business, but is there anything I can do?"

Julia touched my arm. "I'm sorry, love. This must be more than a tad confusing to you."

"Flying half way around the world to see your husband for three hours isn't a little confusing," I said, forcing a laugh. "It's a lot confusing. But, I'm sure you have your reasons."

"As you know, Hunter has signed up for a third combat tour. I feel he'll never return to our marriage. I told him I have to continue my life without him."

"Does that mean the 'D' word?"

"Perhaps we'll divorce. My partner is on another continent and won't come home. I can't function as if I were married if he refuses to be present in the relationship."

I looked out the window trying to imagine what kept Hunter away from this intelligent and sensual woman. She had apparently accepted two tours but a third was too much. "What makes a man want to do this three times?"

"Fear," Julia blurted out like an involuntary response.

I was startled. "How can you say that? He's putting himself in harm's way every day."

"He fears what could happen in combat, just like everyone else, but he's more afraid of life and its responsibilities. And, he's terrorized by the rewards of combat success that await him in the States."

"Rewards?"

"Promotion, War College, a fighter wing of his own to command, not to mention a woman who loves him dearly."

"Damn," I said, under my breath, feeling angry at the suggestion that anything could require greater courage than flying combat. Didn't she realize they shoot real bullets here? "That can't be. He's one of the bravest men alive. He goes out looking for MiGs to fight."

Julia looked at me with tears in her eyes. "I know, he's brave in that sense, but flying jets and particularly flying combat are the only successes he's ever known." She reflected for a moment before continuing. "Outside the cockpit, he thinks he's a failure. That's why I flew over here to tell him face to face, to confront him with his fear."

That evening in Bangkok, I checked into the Princess Hotel and joined Julia for dinner at the Oriental. There was no further discussion of Hunter. Perhaps she has learned to compartmentalize the sorrow in her life, too. She was a wonderful dinner companion, talking of the future, of her flight to Hong Kong, and her planned shopping trip there.

I sensed Julia had handled the visit better than Hunter. To his credit, Hunter probably didn't know what Julia was going to say and didn't have time to get in touch with his emotions. Of course, I could be wrong. Perhaps he did know and kept his emotions buried. Fighter pilots seemed to be missing a chromosome that allows them to express their feelings.

After dinner we talked over coffee and snifters of cognac. I felt lightheaded as I walked Julia to her room. She must have felt that way, too. Stopping at the door, she put her arms around me and kissed me deeply. It seemed to be more than a friendly kiss. Perhaps I wanted it to be, or perhaps I didn't know what I wanted. Startled at first, I let my arms hang by my sides. Then I embraced her, but she gently pushed me away. She smiled as I stood before her, stumbling over words, trying to think of something to say.

"Good night," she said, and stepped into her room. The door closed. She was gone, and I felt abandoned in the empty hallway. I stood still, eyes closed, the captivating aroma of her perfume enveloping me. The provocative tastes of her lingered on my lips. I stared at the door and considered the possibilities. Raising my hand to knock, I held my arm in the air a few moments while I took a deep breath. Then I turned and walked away.

In the morning we met for breakfast. As I gazed across the table, I relived last night's kiss again and again. If she felt me staring at her, she didn't show it. I had fallen asleep and awakened imagining her passion.

As Cowboy drove us to the airport, my combat decision tormented me with a visceral sense of anguish and urgency. The only person to whom I felt I could confide was leaving in minutes. Reluctantly I asked. "What do you think I should do, stay and fly or go back to the States?"

Julia pressed my hand in hers. "My dear, I can't tell you what you should do. However, I believe I know what you will do."

"Go on." I said, praying she didn't sense my apprehension.

"You'll stay and fly."

"Why do you say that?"

"Because you share a common flaw among fighter pilots. You fear disapproval of your peers much more than you fear the enemy."

At first her answer seemed silly. How could anyone fear simple loss of approval more than death? And yet it was clear that fear of dying didn't keep pilots from flying their share of combat. It didn't keep some from flying much more than their share, risking everything they have or ever will have. Risking not only their lives, but their families' future.

We hurried through the airport to the customs hall entry point. I had gone as far as I could go with her. We held each other and kissed. It was a tentative kiss at first, and then I sensed a deep longing. As half-formed words began to stir from my emotions, Julia placed her finger on my lips. "Please don't say anything."

"I don't understand."

"Sometimes it's better just to feel."

I stared at her in frustration.

Julia's eyes became moist. "Sometimes, Ashe, we meet the right person at the wrong time."

I held her for a moment. There was a promise to write, another kiss, this time on the cheek, and she was gone.

I sat, looking at the departure portal through which she had disappeared. She had been a friend. The only one who treated me like a person since I arrived in Southeast Asia. Meeting Julia had changed me. She was like an alarm that had awakened me to my own emotion.

I didn't want to return to Korat and go through the new guy treatment again. It was bad enough having the enemy shoot at me, but older pilots had no respect for my ability. Perhaps they meant well, but everyone treated me like he was my father. Now it didn't matter. I could live without flying combat; I smiled as my mind colored in the subtle shades of meaning into that thought.

My mind was made up. I would simply exercise my right to go home. But if it was simple, why did I feel so sick in my gut? Julia didn't believe I would quit. I couldn't bring myself to talk with Grover or Hunter, and Tibby's reaction was still embossed on my face. I would show them all. I would go back to the States, marry Jenny, and settle down for a long life in a place where people don't shoot at you. In a few years, I would be out of the Air Force and get a job with the airlines. But what would I say to the folks back home? To my parents? Jenny was the only one who would support my decision. Or would she? She didn't want me to come in the first place, but, now that I'm here, what would she say if I left?

The policy was clear. If you're shot down and remain overnight you can choose to go home. I had fulfilled my obligation in combat. No double jeopardy here. That's why they offered a choice, wasn't it? After carefully weighing the decision in my mind, I found the men's room and threw up.

Two weeks later in Colonel Mike Parker's trailer, as I sat swirling my fourth Tanqueray on the rocks in a frosted glass, the colonel came to the point. "I think I know what your decision will be, but I still have to ask."

I raised my glass to the squadron commander. "Sir, I can't wait to get back into combat." As I took another sip of icy thick gin, it seemed as if someone else had said the words.

Chapter 20

I had second thoughts immediately after walking out of Parker's trailer. After a few steps, I stopped, pirouetted slowly, and faced the door. I stood motionless until admitting I couldn't go back, face Parker, and retract my words.

Parker had been friendly and made me feel comfortable. But it was clear he was in charge of the squadron and ascribed to the nuances and protocols of a combat commander. His acceptance was conditional and reserved for combat flyers.

Nineteen days had passed since I began to wallow in the great sorrow that accompanies indecision. Now I had to snap out of it. I decided to lose myself in the details of getting ready to fly again, starting with the Aircraft Commander's Combat Orientation that I should have completed before my first mission.

Briefings filled the day and covered ground and flight operations, enemy order of battle, search and rescue procedures, rules of engagement, an overview of friendly forces organization and the current bombing campaign named Rolling Thunder.

Our government acknowledged none of the US operations at Thai bases. Officially our presence was classified. Classified from whom, I wondered, since every massage parlor for miles must know the loud jets carrying bombs were dropping them somewhere. The greatest secrecy was reserved for the location of targets, all of which were classified. Details of some Vietnam missions were selectively released to the press but never those in Laos. I had not known we were bombing in Laos until I arrived at Korat.

The F-105 fighter wings at Korat and Takhli flew exclusively in North Vietnam and Laos. Each wing was equipped with three squadrons of twenty-six aircraft. So far, 1966 had been a terrible year for losses; it was the end of May and thirty-seven F-105s had been shotdown. Eighteen of those thirty-seven pilots had not been recovered. Sometimes weather kept us on the ground, but for every three flying days, we lost one F-105 aircraft.

Above the twentieth parallel, in the area officially called Route Package Six, lay the most heavily defended real estate in the history of air warfare and accounted for most of our losses. Any major mission to the Route Pack Six environs would almost guarantee a loss.

After the orientation briefings, I reviewed the rules of engagement and rescue procedures until my eyes hurt. As I left the operations building, I heard we had lost a pilot on the afternoon mission. I headed for the KABOOM Bar. Perhaps there would be another ritual like the one Grover mentioned.

By early evening, pilots from the last flights of the day were drifting into the bar. The bartender poured straight shots from a quart bottle of Jack Daniels and placed them on the bar in a neat row. I watched as pilots lifted a shot and stood at the bar or gathered at a table with friends. I picked up a whisky and asked for a glass of ice water. The Thai bartender raised his eyebrows and gave me a judgmental look as he half-filled a glass and slid it down the mahogany bar. I poured the whisky into the water and struck up a conversation with a table of pilots I hadn't met before. From the length of their handlebar moustaches they had months of experience.

The five pilots made unhurried conversation in low tones until I said. "Heard we lost one today. Anyone know what happened?"

The table fell silent. The others looked toward a craggy faced major they called Bear. He leaned forward, elbows on the table, and spoke as if giving a eulogy. "We don't know for sure, but we think it was Captain Rusty Baker. That fearless son-of-a-gun was my wingman until he became an element leader. Carried himself with an unruffled grace that's rare in any man but particularly a young fighter pilot. It's one of those Hemingway things, grace under pressure and all that."

"How young?" I asked.

"Twenty-nine I suppose," Bear reflected. "Thirty tops. The Air Force sent him halfway around the world to fly sorties into North Vietnam. A ticket back to the States requires a hundred combat missions. Rusty had ninety-six and a half."

"Couldn't feel worse if he was family," one of the pilots said to me or to the others—I couldn't tell which.

Another flyer added, "Of all people. Why him?"

They had only sketchy details. They weren't positive it was Rusty. But somebody was down, and they had gathered at the bar to wait for news. Shortly after sundown it came.

The club turned silent when Rusty's wingman appeared, knocked back a shot of whiskey then grumbled, "He went in with the jet. There'll be no rescue attempt."

We murmured over the possibilities. Aerial combat happens so fast that pilots have to question what they see with their own eyes. But evidence had mounted to verify the wingman's fears. Rusty had been missing for three hours. No parachute emergency locator beacon was heard, and he didn't transmit on his survival radio. It was clear. Rusty was gone.

For the next hour I listened closely to get a sense of the feelings around the table. Everyone joined in but it was Bear that talked the most. He seemed to have a deep flowing sensitivity that was a marked contrast to his gruff appearance.

For months, F-105 pilots had littered the terrain of North Vietnam. The hastily built combat base lacked facilities to mourn them. There was no place of worship and since downed pilots don't come back, there is no trace of physical evidence to grieve.

In the bad times, like today, they congregate in the holiest of places where fighter pilots assemble: the bar. Of course they gather there in good times, too, but it was their special sanctuary to honor the fallen. During vespers, someone, whomever felt moved and particularly close to the missing man, would propose a toast. It usually seemed spontaneous and natural, a fitting tribute if it happened early in the evening but less so later if Jack Daniels was talking.

After communing, they would retreat into silence. Braced with fluid courage, the living must press on, continuing to fly combat the next day and the next. Thus, they worked through a triage of their emotions.

Bear said he didn't know when it started, but things had begun to come unglued. He even mentioned that the chaplain had been acting strange. That didn't surprise me. He said when others didn't show normal signs of grief, the chaplain tried to have the feeling for them. That's what Doc Morgan had said, too. His exact words.

I sensed that kind of emotion was an insidious trap and easy to fall into. Combat pilots buried grief and built walls of silence punctuated with an ironic humor that passed for strength. It seemed the older pilots had become practiced at burying grief, but I hadn't. I wasn't able to ignore the chaplain either.

Then, by some signal that I must have missed, everyone stood up. I followed the mourners to the bar. Each of us took a new shot glass of whisky and quietly placed it in front of us on the solid mahogany altar. Then, during this period of tranquility, the padre made a serious mistake. He presumed to preside over the ceremony of silence. Perhaps realizing his error, he turned ashen and began to stumble over his words.

"Shut up," Bear growled at him. "Let us drink in peace."

"That's no way to talk to the clergy," someone in back replied in a barely audible voice.

As other grieving pilots joined us, the bartender kept pouring. The chaplain's lips were still moving, this time in silent prayer, I guessed.

Then the pilot next to me slammed his fist on the bar.

"Damnit to hell," he said, placing his face in his hands.

Others drifted in and bellied up with the congregation. I heard a few whispers then someone spoke for all of us. "It's not working. Not this time. Not for Rusty."

I sensed the last few months had taken too much and given back too little. I felt I was witnessing the end of something, but didn't know what. One pilot turned and left, then another and another. Standing alone after the exodus, I looked down the bar at the row of glasses. Only one was empty.

Because I had inherited my family's gift for stoic optimism, and because I had been full of Tanqueray, I had signed up to fly my full tour when I could have gone home. Now Jack Daniels had again raised the fear that I had made a mistake. Not only were the odds against me, but I had lost confidence in myself. I had fooled myself. I had thought I was fighting to keep my courage from leaving, but I realized it had departed weeks ago.

Chapter 21

I was either having a breakdown or an epiphany. I wasn't sure which. Julia had it figured out. She knew I had every intention of quitting, but she also knew I would not be able to say the words—not to my squadron commander, Hunter, Grover, or Jenny. As I wondered why, I sensed I would have to search deep inside myself, far below the surface of my emotions, looking into places I had neither the time nor the inclination to go.

My ear had healed faster than expected, and I was back on the schedule twenty days after my shootdown. I had felt alone and adrift on an ocean of politics and war, lacking both compass and rudder. My emotions were even more confounded when I looked at my name, grease-penciled on the scheduling board. For reasons I couldn't imagine, I began to feel strangely drawn towards combat. Stranger still because the loss rate had increased dramatically in the few weeks I had been out of the cockpit. Before, one aircraft was lost for each ninety-six missions into North Vietnam. Yesterday the figure had dropped to ninety-two. The chance one would be shotdown in a one hundred-mission tour was dangerously close to a statistical guarantee. Trying to look at the odds in the most positive light, perhaps I got my shootdown out of the way early. On the other hand, perhaps not.

To stay busy I walked to the Base Exchange where I bought a "Go to hell" campaign hat. It was a cross between an air commando jungle hat and the kind they wear in the Australian bush. One side of the brim was pushed up flat against the crown. Almost all of the pilots wore them and recorded their "counter" missions into North Vietnam with marks on the hatband. I started mine out with the fraction one-half.

Having made my decision to fly, I also resigned to rid myself of fear and anxiety or accept the consequences. Fear had dropped anchor near my bunk last night and remained until I showered and put on my flight suit. Anxiety followed me to breakfast in the KABOOM dining room. Hunter dined alone at his regular table, back to the wall, reading the *Stars and Stripes*. Grover, at a closer table, motioned me over.

Looking half-awake, Grover cradled his cup with both hands and took a noisy slurp. "You ready?" he asked, not looking up.

I nodded to a waitress, held up two fingers for a number two breakfast and pointed to Grover's coffee. "If I complete this mission, I'll have one and a half."

Grover grimaced. "You're not going to count that half, are you? You weren't flying the jet."

I rolled my eyes, pointed to the mark on my hat, and said, "With what I went through, I've earned it." The waitress poured a steaming cup. I waited until she moved on to another table. "Not much of a target this morning," leaning forward, I spoke in a low voice. "Submerged sandbar. Intelligence calls it a pier."

"Keep it down," Grover cautioned. "We can't talk classified here."

"What a stupid target."

"A stupid, secret target so shut up about it."

I smiled. "But who'd believe we'd attack a submerged sandbar?"

Grover glanced up. "Except we've bombed it before."

"Forget it, Grover. That's no reason to do it again. Don't we ever attack targets we can destroy and not have to go back again? Maybe you like risking your tail for nothing, but I don't." I realized I was taking my anxiety out on Grover and tried to change the subject. "How did it feel, flying your first real mission?"

"Not as exciting as yours I'll bet," Grover smiled.

"No, Grover. I'm serious. How'd it feel to put it all together? To do all the events from training on a real mission in a heavyweight jet with live bombs."

"Refueling was a pain," Grover said holding a piece of toast in the air, moving his hand under it like a fighter ready to hookup and transfer fuel. "You have to be super smooth. There's no throttle to spare with a combat load. You'll find out this morning."

"Hey," Lucky Slater said, greeting us as he pulled out a chair. "Well, if it isn't a table full of cannon fodder." In an instant a waitress placed a plate of eggs, sausage, and toast in front of Lucky.

"Fast service," I said.

"Got it from the kitchen. I garbage up on whatever's ready, but the waitresses still insist on carrying it out."

I nodded, "They know the only thing pilots don't spill is their drink."

"Our flight is almost all here," Grover said, then smiled. "We could have a meeting if we had a flight commander that would eat with us."

I motioned toward Lucky. "Hope he doesn't hold us back today, Grover."

"Hold you back, my dying butt," Lucky said, through a mouthful of scrambled eggs.

"Why are you in a flight with us new guys?" Grover asked.

"Somebody's got to be deputy lead for you hotdogs. Besides Hunter's upgrading me to a flight leader position."

"Congratulations," Grover said. "What's a checkout by Hunter like?"

Lucky speared a sausage and waved his fork in Grover's direction then punched the air with it to emphasize his point. "No formal program, no syllabus, just flying combat with Hunter. When he says you're ready, you're ready."

"I heard ten sorties," Grover said.

"Sounds long to me," Lucky replied. "The paperwork's a formality with Hunter. He's all combat and doesn't cater to any training program designed by some staff officer. We'll be a flight of four, just like everyone else who flies in a flight of four. We'll go on some easy missions then some tougher ones."

"So what's Hunter like?" I asked.

"Why ask me? You should know," Lucky said, glancing over his shoulder toward Hunter's table before he continued. "You went hiking in the jungle with him."

"I meant as a flight leader," I said. "We didn't talk about flying or much of anything else for that matter."

Lucky chuckled to himself, ignoring my question. "You even know the wife, meeting her in Bangkok and all. You're practically family."

I flinched. "How'd you...?"

"It's a small base," Lucky lowered his voice to a whisper. "When's the divorce?"

"What divorce?"

"You can bet it's coming," Lucky said. "Hunter will never leave combat. No woman would put up with that forever."

"So what can we expect from our flight leader?" I persisted.

Lucky leaned forward. "Hunter will give you philosophy. 'The air is not different here,' he'll say. 'Neither is gravity, the laws of physics or the ground. If you fly your jet different here than you did in training, you'll be an accident waiting to happen.'"

"Except a combat-loaded jet is three tons heavier than anything I ever flew in training," I said.

"Yeah," Grover nodded. "So why didn't we train with live bombs?"

Lucky feigned a whisper. "Because there's a bomb shortage. Forget that McNamara, our beloved Secretary of Defense, says there're plenty of bombs. What he doesn't say is that the major parts like fuses, fins, and bomb bodies are on different continents. And in some cases, owned by different nations. That may not be called a shortage in Washington but it sure as hell is here."

"Out of bombs?" I asked.

"Not out, but close," Lucky said. "The government sold the World War Two stockpile to a fertilizer company. They're filled with TNT. Nitrates, you know, and of course there's scrap metal in the casings."

"Why sell them?" I asked.

"To buy new weapons with a better explosive. But they can't make the new ones fast enough and have bought back TNT bombs at an enormous markup. We're almost out of new bombs. If you see three yellow rings painted on the nose, they're the old TNT filled weapons."

After breakfast we walked to the mission planning room at Fort Apache. I stood at a planning table, leafing through strips of map I'd cut and pasted into a target folder. I traced the 40-mile flight path from the initial run-in position to a triangular symbol containing the target. My finger inched slowly, but my mind raced over the nine miles of map terrain we would cover each minute of flight. My eyes saw contour lines, but my mind visualized the landscape's topographic details that would pass beneath us in a blur at 540 nautical miles per hour.

Lucky nudged me and pointed to Hunter.

"Memorizing the run-in to the target?" I asked.

"You got it."

"Looks like he's in a trance."

Lucky nodded. "He could probably do the mission blindfolded but studies harder than anyone. Flies every mile in his head before he crawls into the jet."

As we moved into the main briefing room for the overview, Roscoe trailed behind Lucky and sniffed at his flight suit. Lucky hunched down, retrieved a folded napkin from his ankle pocket, and unwrapped a sausage.

"Good dog," Lucky said feeding Roscoe. "Time to sleep now."

I shook my head, as Grover wiped his greasy fingers on Roscoe's paw. Roscoe walked slowly to the wing commander's chair. The mascot turned and surveyed the room, jumped on the seat, curled up, and licked his paw with long deliberate strokes.

Two briefers sat on the edge of the stage.

A captain presented the weather report, holding two charts he didn't show. "Weather's a piece of cake," he said. "Not a factor at homeplate, the target area, or anywhere in between. Predictions you were provided for mission planning are still valid. Some thunder-bumpers will develop in North Vietnam this afternoon, but you should be in and out before that happens."

Next, Lieutenant Colonel Baker stepped to the podium. I recognized him as the intelligence officer who had supervised our debriefing after we were rescued from the jungle.

"Your target is a submerged ferry pier on Coast Highway Route One. It's near the village of Ron," Colonel Baker said in a clipped, erudite manner.

Pure Ivy League, I thought while I watched Hunter stir impatiently in his seat. Hunter seemed to have a dislike for intelligence people. He had treated the CIA debriefing like an interrogation and the Korat drill was no picnic either.

"The ferry is active at night and camouflaged during the day. All traffic on Route One must cross it. Your aim point is the underwater sand pier on the north side." Baker dimmed the lights and a Vu-graph appeared. "This photo shows the pier. It extends eighty feet..."

"How old is that photo?" Hunter interrupted, making no attempt to hide his sarcasm.

"Ten months," Baker said.

Hunter folded his arms, "Got any photos taken in our lifetime?"

"As you know, we consistently display the most recent that Saigon has released," Baker said.

Hunter turned in his chair. "Ashe. Grover. Here's something about this dumb-ass intelligence business you need to know. Headquarters has up-to-date photos of the targets for themselves, but they classify them higher than Secret so combat pilots can't see them."

"Why would they do that?" I asked.

"They don't want pilots, susceptible to capture, to know much about our satellite intelligence collection capabilities,"

Hunter said, appearing to wait for a reaction.

"So what are we looking at here?" I asked.

Hunter motioned toward the photo. "Probably F-101 recon-naissance aircraft file footage. They select a picture that looks like the good stuff they see from satellites then send it to us. They're so busy playing games they've forgotten who their cus-tomer is."

"What's the classification level of satellite photos?" Grover asked.

"SI and TK," Hunter said. "Sensitive Information, Talent Keyhole. There are other code words that can't be said aloud unless everyone is cleared above Top Secret. It's one of those we got to kill you if we tell you kind of things."

"I didn't know there were levels higher than Top Secret," Grover said.

Colonel Baker cleared his throat. "We can't discuss that here."

Hunter waved off the colonel. "You're right. But we're get-ting worthless intelligence photos and they need to know it. Let's move on."

Colonel Baker raised his pointer to the vu-graph.

"And another thing," Hunter said. "What's the tide level at our Time On Target?"

The colonel made a painfully slow turn, directing his point-er toward the weatherman who was rifling through his papers.

"At your TOT, the tide will be twenty minutes past high tide."

"Oh, just terrific," Hunter said. "What are the planners thinking? This target should be hit at low tide. Our bombs will blow away water when we should be blowing sand. Plus, an afternoon strike would give the bad guys less time to plan for repairs tonight."

"You're absolutely right," the colonel said, appearing annoyed. "I'll pass that comment to the planners at Seventh Air Force."

"Damn the Headquarters in Saigon," Hunter shouted. "We need more control of our TOT's."

"Easy," Lucky said. "You'll wake up Roscoe."

"Too late," Grover said. "He's awake."

"Oh no," Lucky put his hand on the side of his head. "Bad luck's coming."

Hunter scowled. "It's not enough I have intelligence photos from the dark ages. I've got a superstitious fart named Lucky for my deputy lead."

"We're running a little late," the colonel said, tapping his pointer against the palm of his hand. "Perhaps you would like to use the rest of your time for a flight briefing."

"Sure. Thanks for the overview," Hunter turned and leaned on the back of the front row of seats. "It's a simple straight-forward mission. We'll take off, join up as a four-ship formation, rendezvous with the refueling tanker and take on a full load of fuel."

I flinched, dreading my first heavyweight refueling. I hadn't flown in over three weeks, the longest dry spell in my short flying career. Refueling was twenty minutes after takeoff, not much time to shake off the rust.

"Then we proceed across Laos at twenty thousand feet," Hunter continued. "At the North Vietnam border, we'll be 40-miles from target. I'll start a descent to tree top level maintaining 540 knots. Normally we go 580 or 600, but today I'll leave some throttle for you to play with."

I wanted Hunter to review heavyweight-refueling techniques, but he was past it now. I didn't ask, not wanting the flight members to sense my anxiety.

Hunter continued, "We'll navigate as a flight. Your primary job is to stay in formation. However, I want you to memorize the run-in to the target. The same for egress. The coast will be an excellent reference. Since the target is on a river 4,000 feet inland, we should have good visual cues."

Hunter focused on the map again. "Exactly seven miles prior to bomb release is a knoll 1070 feet high. We'll fly to the right of it, hugging the treetops. When we pass the knoll, I'll count one potato, two potato, three potato and light the afterburner then make an abrupt pull-up to 12,000 feet. When we reach 12,000, we'll roll into a 45 degree dive bomb attack on the target."

"What's minimum speed at the top of the pop carrying this load?" Grover asked.

"Not below 400 knots," Hunter said. "Slower and you're just a poster child for the laws of physics. Try a combat maneuver below 400 and only Isaac Newton would understand what happens next. But always fly your own jet. Don't blindly slow down with your leader until your jet stops flying because you can't be positive of your leader's condition. He may be preoccupied or overloaded."

Or hit by enemy fire, I thought, haunted by Hunter's incapacity after we had been hit.

"The air is not different here," Hunter said. "Neither are the other things that affect flying in North Vietnam, like gravity, the laws of physics, and the ground."

I watched Lucky with ironic humor. Lucky knew Hunter's speech word for word but was reacting as if he was hearing it for the first time.

Hunter continued as I mouthed the words. "If you start flying your jet different here than you did in training, you'll be an accident waiting to happen."

I reflected on the mission—alone in the cockpit, live bombs, refueling, and dive bombing with a jet three tons heavier than I had ever flown before.

Hunter looked at his watch. "It's time to suit up and step to the aircrew van. Any questions?"

"Yeah," I moved to the edge of my seat. "What about defenses? You haven't said a word about the enemy."

"This target's not heavily defended. Small and medium anti-aircraft guns. That's it. The biggest hazards today, in order of priority, are yourself, Newton's laws, and the enemy. From a Probability of Kill standpoint, the PK of the enemy is a distant third."

I picked up my mission folder and suppressed a growing impulse to tell Hunter to go to hell. I hated the implication that I was a danger to myself as well as the other members of my flight.

Hunter paused, "Just the basics today. If you don't kill yourself on this mission, we'll let the enemy take a crack at you later."

Chapter 22

I began a preflight inspection before the aircrew van stopped, looking over the jet as soon as it came into view. The configuration was six bombs on her belly, a 450-gallon fuel tank under each wing, and an AIM-9 Sidewinder air-to-air missile on a left wing pylon.

I fished the checklist out of my kit bag, dropped my flight gear in a pile at the foot of the cockpit ladder, then began a walk-around inspection as if I was going to buy the jet and pay for it with my own money. My mind raced through each detail. Wanting to be perfect. Needing to prove myself. To Hunter. To myself.

I paused only once, placing my hand against the olive drab metal surface of a bomb that was still cool and moist from the long night. The seemingly inert mass of metal would soon explode into its singular purpose on a sandy underwater pier in North Vietnam. I tried to picture the instant of detonation but could not imagine how such an enormous force resided in an iron shape that looked so harmless and mundane.

Climbing the ladder to the cockpit, I strained under the heavy weight of my parachute plus survival vest and G-suit pockets crammed with gear. The crewchief helped me wedge into the ejection seat and secure the shoulder harness and seat belt. After putting on my helmet and attaching the oxygen and radio connections, I was ready for engine start.

Placing my finger over the cartridge start button, I shuddered thinking that pushing the button would represent a symbol of commitment. Starting the jet would lock me into finishing a combat tour and wipe away the opportunity to elect to go home. Taking a deep breath, I realized the illusion of choice. It was already too late. With eyes closed, I sat motionless except for my tense-shaking arm. Then slowly, with my whole being, I leaned forward.

As the black powder starter cartridge exploded to life, my eyes opened and shot to the instrument panel. Oil pressure—rising. Engine RPM—climbing. Throttle—forward. Turbine temperature—racing to but stopping short of the red over-temperature line. Electrical power and hydraulic pressure gauges—stable. Each important gauge and dial had that system's limitations color coded on its face. Green—normal. Yellow—caution. Red—emergency. My eyes quickly scanned the panel to confirm that all systems performed in the green.

Now outside myself, I buried the sickening feeling of fear in an endless series of checks and counter checks, forcing myself to think of the next step instead of the waiting enemy. I had clear responsibility as a wingman. The rest of the flight would depend on me for protection and I on them.

"Nash flight, check in," Hunter said on the radio.

"Two," I radioed, spitting the response into the microphone inside my oxygen mask. I had strapped the mask so tightly the mike was touching my lips.

"Three," Lucky said.

"Four," echoed in a drawl that was unmistakably Grover.

"Korat Tower, Nash flight ready to taxi," Hunter transmitted.

The jets lumbered into the arming area where I rechecked the cockpit switches and then placed my hands high on the canopy rail. After the weapon's chief held up a handful of pins with red "remove before flight" streamers and gave me a thumb up signal, my jet was armed for combat.

Hunter led our flight onto the runway where our four aircraft positioned in fingertip formation. Pushing the throttle full forward, I braced against the seat, locking my legs against the brakes as the plane strained to roll forward. The jet noise was deafening even through the closed canopy and form-fitting helmet. The roar of engines vibrated my bones and gave me the sense of sitting aboard a thundering rocket.

When all of the flight members were ready, Hunter tapped his forehead then nodded as he released brakes and selected afterburner. His jet rolled only a few feet before a twenty-foot blue flame erupted from its tail as the afterburner exploded to life with a force that could be felt. I counted seven lens-shaped shock waves in Hunter's afterburner flame, which provided the best indication of a healthy engine.

I was supposed to delay ten seconds for takeoff roll spacing in a jet carrying bombs but released brakes after only seven. Raising my eyes out of the cockpit, I concentrated on procedures to take off and join up on Hunter's wing as fast as possible. I could hear the hollow sucking sound of my breathing, gulping oxygen in deep gasps. Slow down, I whispered to myself as a reminder not to hyperventilate.

At 150 knots the ground was a blur and my plane was no longer capable of stopping on the remaining runway. I was committed to takeoff. If the engine failed now, I would have to eject or the bomb-laden jet would carry me past the end of the runway and into the field beyond. In cultivated dirt, the landing gear would break off and fuel tanks would rupture and explode and engulf me in tons of burning fuel and over-heated bombs.

Approaching nose wheel liftoff at 180 knots, I eased back on the stick and the airplane flew off the runway at 195. At 220 knots, I retracted the landing gear and raised the flaps.

Hunter had briefed 350 knots for join up, but I accelerated to 420. Closing on my leader faster than expected, I pulled back the power and extended the speed brakes. The momentum of the heavy jet was too great and I overshot, flying under Hunter's plane, then to the outside of his turn. Yanking back on the control stick to correct, I felt the terrifying airframe rumble of a high-speed stall.

"OK, dummy, fly the jet," I shouted to myself as I eased back-pressure on the control stick. As the plane slowly responded, I pumped my body in forward motions as if trying to scoot the jet into position. Finally, Hunter changed heading to help me fall into formation. Wet with sweat, I realized I hadn't made a timely correction. Hunter had done it for me. It was a flight leader's gift to a wingman in trouble.

I took several deep breaths then focused on the next event. Approximately 30 miles from the refueling point, I scanned the horizon. At 21 miles off of our nose, the tanker appeared at 20,000 feet altitude. Hunter was closing at 450 knots. We had 150 knots of thundering overtake speed. I thought our flight might over-run the tanker, but Hunter proved a master of wingman consideration. He made only one throttle correction and speed started to dissipate. We eased into perfect formation with the KC-135 Stratotanker.

"Nash flight, noses cold," Hunter radioed to indicate the combat weapons switches were on safe and the pre-refueling checklist was complete. It was a radio call he would not make when we were more experienced, a training call that jogged our memory as well as alerted the tanker boom operator that a new guy was in the flight. I watched Hunter slide under the tanker and move his jet forward until the refueling boom was just inches away from the receptacle in the nose of his aircraft. Hunter stabilized his plane then gently nudged the refueling receptacle against the boom until it locked in place.

While looking out the side of my canopy, flying formation using peripheral vision, I felt for switches to complete the noses-cold and refueling checklist that I acknowledged completing but had not. I seemed to be operating in a haze and not anticipating events. My grounding had left me out of practice and mentally unprepared. I had squandered my time thinking about how to get out of combat flying instead of focusing on how to do it. Glancing back in the cockpit, I located the oxygen switch and selected 100% in case jet fuel vapors appeared during refueling. Leaning forward, I began to reach for the air refueling door handle as the radio blared in my helmet.

"This is Big Eye on guard channel, Bandits Alpha Golf Three, Repeat, Bandits Alpha Golf Three," I recognized the radio call from a C-121 airborne radar control aircraft. A bandit call was a warning of MiG activity, but where were the MiGs? Where was Alpha Golf Three?

Hunter completed refueling and moved out of boom position to the far right side of the flight. I flew under the tanker to the pre-contact position and stabilized. So far, so good, I thought. On the belly of the tanker, position control lights motioned me forward and up. Above me, I could see a window on the belly of the tanker that framed the face of the boom operator. The boomer was wide-eyed and made rapid motions, cupping and uncupping his hands. Then he frantically pointed to the nose of my jet.

"Nash Two, your refueling door is closed," the boomer radioed.

"You idiot," I screamed to myself. Distracted by the MiG call, I had forgotten to open the refueling door. What was I thinking? MiGs aren't a threat in the refueling area. Lunging toward the door handle, I nudged the control stick. The nose of the heavy jet moved down, and I immediately overcorrected. Then the nose shot up toward the tanker. I had induced a porpoise maneuver and every attempt to control it made it worse.

"Ashe, let go of the stick," Hunter radioed, using my first name in an uncommon breach of radio discipline. "Let go of the stick."

I released the control stick and the porpoise maneuver stopped. Gently I placed my fingertips back on the stick and stabilized the aircraft in pre-contact position. I paused, took a deep breath and inched forward.

"Be smooth, be smooth. Breath deep, breath slow," I chanted to myself in the droning tones of a mantra.

The jet responded by gliding into refueling contact position in one positive motion. The boom operator cautiously retracted his instrument a few inches.

"Hope I didn't scare you too bad," I whispered to myself as the boomer initiated contact with a metallic clunk that vibrated through the fuselage of my jet.

The operator looked down and gave me a thumb up to indicate we were transferring fuel. For three minutes, I held position well enough to refuel but still over-controlled the jet in roll. As the plane filled up, the added weight caused the rolling moment of the plane to increase. I fought the flight controls but couldn't stop the motion.

Finally, another thumbs up and I disconnected and backed away from the tanker. I was exhausted and drenched with sweat. The other flight members refueled without a problem. Grover was particularly solid, looking over and nodding at me while connected to the tanker and transferring fuel. Disgusted with my performance, I tried to put the experience behind me and turn to the next phase of the mission.

After we departed the tanker and accelerated to 540 knots, we were exactly 90 nautical miles or 10 minutes from the target. I didn't feel prepared. What I did feel was distracted and powerless to concentrate.

"Nash Flight, green'em up," Hunter said slowly and distinctly on the radio.

The call meant more than arming the weapons. It also indicated we were over North Vietnam.

I had memorized a checkpoint, five limestone karst formations near a village, but at four minutes out, 36 miles from the target, I forgot to look for them. In the distance, I could see the ocean. I could make out a point of land on the coast at Quang Binh that should be to the left and beyond the target. The ground was going by at blinding speed, everything happening so fast that I couldn't keep up. The next checkpoint, the Reo Nay River, should appear thirteen miles prior to the submerged ferry pier.

Hunter bottomed out of a descent at 200 feet, 540 knots. I flew in formation, stacked a few feet high and to the left of Hunter. Lucky's element was line abreast on Hunter's right at 300 feet above the treetops.

The speeding jets pushed through warm moist air forming a surreal vapor that curled and trailed from the wingtips like satin ribbons. Another stream of vapor encased each fuselage, from canopy to tail, in a silky white cocoon. The Rao Nay River slipped beneath the flight in a heartbeat. It was small, what we'd call a creek back home and not helpful for my low-level navigation. We were less than a minute from the pull-up point when Hunter descended to fifty feet, booming over the jungle canopy and forming a wake in the treetops.

The terrain was a blur. I didn't see the white temple or the knoll that was the pull-up checkpoint. My first indication was Hunter zooming into a 45-degree climb. I hung in formation, crushed into my seat by G-forces. I lost sight of Lucky's element but knew they would follow with an identical pop-up maneuver.

Flying in formation with Hunter's jet, I waited for his cue to roll into a dive. I glanced to the left and thought I located the target area but didn't see the pier. There were visual checkpoints up the yahzoo—a river intersection with the ocean and a distinct coastline. There was little excuse for a new guy not to find this target. Still I couldn't find it. It was reassuring to know that, if I stayed on Hunter's wing, I would wind up in a 45-degree dive with the target centered in my bombsite. I focused all my energy and stayed welded in formation with Hunter.

Approaching 12,000 feet altitude, Hunter rolled the plane upside down and pulled the nose of his jet through the horizon, converting the climb to a dive. I hung on my back in the maneuver, looking at the ground through the top of my cockpit canopy. I saw the target area again but lost it as we rolled upright into a dive. Only seconds were left before bomb release.

Descending in a 45-degree dive, my airspeed approached 550 knots and was increasing rapidly. I had practiced formation flying many times. I should be able to concentrate on the dive bomb run without worrying about flying formation or running into my leader. But my body seemed to be pumping tons of adrenaline. I felt wired up as if I could do a thousand things a second, but could I do them well?

Below was a road intersecting the river. Not what I expected. Highway Route One was a small dirt trail pock-marked on both sides with water-filled bomb craters. Finally I saw the faint outline of a pier obscured by mud-stained water.

Airspeed increased rapidly as I put my red aiming reticle on the target. Beside me, the bombs came off Hunter's jet, and he pulled up to recover from the dive. Distracted for an instant, the red dot on my aiming reticle passed the target. Instinctively, I tried to correct by pushing forward on the control stick.

Airspeed shot through 610 knots, increasing rapidly. I was too fast and below safe bomb release altitude. If I released much lower the bombs would be more of a threat to me than to the enemy. Worse, I was flying formation with Hunter's bombs and was gaining on them.

I power-dived toward the ground at 1,000 feet per second while considering my options. Delay one more second and my own weapons would probably kill me. I tried to adjust my aim point millisecond by millisecond but couldn't keep up. I felt like I left my brains back on the ramp and was about to splatter the rest of my body into the jungle. Finally, in one motion, I pushed the pickle button to release and yanked the control stick back into my gut.

G-forces crushed me against the seat. My head flopped toward my chest, neck muscles unable to hold against the force. The jet bucked and rolled like an old car on a washboard road. Holding the control stick back in my lap with both hands, I grunted through the smashing Gs until the nose of the plane pointed above the horizon. Rolling left, I saw Hunter's bombs explode at the water's edge exactly as planned.

The impact of my bombs made my heart sink. They hit on shore, 200 feet from the water and 500 feet north of the pier. Then Lucky's bombs exploded on target followed by Grover's precisely on the T-head pier. A plume of sand and water shot skyward and obscured the target area.

"You screw-up," I repeated to myself about a thousand times while enroute to post strike refueling. I knew I lost concentration but had felt powerless to correct. It was a lonely, quiet flight back to the tanker.

Hunter directed me to refuel first. Then, after the rest of the flight gassed up, had me make several practice hook-ups on the boom. I was exhausted, but now with a lighter jet, refueled successfully on all attempts. Next, Hunter led the flight to an area south of Korat and practiced close formation aerobatics for a full thirty minutes before landing.

I tried to collect my thoughts as I unstrapped and crawled out of the plane. Lucky joined me and we waited for the aircrew van.

"Rough day, huh," Lucky mumbled as he looked up to the sky.

"Lucky," I said. "I can't believe I messed up so bad and so often."

"Well, Shooter," Lucky said, as he stretched his arms then stood with his hands on his hips. "Today you turned buffoonery into a precise science."

My body trembled as the flight assembled in the debriefing room. I had started to throw up in the latrine a few minutes earlier, but it turned into the dry heaves. I couldn't do anything right. I felt dehydrated and emotionally exhausted plus my neck hurt from the G-forces. I expected the flight debriefing would go on for hours to cover all the judgment errors I had committed. Not wanting to make eye contact with Hunter or any other flight members, I made senseless notes on my flight line-up card until he started the briefing, and I could avoid him no longer.

"We all made mistakes today," Hunter said taking a deep breath. "And we all need to think about them and make corrections so they don't happen again. Get some rest and we'll do it again tomorrow."

That was it. That was all he said. The shortest flight debriefing I'd ever heard about was the postmortem on the worst flight I'd ever had. I couldn't believe I didn't get chewed out for hours. In a way, it was worse. I thought it to be an acknowledgment that I wasn't worth the effort to debrief. Now others would believe I was one of those new pilots that put himself and everyone else in danger. I knew they would feel that way because I felt it myself.

Chapter 23

My first combat mission after the grounding had revealed a new enemy—me. In the flight briefing, I had taken offense to Hunter's suggestion that there might be a problem. But the result was undeniable. While DNIF, I lost more than the sharp edge of my flying skills. I had become indecisive and lost the ability to concentrate. It had been an insidious process and before the mission I didn't have a clue that it would affect my ability to fly.

Lucky took me aside. "Hunter's letting you handle it yourself, Ashe. You have to kill your own demons."

"I don't know where to start."

"Flying fast jets is a humbling experience," Lucky said. "And we've all been humbled. I have. Even Hunter has although with him it's hard to imagine."

I sat with my head in my hands.

Lucky paused and lit a cigarette. "Fighter pilots respect each other, because we've all 'been there'. That's what 'been there' means to fighter guys. It's not just the beauty of flying that bonds us together. It's being alone and conquering demons in a way that leaves you stronger. In a way that leaves you with grit and audacity."

"But why is Hunter so tough?" I asked.

"How's that?"

"It's his instructing style, all that..." I searched for the words. "Insinuation and exhortation."

Lucky grimaced. "Whoa. I don't know what all that means. Hunter's life hasn't been a piece of cake. Nothing has come to him easily."

"I suppose. But why does he have to take it out on me?"

"You're too sensitive." Lucky said, waving off the remark. "It's not about you. He's like thunder and lightning. The storm is here one minute and blows away the next."

"Thunderchief," I smiled. "That's a good name for him."

"You mean like the F-105 Thunderchief?"

"Exactly," I said. "Both man and machine are like Old Testament Gods. Lots of rules and no forgiveness."

Lucky laughed. "I like it. It fits. But better not say it to his face."

Over the next three days of flying, I began to regain focus. Hunter scheduled me on his wing everyday for a week before we took a day off.

While debriefing the fifth or sixth mission, I couldn't remember which, Hunter said. "I know why you were Top Gun in your class. You have a gift for flying fighters."

I sat speechless at the briefing table in front of Hunter, Lucky, and Grover. My eyes began to well up. Coming from Hunter it was the ultimate compliment. The affirmation I never received from my father.

While we were flying relatively easy missions to checkout Grover and myself, other pilots were still flying the tougher missions farther north. Weather in the Hanoi area hampered many operations but for missions that did fly up north, the loss rate had increased once again. Four pilots had been lost in the last seven missions that flew above the Red River.

A major who tallied the daily statistics had inherited the nickname "Stats". Each day Stats put a number on the grease pencil board in the mission planning room. The number wasn't labeled; it just had a circle around it but everyone knew what it meant. It was the average number of missions a pilot could expect to fly before being shot down.

While I was planning my eighth mission, Stats walked up to

the board and wrote in the number 86. The room was still as everyone stared.

Finally, from the back a voice said. "Now there are only three ways to get out of here: desert, become a POW, or die."

Another pilot gave a tired sigh and said, "Why don't you just shut your face and die like a man."

It was the first time the number had dropped below ninety and it seemed to stun everyone. It was a shock to headquarters too. Replacements were needed fast. But all the newly trained lieutenants that were ready to come in from Nellis wouldn't replace the week's losses. Clearly more would be needed fast and headquarters took steps to speed up the training pipeline and increase the supply of F-105 pilots and planes. No longer did anyone speak of highly experienced replacements. If the loss rate stayed anywhere close to current levels, there would be a scramble just to fill cockpits.

Another troubling bit of data was circulating and almost immediately attributed to Stats. Rumor had it, the recovery rate of shot down pilots had dropped below fifty percent. The figure sounded believable. Compared to Route Pack Six, the rest of Vietnam was much more survivable. Most of North Vietnam is narrow bordering Laos on the west and the Gulf of Tonkin on the east. The F-105, a robust combat jet, could usually fly a considerable distance after it was hit. But flying a wounded jet south to safety from Route Pack Six tested even the Thud's reserve.

On the last Sunday in June, I was scheduled for my twentieth mission into North Vietnam. I knew it was Sunday, rather than any other day in the week, because a bottle of malaria pills appeared on each table in the KABOOM dining room.

Hunter was grumpy. Once again our primary target was the Doumer Bridge. Normally that would make him happy considering his obsession with downing the magnificent structure. But the weather in Pack Six was crummy. It was the kind of day one sensed we were doing a lot of mission planning for nothing.

I was to fly as number four on Lucky's wing. The weatherman

confirmed our fears. The primary target was clobbered with clouds. Our alternate target was clear, but a line of storms crossed the ingress route. Weather would force us to the alternate and fuel would be a major consideration. If we found a hole in the line of storms, there would be plenty of fuel. If not, we would have to jettison our bombs and return to home base.

"Here's what we're going to do," Hunter said in the flight briefing. "We're not going to piddle away all our gas trying to do a weather check on the primary target. We'll go straight toward the alternate. I'll find the weakest point in the storms and penetrate through it. If the weather's okay, we'll make one dive bomb pass.

"You all have a picture of the alternate target so you know what it looks like. Lead and three have bombed it before so we shouldn't have much trouble finding it again. We'll bomb in element formation. In the dive bomb pass, stay in formation with your leader. Then, when it's time to release, you should be able to glance through the bombsite and see the target. If you don't see it, pickle your bombs off when your leader drops. After release we'll head straight for our next target which is our real objective for today. I'll show it to you now."

Lucky tried to suppress a nervous laugh, "I take it this is one of your Hunter specials?"

"Bull's-eye," Hunter said as he pulled a crumpled packet of target materials from the ankle pocket of his flight suit and slapped it on the table. "I been waitin' to blow hell out of this one and today's the day."

Lucky looked excited as he spoke. "If you're talking about what I think you're talking about, I'm ready."

"The target is this troop area right here," Hunter said, tapping his pencil on the map twenty miles south of Hanoi.

"That's it. Let's do it," Lucky said with a grin. "That place has always teed me off. Those troops are sleeping in scrubbed-up French-built barracks when they ought to be living in the mud."

"Here are some pictures," Hunter said. "Take a good look

because we'll leave all target photos on the ground." "We are after four targets in the complex. Left to right they are the generator building, a radio tower, and the two barracks buildings. The flat area in front of the barracks was probably a French parade ground but now is bristling with dug-in fifty caliber gun positions. We'll be flying over them pretty low.

"We'll use a low angle strafe pattern with the following target assignments. Lead will aim at the transmitting tower. Two, take the generator building. Three, strafe the left barracks building. Aim at the entrance and walk the stream of bullets around with the rudder pedals. Four, do the same with the other barracks."

"I don't see a target number on the card. Is this an approved target?" Grover queried, asking the question that I was thinking but not saying.

"We'll be flying armed reconnaissance," Hunter said. "If they happen to shoot at us, we'll respond with force. It's a flight leader's decision so I'll tell you if they're shooting. If there are no more questions, it's time to suit up and step to the aircrew van."

It bothered me that Hunter's target was not on the approved list, but I didn't raise the issue. He was attacking under the rules for armed reconnaissance, which allowed us in selected areas to fire back if fired upon. But we were preplanning the attack, and I sensed Hunter would hit the target regardless of enemy response or lack of it.

"Korat tower, Ford flight taxi," Hunter radioed.

I tried to focus on the flight as we taxied, armed, then lined up on the runway. Still, I had nagging thoughts about attacking a target that was unauthorized. But, I also remembered the last time I lost focus on a mission. It wasn't worth it. Whether to attack this target wasn't my choice to make. I wasn't the flight leader, and I couldn't stop the world or even slow it down to resolve my personal feelings. My job was to focus and fly combat. My last few missions had been good, and I knew I could do it right if I kept my head on straight.

As I eased back on the control stick, the bomb-laden Thud lifted off the runway and gathered airspeed. Patiently, I waited for the indicator to read three hundred knots then started a gentle turn to join up on Lucky. The hollow click of my oxygen valve ticked off slow, measured, reassuring breaths. I felt comfortable and in control again, anticipating power settings and closure rates well in advance.

With a single motion, I stripped away the bayonet clip on the right side of my oxygen mask and let it dangle from the left strap. I wiped away the condensed moisture from my nose and mouth with the back of my leather glove. With rapid eye movements, I incorporated the other aircraft and the dials on the instrument panel into my crosscheck. But lurking in my peripheral vision, far ahead on the horizon, were sinister looking thunderstorms.

"Brigham, this is Ford flight," Hunter radioed to the area control center. "Ford, airborne, looking for Mongo four one."

"Roger, Ford, your tanker is on station, zero-four-three degrees at fifty-six miles from your position," Brigham replied.

Once on the tanker, all four jets took on a full load of fuel. Then each shuttled onto the refueling boom for a quick final drink to top-off the tanks. Flying the number four position, I finished refueling at the northern tip of the refueling track as it was time to depart the tanker. Our flight had executed the refueling track-timing problem and pulled it off without a single radio transmission with the tanker aircraft.

Hunter held the flight on a northerly heading as the large, lumbering tanker began a gentle arcing turn towards the south. I watched the refueler fade off into the distance. It would be our last contact with friendly forces for over an hour.

An ugly wall of thunderstorms with towering cumulus clouds lay several miles ahead. The individual cloud cells were immense. The storms rose to forty or fifty thousand feet with well-developed anvil formations at the top. An alarm sounded in my brain. Anvils were the sign of enormous turbulence that could spit hail for several miles into clear air.

The cloud formation spelled danger, a sign to be avoided, but Hunter maintained a steady course toward the ominous dark wall.

In my earphones, I heard sharp crackles and punctuated bursts of static electricity from lightning. I had a hunch the other flight members were as concerned as I about penetrating the storm. I studied the amber screen of my radar for a weak point but suspected Hunter would take us through the line of storms whether or not he found a hole.

Hunter flew straight up against the wall of storms and, at the last possible second, turned east. From my position on the right, inside the turn and low, I looked up at an angle through the other three jets. The storm appeared larger than a mountain. Electricity shot through the towering clouds illuminating them from inside like ten-mile high fluorescent tubes.

Taking my hand off of the control stick, I alternately clenched and stretched my fingers to relax the muscles in my wrist and forearm. Once again I committed the cardinal sin, worrying about an event before it actually happened and wasting emotional energy I was going to need later.

A hurried wag of Hunter's wings signaled the event I dreaded. In a few seconds we would enter dense clouds and visibility would drop to a few feet. Our flight took the cue and tightened formation, overlapping wingtips about eighteen inches so we would be able to maintain visual contact. My flight position, slightly aft of Lucky's jet, placed his wingtip even with my canopy. It seemed I could reach out and touch it. Pounded by turbulence, I pushed the trim button forward for a full second to make the control stick heavy toward the nose of the jet. It seemed easier to maintain tight formation if I flew against several pounds of control stick pressure.

As my eyes stayed riveted to Lucky's wingtip, I resisted looking at the radar to see the size of the hole Hunter chose. Maybe there wasn't a hole. I hoped against hope that Hunter had seen something that I had not. I was rationalizing and I knew it, believing Hunter might fly through the belly of the storm just to prove his boys could hack the weather. I laughed at the irony. He would probably look for the worst part and drag his flight through it as a character building exercise.

I didn't have a comfortable feeling but knew what I had to do inside the storm, shut out the world, ignore my physical senses, and concentrate on flying formation with Lucky's wing tip.

We were in clear air—then, suddenly, after a bump of turbulence the world disappeared and our flight was inside a cloud. Instantly visibility dropped to near zero. I could barely see Hunter's jet on the other side of Lucky. Turbulence tossed me against the lap belt and shoulder restraint harness. We were flying in a milky white cloud that was rapidly becoming darker and darker.

I could still make out the outline of Lucky's canopy but couldn't see Hunter or Grover on the other side. Water pounded my windscreen at 480 knots, and wide rivulets streamed back across the canopy and blurred my vision.

My senses indicated I was upside down. I kept telling myself orientation didn't matter. Ignore it. Just keep flying. I fought myself, battling sensory input that screamed danger. A few seconds later, Lucky's wing tip was all that remained visible in the world. The rest of creation was a dark milky mass. For all I knew, I was flying inside a cow.

"Stick on Lucky's wing," I shouted into my mask knowing no one else could hear. My whole being sensed that I was upside down and yet, in my head, I knew I was not. It was as if the devil had control of my senses, trying to drive me crazy. Sweat poured off my forehead and into my eyes, but I couldn't take my hands away from the controls to wipe it away.

Then our four screaming jets burst out of the cloud and into blinding sunlight that filled the cockpit with warmth and a sense of being borne back into the world. Glancing to the heavens, I acknowledged the new layer of humility that comes from each encounter with the enormous strength of nature.

Between thunderstorms, I saw a clear path in the direction of our target. Hunter didn't descend but continued at alti-

tude. We flew at 12,000 feet, 480 knots, which would conserve
fuel for the special target.

"Ford flight, this is lead," Hunter radioed. "Target's at our
ten o'clock. Confirm you have a visual."

"Ford Two, tally ho."

"Three, tally."

"Four, has a tally."

Clearly Hunter was more concerned with saving fuel than
avoiding the enemy. I felt uneasy about cruising into the target
at altitude, ignoring the surface-to-air missiles that could be
masked by clouds. Apparently Hunter counted on the storm
clouds being too dense for SAM radar to penetrate.

Hunter's right wing dip signaled the flight to leave fingertip formation and echelon right. The number two aircraft
crossed under Hunter and positioned between lead and
three. Now our jets flew in a right oblique stair-stepped line,
each positioned for a left roll-in to dive bomb in flight order.
Hunter began a gentle turn to the left. The flight maintained
formation while getting a long look at the target located near
a karst monolith.

Hunter and Grover rolled into a dive followed by Lucky and
me in loose formation. There seemed to be plenty of time. I
didn't see any flak and my eyes were searching the ground for
any sign of a SAM launch.

The bomb run was anticlimactic. All the weapons impacted in the jungle area that was supposed to be a suspected
truck park. I didn't see a single truck, secondary explosion,
or anything else that made this look like a valid target. All I
could see was jungle. Another target selected by Washington
bureaucrats. It's not like there's a shortage of good targets, I
thought. Airfields. Railroads. Port facilities. We often flew
over real targets to hit these worthless suspected truck parks
in the jungle. Targets handpicked in Washington. We were
being directed by the unwise to do the unthinkable.

As we recovered from the attack and turned in the direction
of Hunter's special target, we flew through a narrow passage
between storm cells. The weather seemed to be closing in on

us. I wasn't lost: I just didn't know exactly where we were.

It was Lucky's job as deputy lead to keep us in position, but it was my job to assume Lucky's deputy lead position if required. If Lucky got hit by ground fire or lost his radio, I was not confident I could put him on my wing and lead him safely back to home base in inclement weather. There were many things to master and no school but experience. In stateside training, weather this bad would cancel flying and fill the Officer's Club bar.

As the weather closed in at altitude, Hunter began a rapid descent and leveled the flight at 3,000 feet. From our lower altitude, visibility was somewhat better but we were using more fuel. Still, I didn't see a single checkpoint I recognized. Hunter made very positive course corrections, and I took that as a sign he knew where we were. At least I was hoping.

Chapter 24

Hunter led our flight into a wide sweeping turn. I flew loose formation on Lucky as I searched the ground for Hunter's special target.

"Ford flight," Hunter radioed. "We're taking ground fire from a built up area on the left. Arm-up the 20 mike-mike, we're going in."

His radio transmission was unusually long and precise considering we had pre-briefed the target. The transmission was for show, I figured, for any command or intelligence people, whether friendly or enemy, monitoring our frequency.

The complex lay in a cleared area at the edge of a patch of jungle. Each feature stood out, the antenna on the west side, the small generator shack, and two barracks buildings. I didn't see any hostile fire. I suspected there was none but couldn't be positive. I'd been wrong before, not seeing enemy fire when it had been called out, then, later, reviewing photos from the nose-mounted camera, seeing muzzle flashes from anti-aircraft weapons and puffs of flak.

Hunter set up a racetrack pattern with a run-in over the parade grounds in front of the two-story, French-built barracks. I moved into attack position flying line abreast and slightly above Lucky.

"Ford's in," Hunter radioed as he and Grover charged onto final approach for a strafing pass.

Hunter seemed to be flying a training pattern which presented an easy target for the enemy: a downwind leg at 3000 feet, a flat arcing base leg turn, and a shallow dive onto final approach. His flight path made one thing clear: he intended to fire the 20-millimeter cannon at very close range.

Grover flew wing position a hundred feet to Hunter's right. A trail of pulsating smoke burst from the side of each aircraft as they fired. Flashes, like a thousand twinkling lights, covered the base of the transmitting tower then resolved into a huge ball of dirt and debris. The generator building lit up and exploded. The transmitting tower stood fast as the generator building collapsed in a pile of burning rubble.

Then Lucky and I rolled-in to attack. We had slowed down to stay behind Hunter, and now, beginning our bomb run, my speed was only 450 knots. The jet would accelerate to 500 knots by the time I pulled the trigger, but I wished it were 100 knots faster. As we rolled wings level on final approach, I focused on my aim point in the target complex. I could see gun emplacements on the near side of the parade grounds. Surprisingly, none of the guns were manned. The area appeared deserted until my attack angle was low enough to see behind the barracks where trucks parked under trees were making good use of foliage to hide them from above.

I let the aircraft stabilize and watched the aiming pipper track up through the gun emplacements then over the parade ground. The two-story barracks looked like whitewashed plaster over cinder block that had become dull and greenish brown from neglect. Wide cement steps led to a large entrance door.

As the aiming pipper approached the door of the barracks, three men, partially dressed, ran out and pointed toward the burning remains of the generator building. My finger hovered over the trigger. In my gunsight were soldiers. I felt detached from my senses, making decisions in fractions of a second, spontaneously, impulsively, rather than through any process of rational thought. When I was almost in firing range, the aiming pipper settled near the men's feet as their heads snapped up and looked toward my jet.

I fired, walking the pipper into the building as I instinctively moved the rudder pedals back and forth to disperse the rounds. I felt like what I witnessed wasn't happening in real time. It was like watching a movie. But it wasn't a film, and I could feel the scene being etched into my memory.

Hauling back on the stick, I grunted against the pressure of the inflating G-suit as it compressed my lower body. The barracks passed less than 50 feet below the belly of my jet. As soon as the nose of the plane rose safely above the horizon, I rolled hard to the left and looked back over my shoulder.

I had never been this close to the effects of high explosive incendiary ammunition. The main door of the barracks had disappeared. It looked like a freight train had plowed through the building and bulldozed its center into a trail of debris scattered out back. I let out a moan, realizing the three men and the steps they were standing on had disintegrated.

For a second, my world stopped. I had killed. I had probably killed before when I dropped bombs, but there had been no confirmation. This time I knew for sure. I saw it with my own eyes and felt a sickening feeling in my gut.

I recovered from the attack and maneuvered into loose formation with Lucky. To our left, Hunter appeared on a downwind leg as he positioned for another pass. Again Hunter strafed the tower and kicked up a large cloud of debris. The tower tilted slightly but didn't come down. It seemed damaged and looked unusable, but Hunter probably wouldn't be satisfied until he dropped it in the dirt. Grover's target was gone and black smoke bellowed from the debris. Probably a diesel fuel fire. Lacking a primary target, Grover chose to strafe a gun position at the edge of the parade ground.

I followed Lucky onto final approach as soldiers began to stream out of the wrecked barracks. Placing my pipper in the center of the mass of humanity, I watched it track toward the building. Should I strafe the soldiers before they man the guns, or should I hit the barracks again? After a moment's hesitation the choice became an illusion. I pulled the trigger and walked another burst through the structure until I challenged the minimum safe altitude to pullout and clear the ground.

I wrenched the control stick back into my gut and closed my eyes for an instant, praying I didn't fly into a ricochet from my own cannon. Again I slammed into a left bank to check the target, another 30 feet of barracks gone and the remainder burning. Looking left, I found that Lucky had sawed his building in half, the ends still standing but both on fire.

"Ford flight," Hunter radioed. "They're running for the guns. Get'em."

What, aren't we done? I thought. Why are we sticking around? Why don't we egress before someone gets hammered?

Hunter and Grover turned final for a third strafing pass. From downwind leg, I saw a stream of soldiers, scurrying like ants across the dirt. Hunter fired another burst at the tower. It crumpled as if its legs had been kicked out from under it.

Grover directed a fusillade of rounds onto the parade ground. As in slow motion, bodies exploded and flew into the air, raining down pieces. I couldn't have imagined the carnage that unfolded before me.

"Heads up, Shooter, they're firing real bullets," Lucky radioed as we turned onto final approach for a third series of attacks.

We're in a pissing contest with a skunk, I swore to myself as red balls of anti-aircraft tracers sailed by my canopy. We've made too many passes. Stayed too long in the target area. We're flying on borrowed time.

For every tracer I saw, I knew there were 10 or more rounds not visible and the 50-caliber tracer fire was so thick, I couldn't begin to keep score. The parade ground seemed littered with bodies and so much blood I could see pools of red-soaked earth. Among the bodies of soldiers was a water buffalo I hadn't noticed before, collapsed on its side, not moving.

A gun position began shooting at me from the right side of the parade ground. I made an aiming correction and fired. Direct hit. A stream of high-explosive-incendiary ammunition assaulted the revetted position, scouring out any trace of humanity. I stared at the empty hole for the fraction of a second it took my aircraft to overfly the position.

I looked for Hunter. Unbelievably, he was positioning for another attack. I pounded my fist against my G-suit covered leg. What happened to one pass, haul ass, Hunter? I yelled to myself. You're setting up a shooting gallery for the gunners.

Hunter started the fourth round of attacks for the flight. When I fired again, I'd be making the sixteenth pass of an F-105 over the target. We were violating all the rules for survival, and I knew it. Hunter wasn't even jinking, perhaps hoping that sheer audacity would confuse the gunners. We had been on this target over fifteen minutes, and audacity must be wearing thin as a tactic. Now the gun positions were all manned and shooting.

I became transfixed as Hunter rolled-in on final with Grover welded on his wing flying superb formation. It was like watching the Thunderbirds aerial demonstration team perform in the midst of a Fourth of July fireworks display. The parade ground sparkled with surreal flashes as Hunter and Grover belched cannon fire into the gauntlet the ceremonial ground had become.

"Ford Two, is hit," Grover yelled.

My eyes shot to Grover's jet, as he pulled off target, dropping well behind Hunter.

"Ford Two, this is Lead. Turn to heading two-zero-zero and climb. I'll be on your wing in a second."

Hunter was 2,000 feet in front of Grover. He flew a wide arcing high-G roll over the top of Grover's flight path. Hunter must have cross-controlled, applying full rudder. His jet appeared to be flying sideways. In seconds he lost 2,000 feet of horizontal distance but rolled out co-airspeed in close formation with Grover. It seemed as if he had thrown his jet in reverse and backed up onto Grover's wing. The maneuver hawked back to the days before aircraft had computer-coordinated flight controls and now had been almost forgotten. Probably only a handful of pilots could still execute a perfect

high-G barrel roll to the outside. It was clear to me that Hunter
had elevated stick and rudder flying into an art form.

"Ford Two, this is Ford Leader," Hunter radioed to Grover.
"Looks like you took a 50-caliber in the nose of your drop tank.
It split like a banana and a strip of aluminum folded over the
top of your wing. Do not jettison. Repeat. Do not jettison. Give
me some feedback on handling qualities and warning lights in
the cockpit."

"Ford Lead, this is Two," Grover radioed in an uneasy voice.
"It's flying like a barn door. No lights or other problems. Feels
like the speedbrake is out. I can barely maintain 280 knots with
full power."

"This is Big Eye on Guard Channel, Bandits, Bullseye heading 180 degrees for 10 miles, Repeat, Bandits, Bullseye heading 180 degrees for 10 miles. This is Big Eye, out."

Big Eye, a large lumbering radar control aircraft over the
Gulf of Tonkin, apparently had been tracking our flight and
was aware of our dilemma. The enemy must be aware, as well,
since MiGs were moving toward us like birds of prey under
radar control. According to Big Eye, the MiGs were 10 miles
south of Hanoi which put them less than 20 miles north of our
position. The MiGs could attack in less than three minutes.

"Ford Flight, this is Lead," Hunter radioed in a stern voice.
"Ford Three, take your element high and provide top cover."

I moved out to air-to-air fighting formation, a thousand feet
from Lucky's wing, and began looking over my shoulder for
MiGs. We had several problems. Hunter and Grover were sitting ducks at 280 knots. Lucky and I needed to maintain a higher altitude if we were to protect the flight against a MiG attack.
Lucky, as element lead, would have to keep Grover in sight
while traveling at least 150 knots faster. Last, but not least
important, I was out of ammunition. Fortunately, the MiGs
wouldn't know our weapons status, but we couldn't fake it for
long.

It bothered me that the MiGs reacted so fast. Our intelligence briefings characterized MiG pilots as burdened by a

command and control, slow to take the initiative and to press the attack. All of that may be true, but today they seemed pretty darned good.

I felt vulnerable trying to protect Grover with enemy fighters on the way. My skin crawled at the thought of engaging a MiG with no ammunition. I cursed Hunter's repeated attacks. Thankfully we had Big Eye. I wondered how Big Eye did it and wanted to know more. I wanted to confirm some level of confidence in Big Eye's information, since I was betting my life. But Big Eye's mission was too highly classified, another Top Secret compartmented program to which I didn't have access. If captured I couldn't reveal what I didn't know, but I sensed Big Eye knew a great deal about the minute-to-minute activities of MiGs. Still, I wanted reassurance that I was getting better information than the MiG pilots.

I weaved back and forth in fluid formation across Lucky's flight path. Like a hawk, Lucky kept station high above looking for prey. I suspected Lucky, like Hunter, would provoke an attack if a hint of opportunity came. Both would welcome the challenge and probably not consider the risk to themselves or their wingmen.

I remembered Hunter speaking almost with reverence. "There are transcendent moments when you engage another pilot in air-to-air combat. It's a moment that makes you feel alive. The clashing of warriors flying supersonic fighters. Just one man against the other."

"Ford flight, this is Dallas Leader," a voice radioed with the call sign of an F-4 Phantom air-to-air flight.

"Dallas, Ford Leader here," Hunter responded.

"Dallas has been talkin' at Big Eye on another channel. Understand you got a problem."

"Roger that," Hunter said. "One of my chicks got his feathers clipped. Can you keep the buzzards off our back while we head to the roost?"

"Our pleasure, Ford Leader. We got you on radar. We'll pass over your position in three minutes. Give me a shout when you see us."

I knew I should still keep a visual lookout behind us, but I caught myself glancing forward every few seconds looking for Dallas.

The next minute seemed like the longest of my life. Then four dots appeared in the sky each tracing a wispy trail of black smoke, the characteristic signature of F-4 engines. Dallas raced toward us. Our combined closure rate was 14 miles a minute. I never again looked back for MiGs. I focused instead on Dallas flight tracking straight and true across the sky and coming to our rescue, literally faster than a speeding bullet.

"Ford, Dallas here. Over your position now."

"Roger, Dallas," Hunter radioed. "You're a pretty sight. Wish we could go with you."

"Roger, Ford Lead, we'll be changing radio channels. Have a nice day. Dallas flight, button ten, go."

I let out an exhausted sigh. At least the MiGs were off our back. Dallas had long-range missiles and the enemy fighters would run for cover when they realized they were being aggressively pursued.

Hunter located a hole in the line of thunderstorms and the flight made it across Laos in visual flight conditions.

"Ford flight, this is Lead," Hunter radioed. "Lead will escort Two to NKP. Ford Three, proceed to the tanker, then to homeplate."

"Ford Three, roger that," Lucky radioed.

It'll be a long day for Grover, I thought. He'll land at Nakhon Phanom then catch a helicopter to Korat.

As Lucky started a slow climb, conserving fuel as we headed towards the tanker, my thoughts turned back to the carnage on the parade ground. The attack reeled through my mind in animated slow motion. I broke out in a cold sweat. I fought off the emotion and turned my attention to a dull pain that slowly traced down my arm. Hunching over, I raised my shoulder and rotated it to loosen up, but my forearm and trigger finger were numb and seemed frozen. My hand ached and I found it difficult to grip the control stick. The numbness grew worse as we approached the refueling tanker.

I watched Lucky refuel effortlessly, as I flexed my hand trying to restore the feeling. As it came time for me to refuel, I

laid my hand on the top of the control stick and used down-
ward pressure rather than a grip. I flew into the pre-contact
position and the boomer shot the probe down to connect
immediately. The tanker could spare only 2,000 pounds of gas
and the offload took much less than a minute.

As we departed the tanker, Hunter checked in on refueling
frequency. "The chick's in the coop," Hunter radioed, indicating Grover had made a successful emergency landing at Naked
Fanny.

After engine shutdown, I sat in the cockpit and stared at my
trigger finger. It felt as if it didn't belong to me. My hand and
arm were numb to my shoulder, as if they weren't connected to
my body.

As the crewchief began his post flight inspection, Lucky
sauntered over to my jet and climbed the ladder to the cockpit. "Better pull your gun camera film, Ashe."

"Because it's not on the target list?" I asked.

"You got it."

"What do I do with it, if I don't give it to Intelligence?"

"Hell, I don't know," Lucky said. "Expose it, burn it, save it
for after the war. I just know what you shouldn't do with it."

"What about the intelligence debrief?"

"We'll debrief as a flight," Lucky said. "Except Grover won't
be back in time. Hunter will do all the talking, and you won't
have to say a word."

Chapter 25

The sixth of July was an anniversary of sorts; our flight had been together for exactly three months. I had flown forty-three total missions, twenty-five into North Vietnam and eighteen non-counters into Laos. I felt relieved that a quarter of my tour was over, but, most important, I'd established credibility as a wingman. That's what Hunter started saying last month after I had twenty total missions under my belt, and, because Hunter said it, the other pilots accepted me.

Lieutenant Colonel Mike Parker was a squadron commander who believed in flight integrity over the long term. As a result, Hunter, Lucky, Grover, and I always flew together except when one of us had the green apple two-step or some other malady that kept us off the schedule.

The four of us were together everyday, even when we weren't flying. The anniversary created another excuse for us to celebrate on R&R in Bangkok. Through the strange baptism of enemy fire, our flight had grown closer. We were family, although none of us had ever used that word to describe our strange mix of pilots in a bizarre war. We were an unlikely group brought together in an unlikely situation. Except for our common interest in flying fighters, none of us would have given the others a second thought.

We had bonded out of necessity and tolerated each other's habits. Hunter—the gruff, stoic patriarch. Grover and I—unwittingly in the role of two young sons learning the craft. Lucky— the mediator, holding the group together. Lucky communicated feelings when the rest of us were either too proud or too quixotic to express them. And Lucky was the conflict resolver. In many ways he seemed like a mother.

As with many families, we had dysfunctional elements. Lucky had an affinity for the prostitutes in Bangkok and Grover griped at him about it. Grover chain-smoked cigars and everyone complained to him about that. Hunter was just Hunter; there was no easy classification for him. If he indulged in the sexual smorgasbord available in Bangkok, it wasn't apparent. Perhaps his only vice was drinking himself into a stupor and talking incessantly about combat.

"We don't need four days R&R every month," Hunter complained. "We're wasting our time in Bangkok. We should be flying combat."

Our first mission after R&R was a routine strike on another of the elusive suspected truck parks near the Ho Chi Minh trail and about forty miles south of Hanoi. I flew on Hunter's wing and Grover on Lucky's. Our four-ship made a low-level ingress, popped up, and dive-bombed the target in a textbook attack. As Hunter had predicted, there were no secondary explosions or significant signs of activity in the target area. After our bombs dropped, a few anti-aircraft gunners fired, but that was all.

I had begun to feel confident on missions, almost invincible, except in the far north around Hanoi, and a few other well-defended targets like the Than Hoa Bridge. In those areas, combat seemed impossibly hard and luck played a large part. But luck had been redefined; now it meant losing only one pilot on each mission to a heavily defended target. We had been going to the Hanoi environs only four to six days a month but it was time for the northeast monsoon season to end and we would go more often.

In the south part of North Vietnam and Laos, missions seemed too easy. We flew in, dropped bombs, the gunners woke up and fired a few rounds, and nobody got hurt. Of course, it took me a few missions to learn how to pull that off. But it's a fact: if one lives through the first ten combat missions a pilot's chances of survival go way up.

But relatively easy targets were discouraging in their own way, considering the hours of preparation coupled with the inherent risk of any flight over hostile territory. The enemy didn't defend worthless targets, and sometimes it was depressing to fly across a target and not draw hostile fire. For a day to be considered worthwhile, the enemy had to show up—and shoot.

I wondered if the wizards in Washington realized that a triple tree canopy, in places more than a hundred feet thick, covered many of their hand-picked targets. They could have asked me since I had parachuted through it. But of course, they didn't. The canopy prevented visual acquisition of many targets, but it also kept the gunners from being effective. Many missions weren't worth the effort; perhaps Hunter thought so, too. Perhaps that's why he briefed special targets.

After departing the jungle-covered suspected truck park, Hunter turned north toward Hanoi. Fifteen minutes later, we skirted the east side of the city at 10,000 feet and were met by a hail of anti-aircraft fire. My heart raced as I checked out the defenses. Puffs of flak appeared in all quadrants. Hunter sure knew how to pep-up a dull day. Apparently ignoring the enemy, he set a course for Phuc Yen airfield on the north edge of the city. Enroute we were taunting the most experienced gunners in the world.

Hunter descended to 3,000 feet. I could see Phuc Yen in front of us and expected him to turn away. He didn't. Instead he headed directly toward the runway. Below, I could see MiGs parked off the airfield in little cul-de-sacs of revetments, each connected to the runway by a long ribbon of taxiway.

Three MiG-21s held in takeoff position on the far end of the runway. It gave me the willies, sensing we were the intended targets of the three jets lined up in Soviet air defense formation. I wondered if Russian pilots were flying today. If they made a formation takeoff, they could attack us in minutes.

I cursed the Rules of Engagement. The ROE prohibited attacking MiGs on the ground. We couldn't bomb any part of the airfield for any reason, even under the catchall category of armed reconnaissance. Gunners on the airfield could shoot all day, and we couldn't return fire. No exceptions. I remembered seeing it in bold print. I was stunned by the thought. Why give them a sanctuary on their own base when we have to fight deep in enemy territory?

As Hunter rolled out over the base a chill ran up my spine. I couldn't believe I was in a formation of four jets, straight and level, over Phuc Yen. Hunter had a set of nuggets all right, perhaps where his brains should be. I half expected him to pitch out into the landing pattern and do a low approach over the runway.

At the far end of the runway, Hunter wagged his wings to call our flight into close formation. He descended to 800 feet while making a sweeping turn back toward the airfield. I clenched my teeth until my jaw hurt. Hunter was going to do it again. Beyond belief, I thought, he's crazy. Reluctantly, I tightened up close to Hunter's wing as Grover did the same on Lucky's.

But Lucky didn't close in on Hunter, keeping his element in fighting wing formation, spread line abreast to Hunter's jet 1,000 feet away. Again Hunter led the flight straight and level over the Phuc Yen runway, putting on an air show over the base in the midst of flack, which seemed to come from everywhere.

"Buick Three, fly top cover," Hunter radioed.

Lucky pulled up, leading Grover to a position 6,000 feet above the airfield. Hunter made a wide sweeping arc, turning and descending to 500 feet as he built up our airspeed to 600 knots.

"Buick Lead, three bandits on takeoff roll," Lucky radioed.

Hunter tightened his maneuver and continued descending which forced me outside of his turn to avoid hitting the ground. Usually, Hunter was a considerate leader, but, in this turn, at full power, he left me well behind. Give me some throttle, I thought as I grunted against the G-forces, not wanting to waste fuel in afterburner.

Hunter flew lower and was still accelerating as he leveled off at 200 feet. I couldn't go much lower and was still falling behind with little hope of catching up. As we approached the runway, some soldiers ran across the parking ramp while others pointed rifles in the air. The flack had almost stopped. Were the gunners holding back because we were too low or because their own jets were in the air?

We crossed the runway in a flash. From my position, lagging in trail behind Hunter, I watched him track the arrowhead formation of MiGs. But he was closing fast. Too fast. Suddenly, the speedbrakes on his jet unfolded like petals on an aluminum flower. Instinctively, I extended my speedbrakes and slammed my throttle to idle.

I was thrown forward against the shoulder harness with bruising force as the four petals, 64 square feet of metal, popped into the 650-knot air stream. Hunter had misjudged the MiG's speed. His closure rate was horrendous. The MiGs had just retracted their landing gear and flaps and were probably accelerating through 200 knots.

A smoke trail erupted from the nose of Hunter's jet, signaling his desperate attempt with the 20-millimeter cannon. There were no hits as his jet flashed past the MiGs like a rocket. Hunter, now in front of the MiGs, became the hunted as he blundered into their gunsights. But trailing behind put me in perfect attack position.

The three-ship of MiGs rapidly loomed large in my windscreen. My mind raced. The MiGs were Hunter's to shoot, but he had blown it. I lined up the aiming pipper on the fuselage of a MiG. As my finger tightened on the trigger, I winced, seeing Hunter's jet lingering in my sight picture down-range of the MiG. I couldn't fire with Hunter in the path of my cannon, and I was on a collision course with a MiG.

"Hunter, break left," I shouted over the radio. "Break left."

The MiG filled my windscreen. I no longer had to aim. I could see the rivets in the jet's aluminum skin. In a heartbeat, I was going to eat this MiG. Finally, Hunter broke, and I fired. Instantly the MiG exploded, and I was engulfed in his fireball. Pieces of MiG peppered my jet like aluminum rain. I gasped, expecting to collide with a major hunk of metal and die.

Before I could react, I flew through the fireball and back into clear air.

"Buick Two, confirmed splash," Lucky cheered over the radio.

I retracted my speedbrakes, plugged in the afterburner, and hugged the ground. My speed was down to 350 knots, and I had two accelerating enemy jets behind me. Holding course for an instant, I looked for Hunter.

"Buick Two," Hunter radioed. "Lead's at your ten o'clock in a left turn."

I joined on Hunter as he turned north. I thought he might be going back for the two remaining MiGs. There were black marks on my canopy so thick I had to look around them to fly formation, and I noticed a long tear in the skin of the radome on the nose of my jet. Some of the radome fiber was folded back and fluttering in the wind stream.

Then I saw what Hunter was chasing, a MiG that was heading due north. We were over the hills north of Hanoi. Up ahead, less than a minute's flying time, was the Chinese buffer zone.

"Buick flight, burners now," Hunter said.

I selected afterburner, realizing Hunter would go after the MiG even if he had to follow it across the Chinese border. Two seconds elapsed, and my burner didn't light. I recycled the throttle inboard, then outboard again. Nothing. Hunter's jet was still accelerating away.

"Buick Lead, Two has negative burner," I radioed and moved the throttle inboard again.

"And Lead, Buick Three is bingo fuel," Lucky radioed then continued in a concerned voice. "We're pretty far north."

"Roger, Buick Three, Lead copies," Hunter said.

Hunter's afterburner flame extinguished, and his jet racked into a hard turn to the south. He began a gradual climb, apparently assessing the long flight to the tanker and the possibility of engaging MiGs on egress. I cut off Hunter's flight path in the turn and joined up two hundred feet off his left wing. Hunter looked over at my plane, shaking his head.

"Buick Two, Lead here. Fly straight for a minute. I'm going to have a closer look."

Hunter moved into tight formation then disappeared beneath my jet. After a few seconds, he sprung up on the opposite side and rolled over the top of my plane, canopy to canopy, before he stabilized beside me.

He gave a quick hand signal indicating that he had assumed the formation lead again and radioed. "Buick Lead here. Damn, son. You shoot that MiG or ram him? You got a busted radome, and ripped skin all over the jet. Is it flying okay?"

I checked my instrument panel.

"Buick Lead, Two, seems okay except my angle of attack is indicating full up."

Hunter pulled in close again. "Buick Two, Lead. Your angle-of-attack vane is gone. Probably got knocked off and went down the engine. It running okay?"

"Roger, Buick Lead, okay so far."

I scanned the engine instruments carefully while I wondered how badly the engine was damaged by ingesting the solid metal vane about the size of a can opener. This was no place to lose my only engine. The Thud had a strong constitution, but it wasn't designed to eat solid chunks of metal. A wave of loneliness washed over me. If my engine quit for any reason, I would be on the ground again but without Hunter. I was too deep in enemy territory for any hope of rescue.

Finally, as we approached the Laotian border, it sunk in. I had shot down a MiG. I unfastened the bayonet clip on the side of my facemask and shouted at the top of my voice. "I killed a MiG." As soon as the words came out I bit my lip. There'd been a pilot in that jet, perhaps someone like me. My heart sank.

Strangely, I wanted to know about my adversary. Who was he? Was he Russian, Chinese, or Vietnamese? Hell, he could have been a Cuban exchange pilot. What were his hopes and dreams? Did he eject? Probably not, his fighter blew up so fast. Maybe the Big Eye control aircraft knew something. But could I ever find out?

My engine held together on the flight back although several times I thought I heard strange noises. Perhaps I listened too closely to every creak and groan.

Waiting for me on the ramp was a crowd of pilots including the wing commander and my squadron commander. As soon as my foot touched the ground, they drenched me in champagne. Good thing too, as the bubbly masked the tears of joy and relief in my eyes. The throng pounded my back with congratulations and lofted me on their shoulders for a round of cheers.

"Move on to the club," Lieutenant Colonel Parker said to the crowd. "Let Ashe debrief. He'll join you later."

"Thanks, sir," I said, wiping champagne out of my eyes.

"What happened to your jet, son?" Parker asked, pointing to the broken radome and pieces of aluminum lodged in the aircraft's skin.

"Unbelievable," I said looking at the heavy damage I hadn't been able to see from the cockpit.

"Looks like you flew through that MiG," Parker said. "Could be 200 holes in your jet."

"I was pretty close," I said, continuing to survey the damage.

Parker walked to the empty bomb rack on the belly of the plane and pulled out a piece of aluminum the size of his hand. "And you brought back a souvenir. A piece of MiG. Guess you wanted to make sure you got credit for this kill."

I shook my head. "I was way too close. Just lucky I didn't hit the engine."

"Real lucky," Parker nodded. "But you downed a MiG and brought your F-105 back home. No one will second-guess that kind of success. The Thud's a tough bird, and it can be repaired. The important thing is that you're safe.

Hunter walked up followed by Lucky and Grover. He dropped his flying gear and gave me a bear hug that lifted me off of the ground.

"You're a MiG killer," Hunter yelled. "That's so hot I can't believe it."

Lucky pounded me on the back. "And a fine shot. It just disintegrated."

I looked at Hunter. "Thought you had him."

Hunter shook his head. "So did I. I misjudged the overtake. I fired a burst but never touched him."

"Ashe, why'd you take so long to shoot?" Lucky said.

I paused, not wanting to say that Hunter had lingered in my line of fire.

Hunter tapped himself on the chest. "Because of my screw up," he said. "If he'd fired earlier, he'd have shot me too. I was so hacked off when I missed the MiG that I forgot to break away. Ashe did the only thing he could have. Probably saved my life, shooting that MiG driver before he shot me. And that's the way I'll debrief it to Intelligence."

Chapter 26

Our fighter wing maintenance officer estimated that it would take two months to repair the holes in my jet not counting the lead time for a new engine and radome that would have to be flown in from the States. In the back of my mind, I thought I would bear some criticism for the damage. I didn't know how many tens of thousands of dollars it added up to, but it was going to be plenty. To my surprise, instead of being chastised, I was ordered to Saigon to receive the Silver Star for gallantry.

"They're always looking for someone to call a hero," Hunter muttered. "You're the first newly trained F-105 lieutenant to shoot down a MiG. It's your turn in the barrel."

I suppressed a laugh. "Hero is not a word you care for, is it?"

"It's a politician's word," Hunter said. "Get labeled a hero and you're no longer in combat, you're in public relations. It's a pain in the butt, going places, giving speeches. And I hate public relations people."

"More than intelligence officers?" I asked.

"I suppose it's a toss up," Hunter said. "One time a PR guy wanted me to say...my life is bound by danger, isolation, and the privilege of sacrifice."

"Very Hollywood."

"That's what I thought," Hunter said.

The wing commander cut orders for Hunter to travel with me to provide a buffer against both the brass and the press. For our

232

flight to Saigon, two F-105's were touched up with fresh camouflage paint and the equipment section produced new flight suits with new patches. Hunter and I were chauffeured to the planes in the back seat of the wing commander's staff car while a photographer rode shotgun. It seemed like the cameraman took a hundred pictures. He even clicked away in the car. It appeared as if he made an effort to include the wing commander in every shot.

Hunter led the flight and I flew on his wing to Tan Son Nhut Airport where we were met by a staff car and driven to Seventh Air Force Headquarters.

When we arrived, a major opened the car door then saluted. "The name's Dan Steinbeck, but you can call me 'News,'" the major said, thrusting his hand out to Hunter.

"Public relations," Hunter scowled, not shaking hands, pointing to me instead. "He's the one you want. I have things to do. I'll see you guys at the ceremony."

News took me to a cramped office crowded with four desks. Seeing no empty chair, I sat on the side of his desk and leaned against the wall.

"How'd you shoot down that MiG, Lieutenant?" News asked.

Using my hands, I demonstrated the tail chase. "We cruised up behind him, but we were going too fast. When my windscreen filled up with MiG, I pulled the trigger. It really blew the hell out of him. His jet disintegrated into a thousand pieces."

"I see," News said as he raised his eyebrows and looked over the top of his glasses. "Perhaps we could work on your statement. Don't think 'blew the hell out of him' will fly on stateside television."

I felt embarrassed. "I thought it was just you and me talking."

"I know," News said. "That's why I'm here. This place is crawling with reporters, and what they don't hear with their own ears, leaks out. You'll have to watch what you say and how you say it."

"We don't have reporters at Korat."

News ignored my remark and picked up a pen. "Let's see..."

"I don't want to talk to the press," I said. "What if I get shot down again? The Vietnamese would really be hacked off, and they'd have pictures."

"We don't get many MiG kills. When it happens, it's an event. General Markum likes to advertise success, and we've been very short of it lately. He's not going to pass on your MiG."

"So I have no choice?"

News frowned. "Not if you want to keep flying Markum's fighters. Unless you want to haul trash on a cargo plane, you'll go on TV and say something uplifting and patriotic."

"Like what?" I shot back.

"I'm writing suggested remarks," News said.

"Suggested?"

News nodded, "Highly suggested."

"How can you write about it? We haven't talked about the fight and you weren't there."

"I don't have to be there. I'm the writer," News said as he scribbled on a legal pad. "I write it. You say it, then...that's the way it happened. People tend to forget, the most important part of combat is how one records it for history."

I laughed. "And you probably think fighter pilots are arrogant."

"Yes," News replied, not looking up. "I do."

Later at the awards ceremony, I stood at attention while four-star General Levi Markum pinned a Silver Star on my flight suit. I turned to the cameras and paused while my eyes adjusted to the lights. News's remarks were crammed into the leg pocket of my flight suit. I had read them and decided News and I were fighting a different enemy.

"Thank you, General Markum," I said as Hunter sat in the audience grinning like a proud father. "I'd just like to take this opportunity to thank all the maintenance and support personnel for the commendable job they do everyday. They ensure we have the best combat-ready planes available to fly.

This medal, rightfully, should go to them. Now I'm looking forward to getting back to my base, flying combat with my squadron, and especially getting this war ended as soon as possible."

As the audience applauded, I said under my breath, "And I thank that poor dead MiG driver for his total commitment."

On the return trip, Hunter asked me to lead the two-ship flight while he flew formation on my wing. To have Hunter as a wingman, even for one flight, was as important to me as receiving the Silver Star. The day had been a wonderful acceptance and a validation of my abilities as a fighter pilot. My recollection of the cold, lonely rite of passage into the fighter pilot fraternity was now a fading, but not forgotten, memory.

Before landing, I led Hunter through a series of formation aerobatics. I was relaxed, having flown almost every day for months. I felt at the top of my form. The jet was part of me, an extension of my being. I knew its sounds and could tell if it was healthy just by listening. I knew I was healthy too, confident in my ability and no longer plagued by self-doubt and irrational fear. Route Pack Six missions still filled me with fear but that feeling wasn't irrational.

I kept glancing over at Hunter flying on my wing. Our two jets seemed to be welded together by an invisible thread of skill and precision. I felt the euphoria that comes from witnessing perfection. I knew I would always remember the sight of Hunter, tucked in close wing position, as we rolled inverted over the lush green landscape of the Thai countryside. As pre-briefed before takeoff, Hunter stayed in formation on my wing as we pitched out over Korat Base and turned onto final approach. We landed in close formation, my jet on the left side of the runway and Hunter's on the right.

The Saigon trip was a break in my routine and gave me time to reflect. I loved to fly supersonic planes but couldn't deny their role. I had become one with the power and esthetic beauty of a machine whose singular purpose was destruction. War seemed foreign to my nature but was an integral part of the choices I had made. I was embroiled in it. Since I was one with my plane, I, too, had become an instrument of destruction.

The mind is practiced at accommodation and reconciliation. I didn't like war, but if my country chose to be at war, I wanted to be a part or it. Finally I admitted that I liked flying supersonic jets in combat. But most importantly, I liked myself.

When we returned to combat the seemingly impossible happened. Hunter's hate for the Doumer Bridge and his appetite for air-to-air combat became even more focused. He stepped up his efforts to intimidate MiG pilots by flying through their traffic pattern and taunting them to come up and fight. It was much like he taunted me when I first met him. He put them off balance, confounded their expectations, and shaped their behavior to achieve not what they wanted but what he intended. He was well practiced at the cerebral aspects of air combat.

Hunter was short on words, especially compliments, letting his actions speak for him. As he renewed his effort to kill his fifth MiG, to my surprise, Hunter chose me to be his permanent wingman. In the fighter pilot pecking order, it was like sitting at the right hand of God.

Chapter 27

By November 8, 1966, my hatband had seventy-two marks on it. I had flown one hundred sixteen total missions, seventy-two counters into North Vietnam and forty-four non-counters into Laos. My monthly average was sixteen missions while spending twenty-six or twenty-seven days at Korat and four on R&R in Bangkok. Hunter had been my mentor for seven months when he requested I meet him alone at the squadron a few minutes before a mission.

"Lucky's going to move on and lead his own flight," Hunter said.

"Who's going to be our deputy lead?"

Hunter took a drag on his cigarette and stared at the wall, expelling the smoke in a long breath. Then he turned to me, looking me square in the eyes. "You, if you feel ready."

"Me?" I said, in disbelief. "I thought lieutenants had to be wingmen forever. There are plenty of captains and majors with more experience. Do you think I'm ready?"

"I think modesty is an unbecoming trait in a fighter pilot. You were Top Gun in your class. More important, you can think in the air. Although you don't always do it."

I rolled my eyes. "Thanks a bunch."

"And you have credentials. You're a bona fide MiG killer."

"I got that shot because I screwed up and fell behind. If I were a better wingman, I wouldn't have had the opportunity."

"You're a great wingman. I threw you out of formation with a hard turn close to the ground at full power."

I shook my head. "Hunter, I was just lucky and you know it. You put the MiG right in front of me."

He pointed at me with his cigarette. "You capitalized on the situation, the fog of war and all that. You reacted to an unforeseen event and used it to your advantage."

"But you set me up for the shot."

Hunter paused, shaking his head. "You give me too much credit. I tried to shoot that MiG with every ounce of my being, but I missed. I'm fortunate the MiG pilot didn't shoot me. He probably would have except you killed him first."

I looked up, wondering if I would ever get used to the idea that I had killed. Somehow it sounded worse when Hunter said it. "I happened to be in the right place at the right time."

"That's a load of rubbish," Hunter said. "Results come from skill, not luck. We've seen enough of your results to know they didn't happen by accident."

"Who's we?"

"Your squadron commander, the wing commander and General Markum at Seventh Air Force."

I raised my eyebrows. "Why all the horsepower?"

"The first of the new lieutenants in the F-105. You know the drill."

"That again. Do you think a lieutenant will ever rise above the status of green-ass in their eyes?"

Hunter shrugged, "Maybe when they have enough ice cubes in hell."

"But what do you think? You're the only one that really counts."

Hunter broke into a wide grin. "You're absolutely right. You start today."

I assumed the number three position in our flight as Hunter's deputy lead. Now, the flight line-up was Hunter as leader; Bart, a new lieutenant with only two combat missions, in the number two slot flying Hunter's wing; me in deputy lead position as number three; and Grover in the number four position flying on my wing.

Our target was another suspected truck park in the jungle.

Having been to the target before, the only new experience for me was having my own wingman to consider while staying in position on Hunter's lead element.

During the mission, I watched Bart fly Hunter's wing. I remembered Bart from Nellis F-105 training. He had arrived on base as I finished the program. I didn't know much about him and found myself less than curious. I could see everything I needed to know in his performance. I saw Bart's uncertainty during join-up and heavyweight refueling, as well as his tentative nature when performing difficult maneuvers for the first time under the critical eye of his peers.

When I looked at Bart I saw myself six months before, and finally realized why I emotionally distanced myself from him: waiting for him to prove himself before I extended my friendship. I saw myself not wanting to go through the agony of letting someone near, then losing a friend. I realized I was treating Bart in the remote way I had been treated when I was new. Remembering how I had felt, I vowed to change my attitude and befriend him after the mission.

Bart seemed a fairly solid aviator as we bombed the tree canopy where a truck park was reported to be. While recovering from the dive bomb pass, I expected to see Hunter turn south but he didn't. As I feared, he turned north toward Kep Airfield.

"Buick Flight, Top Cover," Hunter radioed.

As Hunter led our flight low, through the traffic pattern of Kep airfield, a lone MiG sat on the runway in takeoff position. Buick Flight had surprised the defenses, but the MiG pilot sat still, perhaps hoping American pilots would obey their own rules of engagement. Buick Flight was traveling 500 miles an hour in a jinking, arcing pattern around the airfield. The seconds seemed endless as we waited for the MiG pilot to make a move.

"Buick Three, come off of top cover and make a dry pass on that MiG," Hunter radioed. "Get in the dirt and let him know you're there."

Flak bursts crawled up the sky forming a wall as I followed

Hunter's instructions and arced around a base turn to final approach, setting up a high-speed pass from the MiG pilot's two o'clock position. I used an uncomfortably shallow dive for the attack, just steep enough to get my point across without giving the gunners too much of an opportunity. An instant before I reached firing range, the MiG pilot started to inch forward out of the path of my F-105's cannon.

I zoomed past, less than 30 feet over the MiG driver's canopy, wanting to intrude and invade by making certain the pilot heard the thunder of my engine reverberate through his cockpit. Grover dropped back far enough to pick up the fake pursuit as I pulled off the pass.

With Grover continuing the attack, the MiG kept rolling, picking up speed to stay ahead of Grover's gun sight. As Grover extended his speedbrakes and slowed down, his fake attack became more convincing. By the time Grover completed his pass, the MiG pilot was rolling fast and committed to takeoff. Hunter was stationed on his perch like a bird of prey, waiting for the right moment.

Hunter, anticipating the takeoff, positioned to fire as soon as the MiG broke ground. The rest of our flight maneuvered our jets to watch. Even the ground defenses appeared to ease as Hunter's dramatic attack played out against the sleek silver enemy fighter.

Hunter was closing fast. Too fast. Not again, I thought as I pushed my helmet back against the headrest, trying desperately to will the MiG into the air. The nose of the enemy jet rotated up tentatively, then, after a brief pause, came up slightly more.

Fire spewed from Hunter's cannon as it belched high explosive incendiary ammunition. A stream of fire traveled over a 1,000 miles an hour and hit the runway a few feet short of the MiG. The impact caused a fusillade of exploding metal and macadam that ricocheted at a low angle and ripped the landing gear from under the plane. With most of the weight off the landing gear, the MiG hung suspended by its wings for an instant until cannon fire walked up through the fuselage and ripped the jet in half behind the cockpit. The MiG shuddered, tumbled, and exploded, then slammed down on the runway, skidding a quarter of a mile, shedding parts and trailing burning fuel.

"Buick Lead, Three here," I radioed. "Confirmed splash."

Four hours later, North Vietnam lodged an official protest claiming American air pirates had attacked an aircraft on the ground. The most convincing evidence was the wreckage, which fell in a scattered trail on and beside the runway at Kep. It would be easy for the Vietnamese to claim the bird was on the ground when attacked. Even I had doubts, and I was there.

Analysis of Hunter's gun camera film seemed to show the weight of the MiG was off the main landing gear. But it was less clear if the wheels had left the ground.

"There's going to be hell to pay for this one," Wing Commander Fallbrook said after reviewing Hunter's film with our flight and his staff. "It looks like we're quibbling, and it appears that way because we are. This never should have happened. There's going to be a wave of political heat."

"I'll leave politics to the guys in Washington," Hunter said. "The way I see it, I'm the first Ace of the war. Out here, a kill's a kill, and I'm filing for official confirmation of my fifth MiG."

Fallbrook pointed his finger at Hunter. "We've been friends for twenty years, Hunter. But now you've made it too difficult to help you. Don't ever forget, you could be one of those guys in Washington soon."

Hunter scowled at Fallbrook for a long time then broke into a broad smile and said, "Like hell I will."

Chapter 28

I woke up at dawn and was halfway through my usual ritual in the latrine when I heard the word. Flying had been canceled because of bad weather in the target area. And it's not too shiny here, I thought as I heard the ominous rumbling of distant thunder.

It thought it would be a good day to write Jenny. I tried to do it but nothing came out. Somehow, thinking about Jenny meant thinking about her world, and her world and my world had grown, as they say, worlds apart. She was back in the States and it was increasingly painful for me to think about home.

It seems the only time anything interesting happens to me is in the heat of battle, but I can't write about any of that. When I'm not flying, days differ only by the degree of boredom. By 1000 hours, I hadn't written a word. Finally, I took a shower then walked to the Officer's Club where I saw Chaplain Johnson sitting alone.

Although I had been on base for several months, I didn't feel that I really knew Johnson, but I knew about him. To protect our pilots from harm, the chaplain often prayed until he achieved a profound, trance-like state. Since he felt personally responsible for the safety of all of our pilots at Korat, the chaplain carried a heavy burden.

That marked a difference between the chaplain and me. To me, combat was three hours of flying punctuated by thirty minutes of terror over North Vietnam. The rest of the day I had no worries. On weather days, like today, I spent time at the KABOOM. The O-Club was an interesting diversion, but I'd rather be flying. Chaplain Johnson, on the other hand, never had a minute of relief. He tended his flock night and day, rain or shine.

I stepped out of the club to get a Stars and Stripes newspaper. I was only gone for a minute. Before I returned, the chaplain's burden had become so heavy he fell off his barstool and nicked his head on the jukebox. Fortunately, Doc Morgan appeared on the scene and cleansed the abrasion with a bar towel and some good Russian vodka.

After a while, I followed Doc Morgan, Chaplain Johnson and several others to the dining room. They wanted an early lunch or late breakfast; I didn't know which. I wasn't hungry but decided to have coffee and stay for the conversation.

"Eat something," the flight surgeon said to me. "Besides, it's time for your medicine, everyone else has had theirs." The Doc picked up a large bottle from the table and rattled the pills in front of me. "Quinine should be taken with food. Doctor's orders."

"Okay Mom," I said. "It must be Sunday."

Doc nodded. "It's Sunday all right, and that means it's time for your medicine."

"You have any pills that don't taste disgusting?" I asked, then realized I may have sounded grumpier than I intended.

"If I did I'd take them myself," Doc said. "I know it's bitter, but quinine's a medical miracle; a crystalline alkaloid derived from cinchona bark and used to prevent malaria."

"Despite your technical, trivia for the day, definition", I said. "They still tastes like buffalo chips in a bottle."

"All you aviators do is complain. If you're not going to have lunch, then wash down a pill with toast and coffee.

"Was trivia a full credit course in medical school?"

"How did you know?" Doc said.

"You must have graduated with honors," I said.

Doc smiled. "Let's go to the bar and have a beer."

"Normally, I wouldn't drink this early," I replied. "But today's boring. I'll make an exception."

"Boring," Chaplain Johnson mumbled. For several minutes, he had been holding a sandwich in unsteady hands, suspended in front of his face as if studying an object from outer space. Finally, he put it back on his plate without taking a bite. Johnson looked pale and spoke slowly, separating and emphasizing each syllable. "Yes," he said. "To the bar."

"Chaplain," Doc said. "You mean it's almost noon and you haven't had a beer?"

"Maybe one," Johnson said as he glanced at Morgan and forced a grin. "Perhaps more than one."

After lunch we migrated to the bar and sat around a table by the window. Somewhere, between the dining room and the bar, the chaplain disappeared. The rest of us sat and talked. No one seemed particularly interested in drinking, but there wasn't any place to go in the drizzling rain. We debated whether to look for the chaplain, but decided, since he was drunk on Sunday morning, he was the Almighty's responsibility. Finally, our small group drifted off until only the flight surgeon and I remained.

"I guess I should feel sorry for the chaplain," I said. "But I don't. I can't remember the last time he held a service. Not that there's a place to hold one. If a flyer gets sick we can replace him on the schedule. We don't have another chaplain—or anyone else like a psychiatrist or counselor—to look after the mental health of our pilots. Without a chaplain, you're it, Morgan."

Doc shrugged. "Not me. All I can do for drinking or emotional problems is send them home. Which would ruin the career of a pilot or priest."

"I suppose Johnson ministers to some folks, but who knows who they are and how he does it."

"Feeling the need for a service?"

"Probably wouldn't go if he had one. But a chaplain should be helping instead of wallowing in his own grief."

Doc leaned back in his chair, "Hmmm."

"Forget it. I just need something to complain about. But I'm curious, what are you going to do with the chaplain? Send him home?"

Doc shrugged. "To be honest I'm going to put off a decision as long as possible. Permanently if I'm lucky. I'm not a psychiatrist. If they were put to a test, I'm not sure who I would label crazy."

"You're afraid of the decision."

"Not the decision. What I'm afraid of is the paperwork."

Morgan's radio blared out from its position on the bar, "Duty flight surgeon, this is the command post, how do you read?"

"Excuse me, Ashe. My brick is yelling at me," Doc said as he picked up his handheld radio. "Morgan here, go ahead."

"Roger, sir. We have a medical emergency inbound. Request you respond. There is a C-123 Provider that will land shortly."

"Morgan here. Copy. Anything else you can tell me?"

"Negative, sir. Just got the call. That's all we know. The plane is now seven miles out on final approach."

Morgan stood up. "Looks like I have to go to work. Ashe, if you're not busy, want to ride along?"

"Count me in. I was supposed to meet Sophia Loren for a beer, but it looks like she's a no show."

We rode in a small Toyota pickup truck that served as Doc Morgan's emergency response vehicle and were on the ramp before the Provider taxied in. Morgan drove onto the taxiway and followed the plane until they shutdown engines and lowered the rear cargo door. The back of the plane seemed empty until we hopped up on the ramp and walked inside.

An airman, the loadmaster I presumed, motioned toward a body sprawled on the floor in a pool of blood.

The stranger looked like a rugged outdoor type: fit but a tad stocky, short blond hair, pencil-thin mustache, and leathery skin that had seen too much sun for his years, which I guessed to be late thirties. He was dressed in civilian clothes—a hiking outfit that could have come from L.L.Bean, muted blue-plaid shirt, sand-colored safari jacket with matching pants, hat, and boots. As we moved closer, I noticed he clutched a high-powered rifle that was not like any military piece I had ever seen. It had a long-range sighting scope, the kind a serious hunter might use in the mountains or a sniper might carry.

Morgan opened his medical case and started to work. In a few seconds, a captain wearing pilot wings and lieutenant navigator came out of the front of the airplane and stood over the flight surgeon.

"What do you know about this guy?" Morgan asked.

"Nothing," the pilot said. "Except I think he's been shot. We don't know who he is, where he's from, or how it happened."

Morgan glanced up at the crewmember. "Well...how did he get in your plane?"

The navigator appeared nervous as he spoke. "We dropped off some cargo at a classified base in Laos. Just before we left, four men carried him in and dumped him on us."

Doc Morgan spoke without looking up. "Is this guy one of us? On our side?"

"We don't know," the pilot said. "His friends said don't bother looking for identification. They didn't talk much, but what they did say was in English. If that helps."

"What else did they tell you?" Morgan asked.

The pilot and navigator looked at each other shaking their heads, then the loadmaster spoke, "They said he needed medical attention."

"Well," Morgan replied, sarcastically. "I don't suppose they mentioned a priest."

"We asked who he was. Really we did," the pilot said. "They told us someone would come for him after he gets medical attention. We told them we couldn't take him unless we got approval. They pointed guns at us and said get him out of here, get him to a hospital. Can you believe it?"

"We don't have a hospital here," Morgan shot back as he began to work faster over his patient. "All we have is a little, nickel-dime clinic. This patient needs a first class operating facility. Why didn't you land at Nakhon Phanom? You probably had to fly right over it to get here."

"We didn't know. We brought him here because it was our next stop."

Morgan seemed increasingly frustrated and appeared to be taking it out on the crew. "This man is going to die. Why didn't you call somebody on the radio and ask where you should take him?"

The young navigator's eyes began to well up with tears as he stared at the blood-soaked stranger. "They told us not to tell anyone he was on-board. They had guns, big guns."

"One of them had hand grenades," the pilot added.

"They asked us where we were going, and I told them. I thought they wanted him here. They weren't the kind of people you have a long conversation with. We thought some of their friends might be waiting for us when we landed."

"How did the command post know I was supposed to meet the plane if you didn't tell anybody he was on-board?"

"About 20 miles out, I thought he was going to die on the spot," the loadmaster said.

"And he told me," the pilot added. "When I changed over to approach control frequency, I radioed that one of our crewmembers was injured. I didn't know what else to say. We didn't want to reveal anything classified over the radio. We didn't have a clue about this guy, or the others, but we knew they were somebody we couldn't ignore."

While we talked, the man began to go into convulsions. They were mild at first as if he were trying to cough up something, but as minutes passed, they gradually tapered off until he appeared to be in a peaceful sleep. The Doc tried to revive him as we silently stood watching.

When someone dies right in front of you, you don't need a medical degree to know he is gone. I felt his passing, life draining out of him, and could identify the moment it happened. I wondered what it was about the dead that informed the living. What triggered thoughts of one's own mortality and the fragile nature of life? The mind usually deceives us to our own advantage and protects us from emotional danger. But as we witness the dead or dying, it confronts us with the ultimate consequence of life.

Five minutes went by as Morgan struggled with the body, grunting with each compression on the crimson-soaked, plaid shirt. Sweat dripped from his face and blood smeared onto his hands and forearms. I wanted to tell Doc the stranger was dead, but I sensed he knew and continued out of his own need long after the afflictions of his patient had expired.

Finally, after more excruciating minutes through which the only one who didn't look tormented was dead, Morgan sighed in an exhausted and resigned way that conveyed he had lost the battle.

"He's gone," Doc said, pushing away from the body, sitting on the floor of the plane then leaning back on his hands, filling his lungs and uttering low moans. "Anyone here know how to pray?" he asked. "We could call the chaplain, but this guy's day has been tough enough without adding the padre to it."

"What do we do now?" I asked.

"Could you get my brick?" Morgan asked. "I need to radio the wing commander and have him take a look."

I started toward the truck to retrieve Morgan's radio, but the wing commander pulled up in his staff car before I could get it.

"What's happening?" Colonel Fallbrook asked.

"There's a dead man in the plane. He wasn't, but now he is. If you know what I mean."

The colonel bounded up the ramp and put his hand on his hips as we stood over the stranger. "Who is he?"

"*Was* he, sir," Morgan said. "I don't have a clue, and neither does the aircrew."

"Well. Where did he come from?" the colonel asked, looking frustrated.

Morgan slowly lifted his gaze towards the pilot.

"Long Tieng, Laos," the pilot said then flinched. "But sir,

I'm not supposed to say that. The place doesn't exist. If you know what I mean."

"Yes, I do know. But speak freely, we have a situation here," the colonel said, then pointed to the pilot. "Is this all of your crew? Three of you and no passengers that lived?"

"Yes, sir."

"Doc, I'm going to take the aircrew over to Intelligence so they can debrief this whole affair. Perhaps you can take care of our friend here. Take him to the mortuary if you're sure he's dead."

"We don't..." Morgan said, as he shook his head. "We don't actually have a mortuary, sir. But I know what to do with him."

"And his rifle," the colonel said, as he motioned to the loadmaster. "Clear the chamber and put it in the trunk of my car."

Doc Morgan slowly stood and made a gesture to brush the blood off of his flightsuit. Then he motioned to the aircrew members and me and said, "I need a little help carrying this guy out to the truck."

We all stood silently staring down at the dead man. He was only the second human that I'd seen die. No one moved. It was as if we were at a gravesite except that no one was speaking.

Morgan became impatient, "Let's haul this guy. We can't stand here forever."

As we drove across base, I sat at an angle on the passenger side of the pickup, looking over my shoulder at the body in back. Doc Morgan had placed a blanket over him, but he jiggled in a macabre way when we turned a corner or hit a bump. As I stared, chills went up my spine.

"You don't have to watch him," Morgan said. "He's not going anywhere."

"I know, but it's weird. You're probably used to seeing dead bodies, but I'm not."

"It's strange for me too," Morgan said, as he glanced over his shoulder. "This place is not like working in a hospital. A flight surgeon for fighter pilots has a limited practice. Pilots don't get sick often and when they do they lie about it to keep flying. This is the first death I've witnessed at Korat, and I've been here almost a year."

"But we lose a lot of pilots."

"I know," Morgan nodded. "But they don't come back to see me. They fly away and never return. I don't even see the injured. At least, I don't see them first, since they land at Nakhon Phanom or some other base close to the border. Of course, if injured bad enough, they go straight to the Philippines or back to the States."

"They don't come back," I said as I thought about that for a while. "I don't know whether that's bad or good."

"A mixed blessing, I think," Morgan said, glancing toward me without making eye contact. "My father was a B-17 co-pilot in the big war in Europe. A member of the One Hundredth Bomb Group during the time when they lost half of their crews and earned the nickname Bloody Hundredth. They had big-time losses, like six planes with ten crewmembers each on one raid against Schweinfurt. He told me what it was like for them, seeing the injured come back and carrying dead crewmembers off the planes."

"I know it happened, but it's hard for me to imagine," I said.

Doc grimaced. "Dad told me it was especially hard when a whole crew disappeared. Someone might see them get shot out of the sky, or see them descending, smoking, or burning. Then not a trace would make it back to home base. That was the worst, he said, the not knowing, having nothing left to grieve. My father survived but returned home with deep, unshakable feelings of loss. For the rest of his life, it affected his relationships. He was reluctant to make friends and silently mourned for the loss of people and loss of life's meaning."

"He told you all that?"

"No. I often wished he could have talked about it more, but he kept a lot inside. I had to figure it out for myself. I didn't understand until after he was gone and then, not completely until I came here and witnessed what combat does to people. It seems to be a universal experience of war."

"Are you trying to tell me something?"

He glanced over at me. "Perhaps."

At the hospital, we were met by two medical corpsmen and turned the body over to them. While one of the corpsmen wiped blood off the seat of the pickup, Morgan and I stood and looked off in the distance. I sensed that neither of us knew how to feel about what had happened. The blood on Morgan's flightsuit gave me the willies. It was a chilling reminder of the stain the young soldier's death had left on me.

"You probably want to get cleaned up," I said. "And I've got some on my hands too."

Morgan nodded without speaking.

I went to Doc Morgan's hooch and waited while he showered and changed. Then he waited at my hooch while I did the same. For the rest of the afternoon, we spent silent time together. Intuitively, I knew that neither of us wanted to be alone. I thought it comforting to be with someone who had shared the experience and sensed Morgan could understand what I was feeling without much explanation.

As the rain passed and the sun hung low in the sky, we dropped off the truck at the motor pool and asked them to give it a thorough wash inside and out. Then, we walked slowly, as one walks when there is no place to go, until we were in front of the KABOOM.

Morgan nodded toward the bar. "Let's go talk to Jack Daniels," he said.

Chapter 29

Half awake, I opened one eye as the silhouette of someone appeared over my bunk. I recognized the voice.

"Wake up, Shooter," Hunter said.

"Oh, no," I answered, pulling the pillow over my head. "What time is it?"

"Time to get up."

I rubbed my eyes. "It's still dark. We don't brief until ten."

"Our target's been changed."

I propped myself up on one elbow. "Anything worth getting up for?"

Hunter nodded then whispered, "How about a sixteen ship raid on the Doumer Bridge?"

"You're kidding," I said, flopping back on the bunk. "Been there, done that."

"I knew you'd be excited," Hunter whispered. "Now get your posterior out of bed."

"You're talking about the big bridge on the north side of Hanoi?"

"Exactly."

"Thought so. Haven't we hit that place four or five times already?"

"Hit is not technically correct." Hunter replied. "Tried to hit is the phrase you're looking for."

"Didn't we walk home once?"

"Yup," Hunter said. "Of course, if you don't want to go, we can..."

"Are they going to shoot at us?" I said. "Because if they're not going to shoot at us, I don't want to bother."

"I promise they'll shoot at you."

"Okay then, I'm in. You know how I hate indifference in an enemy."

Hunter patted me on the shoulder. "Better wake up Bart and have him work with you on a mission plan. This is his tenth mission. It'll be a good experience for him. I'll see you later at the squadron."

"You want to see the plan before we fill out the mission cards?"

Hunter let out a low groan. "Don't wait for me. Your plan will be fine. I might even learn something."

"You know, Hunter, just once I'd like to destroy a target and not have to go back."

Hunter nodded, "Yeah, I know. It's not worth losing someone if we have to go again."

"That bridge has cost us six so far."

"Maybe more. I lost count."

I sat up on one elbow and watched Hunter's shadowy figure disappear out the door. It's possible he always had more faith in me than I had in myself. I showered and dressed before waking up Bart, wanting some peaceful time for target study before he joined me and started asking questions.

At the squadron, I gulped coffee and tried to clear my head as I leaned over a mission-planning table and studied photos of the bridge. From an intelligence folder, I pulled out a booklet containing design specifications. The source was listed as the original engineering drawings Intelligence had acquired from the French.

The bridge was 5,532 feet long and 38 feet wide, with a 3-meter railroad down the center and a 10-foot wide road on either side. Doumer was the longest bridge in Vietnam by far. I was familiar with the numbers. There were not many things in Vietnam I could use to judge distances and this landmark was a valuable tool. The bridge was a few feet longer than a statute mile, and I had often used it to estimate distance in the Hanoi area.

Bart walked in, put his coffee cup on the planning table, and looked at the map with a sleepy stare. "Which way we going in?"

I traced my finger east from Korat to the Gulf of Tonkin. "In by water," I said, tapping on an oval shaped, refueling track drawn 40 miles off the coast of North Vietnam. "After refueling we'll cross the coast 10 miles north of Haiphong Harbor then set a direct course to the bridge. Egress will be west along the Red River until we clear the city then turn south just short of Son Tay. Post- strike refueling will be over Laos."

"It's the grand tour," Bart said. "How long is the whole enchilada?"

I made a nervous clicking sound with the side of my mouth. "Almost four hours."

"And what if we don't find the tanker over all that water?" Bart asked.

"It is strange," I smiled, knowing exactly how Bart felt. "We're flying into one of the most heavily defended targets in history, and what we worry about most is refueling."

Bart looked up. "If the bad guys shoot me down, my folks will get a nice letter saying I'm a brave patriot, whether it's true or not. But if I eject over water because I can't refuel, everyone will know I'm a bonehead."

At 0755 hours, sixteen pilots filed into the main briefing room and sprawled over the theater style seats. Colonel Parker, today's mission leader, waited patiently until Lucky fed Roscoe a sausage and got him comfortably curled up in the Wing Commander's seat. Lucky, true to form, wiped his hand on Roscoe's paw.

Finally at the end, after the intelligence, weather, and operations briefings, Parker returned to the podium with late breaking news. "We have some new players near our target today. Intelligence has a report that new MiG-21s have arrived at Kep Airfield. So be careful and keep your eyes peeled. They think the MiGs flew in from China, since Intelligence didn't see the usual evidence of aircraft off-loading from Soviet ships at Haiphong Harbor. Overnight, four new MiG-21s just showed up."

The news of the fresh MiGs went through the room like a flash. Lucky's eyes shot to Roscoe whose ears perked up. Hunter looked over at me and winked. I swore Hunter would go to Kep and look for himself. I waited for him to create some excuse for us to fly over the airfield, but Hunter didn't bring up the subject of MiGs in our individual flight briefing.

Later that morning, our four flights of four jets each trailed across the Gulf of Tonkin with one mile spacing between flights. I didn't care for my position in the last wave. The first wave would wake up the anti-aircraft defenses, the second and third would get them fighting mad. Then our flight composed of Hunter, Bart, Ashe, and Grover would fly through the gunners' gauntlet.

Bart had been nervous all day. I had watched him closely, seeing a less experienced version of myself early in my combat tour. It would take several more missions before he had enough heavyweight refueling experience to feel completely confident over water.

It always surprised me how refueling tankers appeared so huge on the ground but so small against the wide expanse of the Gulf of Tonkin. As we searched for our KC-135, I had a lonely feeling in my gut. I still got butterflies although I had refueled so many times I couldn't remember. Low clouds obscured the shoreline and only the sea was visible.

It was a stark reality that one engine supported my world. If it quit, there was no back up except to parachute into the ocean and hope for rescue. Staring down I reflected on rescue's task of finding a pilot in the wide expanse of water. It would be like trying to locate a coconut bobbing in the ocean.

After refueling, Bart's aircraft control seemed to smooth out. I felt more comfortable too. At least now we had enough fuel onboard to make it back into friendly territory.

But considering the rest of my laundry list of desperate choices, I preferred ejecting over hostile territory to the risk of drowning at sea.

The line of coastal clouds stopped short of Haiphong Harbor. The docks, stacked high with weapons and supplies, were clearly visible from our flight altitude. The port facility would be a great target, but the Rules of Engagement put it off limits. It was crazy. The ROE supported Washington's policy of gradual escalation and wouldn't allow a strike that would endanger a Soviet ship. But Soviet ships were constantly off-loading weapons at Haiphong.

Hunter followed the gaggle of planes as they arced from a northerly to a westerly heading. The enemy gunners didn't seem surprised and began hammering away at the first for-mation of planes. In response, each flight took up a slightly different heading, tracking to their initial roll-in points for individual dive bomb runs on the target. The tactic gave the gunners more targets to shoot but less time to concentrate their forces.

The first flight made a diving attack and four loads of bombs bracketed the bridge, detonating in the water. Each plane dropped 6 bombs, sequenced to hit 75 feet apart. A string of 6 bombs covered 450 feet from the first bomb to the last. It was great coverage for a target on the ground but not for an elevated bridge only 38 feet wide. To be effective, a bomb had to hit the roadway or superstructure of the bridge. The second and third flights dived at the target with the same result. By the time we approached, 12 jets had expended 72 bombs on the target and all they had accomplished was get-ting the bridge wet.

I was afraid I knew what Hunter was thinking and turned my eyes toward Bart who was riveted in formation on Hunter's wing. I wanted to tell Bart to be careful. Don't follow Hunter too closely in the dive attack. It was a caution I couldn't share over the radio so I shook my head thinking that Bart was in danger on this mission.

Hunter pointed his plane at the ground. Bart was in position 100 feet to the right and slightly behind him. I followed 2,000 feet in trail with Grover hanging in formation on my left. I knew, at this point in the attack, Bart was aligning the bridge in his bombsight and not focused on Hunter. I held my breath as Hunter and Bart approached the planned bomb release altitude of 4,500 feet.

Bart's bombs rippled off the belly of his jet in a smooth string, but Hunter didn't release. As I feared, Hunter pressed the attack trying for a more accurate delivery. Bart wouldn't be expecting this. I groaned as Bart started a recovery maneuver then stopped and continued in formation with Hunter as he streaked towards the ground.

Bart was in perfect formation, but his bombs were loose in the formation as well. Hunter kept pressing the dive toward the target. Each passing millisecond seemed an eternity. Hunter was leading Bart down into the bomb blast fragmentation envelope where their own weapons could kill them. As Hunter pickled off his bombs, the two jets rotated into a brutal recovery maneuver. Almost immediately one of Hunter's bombs impacted a span of the bridge. A heartbeat later two of Bart's bombs hit the adjoining span.

After Grover and I released our bombs, I glanced back to assess the damage. Our weapons went into the plume of debris left by Hunter and Bart. Clearly they had each hit a span of the bridge. Both Grover and I could claim an assist, but the honors belonged to Hunter and Bart.

Bart had two direct hits and released at a safe altitude. Hunter had pressed the attack, placing both his and his wingman's lives at risk and got one hit. If Bart had missed, as Hunter probably expected he would, Hunter's effort might have seemed worthwhile. Now it just appeared foolish. I didn't care if Hunter risked himself, but his wingman? And, not to put too fine a point on it, Hunter had risked a fine airplane.

Hunter turned west and departed the bridge as his voice boomed over the radio. "Nash Three, fly top cover."

My heart sank. Hunter was going after the MiG-21s. Hunter loved to chase MiGs almost as much as he hated the Doumer Bridge. I started a climb by bleeding off airspeed from the dive bomb pass. Leveling off at 10,000 feet, I tracked Hunter and Bart as they rooted around at tree top level working their way toward Kep Airfield. Then Hunter wagged his wings to signal Bart to tighten up the formation. With Bart flying wingtip-to-wingtip, Hunter flew an air show pass over the enemy runway.

I was furious. "Why don't you sell tickets," I yelled, as my voice was drowned out by cockpit noise.

Flak was getting heavy around Grover and me. The larger caliber guns were shooting at us because Hunter's element was too low for the gunners to be effective. I watched as Hunter turned and started back toward the airfield with Bart in formation. I stared in disbelief as they crossed the approach end of the runway and flew to the center of the field.

"I'm hit," Bart screamed over the radio.

A wisp of black smoke streamed from Bart's plane then blossomed into a heavy trail. A moment later flames lapped from the back of his jet.

"Nash Two," Hunter radioed. "You're on fire, eject, eject, eject."

My eyes were fixed on Bart. I knew I should scan the sky for MiGs, but I couldn't. Bart appeared to be pulling up, perhaps climbing to gain separation from the ground and to bleed off airspeed for a safe ejection. Bart's plane slowed then hung in the sky.

I flinched as his canopy came off and tumbled back over the tail. I counted to three as the seat catapulted out of the cockpit. The butt thruster blew Bart away from the seat and his parachute deployed. I recalled my own ejection and the pounding pain as I ricocheted through the limbs of a tree. Fortunately, Bart was over open terrain. Unfortunately, he was very close to the Kep MiG base.

Bart's parachute locator beacon, operating on Guard Emergency Channel, sent out its irritating beeping tones to all friendly aircraft. Each modulated chirp painfully reminded that Bart was behind enemy lines and hopelessly close to an enemy base. I flipped a switch and cut off Guard Channel then remembered Bart's only way to communicate was on that frequency. I switched it back on and lived with the noise. In a few seconds, the beeper ended. It was a good sign. Bart must have remembered to turn off his parachute beeper so he could transmit voice on his survival radio.

"Nash Lead, this is Nash Two," Bart radioed.

"Nash Two, this is Nash Leader on Guard Channel. We have a visual on your position. Say your condition?"

"I think I'm okay," Bart radioed. "But I can hear gunfire. Lots of gunfire."

"Nash Two, Lead, here. Unstrap your parachute and run away from it. Do you understand?"

"Roger, Two understands."

A truck began to move down a road from the airbase toward Bart. Hunter gracefully maneuvered his jet into an arcing turn and strafed it with his 20-millimeter cannon. The truck crashed off the side of the road and exploded into flames.

"Nash Lead, this is Two. People are coming."

"Two, this is Lead. Find a place to hide."

"I see them coming. Shooting. No place to hide."

I blinked as I heard gunfire in the background of Bart's radio transmission. Then I saw figures moving toward Bart in groups of twos and threes.

"No place to go. They're going to get me."

I felt helpless. I could see Bart, but there was nothing any of us could do.

"Nash Flight, this is Lead. I'm going to strafe ...m."

I panicked. Hunter's transmission was broken; did he say him or them? Either way it was a bad idea. In my head, I knew I had to get Hunter away from Bart and Kep airfield before we lost someone else.

Even though I knew it was senseless for us to stay, my heart ached to help Bart. My mind, stunned into indecision, was trying to separate the emotion of the moment from the sensibility of the longer view. There wasn't anything we could do to improve Bart's position in the slightest. All we had were bullets, and any way we used them would make his fate worse.

I looked at my fuel gauge and lied. "Nash Lead, Three is bingo fuel."

Hunter answered with an irritated voice. "Understand, Nash Three is bingo?"

"That's affirmative. Let's return to base. There's nothing we can do here."

"Nash Lead, roger," Hunter said, in a voice filled with wounded resignation. "Nash Flight, head south. Let's stay off the radio so Nash Two can transmit if he's able."

I had a lonely sinking feeling as we finally accepted the fact we had to leave Bart. I had lied to Hunter. A small lie since I had a few more minutes of fuel. But I was afraid Hunter would endanger the rest of the flight and not change Bart's fate one whit. My whole being was torn between rational and emotional feelings. I felt an intense sense of loss. I couldn't shake the feeling that I was abandoning a flight member although clearly I had no choice. From my position north of Bart, I maneuvered to swoop down over him on my way to join up with Hunter.

A hiss came over the Guard Channel, and I sensed Bart was holding down the transmit button on his hand-held survival radio.

"They're almost here," Bart whispered over the radio. Then a shot rang out and Bart screamed. "I'm hit in the leg. I'm shot. They're on me. No, don't hit me. No, they're killing me!"

As I approached the bloodbath at 100 feet and 450 knots, I saw figures crowding around Bart and savagely pounding him with butt of their rifles. Bart's radio conveyed his tortured response to the impact of every blow. But in the background of Bart's transmission, when not blocked out by his screams, I heard the sound of my F-105 passing over him.

Another shot cracked. Then excited voices in a foreign

language. Then the transmission ended. I knew in my heart, Bart had held down the transmitter button until life had drained out of him.

Chapter 30

As our three remaining members of Nash Flight droned across Laos in silence, my emotions caromed between melancholy and anger. I had always tried to understand Hunter, but it was becoming more difficult. Clearly I blamed him for Bart's death. No target or MiG was worth it.

The truth is I also blamed myself. I felt Hunter was taking too many risks, and I should have spoken out long before Bart joined our flight. Instead, I kept the silence of a loyal lieutenant. It was hard to know what was right. Even now, after Bart's loss, I was unsure. In combat, there's a delicate balance between aggression and caution. Too much or too little of either can cost lives.

Hunter led our flight to the post-strike tanker. Not a word had been spoken since we left Bart's pummeled body on that blood-soaked grassy knoll in North Vietnam. As I refueled, tears streamed down my cheeks. The intense pain felt like a fire welling up in my gut. Even though I had sworn to befriend Bart, I didn't do it and held our friendship at arm's length. Had I allowed myself to get closer to him, the grief would have been unbearable.

What a strange relationship I'd created, sharing trust and a brotherly love in the air, but on the ground, sculpting an elaborate bulwark of emotional distance to guard against loss. A curious way to be a friend, I thought, identifying my feelings as both bond and barrier. I had staked out a buffer zone around my heart.

After landing, I quickly shut down the engine, left my flight gear, and started walking down the ramp toward Hunter's jet. The walk turned into a run. Finally, I scrambled up the ladder to Hunter's cockpit.

"Damn you," I yelled, trying to control my emotion but feeling tears well up in my eyes. "Why did you drag the kid across that airfield?"

Hunter placed his helmet on the canopy rail like a saddle and stared straight ahead.

"You killed him," I shouted. "Just as sure as if you shot him yourself."

Hunter scowled, not moving.

"Damn you, say something."

"I suggest we take this up in debriefing," Hunter said, with an indifferent tone as he unstrapped and stood up in the cockpit. "Now, if you'll get off my ladder."

I didn't budge. "Talk to me, you SOB."

Hunter's eyes flared then immediately relaxed. He shook his head and spoke in a soft but firm voice. "We don't have time for this. We have to go to Intelligence and pinpoint where Bart went down."

"He's dead. I saw it."

"You didn't see anything for sure," Hunter said, brushing his hand out to wave me down off the ladder.

"To hell I didn't. I heard it too."

"You don't know he's dead. Did you take his pulse while you flew over at 500 knots?"

After a few moments, I backed down the ladder and stood on the ramp glaring at him.

As Hunter stepped off the bottom rung, my anger flared again. "I can't believe you got Bart shot down. You put the kid at risk. Too much risk."

Hunter turned toward me and his eyes narrowed. "I'm sick of your greenhorn emotion. We're all at risk here. Risk is the name of the game. I've been shot down twice and you once. You've been in my flight for 82 missions and it's the first time we've lost anyone. Do you know how many F-105s have been lost in combat?"

I glared at him. "You know as well as I do. It's been ninety-eight jets so far this year. Bart was ninety-nine."

Hunter nodded. "And it's only the second week in November. On average, nine a month, one every three days, or to be precise one every eighty hours. But who's counting, right? Have you forgotten that in the seven months I've led the flight, this is our first loss? Pilots die in combat. This is what it feels like to see it, to experience it in your own flight. Maybe next time, and there will be a next time, you'll act like you've been there before."

I flinched. "You're a hard-hearted..." I said, then immediately regretted starting to blurt out the epithet. Hunter had lost many friends. For him, it must be one more loss in a long series. Perhaps that explained why he kept his distance and put up walls to the world.

Hunter gave me a pained look. "I know you hurt inside, but you can't bring him back. Instead of wasting your energy hating me, why don't you do something useful?"

"Like what?"

"Write a letter to his wife."

My feelings of anger resolved into an embarrassing realization. I had isolated myself so completely from Bart that I hadn't asked the simple questions of friendly conversation. "I didn't know he had a wife."

"Well, he does," Hunter shot back.

I felt defensive. "Why me? You're his flight commander."

"You wouldn't want an unfeeling SOB like me writing to his wife, would you?"

A minute ago I didn't think I could feel worse, but now I did. "I don't know what to write."

Hunter took a deep breath and spoke in a whisper. "Son, at a time like this, no one knows what to write. Look deep into your heart and follow what you find there."

I clutched the back of my neck as a muscle spasm pulsed through my shoulder.

"We aren't on the flying schedule tomorrow," Hunter said. "Have a draft to me before lunch."

"Can't I have a couple of days?"

"Absolutely not. She'll receive official notification in a few hours. Your letter will be the only contact from someone on the scene. And another thing, it's better to finish before you fly again. While it's fresh in your mind."

I looked up. "Believe me. It will always be a vivid memory."

"Perhaps, but it could happen again tomorrow."

"What could happen?"

"There could be another letter to write, or it could happen to us, then who would write?"

I nodded, still rubbing the pain throbbing in my neck.

"Remember, regardless of what you think you saw, we don't know he's dead. His status is missing in action."

I spent most of the night awake, trying to compose a letter. An hour before it was due to Hunter, I looked at the two pages I'd created and judged them pitifully unfeeling and inadequate. Worse, I didn't know how to fix it.

Hunter sighed as he read the letter. "Thanks, I'll take it from here." Shaking his head, he turned and started to walk away.

"I'm sorry," I said.

Hunter stopped but didn't turn around.

"I apologize...it's harder...I mean...I know it's not enough..."

Hunter turned and looked at me. Once again I saw in his face an affirmation and empathy that I had always sought from my father.

"I know," Hunter said. "The first time is always the toughest. The first letter...the first guy that takes off with you and doesn't come back."

I felt emotion stirring in my gut then welling up in my eyes. I didn't want to cry in front of Hunter and fought to hold back the tears.

Hunter looked away.

"I thought about what you said. I know other flight leaders have lost plenty of wingmen. Sometimes whole flights have been wiped out. And I'm complaining because we lost one in eighty missions. Hunter, I realize we've been lucky."

Hunter stiffened. "Actually, luck has very little to do with it."

I nodded. "I realize that, too. I'm thankful for your experience, and, yesterday...about what I said..."

Hunter put his hand on my shoulder. "Forget it. We lost one. Like I said, the first time is always the toughest."

The past twenty-four hours had left me emotionally exhausted, and I couldn't stomach the thought of lunch. After a long, cold shower, I stretched out on a grass mat in front of the hootch. Lying on my stomach in the sun, I read a Stars and Stripes article about a B-52 raid on Mu Gia pass. Lately our government had been more public about our presence in Thailand and more open about selected bombing missions. But the articles often struck me as overwritten and more like public relations pieces than battlefield accounts.

Reportedly the attack had caused huge landslides, which permanently closed the road in the pass. Who are they kidding? Even if they did close the road, nothing is permanent here. I had flown through the sloping, jungle-covered hills of Mu Gia and looked at the narrow dirt road winding through the pass. The reporter made the road sound like a busy highway with monumental cliffs on each side.

The B-52s were doing a great job on a lot of targets but I felt angry. Why didn't they write about the heavy bomber's real successes instead of making things up? PR had reached a new level of incredibility. As I read, a shadow eclipsed my newspaper.

"Are you Lieutenant Samuel Wilcox?"

I turned toward the blinding sun to see the black and bright outline of a man in civilian clothes. "You can call me Ashe."

"I'm Agent Bob Abbot," he said hunching down, flashing an Office of Special Investigations identification card. "I'd like to ask you a few questions."

I recoiled with a noticeable twinge. Instantly I suspected this was about Hunter. But why OSI?

"You're Lieutenant Colonel Erasmus Snow's wingman, aren't you?"

I smiled. "You can call him Hunter. In fact, you'd better call him Hunter if he's around."

"So I hear. You his wingman?"

"Sometimes."

"Were you flying on his wing when he attacked that MiG at Kep?"

"Can't recall," I said, remembering how Hunter responded to the OSI after our shootdown.

"What do you mean, you can't recall?" Abbot shot back.

I laughed. "I can't recall hearing your security clearance. For all I know, you're a spy."

"I can assure you, I'm cleared."

"The only thing I'm certain about, where you're concerned, is that I'm trying to get a tan and you're blocking my sun."

"Lieutenant, I'm just trying to do my job," Abbot said, without hiding his indignation. "We can do this easy or we can do it hard. You'll have to talk to me sooner or later."

"Later would be perfect. Much later."

"Why not now?"

"Everything about our mission is classified," I said, then pointed to the newspaper. "Probably so they can print these lies without getting contradicted."

"What lies?"

"Like this B-52 Mu Gia Pass thing. Landslides. Who thinks up this bull?"

"I can assure you I do not, Lieutenant," Abbot said, wearing his impatience like a badge.

I paused. "I can't just talk to you out of the clear blue. Someone has to tell me you have a need to know."

"You mean they haven't?" Abbot said, putting his face down close enough that I could see frustration in his eyes.

"Nope. Not a word."

Abbot looked around, tight-jawed. "There's been a screw-up. You were supposed to know I was coming. I suggest you contact your commander," Abbot said, as he turned and walked away.

I went back in the hootch, put on a flight suit and found Hunter.

"Do you know the OSI is asking questions?"

"Yup," Hunter said, as he lit a cigarette.

"So, what's the skinny?"

"It's about the MiG."

"I figured that. But why the OSI?"

"It's turned into an international incident. Politicians want an independent look. Someone outside the services."

"But I thought..."

"You're right," Hunter interrupted. "The OSI is a service agency, but it's as close as they could come to independence on short notice."

"So what's the big deal? Why can't they award you the kill and pin a fifth Silver Star on your chest? Last time I heard, we're supposed to kill MiGs."

Hunter sighed. "It's all politics. The Rules of Engagement stink. They send us to war, then give us ROE that make us criminals unless we fight with one hand tied behind our back."

"So, what happens next?"

"If they decide the MiG was in the air, I'll be the first Ace of this war."

"And if..."

"Then I'll be the first bad example of the war. Could be a court martial."

I felt flustered. "The MiG was airborne, at least technically. The nosewheel was off the ground. The wings were holding it up, even if the main wheels were still touching the runway. The pilot's intent was to fly, not drive down the runway."

Hunter took a long drag on his cigarette. "Nice try. I appreciate your support, but even I have to admit it could have been either way. I had too much closure rate again. Seems to be my habit where MiGs are concerned."

"Yeah," I reflected. "A guy could make a career out of picking off your leftovers. I can still picture you blowing past that MiG faster than the speed of heat. That scene is etched in my memory, and I'll bet the MiG driver won't forget it either."

"Too bad you weren't behind me to get this one. I would have gladly pulled off and let you have him."

"You had to fire. What else could you do?"

Hunter shrugged. "They'll say I should have broken off and positioned for a re-attack."

"Sure," I said. "They can second guess. It's easy to do from a desk in Washington. How much do they get shot at in the nation's capital?"

"Probably more than you would imagine," Hunter reflected. "And with more sophisticated weapons. That's supposed to be my next assignment."

"What?" I was startled. "I heard the wing commander say something about Washington, but I thought he was kidding. You have an assignment?"

"I've been selected for War College with a follow-on stint at the Pentagon."

"When do you go?"

"The assignment came months ago, but I got rid of it, I thought. Now it's lingering like a fart in a pressure suit."

"So, when will you go?"

Hunter laughed. "Never, if I can keep extending here."

"And if you can't."

"Combat is what I'm born to do. Not go to War College or the five-sided puzzle palace. That would be the end. The bitter, draconian end. I guarantee they'll never take me alive."

I sat shaking my head. "Hunter, what's going to happen to you?"

He looked grim. "They're right you know. I could have disengaged and re-attacked. I had the speed built up and the MiG didn't."

"What about exposure time?" I asked. "They were shooting like hell."

"Yeah," Hunter said. "There're two sides to every story. But it's out of my hands now. It's going to turn into a political frog-wrestle and nothing will seem true or make any sense. No matter how I try to dodge this bullet, I'm going to wind up right in the center of the Pentagon's gunsight."

Chapter 31

If the OSI investigation bothered Hunter, he didn't show the slightest trace. He approached the matter with his usual calm resignation. I was convinced his heartbeat wouldn't show up on an electrocardiograph if he didn't want it to.

I sensed Hunter wouldn't speak on his own behalf. If anything were to be done to help him, I would have to do it myself. Julia had raised this very issue, saying she felt things for Hunter when he couldn't or wouldn't feel them for himself. I was beginning to understand what she meant. What I was feeling—and Hunter was not—was urgency.

Curiosity created a burn I had to extinguish. If the higher-ups were concerned enough to launch an investigation, it could affect target assignments for Hunter and our flight, possibly even grounding us until after the inquiry.

The OSI was like a sponge, taking but giving nothing back. There was nowhere I could go to get information. Or was there? Perhaps I could get an advanced look at tomorrow's schedule, and that might give me a hint of what to expect.

Stopping by the wing operations room, I drank coffee and made small talk. Not wanting to appear obvious, I leafed though a copy of the ROE manual as if I'd come to study. After a while, bored with the charade, I fished around in my flight suit pocket for the letter from Jenny I had picked up at the post office but hadn't read.

The envelope was noticeably thinner than others I'd

received earlier in my tour, when she wrote page after page describing the details of her day. Clearly she was writing less, and less often. Who could blame her? The first few months I tried to hold up my end and write eloquent and lengthy passages. As my combat tour wore on with unrelenting carnage and loss, it became more difficult to describe my day.

To protect my spirit, I had hollowed out a deep grave and interred the corpse of my emotions. But in the process, I had buried the memories I cherished and covered over all traces of enthusiasm, spontaneity, and love. Perhaps I thought someday I could unearth my soul and revive it, and become whole again.

All my days were the same: plan, fly, toast at the bar to whoever didn't come back, celebrate at the bar if everyone did return, and welcome, but not too warmly, the new replacements.

In my disconnected state, I didn't feel love for those I should love, nor did I hate the enemy. Nothing that was normal in life moved me to laughter or tears. I was wounded, and the instrument of my injury was meaningless loss. Finally, I returned Jenny's letter to my pocket without reading it.

In spite of several cups of coffee, I fell asleep in the chair until jolted awake by the splat of a thick operations order dropped in my lap.

"You're probably waiting for this," the operations duty officer said with a smile. "You're on a sixteen-ship raid to the Than Hoa bridge. Tomorrow is going to be a doozy,"

The heavily defended bridge, called the Dragon's Jaw by the Vietnamese, was located about seventy miles south of Hanoi. The Viet Minh had destroyed the original French-built structure in 1945; they simply loaded two locomotives with explosives and ran them together in the center of the bridge. The rebuilt structure, completed in 1964 with help from Chinese engineers, had two steel spans which were solidly anchored, in hills on each side and to a massive concrete pier in the middle. Its reinforced construction made the bridge akin to attacking solid rock. I had bombed the target twice before but only in a four-ship flight. A sixteen-ship raid presented a different challenge. We would lose the element of surprise and probably lose one of the sixteen pilots.

I had mixed emotions. Our flight was still being scheduled, that was good news, but Hunter had assigned Bart's replacement as my wingman. Our target was too tough for a new pilot's initial combat mission, but we were short of pilots and short of easy missions for training.

I didn't think I was ready to check out a new guy. It seemed as though Hunter trusted me, but I had doubts about why I was selected; perhaps he didn't have another choice. I always did this. Wanting trust and respect, then second-guessing when I got it. Perhaps I wanted the trust that goes with responsibility but didn't want to be responsible. Bart's loss had taken the wind out of me. I wasn't looking forward to training his replacement, Gil "what's his name."

Why couldn't I remember Gil's last name? I'd met him three days ago. We only talked for a minute, but I should have been able to remember his last name. I sat with my chin resting on my hand, searching for the brain cell that held the information. Nothing. Was it one of those subconscious things? Forgetting his name because I didn't want to know him? Gil...Gil...Gil what?

Gil was a tall lanky pilot from a small town in Georgia. He had a manner as thick and lumpy as sausage gravy but made up for it with a silver tongue. A review of his flight training records revealed good comments and no significant weaknesses. Gil's last name had been on the top of every grade sheet. Why couldn't I remember?

I was supposed to be Gil's instructor and mentor as Hunter had been to me. But I wasn't Hunter. Not even close to Hunter's talent and experience. I didn't have Hunter's motivation or his obsession with combat. I didn't believe I was ready to train someone else.

Reluctantly, I told Hunter how I felt.

Hunter's eyes seemed to focus on something I couldn't see as they always did when philosophy was coming. "You'll find the answers in yourself. You know more than you think you do. Besides, it'll be good training for a leadership role on your second combat tour."

"What second tour?" I asked.

"The one you'll fly right after you finish this one. You'll be a top-notch flight leader. I'll personally recommend you."

"Thanks for the vote of confidence, but do you really think I'd do this again?"

Hunter paused. "Of course I do. In your heart, you're a warrior like me. You don't know that about yourself because you haven't found your heart."

"What are you talking about? My heart is back in the States where I'm engaged to be engaged and they won't shoot at me everyday."

"Oh they'll shoot at you. They'll just use a different kind of bullet. Here it's black and white. The enemy wears a uniform you can recognize, and you can see the muzzle flashes."

"And back home?"

"Gray areas, blind-side attacks, you don't know who's shooting or when the attack is coming."

"I think that's a pretty cynical view."

"Maybe so, or perhaps realistic," Hunter mumbled, as he twisted his head around as if the muscles in his neck were tight. "You owe it to the fighter corps."

"I've paid my dues. What could I possibly owe?" I said, suspicious about where this was leading.

"You have eighty-eight North Vietnam missions under your belt. You've been trained as only a handful of pilots in your generation. You have talent. You're an asset. A scarce resource."

"And after another twelve missions, I'll be a real scarce one. I'll be gone," I shook my head, dismissing the absurd suggestion. "I've had my turn in the barrel."

"But you're a born flight leader. You know you are. You can save lives."

I felt indignant. "You mean I can share the wound of losing a wingman, or conduct my own private war because the ROE won't let me fight a real one."

Hunter looked pained. "I guess I deserved that, but somebody's got to carry this war to the enemy."

"That makes us no better than the protesters back home. Probably worse because we're killing people in places the ROE tells us to avoid."

Hunter's face reddened as he slammed his fist into his hand. "That pilot was a combatant. It doesn't matter if he was on the ground or in the air. And the barracks, they were soldiers, plain and simple."

"I suppose you could read their name tags going five hundred knots," I shot back.

Hunter's eyes flared. "They were shooting. I saw it and called it out on the radio." Then, as if a wave washed over him, Hunter became calm.

He stared through me with an unfocused gaze as if studying something within me. Then he hummed in a low soothing tone, sounding like an Indian medicine man in the movies. The humor of this scene wasn't lost on me. I almost laughed at him except, as he raised his hands to speak, I could feel he was dead serious.

Hunter smiled and assumed a noble look, "I have taught you much and you have learned well. You're a warrior now. Look into your heart and use your skills as you see them, to do the most good, as you see good to be done."

Hunter appeared to be transfixed in a macabre way. I didn't know to whom he spoke—himself, an Indian spirit, or me. I stood quietly. Finally, after what seemed like an eternity, he turned and walked away.

The next morning, after a restless night's sleep, I sauntered to the KABOOM for breakfast. I had a choice between two tables, a congregation of older pilots and a pride of young lions. For the first time, I chose the young lions.

I pulled out a chair, "Morning, guys."

"Ashe, maybe you can settle this," a lieutenant across the table asked.

I smiled. "Make it easy. It's too early in the day for tough questions."

"Yesterday a forward air controller called in a flight to strafe some water buffalo. He said they were carrying supplies. Would you do it?"

I signaled to the waitress for a cup of coffee. "I never kill animals under any circumstances."

"But you eat steak don't you?"

"Not if it's killed with an airplane."

A voice from the end of the table piped up, "But, Lieutenant Wilcox, that's betraying the interests of your country."

A cold silence fell over the table and everyone stared at the new lieutenant at the end.

"What?" I replied feeling a twinge of anger, wondering where this guy was coming from.

"Yes, Lieutenant Wilcox. It's giving quarter. Captain Rene Fouchs said giving quarter to the enemy is betraying the interests of your country."

"What war was he fighting?"

"He was a French pilot in the First World War," the lieutenant grinned, apparently satisfied with himself.

Pausing to compose myself, I said, "I suspect he meant quarter to other pilots, not water buffalo."

"But he..."

I felt weary and glared at the pilot, stopping him in mid sentence. The kid was youthful and foolish. Young? Probably only a year younger than myself but a combat tour short of experience. The way I see it, by the time you're experienced enough to earn the right to be a smart-ass, you're too tired of combat to care.

Looking at these kids, I saw myself, fresh out of training. I'd been the canary in the mineshaft and had survived. Surviving not because I was brave or talented or smart, but because I had "been there" in the company of an experienced mentor and was fortunate enough to live through it.

At that moment, looking around the table, I felt the first twinge of responsibility, my first sense of a need to pass on my experience. It seemed I was on a rickety ship of state with too many innocents onboard. My concern was no longer about winning an unwinnable war, but saving men from mortal wounds of combat and emotional wounds of loss. Staring at the end of the table, at the young pilot filled with French history at the expense of common sense, I felt I was looking at a man who would soon be dead.

My tablemates finished breakfast and drifted off to plan their mission. I lingered alone, sipping coffee and leafing through the Stars and Stripes. I recognized Gil's controlled voice, as smooth as butter flavored grits.

"Good morning, Lieutenant Wilcox, sir."

His rigid posture gave him away. He was nervous, almost standing at attention. At that moment, I saw Gil as Hunter must have seen me. I scowled but was laughing inside. It was an opportunity too good to pass up.

Slowly, I moved my eyes from the newspaper to the coffee cup and finally acknowledged Gil's presence with a brief glance. "Lieutenant, do you come by your military bearing naturally or is it a product of all that college education?"

"I don't understand, sir."

"We're both the same rank. When you call me sir, I turn around and start looking for my father."

"Sorry, sir...oops, I did it again. Didn't realize..."

"Great SA, Gil."

"SA?"

"That's what fighter pilots call Situation Awareness. Ever hear of that?"

"Sure, I know what SA is."

"Congratulations. You didn't call me sir."

"Look, Ashe, I'm from the south. In my hometown we call everybody sir."

"It's your first combat mission. You scared?"

"No. Well, maybe a little. I'm glad you're going to check me out. Next to Hunter, I hear you're the best. You must do this all the time."

"Nope. Never checked out anyone before. You're the first."

Gil pulled out a chair. "Mind if I join you for breakfast?"

"As you can see, Shooter, I'm finished. I'll meet you down at operations."

"Wait, sir...rats, I did it again. I'll walk with you."

"Wrong," I cautioned. "There are two things you should do before strapping your body into a supersonic jet. Eat a good breakfast and have a good crap. It might turn into a long day. In fact, I didn't come back from my first mission for three days."

Gil nodded. "I heard. Maybe you can fill me in on the details sometime."

I stood up. "One more thing. Can you read my nametag?"

Gil nodded.

"What does it say?"

"Ashe, sir...Oh, rats, you're doing this just to get my goat, aren't you?"

I smiled, in a strange way enjoying this. "Last time I looked, it said Ashe. Just Ashe. Not Ashe, sir. Not Lieutenant Wilcox. Not, oh rats, or goat or anything else. Just Ashe. And that's what I want you to call me, Ashe."

Chapter 32

Slowly, tempered by reluctance I could neither define nor resolve I walked toward the operations building. Finding our flight on the schedule was a relief at first but soon the impact soaked in. We were still in the flying game but the bridge at Than Hoa was going to be a troublesome target.

A sixteen-ship gaggle carried a lot of firepower, but a formation that large was impossible to hide. With the element of surprise lost, the enemy would focus all of its defensive effort. We were about to lose another pilot.

If I didn't know better, I'd think I was getting depressed. Everything in my life seemed detached from its base. I still hadn't written to Jenny, and I was carrying her last letter in my pocket, unread. Before it had always been comforting to hear from her, but now her letters were reminders that I didn't have a positive aspect of my life to write about.

I felt isolated. For months, I hadn't touched a woman except for the brief fling with Tibby. And my conversations with Julia were the only time I felt truly connected with another human.

Julia was a special person but not my special person. Still my thoughts often returned to moments of intimacy with her. Not sexual intimacy, but times when we understood each other through a unique kind of communication. She was important to me in a way that was completely out of proportion with the amount of time we spent together. Maybe she touched everybody like that. Perhaps her magnetism made everyone believe he had a special relationship with her.

I heard footsteps and Lucky's voice boomed behind me. "Hey, Ashe. Check your six."

I turned, "If I'd known you were back there, I would have waited."

"No trouble catching up," Lucky said. "You're walking kind of slow. Anything wrong?"

"Just bored. Nothing to do here. No women to talk to and all of us guys have the same training, do the same job, and hash over the same shallow things."

"No girls? What you need is a trip to the village. I know this massage parlor, put fifteen bucks on the counter and tell them you don't want to come out alive."

"Lucky, you'd take on anything that walked in the door."

He nodded, "Probably."

"That's not for me. I need to feel something."

"Whaddya mean feel something?"

I shrugged, "At least talk the same language."

"Talk! Now there's a concept. But you got it backwards. It's women that need to feel loved to have sex. Men need to have sex to feel loved."

"Lucky, you have an amazing penchant for distilling the essence."

"And you have an amazing whatever for thinking too much. Go to the village. It'll fix you right up."

We walked the rest of the way without saying much, respecting the silence that passes for companionship among fighter pilots. Lucky had a down-home intellect that I wanted to tap. I wanted to talk about many things but held to the protocol.

I wanted to tell him about my loneliness and not feeling comfortable in a place that substituted congeniality for closeness and constructed defenses against emotion.

I wanted to tell him about building walls around myself and wondering if they would come down when the war was over.

But I didn't tell him.

The walls had not come down for Hunter. Julia was clear on that. Of course, he'd been a prisoner. It was much harder for him. One can forgive almost any kind of behavior from a man who had suffered so much for so long.

I felt like a prisoner of war, too. Not interned and tortured by an enemy but trapped and tortured by myself. I sensed others around me were living in the same prison, confined by the idea that losing a friend was so painful that we held friendships at arm's length. I recognized the ironic logic, but the idea seemed as formidable as a stone cell.

Because of combat, I had compartmentalized my life—avoided having friends to avoid the loss of friends, avoided relationships to avoid the loss of relationships. Today I had to climb into a jet and fly another mission. For the next few hours, it was time to open the combat flyer's compartment and turn off emotion in all the others. I had become an expert at turning feelings off, but not so talented at turning them back on.

But even the combat flyer in me had mixed emotions about today's mission. Grover and I had both been scared into a cold sweat the first few times we flew in a sixteen-ship gaggle. It had been like an old war movie with the bombers going in over Germany. You saw flak over the target and knew you were going to fly right through it.

Over the span of my tour I had become seasoned under fire and knew how to defend myself against hostile gunners in the Red River Valley as well as missiles launched from downtown Hanoi. But the enemy had gained experience, too, and the odds kept closing in.

It had been Hunter that guided us through our first few missions and kept us alive long enough to learn the ropes. Now it was my turn to mentor. I had the heavy feeling that Gil's life was my responsibility.

There were too many conflicting rules and it was impossible to follow them all. Hunter had known that all along. Now I had to teach Gil. I had come down hard on Hunter for losing Bart, but now I wondered if I could keep Gil alive for the rest of the day.

I surveyed the operation's scheduling board. Our flight callsign was Buick, and that made me feel uneasy. Not that I was superstitious, but it was my callsign the day I was shot down.

Hunter was listed as the Buick leader with Grover on his wing. I was deputy lead in the number three position with Gil as my wingman. But something was wrong. Before I could copy down the flight data on my line up card, the duty officer began erasing it.

"Hey. What's up?"

The duty officer turned and pointed to the next board. "Over there. You're scrubbed off of the sixteen-ship raid and rescheduled on an alternate mission."

I was startled. "But why?"

"Came down from above."

"Who above?"

"Don't have a clue." The duty officer shrugged, "I just post the board."

Why was this happening? Was it Hunter? That had to be it. Headquarters had taken him off the primary target because of the OSI investigation. But if that were it, they would have cancelled our flight. They simply changed targets, sending us as a four-ship on an easier mission.

There was another possibility. Perhaps it was because of Gil. The operations officer may have realized the target would be too tough for an initial checkout mission. I would have to ask Hunter later. I felt an obscure kind of guilt, as the duty officer grease-penciled another flight into our position in the gaggle.

Our new target was a pontoon bridge on the supply route several miles south of Than Hoa. Intelligence reported that sections of the bridge were tied to the bank under overhanging trees by day and floated into place each night. Sometimes the sections were moved up river and the bridge location turned into a daytime flak trap. But when nighttime supply movements were heavy, as they were now, the pontoons would be in a convenient position near the intersection of the road and the river. They suspected the bridge sections were hidden beneath overhanging limbs, but Intelligence wasn't sure.

I decided to plan the attack and not wait for Hunter. The

conservative approach would be to aim for the intersection of the river and the road and release the bombs high to avoid the flak. But, unsure where the pontoons were moored, we would probably bomb trees again.

I decided on a bold move but wasn't positive Hunter would do it with a new guy on board.

"Here's the plan," I said to Hunter when he finally walked up to the mission-planning table.

He raised his eyebrows, "Let's have it."

"My flight element will go low down the river, tree-top kind of low, moving at the speed of heat while looking under the tree canopy. I'll call out the target's position on the radio."

Hunter nodded, "I like it. What about spacing?"

"Gil will be on my wing. After I locate the target, you and Grover attack while I lead Gil up to bombing altitude for our target run."

Hunter paused with a pensive look then slapped the table with his hand. "Audacious. I love it."

Coming from Hunter, that was high praise.

Hunter studied the map for several minutes. "Just one little change," he said. "Since this is Gil's first mission with us, I'll go in low with Grover. You drop back a bit with Gil and stay at medium altitude. I'll locate the target, zoom up and bomb it. Then you two drop."

I smiled, "You get all the fun."

Later, on the mission, Hunter radioed, "Buick Flight, Top Cover." He used the first four words said over enemy territory to tell the flight he was going down to take a look.

After gathering airspeed, I took Gil high to stay above most of the anti-aircraft fire. We were up on a perch, trolling for AAA guns like bait, changing course every few seconds to confuse the gunner's tracking problem. Hunter split to the east and dropped down into the river valley. Grover flew in close formation, line abreast of Hunter. Using hand signals instead of the radio, I got a fuel check from Gil. Looking back I didn't see Hunter or Grover at first.

Then to the west, I spotted two lines drawing across the jungle canopy. Jet blast indented the foliage like a stick pulled quickly across flat sand. Even before I saw the jets, I knew it was Hunter and Grover traveling over 600 knots across the top of the trees. Then Hunter dropped his jet below the tree line and into the slit in the jungle that contained the river. It was a bold, unexpected move and low enough the gunners couldn't react. Hunter flashed by the target and abruptly pulled into a steep climb.

"Buick Flight, our targets are concealed 500 yards east of the road where the river bends, then for the next 200 yards," Hunter reported.

I glanced at my wingman. Gil gave me a thumb up; he had heard the call and apparently knew what to do. Good thing. No time to stop and explain.

Each flight member adjusted his impact point and dropped bombs on the tree sheltered pontoon sections. The explosions formed shock rings of moisture that ripped into the jungle. Branches and leaves were blown away. Trunks of majestic trees lifted as if in slow motion then fell into the river, cleaved and broken like massive reeds. The floating bridge pontoons were heaved upward and came to rest twisted and torn and covered with tons of splintered tree trunks.

The floating bridge was destroyed in a success Hunter would boast about by saying, "One close look is worth a ton of intelligence reports."

I didn't ask Hunter if he knew why our target was changed. I wanted to believe it was because of Gil's checkout program so that was the reason and the logic I accepted. But in the back of my mind, I wondered.

Chapter 33

The next morning over breakfast, Grover and I were rumi-
nating about Gil's first mission. Seldom does anything in life,
with four fighter pilots involved, come together in such a
seamless way. We both recognized the moment.

"You know, Ashe," Grover said. "Gil had a great mission
for a new guy."

I glanced around to see if Gil was within earshot. "The kid's
a natural. A perfect blend of arrogance and good reflexes."

"Hope he doesn't think every mission will be as smooth as
yesterday."

After breakfast we flight-planned for the afternoon. The target, an earthen dam at the edge of a lake, was located near the
village of Bai Le. The dam supported the roadbed for Highway
One and a set of railroad tracks, which presented a rare opportunity to knock out two lines of communication and an earth-
en dam on one dive bomb pass. The most interesting thing
about the target was its position on the Red River Valley Delta,
twenty-two miles south of the center of Hanoi.

While we suited up in the personal equipment room,
Hunter told stories that all the flight members except Gil had
heard before. Hunter was practiced at spinning yarns and,
through several tellings, had honed his words carefully for the
greatest impact. For me the pleasure was watching him tell the
stories. It was one of the few times he seemed to enjoy himself.

"I faked that unsuspecting MiG pilot right off the runway into
the wild blue yonder," Hunter said. "He didn't know how wild

until he eased back on the control stick," he added as his eyes lit up and he tossed his head back and laughed.

Colonel Fallbrook, the wing commander, came to the door and motioned Hunter outside. I moved near the window and pretended to adjust my equipment. Fallbrook gave Hunter a piece of paper. As he read, Hunter appeared to go limp. His shoulders slumped and his head hung low. Then Hunter waved his arms in broad gestures and appeared frustrated. After several strained minutes, the animated conversation ended with Hunter standing, hands on his hips, staring up at the sky. Finally, the wing commander stuffed the paper in his pocket, nodded, and motioned Hunter toward the door.

As they walked back, Colonel Fallbrook placed his arm on Hunter's shoulder. They shook hands at the door. Then Hunter walked straight back to the equipment rack and put on his G-suit and survival vest. There was an uneasy tension in the room. Everyone was quiet, exchanging glances, seeming to wait for Hunter to comment on the unusual visit.

After a while, Hunter walked over to me and talked in muted tones as if sharing a secret, "It may be worse than I thought. The CO says there is a message coming. A buddy of his called from the Pentagon."

"A message from the Pentagon? Not Saigon?"

Hunter nodded and made a nervous clicking sound with his mouth, "The political pukes are driving it. His friend gave him a heads-up on that too."

"So what's the skinny?"

"He thinks they'll credit me with a fifth MiG kill and pull me out of here fast. Probably for more of that war-hero-tour stuff back in the states."

I patted him on the back, "Congratulations, Ace. Looks like you can go home and write your own ticket."

His brusque voice betrayed his agitation. "Not so fast. I'm not a staff officer or a hero or whatever they're trying to make me into. I'd suffocate in that arena. I'm a fighter pilot. That's all I've ever been or wanted to be. It's the only thing I'm good at."

Hunter's eyes were moist. We had been through hell together, and I knew the signs. He was deeply depressed and afraid, but never had I seen him act more upset when there were others around to see. If I hadn't known him better, I would have been worried. But I didn't worry. In my eyes, Hunter could handle anything. His whole life had been a richly woven tapestry revealing a singular message in bold letters: I am a warrior and a survivor.

Perhaps the last survivor, I thought. The last survivor of a dying breed of fighter pilots if the politics of modern war have anything to do with it.

Hunter's hand clenched a pack of Camels and his arm shook noticeably. Looking down, he fumbled with a cigarette then finally flipped open his Zippo and got it lit. After a long drag, he continued in a tentative voice. "It's all closing in on me. My combat flying days are over," He paused appearing to let the words soak in. Looking at me with a blank stare, he pointed a trembling finger, "Do you hear me? I'm finished."

I stood beside him but looked away out of respect for his pain. "I thought you'd be happy. You'll be an Ace. They'll send you to War College." I was rambling, trying to point out some unseen advantage, not knowing what else to say. "You'll spend a couple of years in the Pentagon then command your own wing. Automatic career progression. General Hunter. How does that sound?"

When I said General Hunter, he jumped as if I'd shot him. I saw raw terror in his eyes as I had when we parachuted into the jungle.

"It won't be General Hunter," he spat out. "I'm not built that way and you know it. I'd never make it through War College. I barely made it through high school. If I graduated, it would be a gift because I was an Ace."

"You could do it standing on your head," I said, then laughed in a feeble attempt to quench his fear. "And you know how to be political. You just refuse to do it."

"Ass kissing. That's what it is. By the ones looking for stars. I could never do a Pentagon tour. They'll never get me. Never." Hunter turned and walked to the gun cage. "Need my pistol, no extra ammo today."

"One basic thirty-eight caliber pistol and one of your basic mil spec rounds coming up," Sergeant Davis said. "Guess you're not going to fight your way out of North Vietnam today?"

Hunter stared at the pistol as if seeing it for the first time. "You ever look at one of these close?"

I was confused. "It's a pistol. What's to look at?"

"It's a beautiful piece, built for a single purpose. It's a weapon for war. It has no place in a peacetime society. Just like me. There's no place for me in peacetime."

"The crew truck's here," Grover broke in. "Time to rock and roll."

Hunter loaded the one round, spun the cylinder closed, and placed the revolver in the shoulder holster of his survival vest. Then he motioned me toward the door. "If this is the last mission I get to fly, I'd better make the most of it. We need to get airborne before that message comes in."

After one deep breath, Hunter's eyes turned bright and alive. I felt relieved to see his attitude change, but an uneasy feeling lingered in my gut.

In the crew truck, he leaned close to my ear and talked in short bursts to be heard above the flightline noise. "Grover's a great pilot. You can't ask for a better wingman. And Gil seems to be a fast learner. He's a good stick, with a maturity in the air that's beyond his age and experience."

"You mean his total combat experience of one mission," I chided.

Hunter ignored my comment and continued. "Keep reminding them how unusual our flight has been. Most fighter jocks go through their whole career and never fly on a team this good. It's a once in a lifetime experience."

I felt captured by his intensity as he paused and looked at

the rows of planes as we drove down the flightline.

"Nothing lasts forever," he continued. "Now it's your responsibility to build for the future. Grover's ready for the deputy lead position, and you've taken on a new wingman. You're in the training business now and you'll have to be less aggressive for a time."

"Oh, right," I said. "Like you've ever been less aggressive on a checkout flight?"

Hunter smiled, "At least stay out of the weeds for a while. Gil will be a top-notch wingman but don't take him along too fast." He nodded toward Grover and Gil. "The next war is theirs to lead. Make sure they come through this one alive."

I felt sad and confused. I knew flying with Hunter couldn't last forever, but for months I had not thought further ahead than the next flight. Today would probably be our last combat mission together. I felt an intense sense of loss. The loss of something special. The loss of someone special. A loss I could never resolve or reclaim.

But it was time to fly. Once again I'd have to put my emotions on hold and deal with the feelings later. Whatever I did, I needed to concentrate and focus so there would be a later. The sensible thing would be to enjoy our last mission together as much as possible.

When the truck stopped at Hunter's jet, he stared at the floor for a few seconds then looked up with a pained smile and announced to the flight, "There's one change in tactics today. When we pull off the target, Grover will break off of my wing and join with Ashe's element."

"Hey," Grover shouted as Hunter hopped out of the crew van and walked toward his jet. Hunter turned and gave Grover a stern look. His words were drowned in jet noise but he seemed to mouth, "Do it."

Grover turned to me, "What's going on?"

"Beats me. I'm just the second-in-command in a one man show."

"What should I do?"

I leaned back against my parachute, "Exactly what your leader told you to do. You know Hunter always has a plan. He just doesn't always share it with us."

Approaching the North Vietnam border, Hunter accelerated to 600 knots. He descended to 500 feet as the ground blurred beneath us at 10 miles a minute. Moist air condensed into visible trails, streaming white ribbons of vapor from the wingtips of each plane as we streaked past massive cliffs of limestone karst. I felt like I was riding a bullet as the verdant jungle unfolded like a lush sun-drenched carpet.

Every few seconds, Hunter looked from one side to the other at his wingmen. As a flight leader, he was always professional but was exceptionally crisp this morning. Eight miles from the target, we left the jungle canopy behind and traversed across the plains of the Red River Valley. Thirty miles ahead, the city of Hanoi flattened out across the valley floor and appeared capped with a dull brown layer of smog. Just ahead, and slightly offset to the left, was the lake. We were in perfect position to begin an attack on the dam.

Our flight followed Hunter's lead through a precise pop-up and roll-in. When we stabilized in a dive, I shifted my eyes from Hunter to my own attack. The target filled my bombsight as we dove in loose formation. Our bombs ripped away much of the road structure and cut through the dam and railroad tracks. Then it occurred to me, only three loads of bombs had detonated.

"Buick Lead, you still have your ordnance," Grover radioed.

"Roger," Hunter acknowledged.

My eyes snapped toward our planned egress to the south but Hunter wasn't there. I found his jet heading north in afterburner. Grover had pulled off Hunter's wing and started to join up with my plane. Our flight discipline was in shambles. I was deputy leader with both wingmen, and our flight leader was egressing in the wrong direction. I considered calling Hunter on the radio, but there was nothing I could say that wouldn't be heard and have to be explained later. I wasn't sure I could explain.

What I should have done, if I had any spunk at all, was leave Hunter's arrogant butt shining up there alone. But, of course, I didn't. Reversing my turn, I rolled out on a northerly course to intercept Hunter who was now well ahead and several thousand feet above our altitude.

Grover completed his join-up on my left wing with a fierce closure rate. As he stabilized, we glanced at each other. He took both hands off the controls and smashed his gloved fists against the top of his canopy. I nodded, sharing his frustration. We both knew Hunter was on another one of his missions from The Great Spirit.

I was tired of this game. We were blundering around close to Hanoi, and I had no idea what Hunter intended. The city was rapidly unfolding before us. He might be going after the Doumer Bridge, and if he were, he would drag us right across the city. From our position, the bridge was visible but so was the Gia Lam MiG base to the right. Hunter could be going after Gia Lam, the bridge or possibly the Kep MiG base further north.

Whatever his intentions, he was still accelerating away from us even though he had bombs and we didn't. I selected afterburner to keep him in sight, but I couldn't stay in burner for long or we would run out of fuel. I couldn't believe what was happening. If Hunter wanted to bomb another target up north, why didn't he say something before takeoff?

I shook my head. We weren't gaining on him, so there was only one alternative. I could take the flight low. As I considered the choices, Hunter passed over the edge of the city and was met by a barrage of 85-milimetter AAA. The exploding puffs of flak were all I needed. I didn't know if lower was safer, but I wasn't going to expose my wingmen to those 85s. I accelerated to near supersonic speed and descended over the city of Hanoi.

At 500 feet, I leveled off. Our speed was 12 miles a minute. We didn't seem to be closing on him, but we weren't falling back much either. Hunter, 15,000 feet above us, looked like a speck in the sky. I waited for him to roll in on the bridge, but he made a left turn instead. Half way through his turn, two surface-to-air missiles launched from our right.

I smashed down my microphone button, "Buick Leader, this is Buick Three, two SAMs airborne, ten o'clock at five miles from Gia Lam. Headed your way."

Hunter made a hard turn. His plane seemed to hang on its afterburner like a rotating dot in the sky. The jet turned gracefully until its nose dropped and pointed straight at the Doumer Bridge.

"Buick Lead is in for the last pass. Wish me luck," Hunter said, in an uncommon breach of radio discipline.

"Good luck, Lead," I replied, as we roared at supersonic speed through the traffic pattern of Gia Lam and started an arcing turn toward the Doumer Bridge.

The bomb-laden fighter was in a steep dive. As Hunter went through the sound barrier, moist air formed a cloudy contrail that engulfed the fuselage and wings of his fighter from the cockpit to well past the tail. Hunter was in a supersonic dive in full afterburner. The velocity was incredible. The airborne SAMs began a correction toward his diving aircraft but couldn't make the turn. They passed behind him, exploding in two huge fireballs.

Hunter's track was straight and true and quick as a comet. Why hadn't I known? I had seen the signs in Hunter but not the full measure of his desperation. Only now could I share his terrible feeling of meaningless loss.

I watched in horror as the diving jet and its shadow converged into one. The bomb-laden fighter crashed into the bridge with the unholy power of a meteorite. The impact hurled a span of the bridge down into the river. Then the explosion elevated a plume of water, cement, and steel more than a mile into the sky.

My world shook with the impact. The road below that had been as active as an ant track with bicycles, tuk-tuks and hand-carts was now devoid of motion. The gunners stopped firing.

Movement stopped as if everyone knew he had witnessed a cat-
aclysmic event.

I circumnavigated the site in a wide arc, staring at the dis-
turbed water while thousands of fragments of steel and
cement began to rain back into the river. The remains of a
monumental bridge, a magnificent air machine, and a great
warrior pilot descended together from the sky and fell to their
final resting-place, entwined forever in a monument to strug-
gle.

After several minutes, I wagged my wings as a signal to close-
in the formation. With Grover on my left and Gil on my right,
I flew south across the city at a thousand feet straight and level.
Perhaps I felt indestructible. Perhaps I didn't care. Looking
down at people on the streets, I saw them looking up. No one
fired a shot at us as far as I could tell. When past the southern
boundary of the city, over the wide expanse of the Red River
Valley, I began a gentle climb and headed home.

Epilogue

Dear Julia,

By the time you read this, you will know that Hunter is gone. We have both suffered a great loss. A letter like this is supposed to help comfort you, but I don't know what to say, especially since you understood him far better than anyone.

I grew to respect and love Hunter more than any man I have ever known. He followed his own compass, and in many ways will always remain a mystery to me. But I did not think the loss of anyone could affect me so deeply.

I was on the mission with him. He has been declared missing in action because he went down in enemy territory and there's no physical evidence of his death. The government is always reluctant to make a final determination on the basis of pilot observations alone. A lot happens quickly in combat and much of what is observed and reported with the best of intentions is not complete or not what it seemed. But I was there. I saw it all, and he is gone.

Hunter was a true warrior, an exemplar, and a teacher for us all. He did not suffer. I think he went the way he wanted to, in combat, with great dignity, doing what he believed he was called to do.

Enclosed is the Silver Star that I was awarded for shooting down a MiG. Since I can't give it to Hunter, I want you to have it. It is rightfully his. He put the MiG in my gunsight. All I did was pull the trigger when the poor SOB flew right in front of me. As you know, Hunter's Silver Star for his fifth MiG kill and his status as Ace are being held up because of an investigation. I don't know what the outcome will be, but I want him to have mine.

As it turns out, you also understood me better than I understood myself. I volunteered for a second combat tour. When I talked to Jenny, she was crushed. I had planned to spend two weeks with her in the States between tours, but she broke off our relationship for good.

I tried to explain why I have to stay and fly, but Jenny couldn't understand that my second hundred missions would be safer than my first. She said she couldn't take another tour, and I couldn't convince her why I have to do it. Perhaps I was not convincing because I'm not convinced. I don't know why I must stay and fly combat, but I know I have to do it.

Sincerely,

Ashe